THE GRAVE TATTOO

Val McDermid grew up in a Scottish mining community then read English at Oxford. She was a journalist for sixteen years, spending the last three years as Northern Bureau Chief of a national Sunday tabloid. Now a full-time writer, she divides her time between Cheshire and Northumberland.

Her novels have won international acclaim and a number of prestigious awards, including the Gold Dagger for best crime novel of the year, the Anthony Award for best novel, and the *Los Angeles Times* Book of the Year Award. Her thriller series featuring Dr Tony Hill, criminal profiler, has now been adapted for television under the generic title *Wire in the Blood* and stars Robson Green.

For the latest news, visit www.valmcdermid.com.

Visit www.AuthorTracker.ca for exclusive updates on Val McDermid.

Acclaim for *The Grave Tattoo*

'Absorbing modern mystery. . . . McDermid's mix of historical and literary clues with modern detection is handled with panache.'

—*The Times*

'One of the world's leading mystery writers, combining acuity of perception about the pathological mind with a rare talent for blindsiding the reader and graphic descriptive powers. Thomas Harris crossed with Agatha Christie, if you will . . . . *The Grave Tattoo* is a great read. England's heritage history has never been so chilling.'

—*The Observer*

'McDermid has lion-hearted courage as a writer. . . . The complex plot is handled with [her] usual narrative confidence.'

—*The Independent*

'[A] cleverly plotted thriller. . . . Lost manuscripts, 200-year-old enigmas, an isolated Lake District village mystery and oodles of atmosphere: McDermid concocts a fascinating brew which is miles away from her customary bloody excursions into the realms of the perverse. It should gain her a crowd of new fans.'

—*The Guardian*

'One of our most accomplished crime writers. . . . Compelling.'

—*The Glasgow Herald*

'Cunning . . . gripping. . . . [McDermid is] so adroit in her pulling together of various items of historical conjecture and marrying them up to a murderous plot that has as many twists and turns as one of her Tony Hills. . . . A substantially entertaining novel which grips the reader's interest from the first page until the final deeply satisfying sentence.'

'Bodies pile up—one with bizarre tattoos—and trying to solve a 200-year-old mystery becomes increasingly lethal.'

'Safe for the squeamish. . . . One of her best.'

'An irresistible combination of contemporary psychological thriller and historical mystery filled with the moody atmosphere of the Lake District. In Wordsworth scholar Jane Gresham, McDermid has created a character whose keen intellect matches her generous heart.'

Also by Val McDermid

Cleanskin
The Distant Echo
Killing the Shadows
A Place of Execution

TONY HILL NOVELS
The Torment of Others
The Last Temptation
The Wire in the Blood
The Mermaids Singing

KATE BRANNIGAN NOVELS
Star Struck
Blue Genes
Clean Break
Crack Down
Kick Back
Dead Beat

LINDSAY GORDON NOVELS
Hostage to Murder
Booked for Murder
Union Jack
Final Edition
Common Murder
Report for Murder

NON-FICTION
A Suitable Job for a Woman

VAL McDERMID

The Grave Tattoo

■ HarperCollins*PublishersLtd*

The Grave Tattoo
© 2006 Val McDermid. All rights reserved.

Published by HarperCollins Publishers Ltd

Originally published in trade paperback by HarperCollins
Publishers Ltd: 2006
This mass market paperback edition: 2007

HarperCollins books may be purchased for educational, business, or
sales promotional use through our Special Markets Department.

HarperCollins Publishers Ltd
2 Bloor Street East, 20th Floor
Toronto, Ontario, Canada
M4W 1A8

www.harpercollins.ca

Library and Archives Canada Cataloguing in Publication

McDermid, Val
The grave tattoo / Val McDermid.

ISBN-13: 978-0-00-639159-3
ISBN-10: 0-00-639159-1

1. Christian, Fletcher, 1764–1793—Fiction. 2. Wordsworth,
William, 1770–1850—Manuscripts—Fiction. 3. Lake District
(England)—Fiction. I. Title.

PR6063.A168G73 2007   823'.914   C2007-902794-6

OPM 9 8 7 6 5 4 3 2 1

Printed and bound in the United States

For Kelly – my blossom of snow

Acknowledgements

The seed for this book came from a talk Alan Hankinson gave some years ago to the Northern Chapter of the Crime Writers' Association. I am indebted to Reginald Hill for organising it and to Robert Barnard for filling in some of the gaps in the immediate aftermath. I was encouraged to continue by Wordsworth expert Juliet Barker. The late Robert Woof, Director of the Wordsworth Trust, gave generously of his time and encyclopaedic knowledge. Professor Sue Black provided invaluable information about the work of a forensic anthropologist and on the forensic details in the text. Any inaccuracies are entirely my responsibility. Thanks too to Cherry Cappel who steered me towards a title when I was becalmed. The book would never have been completed without the wholehearted support of my editor Julia Wisdom, my agent Jane Gregory and Anne O'Brien, the Jedi master of copy-editing. Finally, I want to thank Kelly Smith who made the dark places light.

O Reader! had you in your mind
Such stores as silent thought can bring,
O gentle Reader! you would find
A tale in every thing.

William Wordsworth, *Simon Lee*

Line of primogeniture

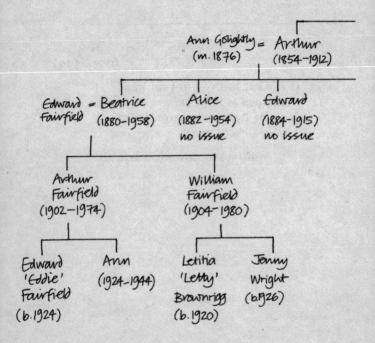

Ann Golightly = Arthur
(m. 1876)   (1854–1912)

Edward = Beatrice
Fairfield (1880–1958)

Alice
(1882–1954)
no issue

Edward
(1884–1915)
no issue

Arthur
Fairfield
(1902–1974)

William
Fairfield
(1904–1980)

Edward
'Eddie'
Fairfield
(b.1924)

Ann
(1924–1944)

Letitia
'Letty'
Brownrigg
(b.1920)

Jenny
Wright
(b.1926)

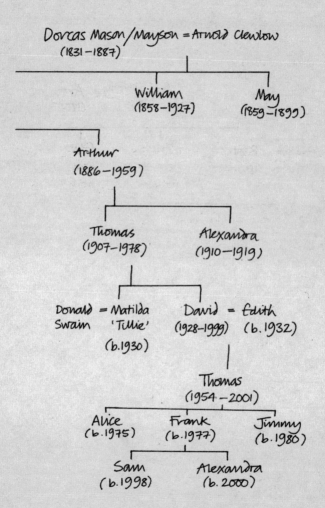

Dorcas Mason/Mayson = Arnold Clewlow
(1831–1887)

William   May
(1858–1927)   (1859–1899)

Arthur
(1886–1959)

Thomas   Alexandra
(1907–1978)   (1910–1919)

Donald = Matilda   David = Edith
Swain   'Tillie'   (1928–1999) (b.1932)
        (b.1930)

Thomas
(1954–2001)

Alice   Frank   Jimmy
(b.1975)   (b.1977)   (b.1980)

Sam   Alexandra
(b.1998)   (b.2000)

The Prelude

September 2005

All landscapes hold their own secrets. Layer on layer, the past is buried beneath the surface. Seldom irretrievable, it lurks, waiting for human agency or meteorological accident to force the skeleton up through flesh and skin back into the present. Like the poor, the past is always with us.

That summer, it rained as if England had been transported to the tropics. Water fell in torrents, wrecking glorious gardens, turning meadows into quagmires where livestock struggled hock-deep in mud. Rivers burst their banks, their suddenly released waters finding their own level by demolishing whatever was vulnerable in their path. In the flooded streets of one previously picturesque village, cars were swept up like toys and deposited in the harbour, choking it in a chaos of mangled metal. Landslips swamped cars with mud and farmers mourned lost crops.

No part of the country was immune from the sheets of stinging rain. City and countryside alike struggled under the weight of water. In the Lake District, it sheeted down over fell and dale, subtly altering the contours of a centuries-old landscape. The water levels in the lakes reached record summer highs; the only discernible benefit was that when the sun did occasionally shine, it revealed a lusher green than usual.

Above the village of Fellhead on the shores of Langmere, ancient peat hags were carved into new shapes under the onslaught of water. And as autumn crept in, gradually the earth gave up one of its close-held secrets.

From a distance, it looked like a scrunched-up tarpaulin stained brown by the brackish water of the bog. At first glance, it seemed insignificant; another piece of discarded rubbish that had worked its way to the surface. But closer inspection revealed something far more chilling. Something that would reach across the centuries and bring even more profound changes in its wake than the weather.

My beloved son,

I trust you and the children are in good health. I have found this day troubling matter in your father's hand. It may surprise you that, in spite of the close confidence between us, I was in ignorance of this while he lived, and wish heartily I had remained in that state. You will easily see the need for secrecy while your father lived, and he left me no instructions concerning its disposition. Since it closely touches you, and may be the occasion of more pain, I wish to leave to you the decision as to what should be done. I will convey the matter to you by a faithful hand. You must do as you see fit.

Your loving Mother

1

The way it rained that summer
It would have broken your heart to see.
It smashed its sheets to smithereens
And flowed down the corrugated roofs
Of dismal railway stations.
And I would sit waiting for trains,
Feet in puddles,
My head starry with rain,
Thinking of you miles from me
In Grecian sunlight
Where rain never falls.

Jane Gresham stared at what she had written then with an impatient stroke of her pen crossed it through so firmly the paper tore and split in the wake of the nib. *Bloody Jake,* she thought angrily. She was a grown-up, not some lovestruck adolescent. Sub-poetic maundering was something she should have left behind years ago. She'd had insight enough to know she was never going to be a poet by the time she'd finished her first degree. Studying other people's poetry was what she was good at; interpreting their work, exploring thematic links in their verse and opening up their complexity to those who were, she hoped, an assorted number of steps behind her in the process. 'Bloody, bloody Jake,' she said out loud, crumpling the paper savagely and tossing it in the bin. He wasn't worth the expense of her intellectual energy. Nor the familiar claw of pain that grabbed at her chest at the thought of him.

Eager to shunt aside thoughts of Jake, Jane turned to the stack of CDs beside the desk in the poky room that the council classified as a bedroom but which she called, with knowing pretentiousness, her study. She scanned the titles, deliberately starting at the bottom, looking for something that held no resonance of her . . . what was he? Her ex? Her erstwhile lover? Her lover-in-abeyance? Who knew? She certainly didn't. And she doubted very much whether he gave her a second thought from one week to the next. Muttering at herself under her breath, she pulled out Nick Cave's *Murder Ballads* and slotted it into the CD drive of her computer. The dark growl of his voice matched her mood so perfectly, it became a paradoxical antidote. In spite of herself, Jane found she was almost smiling.

She picked up the book she had been attempting to study before Jake Hartnell had intruded on her thoughts. But it took her only a few minutes to realise how far her focus had drifted. Irritated with herself again, she slammed it shut. Wordsworth's letters of 1807 would have to wait.

Before she could decide what to attack next, the alarm on her mobile phone beeped. Jane frowned, checking the time on her phone against the watch on her wrist. 'Hell and damnation,' she said. How could it be half past eleven already? Where had the morning gone?

'Bloody Jake,' she said again, jumping to her feet and switching off her computer. All that time wasted mooning over him when there were better things to be passionate about. She grabbed her bag and went through to the other room. Officially this was the living room, but Jane used it as a bedsit, preferring to have a completely separate space to work in. It made the rest of her life even more cramped by comparison, but that felt like a small price to pay for the luxury of having somewhere she could lay out her books and papers without having to shift them every time she wanted to eat or sleep.

The small room could barely accommodate even her Spartan existence. Her sofa bed, although folded away now, dominated the space. A table sat against the opposite wall, three wooden chairs tucked under it. A small TV set was mounted on a bracket high on the wall, and a bean bag slouched in the furthest corner. But the room was fresh, its soft green paint-work clean and light. On the wall opposite the sofa hung a series of digital colour photographs of the Lake District, blown up to A3 size and laminated. At the heart of the landscape, Gresham's Farm, where her family had eked out a meagre living as far back as anyone could trace. No matter what was outside her windows, Jane could wake up in the morning to the world she'd grown up in, the world she still missed every city day.

She stripped off her sweatpants and fleece top, swapping them for tight-fitting black jeans and a black v-neck stretch top that accentuated generous breasts. It wasn't her first choice of outfit, but experience had taught her that making the most of her assets meant better tips from customers. Luckily her olive skin meant she didn't look terminal in black, and her co-worker Harry had assured her she didn't look as lumpy as she felt in the tight top. A glance outside the window at the weather and she grabbed her rainproof jacket from its hook, shrugging into it as she hurried towards the front door. She didn't care that it lacked any pretence of chic; in this downpour, she cared more about arriving at work dry and warm.

Jane took her invariable last look at the Lakeland vista before walking into a completely different universe. She doubted whether anyone in Fellhead could conjure up her present environment even in their worst imaginings. When she'd told her mother she'd been granted a council flat on the Marshpool Farm Estate, Judy Gresham's face had lit up. 'That's nice, love,' she'd said. 'I didn't know you got farms in London.'

Jane shook her head in amused exasperation. 'There hasn't been a farm there in donkey's years, Mum. It's a sixties council estate. Concrete as far as the eye can see.'

Her mother's face fell. 'Oh. Well, at least you've got a roof over your head.'

They'd left it at that. Jane knew her mother well enough to know that she wouldn't want the truth – that Jane had so few qualifying points that the only accommodation the council was going to offer her was exactly the sort of place she'd ended up with. A hard-to-let box on a run-down East End estate where almost nobody had any form of legitimate employment, where kids ran wild day and night, and where there were more used condoms and hypodermic needles than blades of grass. No, Judy Gresham definitely wouldn't like to think of her daughter living somewhere like that. Apart from anything else, it would seriously impair her ability to boast about how well their Jane was doing.

She'd told her brother Matthew, however. Anything to blunt the edge of the resentment he carried because she was the one who had got away while he'd been left, in his words, to rot in the back of beyond because somebody had to stay for the sake of their parents. It didn't matter that, as the elder, he'd been the first to fly the nest for university and that he'd chosen to come back to the job he'd always wanted. Matthew, Jane thought, had been born aggrieved.

The irony, of course, was that Jane would have swapped London for Fellhead in the blink of an eye if it had held the faintest possibility of doing the work she loved. But there were no jobs for academics in the Lakes, not even for a Wordsworth specialist like her. Not unless she wanted to swap intellectual rigour and research for lecturing to schoolkids about the Lakeland poets. Nothing would kill her passion for the words faster than that, she knew. So instead, she was stuck in the worst kind of urban hell. Jane tucked her head into her chest as she walked along the galleried balcony to the stairs. By what she could only believe to be the evil whim of the architect, her block had been constructed so that the prevailing wind was funnelled down the walkways, rendering even a gentle summer breeze blustery and uncomfortable. On a showery autumn day, it drove the rain into every nook and cranny of the building as well as the clothes of any inhabitants who bothered to emerge from their flats.

Jane turned into the stairwell and gained a brief respite. No point in even trying the lift. Ignoring the badly spelled graffiti, the unsavoury collections of rubbish blown into the corners and the stink of decay and piss, she trotted downwards. At the first turn of the stairs, her stomach flipped over. It was a sight she'd seen so often she knew she should have been inured to it, but every time she saw the tiny frame perched precariously in the lotus position on the narrow concrete banister three floors up, Jane's knees trembled.

'Hey, Jane,' the slight figure called softly.

'Hey, Tenille,' Jane replied, forcing a smile through her fear.

With what felt like death-defying casualness, Tenille unfolded her legs and dropped down to the dank concrete next to Jane. 'Whatchu know?' the thirteen-year-old demanded as she fell into step beside her.

'I know I'm going to be late for work if I don't get a move on,' Jane said, letting gravity give her momentum as she took the stairs at a faster pace. Tenille kept stride with her, her long dreads bouncing on her narrow shoulders.

'I'll walk wi'chu,' Tenille said, her attempt at a swagger a pathetic parody of the wannabe gangstas that hung around the dismal maze of the estate learning their trade from older brothers, cousins and anyone else who managed to stay out of custody for long enough to teach them.

'I hate to sound like a middle-aged, middle-class pain in the arse, Tenille, but shouldn't you be in school?' It was an old line and Jane mentally predicted the response.

'Teachers got nothin' to say to me,' Tenille said mechanically, lengthening her stride to catch up with Jane as they hit street level. 'What they know about my livin'?'

Jane sighed. 'I get so tired of hearing the same old, same old from you, Tenille. You're way too smart to settle for the crap that's coming your way unless you get enough of an education to sidestep it.'

Tenille stuffed her hands into the pockets of her skinny fake leather jacket and raised her narrow shoulders defensively. 'Fuck dat,' she said. 'I ain't gonna be no mo'fo's incubator. None of that baby mamma drama for Tenille.'

They cut through a walkway under the block of flats and emerged beside a stretch of dual carriageway where cars surged past, their drivers rejoicing at finally getting out of second gear, their tyres hissing on the wet tarmac. 'Hard to see how you're going to avoid it unless you harness your brain,' Jane said drily, keeping well away from the kerb and the spray of the passing vehicles.

'I wanna be like you, Jane.' It was a plaintive cry that Jane had heard from Tenille more times than she could count.

'So go to school,' she said, trying not to let her exasperation show.

'I hate the useless stuff they make us do,' Tenille said, a lip-curling sneer transforming her unselfconscious attractiveness into a mask of scorn. 'It's not like what you give me to read.' Her speech had shifted from street to standard English, as if leaving the confines of the estate allowed her to slip from persona to person.

'I'm sure it isn't. But I'm not where I want to be yet, you know. Working part-time in bars and seminar rooms while I get my book finished so I can land a proper job is not what I had in mind when I started out. But I still had to go through the same crap to get even this far. And yes, mostly I did think it was crap,' she continued, drowning whatever Tenille had been about to add. She wished there was something she could offer apart from platitudes, but she didn't know what else to say to a thirteen-year-old mixed-race orphan who not only adored but also seemed to grasp the significance of the writings of Wordsworth, Coleridge, Shelley and De Quincey with an ease that had taken Jane herself a decade of close study to achieve.

Tenille sidestepped to avoid a buggy containing a moon-faced toddler, chocolate smeared across its cheeks, a dummy jammed in its mouth like a stopper designed to keep the chubby child inflated. The pram pusher didn't look that much older than Tenille herself. 'I'm not going to make it that way, Jane,' Tenille said despondently. 'Maybe I could use the poetry another way. Be a rapper like Ms Dynamite,' she added without conviction.

They both knew it was never going to happen. Not unless someone invented a self-esteem drug that Jane could pump into Tenille's veins ahead of the heroin that kept what seemed like half the estate sedated. Jane halted at the bus stop, turning to face Tenille.

11

'Nobody can ever take the words out of your head,' she said.

Tenille picked at a chewed fingernail and stared at the pavement. 'You think I don't know that?' she almost shouted. 'How the fuck else do you think I survive?' Suddenly she spun round on the balls of her feet and she was off, scudding down the uneven pavement like a gazelle, long limbs surprisingly elegant in motion. She disappeared into an alley and Jane felt the familiar mixture of affection and frustration. It stayed with her on the ten-minute bus ride and it still nagged her as she pushed open the door of the wine bar.

Five minutes before noon, the Viking Bar and Grill felt hollow with emptiness. The blond wood, chrome and glass still gleamed in the halogen spots, evidence that nobody had been in since the cleaner finished her shift. Harry had put Michael Nyman's music from *The End of the Affair* on the CD player, and the strings seemed almost to shimmer visibly in the calm air. In twenty minutes' time, the Viking would be transformed as the city slickers piled in, desperate to cram as much food and drink into their short lunch breaks as they could. The air would thicken with conversation, body heat and smoke, and Jane wouldn't have a second to think about anything other than the press of bodies at the bar.

For now, though, it was peaceful. Harry Lambton stood at one end of the long pale birch curve of the bar, leaning on his forearms as he skimmed the morning paper. The light gleamed on the spiky halo of his short fair hair, turning him into a post-modern saint. He glanced up at the sound of Jane's feet on the wooden floor and sketched a wave of greeting, a smile animating his sharp, narrow face. 'Still raining?' he asked.

'Still raining.' Jane leaned in and planted a kiss on Harry's cheek as she passed him on her way to the cubbyhole where the staff hung their coats. 'Everybody in?' she asked as she returned to the main bar, corralling her long dark corkscrew curls and pushing them into a scrunchy.

Harry nodded. That was a relief, Jane thought, slipping past Harry's tightly muscled back and checking everything was where she needed it to be for her shift to run as smoothly as possible. She'd landed this job because Harry's boyfriend Dan was a friend and colleague at the university, but she didn't want anybody accusing her of taking advantage of that relationship. Besides, Harry claimed that managing the bar was only a stopgap. One day he might decide what he wanted to do with his life and Jane didn't want to provide her co-workers with any excuse to grass her up to a new boss as lazy or incompetent. Working at the Viking was demanding, exhausting and poorly paid, but she needed the job.

'I finally came up with a title,' she said, tying the long white bistro apron round her waist. 'For the book.' Harry cocked his head interrogatively. '*The Laureate of Spin: Politics, Poetics and Pretence in the Writings of William Wordsworth*. What do you think?'

Harry frowned, considering. 'I like it,' he said. 'Makes the boring old bastard sound halfway interesting.'

'Interesting is good, it sells books.'

Harry nodded, flicking over a page of his paper and

giving it a cursory look. Then his dark blue eyes narrowed and frown lines appeared between his sandy brows. 'Hey,' he said. 'Isn't Fellhead where you come from?'

Jane turned, a bottle of olives in her hand. 'That's right. Don't tell me somebody finally did something newsworthy?'

Harry raised his eyebrows. 'You could say that. They found a body.'

I am minded tonight of the time we spent at Alfoxden, & the suspicion that fell upon Coleridge and myself, viz. that we were agents of the enemy, gathering information as spies for Bonaparte. I recall Coleridge's assertion that it was beyond the bounds of good sense to give credence to the notion that poets were suited for such an endeavour since we see all before us as matter for our verse & would have no inclination to hold any secrets to our breasts that might serve our calling. In that important respect, he was correct, for the events of this day already ferment within me, seeking an expression in verse. But in the more important respect of maintaining our own counsel, I pray he is mistaken, for my encounter within the secluded bounds of our garden has already laid a heavy burden of knowledge on my shoulders, a burden that could yet bear down heavy on me and on my family. At first, I believed myself to be dreaming, for I hold no belief in the ghostly manifestations of the dead. But this was no apparition. It was a man of flesh and blood, a man I had thought never to see more.

2

Matthew Gresham gulped his last mouthful of coffee and dumped the mug in the sink. Members of staff were supposed to do their own washing up, but Matthew reckoned there had to be some advantages to rank so ever since his promotion to head teacher he'd left his dirty crockery for someone else to deal with. Besides, he had more important things to occupy him. So far nobody had commented on his presumptuousness, though he'd noticed disapproving glares from Marcia Porter more than once. But Marcia was a busted flush. When he'd leapfrogged her into the top job, she'd stopped trying to get the world to bend to her will. It was as if she'd thrown in the towel. She might not like what Matthew did, but she didn't attempt to challenge him. Not like before, when they were theoretically equal except for her constant assertion of her seniority. These days, she gave him as wide a berth as was possible in a village school with a staff of five teachers and four teaching assistants.

Teaching assistants. That was a joke. Mothers with time on their hands and the misplaced notion that somehow, merely by giving birth, they had the inside track on how to educate kids. But they'd gone through the school system before SATs and the National Curriculum. They didn't have a bloody clue about the pressures that real teachers like him had to live with on a daily basis. Matthew missed no opportunity to remind them of how much the world had changed. The main result was that, as with the rest of his staff, they spent as little time as possible slacking in the staffroom. That suited Matthew fine; his office was, to his way of thinking, barely adequate for his needs. He much preferred working in the staffroom, where he could brew himself a coffee whenever he felt like it.

He had to stoop to glance in the mirror above the sink which had been placed to suit the stature of female teachers rather than six-foot headmasters. Dark blue eyes stared back at him from olive skin a couple of shades darker than the local norm. The legacy of his Cornish grandfather, passed on to Matthew and Jane from their mother. He ran a hand through the dark mop of mutinous curls, inherited from the other side of the family. They looked glorious on his sister but simply made him feel like a poor man's Harpo Marx. He smiled wryly, thinking of the lesson he was about to teach the top two classes. Genealogy and genetics, those twisted strands that wrapped around each other like the double helix of DNA, complete with the kinks that could have all kinds of unforeseen consequences. There was no doubting his relationship to his sister nor his parentage. Their father had the same corkscrew curls, as had his father before him.

The bell rang for afternoon classes and Matthew hurried out of the staffroom. As he approached the classroom, he heard a low murmur of conversation which stilled when the fifteen children saw him appear in the doorway. One of the benefits of small rural schools, Matthew thought. They still learned manners along with the National Curriculum. He didn't envy the poor sods who had to teach the kids on the estate where Jane lived. 'Good afternoon, children,' he said, his long legs quickly covering the short distance to his desk.

'Good afternoon, Mr Gresham,' the class chorused raggedly.

He opened up his laptop and hit the key to take it out of slumber mode. Immediately the interactive whiteboard behind him showed a screen which read *Family Trees*. Matthew perched on the edge of his desk, from where he could easily reach the keyboard. 'Today we're beginning an important new project which will form part of the village Christmas celebrations. Now, one thing every one of us has is ancestors. Who can tell me what an ancestor is?'

A small boy with a thick mop of black hair and a face like a baby spider monkey shot a hand into the air. He bounced on his chair with eagerness.

'Sam?' Matthew said, trying not to sound weary. It was always Sam Clewlow.

'It's your family, sir. Not your family that's alive now, but all the ones that came before. Like, your grandparents and their grandparents.'

'That's right. Our ancestors are the people who came before us. Who made us what we are. Every one of us is who we are and what we are because of the way our genes were combined down the ages. Now, does anyone know what a family tree is?'

18

Sam Clewlow's hand rose again. The others looked on in indifference or satisfaction that Sam was doing all the work and saving them the bother. This time, he didn't wait to be asked. 'Sir, it's like a map of your family history. It's got everybody's birthdays, and when they got married and who to, and when they had children and when they died and everything.'

'You've got it, Sam. And what we're going to do over the next few weeks is to try to map our own families. That'll be easier for some of you than others – those of you whose families have lived locally for generations will be able to track them from parish records. It will be harder for those of you whose families are relative newcomers to the area. But one of the things we'll be doing during this project is exploring the many different ways we can go about mapping our past. The thing about this project is that it's one where you'll have to work with the other members of your family, especially the older ones such as grandparents and great-aunts and -uncles.' Again, Matthew felt grateful that he wasn't stuck in some inner-city sink school. A project like this would be impossible to contemplate there, with its fragmented lives and alternative views of what constituted a family. But in Fellhead, either they'd lived in extended families for generations or else they were incomers from the sort of nice middle-class family where, even when they pretended to be New Age, marriage certificates were still the order of the day more often than not.

'To show you the kind of thing we'll be doing, I'm going to show you my own family tree.' He clicked the mouse button and his name came up on the screen. Underneath it was his date of birth. He clicked again and this time his name was linked to Diane Brotherton with an 'equals' sign. 'Can you guess what that sign means? Jonathan?' he asked a chunky red-haired boy, ignoring Sam's eager hand.

Jonathan Bramley looked faintly startled. He frowned in concentration. 'Dunno,' he finally conceded.

Trying not to show his exasperation, Matthew said patiently, 'It means "married to". Mrs Gresham was Diane Brotherton until she married me.' He clicked again and a vertical line appeared, connecting them to Gabriel Stephen Gresham.

'That's your baby,' one of the girls piped up unprompted.

'That's right, Kylie.' Matthew clicked again. Now little thumbnail pictures appeared beside each of the names. 'We can even add photos. That way, we can see how family resemblances move between generations. Now, we can all start our family trees with what we know already.' He tapped the keyboard and brought up another screen. This showed his parents and his sister, complete with photos, places of birth and occupations.

'But we're going to do more than that. We're going to delve into the past and trace our family trees as far as we can.' This time, the family tree he displayed included his grandparents – one grandfather an incomer, a refugee from the Cornish tin mines who had come to the Lakes to mine slate, the other a Cumberland shepherd – and his aunts, uncles and cousins.

'And one of the things we are going to learn about is the way a community like ours has grown through the years. We'll find all sorts of connections between families that you might not even have known about yourselves. You may even discover common ancestors, and you'll start to get a sense of how people's lives have changed over the centuries.' Matthew's gift for sharing his enthusiasm was working on the children now. They were hanging on his words.

'We're going to begin with your immediate family. Look at my family tree on the board so you know how to lay it out on the page. And tonight, when you go home, you can ask the rest of the family to help you fill in the gaps. As we continue, we'll explore different ways of discovering more information about your history and your ancestors. Now, find a fresh page in your workbooks and make a start.'

Matthew waited till they had all got going, then he sat down behind the desk. He pulled a pile of maths workbooks towards him and started marking the children's work. His absorption was disturbed by a muttering and sniggering that ran round the room. When he looked up, Sam Clewlow was flushed, his eyes bright with unshed tears. Jonathan Bramley looked gleeful.

'What's going on?' Matthew demanded, getting to his feet. Nobody met his eye. 'Jonathan? What's going on?'

Jonathan's mouth compressed in a tight line. He didn't know it yet, but he would spend the rest of his life being caught out by his own stupidity and the concomitant inability to dissemble. 'Nothing,' he muttered eventually.

'You can tell me now or you can stay after school and tell me then,' Matthew said, his voice hard. He'd never understood the complaints of teachers who claimed they couldn't control the kids. You just had to show them who was boss, and keep on showing them.

'I just said . . .' Jonathan's voice trailed off as he looked around desperately for support that was not forthcoming.

'You just said what?'

'I said we all knew who Sam's ancestor was,' he mumbled.

'I'm fascinated to hear it,' Matthew said. 'And who exactly did you have in mind?'

Jonathan's ears were scarlet and his eyes were fixed on the floor. 'The Monkey Man up on the moor,' he said in a voice barely above a whisper.

'You mean the body in the bog?' Matthew guessed. The grisly discovery had been the talk of the village for the past few days.

Jonathan nodded and gulped. 'It was just a joke, like.'

'Jokes are meant to be funny,' Matthew said repressively. 'Insults aren't a joke. And it's not appropriate to make jokes about the dead. When that man was alive, he had friends and family who loved him, just like you. Imagine how you'd feel if someone you loved died and some thoughtless person made a joke about it.'

'But, sir, there's nobody alive to care about the Monkey Man,' the irrepressible Kylie said.

Matthew groaned inwardly. It was going to be one of those conversations, he knew it. He believed in his job, but sometimes he wished he hadn't done quite such a good job of helping them develop enquiring minds. 'Why do you call him the Monkey Man?' he asked.

'Coz that's what they look like,' a boy piped up. 'There was a programme on the telly about that one they found down in Cheshire. He looked like an ape.'

'So that's why we call him the Monkey Man,' another chipped in.

Sam Clewlow snorted. 'That's stupid,' he said.

'Why is it stupid, Sam?' Matthew asked.

'Because the man they found in the peat in Cheshire died back in the Stone Age. That's why he looks the way he does. But the one on the fell isn't that old. So he doesn't look like a monkey, he looks like us,' Sam said firmly.

Snorts of derision met his words. 'He don't look like me,' Jonathan blurted out. 'Our Jason said he looked like an old leather bag with a face. And he should know, he plays darts with Paul Lister that found the body.' Jonathan leaned back in his seat, his earlier humiliation forgotten as he basked in their attention.

'So maybe he is one of our ancestors,' Sam chipped in.

'Yeah,' Kylie said enthusiastically. 'Maybe he got murdered and buried on the fell.'

'That's right. Coz how else would he have ended up in the peat?' another said.

'He might simply have had an accident when he was out on the hill,' Matthew said, trying to dampen down their ghoulish enthusiasm. 'He might have gone out to tend his sheep, taken a tumble and died out on the fell.'

'But then somebody would have gone looking for him and they'd have found his body,' Sam pointed out reasonably. 'The only way he could have ended up under the peat is if somebody buried him there because they didn't want anybody to know what had happened to him. I think Kylie's right. I think somebody murdered him.'

'Well, until the scientists have done their tests, we won't know anything for sure,' Matthew said firmly.

'It'll be like *Silent Witness*,' Kylie said. 'The doctor will figure out how he died and then the police will have to find out what happened.'

Matthew couldn't help grinning. 'I don't think it'll be quite like that, Kylie. From what I hear, if the body in the bog was murdered, his killer will be long dead too. But until we have some facts, I suggest we all get back to what we do know about.' He held up a hand to silence their chatter. 'And who knows? Maybe one of you will discover an ancestor who went missing at the right time.'

Sam Clewlow gazed at him, open-mouthed. 'That would be fantastic,' he breathed.

I was engaged in my poetical labours upon the long poem on my own life, pondering how best I might find apt illustration of those matters I hold dear when I saw a figure at the gate. At first glance, I took him to be one of those travelling or wandering men who from time to time arrive at our door in search of sustenance. My sister is accustomed to provide them with food & drink before setting them on their way. On occasion, she has gleaned tales from them which have provided me with matter fit to be translated into poems & so I do not discourage her in this small charity. The man at the gate seemed to be one such, with travel-stained clothes & a large-brimmed hat to shelter him from sun & rain alike. I was about to direct him to the kitchen door when he spoke. To my astonishment, he greeted me by my Christian name, addressing me with some warmth & familiarity. _William, I see you are hard at it. I was told you had become the Poet of the Age & now I see it for myself._ I still had no notion of who the man was, but he opened the gate without further ado & walked across the garden towards me. His bow-legged gait had a nautical flavour to it, & as he drew closer an impossible suspicion grew large in my mind.

3

By three thirty, the Viking had almost returned to its default state of vacant tranquillity. A couple of the rear booths were still occupied by pairs of men talking business over their espressos. They'd already paid their bills; the staff were invisible to them now. Jane loaded the washer with the last of the glasses then hitched herself on to a stool at the end of the bar to give her aching feet some relief. Harry emerged from the kitchen carrying a plate of left-over sandwiches.

Jane reached for a sandwich as Harry pulled up a stool and sat down beside her. 'Where did you put the paper?' she asked.

'I'll get it.' Harry jumped off his stool and went behind the bar. He pulled the paper out from one of the shelves and handed it over.

Jane went straight to the story she'd not had time to read properly before the lunchtime rush.

RIDDLE OF BODY IN LAKELAND BOG

The body of a man found in a peat bog in the Lake District may be hundreds of years old, police said yesterday.

At first, it was thought the remains might have lain undiscovered for thousands of years, like Stone Age corpses recovered from similar sites.

But initial forensic examination indicates that the body is far more recent. Detective Chief Inspector Ewan Rigston said, 'We believe the body has been in the ground for a very long time, perhaps hundreds of years. But we don't think it's anything like as old as some of the remains unearthed in other places.

'We will know more after the forensic specialists have done their work.'

When asked how the man had died, DCI Rigston said it was too early to tell.

The body was discovered by a local shepherd searching for a lost sheep. Police believe the heavy summer rain had eroded banking within the ancient peat deposits at Carts Moss near the village of Fellhead.

Paul Lister, 37, of Coniston Cottages, Fellhead, spoke last night of his gruesome discovery. 'I was following my dog over Carts Moss, looking for a stray lamb. I slipped on the wet grass and fell down into one of the channels between the peat hags.

'My hand slipped on something and I looked down. At first, I couldn't figure out what I was looking at. I thought it was a cow hide or something. Then I realised it had a human face.

'I couldn't believe it. It was like something out of a horror movie.'

While he was waiting for the police to arrive, Mr Lister had the chance to look more closely at his grim find. 'He had black hair, and it looked like he had black tattoos on his arms and his body. But I don't know if that was just the effect of being in the peat for so long.'

Forensic anthropologist Dr River Wilde from the University of Northern England has been called in to work with local scientific experts in a bid to unlock the mystery of the body in the bog. DCI Rigston said, 'Until Dr Wilde has completed her investigations, there is nothing more we can say.'

Jane almost choked on her sandwich. 'Look at that, Harry,' she said when she had recovered herself. She pointed to the penultimate paragraph.

Before Harry could respond, a hand landed on each of their shoulders. A shaved head insinuated itself between theirs. 'What's so fascinating?' a familiar voice asked.

Jane swivelled round to kiss Dan Seabourne's smooth cheek. 'Dan! What a lovely surprise. Harry didn't say you were coming.'

'Harry didn't know,' Harry said, a trace of acid in his tone.

'My three o'clock cancelled on me, so I thought I'd sneak away and pick you up,' Dan said, ruffling his lover's hair.

'Checking up on Harry and the new Italian chef, more like,' Jane teased. 'I knew we'd never get rid of you once you'd seen Giaco in his chef's whites.'

Dan pretended to clutch his heart in shock. 'So insightful,' he sighed. Then he reached round her and grabbed a stool. 'Jane, I haven't seen you in a week. Are you hiding from me?'

Jane groaned. 'It's the book. I'm supposed to have it finished by the end of the year and right now I think the only way I'm going to manage it is if Mephistopheles walks through the door with an offer I can't refuse. When I signed the contract, I thought it would be a piece of piss to turn my thesis into a book.' She snorted derisively. 'How wrong can one woman be?'

'Maybe you should get out of town for a while, get your head down and get it finished,' Dan said. 'I could cover your teaching for you.'

Jane grinned. She and Dan were both sailors in the same boat; post-doctoral researchers, scrabbling for any teaching that might lead to the elusive grail of a permanent lecturing job, desperate to make an impression on their professor and to make ends meet. They should have been rivals, but a friendship dating back to undergraduate days forestalled that. 'And pick up my wages too? Nice try, Dan,' she teased, digging him in the ribs with her elbow. 'You have no scruples, you know that? You should be getting off your arse and writing a book of your own.'

Dan spread his hands, feigning innocence. 'Hey, I'm just trying to help here. You could benefit from less distraction, right?'

Harry pulled the paper towards him. 'From the looks of this, Fellhead's got distractions of its own.'

He pointed to the article, passing it over to Dan. 'Death stalks the fells.'

Harry and Jane carried on eating while Dan read the piece. 'Well, at least you wouldn't have to worry about a mad axeman on the loose,' he said. 'If this is a murder victim, his killer will have been in the ground almost as long.'

'Never mind murder,' Jane said, pointing to the penultimate paragraph. 'I'm more interested in his tattoos.'

'His tattoos?' Dan asked.

'Black tattoos. What does that say to you?'

Dan shrugged. 'Apart from David Beckham, nothing at all.'

'Eighteenth century, sailors, South Sea islands. Lots of them got native tattoos when they went there. Like Fletcher Christian.'

Dan grinned. 'Your favourite rural legend.'

'What are you two on about?' Harry asked.

'What do you know about the mutiny on the *Bounty*?' Jane said.

Harry shrugged. 'Mel Gibson. Very cute in those tight trousers.'

Jane groaned. 'Good to see you were paying attention.'

'Hey, I'm only joking. I'm not just a bimbo, Jane,' Harry protested. 'I remember the bit where Mel stages the mutiny and casts the evil Captain Bligh adrift in an open boat then sets sail for Tahiti.'

'Very good, Harry. Except it wasn't actually Mel Gibson, it was Fletcher Christian who led the mutiny. And what I'm interested in isn't the mutiny as such, it's the aftermath. After Bligh made his epic voyage to safety and finally got back to London, the navy was alerted to look out for the mutineers and to bring them back to London for court martial. Years later, a group of them were found on Tahiti and shipped back. But the fate of Fletcher and the other hard-core mutineers remained a mystery for a long time. They actually ended up on Pitcairn Island with some of the native women and men and settled down there.'

Harry nodded. 'Pitcairn . . . They had that child sex scandal a couple of years ago, didn't they?'

'Right. Featuring direct descendants of some of the mutineers. But that wasn't the first trouble in Paradise,' Jane said. 'Basically, there weren't enough women to go round. The official version is that the mutineers had a falling-out with the natives and there was a massacre. Supposedly Fletcher Christian was the first white man killed. End of story.'

'But . . .? I mean, there has to be a but, right? Otherwise you wouldn't be getting excited about some dead body with a bunch of black tatts,' Harry said.

'This is Jane's fantasy bit,' Dan chipped in.

Jane looked faintly uncomfortable. 'There's always been a rumour in the Lake District that Fletcher Christian didn't die on Pitcairn. That the massacre was just a cover-up. Somehow he managed to flee the island and make his way back to England, where he lived out the rest of his days hidden from justice by his family and friends. It was a pretty risky enterprise for everyone concerned. If Fletcher had been betrayed or discovered, he would definitely have been hanged for leading the mutiny. And so would anyone who had knowingly had contact with him without handing him over to the authorities.'

Harry's expression shifted through surprise to incredulity. 'You're kidding, right? I mean, this is just gossip?'

'Like I said, it's Jane's favourite rural legend,' Dan said, lighting a cigarette.

Jane shook her head, her long curls catching the light. 'It's not just gossip. John Barrow's book raises the question as far back as 1831.'

'As conspiracy theories go, you have to admit it's a goodie,' Dan said. 'Mr Christian staged a massacre and sailed off into the sunset. Oh no, wait a minute. How *did* he get away, Jane? They burned the ship, didn't they?'

Jane leaned on the bar. 'They did. But the *Bounty* had two ship's jolly boats on board and they've never been satisfactorily accounted for. Also, there's the matter of the missing log.' She grinned. 'That's where you're supposed to say, "What missing log?"'

Dan inclined his head and held up his hands in mock astonishment. 'What missing log?'

'Fletcher Christian was an officer of the watch. He was accustomed to keeping a log. It would have been second nature to him.'

'Makes sense,' Harry said.

'It would be extraordinary if there was no record kept of how they settled Pitcairn. There was no shortage of paper and pens. They were still using them years later in the school they set up for their kids. But the only documentary account ever seen was written by one of the other mutineers, Edward Young. And it doesn't start until after the massacre, which implies someone else was keeping notes until that point. Who else but Fletcher? If he'd died, it stands

32

to reason that the journal would have survived him. But if he took to the sea . . .' Jane's voice trailed off.

'He'd have taken it with him, right?' Harry concluded. She could see he was interested too, in spite of his perpetual assumption of cool. 'OK, I'll grant you that that's suggestive, if nothing else. But, as you say yourself, it's all circumstantial.'

'Not quite all of it. Let me tell you about Peter Heywood. He was one of the mutineers who came back. But unlike most of the others who were court-martialled, his family had the cash and connections to secure their blue-eyed boy a pardon. Instead of being hanged, he went on to have a glittering naval career. But the really interesting thing about Peter Heywood is that he was a distant cousin of Fletcher Christian. He grew up on the Isle of Man, where Fletcher spent a fair bit of his own youth. So, as well as sailing with him, Heywood was personally connected to Fletcher. He knew him well,' Jane said. 'And in 1809 or thereabouts, Peter Heywood saw Fletcher Christian in Plymouth.'

Harry frowned. 'But Plymouth was a naval base, wasn't it? Surely he'd have had to have been insane to walk around Plymouth in broad daylight? Here's the most notorious mutineer in the history of the British navy. I mean, even somebody like me with no interest in history has heard of him. And according to you, here's a man who went to extraordinary lengths to stay out of harm's way after the mutiny, a man who'd be a cert for the hangman's rope if he'd ever been caught. And yet here he is taking an afternoon stroll in a city that's awash with naval officers and ratings. And who does he bump into but his old mucker Peter Heywood.' Harry spread his hands in the manner of a man making an unanswerable case. 'And even supposing it did happen, if Heywood and Christian were as close as you say, why would he admit to having seen Christian? It makes no sense.'

'He didn't admit it, Harry. Not publicly anyway. It never came out until after his death. And I can speculate,' Jane said, her voice mild. 'What if he'd arranged to meet Heywood then, at the last minute, Heywood couldn't disentangle himself from one of his colleagues? And when Fletcher saw Heywood wasn't alone, he took to his heels.'

Harry shook his head. 'But why would Fletcher Christian leave Pitcairn in the first place? He was safe there, surely? Why throw that away?'

'I'm not so sure that he felt safe,' Jane said. 'It's clear there were deep divisions between the mutineers themselves as well as the problems with the native men. There's also some evidence that the other mutineers resented his authority as the only officer left among them. And he was a decent man, remember? Maybe he wanted to make his peace, like the Ancient Mariner. Maybe he wanted to explain why he'd been driven to mutiny in the first place,' Jane argued. 'Only, when he got back, he discovered that Bligh had not only survived, he'd become a hero thanks to his amazing navigation of the Pacific. Not to mention the fact that he'd had plenty of time to get his version of the mutiny out there. Whatever Fletcher's motives were for inciting the crew against Bligh, it was too late for him to make his case.'

'But what case could he have made?' Harry asked. 'Mutiny's mutiny, isn't it?'

'There was one defence to mutiny that Christian could have relied on,' Dan said.

Harry's eyebrows shot up. 'Suddenly you're the expert on naval law?'

'No, but I do know something about the history of gay oppression, sweetheart,' Dan said. 'What if Christian alleged sodomy against Bligh? That was a hanging offence back then, wasn't it? If he could demonstrate that Bligh had forced him to have sex against his will, wouldn't that have mitigated the mutiny?' He paused, his brows furrowed, teeth gnawing his lower lip. 'Of course, he would have needed a third-party witness to make it stand up. Back then, because it was such an easy allegation to make and so hard to substantiate, the courts martial insisted on more than one man's word against another. And Christian must have known that.'

'Maybe there was a witness,' Jane said slowly. 'And maybe part of the reason Fletcher led the mutiny was to protect the witness . . .' her voice trailed off and she stared dreamily across the empty bar.

'What do you mean?' Harry was still intrigued.

Jane held up a finger, giving herself a pause to consider her position. 'Let's go back to Peter Heywood,' she said, her eyes focused inward as she searched through the knowledge she'd amassed over years of fascination. 'Fletcher had sailed previously with Bligh and it's on record that he was the captain's favourite. Same story during the *Bounty*'s voyage as far as Tahiti. Then Fletcher spends six months ashore, takes himself a native concubine . . .'

'Concubine, I love that word,' Dan said, rolling it on his tongue.

'Anyway,' Jane said forcefully, 'when the ship leaves Tahiti, Fletcher doesn't want to go back to being Bligh's . . .'

'Catamite. That's the word you're looking for. Another lovely one,' Dan interrupted.

'Whatever. And Bligh starts treating him like shit. And Fletcher's decision has also put him on the horns of a dilemma. He feels he owes a duty of care to young Peter Heywood, his kinsman. Because it was also well documented that Heywood was Bligh's second-favourite after Fletcher. So Fletcher wants to protect Heywood, but not at the expense of submitting again to Bligh.'

'And so he leads a mutiny, knowing he faces certain death if he's ever caught? All to protect the honour of Peter Heywood?' Harry sounded dubious.

'Maybe he's also protecting himself,' Dan said. 'If Bligh had made a move on Heywood too, then he was Christian's witness. Then Christian could argue that mutiny was the only way to stop a sexual predator exploiting his crew far from their home port. Wouldn't that work?'

'It might, I suppose,' Harry said grudgingly. 'Man, you've changed your tune. You were the one calling this Jane's fantasy. Now you're defending her ideas and I'm the one not seeing evidence of anything except Jane's imagination.'

Jane got to her feet and headed behind the bar to finish clearing up. 'That's my womanly powers of persuasion, Harry. And besides, you're wrong. There is something a little more concrete. The mutineers who ended up being court-martialled were the ones who asked Christian to take them back to Tahiti, Peter Heywood among them. Those guys never made it as far as Pitcairn. When the two groups were parting company, Fletcher took Heywood to one side. And when Fletcher said his private farewell to Heywood, he asked him to pass some information to the Christian family back home. But Heywood never disclosed what Fletcher had said. Why would he keep shtum, unless the message was something that would have been viewed as shameful, presumably to himself as well as to Fletcher? That something might have been Fletcher's underlying reason for the mutiny – Bligh's sexual abuse of Christian and Heywood.'

Harry laughed out loud. 'Jane, you should be writing fiction, not criticism. Is this what passes for intellectual rigour in the English Department?' He joined her behind the bar, taking glasses from the dishwasher and replacing them on the shelves.

Jane leaned on the counter and grinned. 'Maybe I should turn to fiction. And if I did, I'd start with William Wordsworth's lost epic.'

'Wordsworth's lost epic?' Harry said, sounding bemused.

'She's kept the best till last, Harry,' Dan said. 'This is the "woo-woo" moment. You're going to love this one.'

Jane carried on regardless. '"Innocence and Corruption; the True History of the Mutiny upon the ship the *Bounty* in the South Seas." Or something similarly Wordsworthian.'

'Huh?' Harry said.

'They were at school together, Harry. William

Wordsworth, the Lakeland Laureate and head honcho of the Romantic poets, and Fletcher Christian, *Bounty* mutineer, were contemporaries at Hawkshead School. Fletcher's brother Edward was their teacher. He went on to become Professor of Law at the same Cambridge college where Wordsworth took his degree. And he represented the Wordsworth family in an important lawsuit. So who else would Fletcher choose to tell his version of events to but his old schoolfriend? The friend of his family who went on to become a famous man of letters. And even if he knew he could never publish it because of the potentially dire consequences, Wordsworth couldn't have ignored a story as big as that, could he?'

Although I offered him no response, he continued to approach me. The man seemed entirely at ease as he made himself at home on the bench that sits nearby my work table. He stretched his legs before him, crossing them at the ankles. 'Do you not know me yet, William?' he said, a note of amusement in his tone. As he spoke, he pushed his hat to the back of his head, allowing me to see his face fully for the first time. Many years had passed since I had last cast my gaze upon his countenance, but I knew him at once. The vicissitudes of time & experience had left their marks upon him, but they were not sufficient to blunt his essential characteristics. My suspicion turned to certainty & my heart leapt in my breast.

4

Tenille knew all about choices. She understood that although teachers loved to lay out their holier-than-thou shit about creating options for their pupils, deep down they believed that people like her didn't have choices. Not really. Not like the teachers and their own middle-class brats. In their hearts, they thought kids like Tenille were stuck without hope in the life they already had. So whatever their mouths might say, the way they acted shouted something different. The way they acted said, 'You're going to do drugs, go shoplifting, get pregnant in your teens and have a shit life on a scummy council estate till you die a premature death from smoking or drinking or drugs or deprivation. So why am I bothering trying to teach you anything?'

But they were wrong. She did have choices, even though they weren't as obvious or as wide-ranging as most thirteen-year-olds'. But Tenille was damn sure she had more going for her than any of the rest of the no-hopers from the Marshpool Farm Estate. That was why she didn't hang out with the other truants. She wasn't interested in dodging the Attendance

Officers or the security guards in the shopping malls and the amusement arcades. Joining the gangs shoplifting tatty clothes and cheap make-up held no charms for her. Not that she was above nicking stuff. Just not the crap that interested them. She couldn't imagine talking Aleesha Graham and her crew into raiding Waterstone's for books of poetry. Apart from anything else, you put them in a bookshop and they'd stick out like a three-piece suit in the mosh pit at a hip-hop gig. Just the thought of it made her roll her eyes back in her head and curl her lips in a sneer. Nor did she have any desire to spend her days holed up in some shithole of a flat watching nicked DVDs with a bunch of losers who just wanted to get out of their heads on weed or extra-strong cider and alcopops.

It hadn't been so bad when Sharon had been unattached and working down the café. With her aunt safely out the door by ten, Tenille would sneak back indoors, curl up under her lumpy duvet and read until school kicked out and she could colonise one of the computers in the library to get online and hang out in chat rooms. There she could find other weirdoes who read poetry and wanted to talk about it. If she got desperate for the sound of another human voice, she would sneak downstairs and check out Jane Gresham's flat. If Jane was home, she'd usually let Tenille in to raid her bookshelves, and if she wasn't too busy, they'd sometimes sit drinking coffee and talking. Except when Jane got one on her and decided to deliver her lecture about how Tenille shouldn't be dogging it. Like anybody in that dumping ground called Marshpool Comprehensive was ever going to teach her anything that would make her life one single step easier.

It was Jane who had told her about the chat rooms, even letting Tenille use her computer occasionally when Jane was reading and not needing the machine herself. Now they'd become Tenille's lifeline, providing her with a retreat where she could be the person she knew she was deep inside. By most people's standards, it wasn't much. But it was enough to allow a narrow chink of optimism into Tenille's life.

But all that had gone to shit a few weeks before. It had started when Sharon had left the café to take a job in the works canteen of a local plastics factory. Instead of regular days, she was on shifts, so two weeks in three, Tenille lost a substantial chunk of her daytime sanctuary. That had been bad enough, though Tenille was resourceful and soon found ways around the problem. But then Sharon had found herself a new boyfriend.

In the seven years she'd been in the nominal care of her aunt, Tenille had grown accustomed to the steady stream of unsteady men who pitched up at the flat for indeterminate lengths of time. She'd learned early to stay out of the way when they were around. Sharon didn't want her dead junkie sister's bastard putting them off, and she'd made it clear that Tenille should be neither seen nor heard when she was entertaining. So Tenille shut herself in her room for hours on end, tuning out the animal noises that seeped through the walls and under the door, sneaking out when the coast was clear to raid the fridge and kitchen cupboards for whatever she could find to kill the hunger that gripped her. Sometimes she felt like the invisible child, a phantom who slipped into the cracks and corners nobody else wanted to occupy. It wasn't a notion she enjoyed, but recently she'd begun to yearn for that invisibility.

Of course, it had occurred to her before the arrival of Geno Marley in her life that there were distinct advantages to slipping under other people's radar. It made truanting and shoplifting so much easier. But as far as Sharon's boyfriends were concerned, she'd believed the only benefit she gained from remaining unnoticed was to avoid Sharon's wrath if she inadvertently got in the way of her aunt's love life. Although she knew in theory about men who preyed on kids like her, she'd never experienced it first hand. The kind of men who had been attracted to the overripe charms of her aunt had thus far shown no inclinations in her direction. After all, there was nothing childish about Sharon, a tough mixed-race woman who exuded a mature and knowing sexuality that promised the delights of experience rather than the temptations of innocence. She wasn't one of those women who fought a doomed rearguard action against time; Sharon accepted she was past the first flush of youth and understood that mutton can be a far tastier meat than lamb. And so her men tended to be those who wanted a woman who had a firm grasp of the pleasure principle.

If she'd confined her neediness to the sexual dimension, Sharon's relationships would likely have lasted longer than they did. But so far she'd failed to find a man who could put up with the constant nagging demands of her insecurities for more than a few months. Tenille was accustomed to bearing the unreasonable blame for the departure of yet another browbeaten lover and, every time it happened, it reinforced her desire to stay out of the way next time.

She hadn't been fast enough to avoid Geno Marley, mostly because she hadn't been expecting him. Usually, she was already safely closeted in her room when a new man tumbled into Sharon's bed for the first time. But Tenille hadn't factored shift work into her calculations. Sharon had been due to finish her shift that day at two, so Tenille had cleared out in good time. She'd been unlucky at the library that afternoon; a quartet of wrinklies had commandeered the computers and a greasy-haired grandson was teaching them the basics of websurfing. Like they were going to be downloading MP3s and hanging out in chat rooms any time soon, Tenille thought scornfully. She hung around for a while, but it was clear that grey power wasn't about to concede in the foreseeable future.

She'd been surprised to return to an empty flat. Sharon should have been home two hours ago. Tenille assumed her aunt had gone shopping. Hell, she hoped so, because there was fuck all to eat or drink in the place. She'd turned on the TV and slumped on the sofa, too pissed off and hungry to read. The sound of the front door opening barely registered, but the sound of muffled giggling and the deep rumble of a man's voice set her senses on alert. She scrambled to her feet, ready for flight, but there was nowhere to run to.

The living-room door opened on Sharon weaving in an unsteady shimmy, a man's arms locked around her waist, the silly smile of drink plastered on her face, her café-au-lait skin flushed scarlet. Seeing Tenille, a scowl wiped the cheerfulness from her face. 'Whatchu doing here?' she demanded.

'I live here,' Tenille muttered.

A face appeared over Sharon's shoulder, the expression a mix of curiosity and impatience. 'Who's this?' he said, a slur in his voice and the seeds of lechery in his smile.

'My niece. I told you, remember?' Sharon was pissed off, there was no mistaking it.

The man dropped his hands from Sharon's waist and sidestepped her so he could fully enter the room. Tenille recognised an expression she'd seen directed at others but not so far at herself, probably because the anonymous clothes she chose for the street hid rather than flattered her recently developed figure. But here in the privacy of her own home, she was stripped down to T-shirt and hip-hugging jeans. And this man was drinking it in as deep as Sharon had obviously drunk in some afternoon shebeen. Tenille didn't like it one little bit.

'So, little niece, you got a name?' He stepped closer, one hand carelessly draped on Sharon's hip.

'Tenille,' she muttered reluctantly.

'Pretty name for a pretty girl.'

'What's yours?' Tenille demanded abruptly.

He grinned, revealing a gold canine. 'I'm Geno,' he said. 'Like Geno Washington.'

Tenille wondered if she was supposed to be impressed by a name she'd never heard before. She raised her eyebrows in a faint gesture of contempt. 'Who he, man?'

He faked astonishment. 'You never heard of Geno?

45

Girl, you know nothing. Geno was only the greatest soul singer this godforsaken country ever produced.'

Sharon, impatient at so much attention directed away from her, butted in. 'Donchu got some shit of your own to be getting on with?' she said petulantly.

Grateful for the chance to escape, Tenille edged nearer the door. But Geno wasn't for moving. Tenille had to go round him, Sharon moving to one side and kissing her teeth in irritation. Then she was free, out in the hall and suddenly aware of the heightened rhythm of her breathing.

That had just been the start of it. Discomfort and unease attended Tenille whenever Geno was around and she couldn't make a quick getaway. Generally she managed to keep out of his way, but that was getting harder and harder as the weeks passed and it became clear he wasn't about to abandon Sharon any time soon. After three weeks, he had virtually moved in, always around when Sharon was there and sometimes hanging out even when she was at work. Tenille's life came to be lived more and more outside the flat; at Jane's when she could manage it, or on the windswept galleries and dank stairwells of the estate when she couldn't. She pretended even to herself that her actions were the result of choice; it was better than naming the fear she didn't want to acknowledge.

But she couldn't kid herself for ever. Sharon had to do nights sooner or later, and when that week rolled around, Tenille felt no surprise when her aunt announced that Geno would be sleeping over to keep an eye on her. No surprise, just a hot spurt of fear in her stomach. 'I never needed no minder when you did nights before,' Tenille had protested.

'You think it felt right, me leaving you on your own?' Sharon challenged.

'I'm not a baby, I don't need no babysitter.'

'You still not legal alone, girl. It make me feel happier knowing there's somebody here with you.' Sharon gathered her make-up, shovelling it into the fake Louis Vuitton bag Geno had presented her with. He'd preened like a peacock while Tenille had looked on with contempt, knowing he'd picked it up on some market stall for buttons.

'It never bothered you before. You been leaving me shut up in here since I was eight year old.'

'And I was wrong. Geno made me see that. He tol' me about bad things happening lately to girls round here.'

Tenille shivered. 'Nothin' goan happen to me. I don't need Geno to protect me. I don't like Geno,' she tried desperately, feeling somehow ashamed to articulate what really bothered her about him.

'He's a good man,' Sharon said. 'So donchu piss him off, you hear?' There was an air of finality in her voice that Tenille knew better than to argue with. She swept her coat off the chair and made for the door. 'He'll be round later. Donchu mess with his head. You hear me, girl?' she added, whirling round with a look of dark suspicious anger on her handsome face.

Tenille scowled. 'I hear you,' she mumbled. The door had scarcely closed behind her aunt before she was on her feet, pulling on her own coat, throwing her MP3 player and a couple of books into her backpack and heading out into the early evening gloom. She made straight for Jane's flat, but the lights were out and her knock met with no response. Tenille thrust her hand in her pocket and fingered the uneven contours of the key. She'd 'borrowed' the spare from the kitchen drawer months before, had it copied and returned it before Jane even noticed its absence. But she was cautious about its use. It would only be an insurance policy for as long as Jane didn't know she had it. When that useless wanker Jake had still been on the scene, she'd never dared to sneak in, unsure of his comings and goings. She'd only chanced it a couple of times since, both occasions when she'd seen Jane off on the bus and known for sure she'd be at the Viking for the next four hours. Tonight, she had no idea where Jane was or when she'd return. It was too risky.

With a sigh, Tenille turned away and trudged back to the stinking stairwell. A scatter of rain caught her in the face as she turned off the gallery and she swore under her breath. For once, she wished she didn't despise everyone in her peer group. Tonight, the idea of watching some stupid DVD with Aleesha Graham and her crew almost made her wistful. Tenille turned out her pockets. Enough for a couple of regular Cokes. If she carried on past the local Burger King to the one a mile or so away, the chances were there would be nobody she knew inside. With luck, it would be quiet enough for them to let her skulk in a corner for a few hours, nose in a book.

Lost in Byron's *Childe Harold*, the time raced away, and Tenille was surprised when the skinny, acned counter boy leaned on his brush opposite her table and said, 'We're closing.' She grabbed her stuff and made for the door, checking her watch. Half past ten. And the rain had stopped, which meant she could dawdle home, hoodie pulled tight round her head against the wind.

It was quarter past eleven when Tenille inched her key into the lock and opened the front door without a sound. She slid into the darkened hall silent as a shadow, her senses sharpened by the prickle of fear. A cone of faint flickering light spilled into the hall from the half-open living-room door. She could hear the muted drawl of American accents from the TV. Her nose screwed up in a grimace, identifying the sweet of dope smoke and the sour of beer. She risked a quick peek round the door frame. Geno lay sprawled on the sofa, legs apart, one hand lying along the inside of his thigh, the other dangling towards the floor. His head lay back against the greasy mock velvet, his mouth open, a trickle of drool glistening at one corner. *Pissed and passed out*, she thought, relief and contempt mingling satisfactorily.

Tenille crept to her room and silently pulled her chest of drawers across the closed door. Without taking her clothes off, she slid under her lumpy duvet and eased herself to sleep with dark fantasies of a razor-sharp blade making a second red mouth in the invitingly exposed throat of Geno Marley.

'I know you, sir,' I said when I had overcome my surprise enough to speak. I told him that I had believed him either dead or else many hundreds of miles from these parts & that I had thought never to see him more. He said that he was as good as dead if any of His Majesty's men should clap eyes upon him & that he hoped he could count himself safe in my mercy. I gave him assurance that the good offices of his brother had placed me in his family's debt & that I would keep his confidences close in my own breast. He thanked me & shook me by the hand so that I could not fail to notice how yet he suffers the profound perspiration of the palms that so afflicted him as a boy & into his early manhood. Any final doubts of mine were cast to the four winds at that pressing of the flesh.

5

Dr River Wilde tapped the end of her pen against the pad of paper on her desk. 'Look, I appreciate you're busy, but you're not the only one. I've been shunted from pillar to post today. I doubt you have any idea how many people are employed to keep the likes of me from talking to a man in your position. All I'm asking for is a decision. How hard can that be?'

The voice on the other end of the phone sounded exasperated. 'I've already explained. To get a network commission, we have to jump through a series of hoops. I don't have the authority to make that sort of decision on the hoof.'

River made a wicked grimace at the phone. 'Phil, you told me you're Head of Factual Programming for Northern TV. Surely that means you have some say over what appears on our screens?'

'I only have autonomy over a limited amount of regional programming. Anything else has to go through the process.'

River tried to control her desire to shout at the man. She was gradually coming to realise that the bureaucracy of television made university administrators look like amateurs. She stabbed her pen savagely into the paper. 'But this won't wait. I need to begin work on the cadaver as soon as possible. I'm not asking for a fortune. I already emailed you a rough breakdown of costs.' He tried to interrupt but she bulldozed on regardless. 'Look, this is cheap telly, Phil. Cheap as chips. All you need is a camera crew. You shadow my investigation into the body. Your team is present at all the initial work. Trust me, the ambience is fantastic. I've made arrangements with the local funeral parlour to do most of the work on the body there – it's one of those wonderful old Victorian-style facilities, all mahogany and tiled walls, very Conan Doyle, very atmospheric, and a great contrast with all the modern stuff. You can film in the labs where the technical stuff gets done, no problem. You can film at the site where the body was buried. You get my expertise and top expertise from the other disciplines that we'll be bringing to bear on this cadaver, all at bargain basement prices. Come on, Phil. You know your viewers love this kind of thing. Reality TV meets the History Channel. Bog bodies don't turn up that often. And this one's got some really unusual features – those tattoos are remarkable. I'm convinced we're going to get some really fascinating stuff as we go along. This isn't some drunken local who fell into a bog. This is something special. I think we could be talking the South Seas. Just think how much more interesting – and how much cheaper – it will be to shadow the course of a real forensic investigation rather than relying on reconstruction all the time.' She squeezed as much reasonable persuasion into her voice as she could manage.

'Dr Wilde, I agree that what you're proposing would make gripping viewing. But there's no way to short-circuit the commissioning process.'

River snorted. 'What about those instant documentaries that get whipped out of the hat whenever there's some major disaster or political scandal? You find a way of circumventing protocol then.'

Phil Toner sighed. 'A body in a bog in the Lakes isn't a matter of major national significance. Now, if you'd like to come in some time next week . . .'

'Not good enough. Look, Phil, why don't you go out on a limb and make the damn thing anyway? What's the worst outcome? You end up with a riveting regional series that's cost you next to nothing. And if it turns out as good as we both know it should, you can present the network with a great coup that cost peanuts. Come on, you know it makes sense.' She sensed the hesitation on the other end of the line. 'Phil, did I mention I'm bloody gorgeous? And that the camera loves me?' she added, a bubble of laughter in her voice.

She was rewarded with a low rumble of mirth. 'Not to mention that you've come up with a great title. Let me think about it,' he finally said. 'I'll get back to you.'

'When?' River knew she had a reputation for bloody-mindedness; she preferred to think of it as tenacity.

'Close of business today. I'll have an answer for you.'

'Thanks, Phil. I'll look forward to your call.' River put down the phone and punched the air. 'Yes!' She jumped to her feet and hurried out of the glorified cupboard the University of Northern England, in a rare display of wit, described as her office. Ten seconds later she was back through the door, grabbing a folder from her desk and almost running out again.

She found her head of department peering dubiously at a human jawbone. Donald Percival was a man given to doubt. He distrusted certainty unless it was backed up with impeccable scientific data. His small mouth was permanently pursed in disapproval and River would have been prepared to swear that every time she entered his presence, his knitted brows grew ever more tortured. When she bounced into the lab, his shoulders seemed to hunch protectively around his artefact and he made her wait impatiently for a full minute before he turned his watery blue gaze on her. 'Good afternoon, Dr Wilde,' he said.

'Marvellous news, Professor,' River said. 'It looks as if I've got Northern TV on board to make a documentary of the investigation into the Fellhead cadaver. That means we'll be able to go well beyond the basic work you've already granted me funding for.'

Percival frowned. 'Television? Is that a good idea? Do we want the cameras looking over our shoulder as we work?'

River brushed the objection aside with a sweep of her hand. 'They won't get in the way.'

'Is it sending the right message about this department to the wider world?'

'I think it's showing the wider world that we do this well. Which in turn means more outside projects coming to us, bringing money into the department,' River said, shrewdly going for the Achilles heel of all contemporary academics. 'More money means better equipment and more students,' she added, never one to shrink from over-egging the pudding. 'And as far as this project goes, it means we can afford full-body CAT scanning, stable isotope analysis, cemental annulation. The full bells and whistles. And we can get the palaeo-botanists and archaeological sciences people on board without them taking fright over their budgets. Just think of the benefit to the students of such cross-discipline teaching. Great practice for working in the field.'

Percival looked peevishly at the jawbone, turning it over in his gloved hands. 'You're here to teach and research, Dr Wilde, not to use this department as a springboard for personal aggrandisement.'

It was a low blow, but it told River that Percival couldn't come up with a decent professional objection to her proposal. She grinned. 'I'm not pitching to become the next telly don,' she said. 'What I care about is the work. And I'm willing to do whatever it takes to serve the work best.'

Percival gave a weary sigh. 'I know that, Dr Wilde. That is why I chose to employ you here. Very well. You may proceed with this. But make no firm agreement with these people until I have seen the terms and conditions of the arrangement.'

'Thank you, Professor,' River said, resisting the urge to punch the air again. 'You won't regret it.'

He sighed again. 'Let's hope not. Now, before you rush off to make-up, perhaps you could cast your eyes over this.' He held out the jawbone to her in what she recognised as a gesture of reconciliation. 'I find myself somewhat puzzled by the nature of the wear on these molars.'

*　　*　　*

Her own work beyond her, Jane Gresham was attempting to bring her mind to bear on the undergraduate seminar she was supposed to be conducting the following week on the role of the pathetic fallacy in Romantic poetry. So devoid of inspiration had she been that she'd resorted to dredging the bound volumes of the Proceedings of the Modern Language Association for anything that might remotely help shape her session. She was engrossed in a particularly dull article about Coleridge's early work when Dan's head appeared over the top of her library carrel.

'Thought I'd find you here,' he said, sounding faintly smug.

'It's hardly rocket science,' Jane said repressively. 'Considering I always sit in the same carrel.'

He came round the side of the partition and pulled a face when he saw what she was doing. 'My God. If PMLA comes, can despair be far behind?'

Jane pushed the book away. 'It's already here.'

'So let me take you away from all of this and buy you a coffee.'

'I shouldn't, really. I need to prepare this seminar.'

Dan raised his eyebrows and pulled down the corners of his mouth. 'Trust me, you'll feel better about it after a swift injection of caffeine and half an hour in my company.'

Having put up the pretence of a fight, Jane stood up and pocketed her pen. 'I'm leaving my notes here,' she said, warning him that there were limits to the extent of her willingness to be distracted.

Without further negotiation they walked out of the building and round the corner to the Bear and Staff. The pub served decent coffee and, unlike the student refectory, still allowed smokers to indulge their vice. Jane perked up as soon as Dan returned to their corner booth with two large mochas topped with a pyramid of whipped cream. 'You are such a bad man,' she teased.

'I don't believe in half measures.'

'I don't know how you stay so slim,' Jane complained, eyeing the washboard stomach beneath the white T-shirt.

'Lots of exercise, darling. And cigarettes. They kill the appetite, you know.'

'Not to mention those of us who have to put up with your smoke.' Jane took an appreciative sip of her drink, savouring the contrast between the cool cream and the hot brew beneath. 'Mmm. Just the ticket. So, Dan, why am I here?'

He feigned an expression of innocence. 'Jane, I'm surprised at you. It's not like I've never invited you out for coffee before.'

Jane rolled her eyes. 'You've never gone to the trouble of tracking me down in the library and hauling me off to the pub before. I've got work to get back to, so don't make me drag it out of you.' With a shrug he spread his hands in a gesture she recognised. *Small boy playing the cute innocent card*, she thought. *You're getting too old for that one, Danny Boy.*

'What can I say? You nailed me, babe. Yes, I do have an ulterior motive.'

'Well, you better tell me what it is, because I don't have time to play twenty questions. Spill.'

Dan smoothed his eyebrow in a gesture she found familiar from watching him in seminar groups. It was his way of buying time. 'What we were talking about the other day – Christian and Wordsworth? It's been kind of bugging me,' he said.

'Bugging you how?'

'We've been friends for a long time now, Jane. I think I know you pretty well.' He nodded to himself for emphasis. 'I don't think I realised until the other day how much weight you place on the Fletcher Christian story. And I'd say, of all the people I work with, you are the least likely to be taken in by a baseless rumour.'

Jane felt a sudden tension in her neck. 'Very flattering, Dan. But we've all got our blind spots. Arthur Conan Doyle believed in fairies. Hugh Trevor-Roper believed in the Hitler Diaries. I believe in Wordsworth's lost epic. It's really not worth losing sleep over.'

'Good try, Jane, but no cigar. I don't believe you. I think there's more to this than you told me. And I want to help you.'

Jane stared into her cup. She'd held this secret to herself for so long, there had been times when she had wondered if she had dreamed it. She'd told no one, not even Jake, in spite of the fact that she loved him and, if anyone could authenticate what she'd seen, he was the one. Or at least, he would know someone who could. And having denied it to Jake, how could she offer it to Dan? Though it was hard to deny that he might be helpful to her. His own postgraduate work on the linguistic congruences among the Lakeland Romantics could well help to verify anything she found as being typically Wordsworthian in its use of words and grammatical structures. Still, her reluctance held out. 'Please, Dan. Take my word for it.'

'Jane, look at me,' he said, his voice concerned and serious. She lifted her head. 'Dreams are for chasing. How are you going to feel if there is something to be found and somebody else finds it?'

The question she had asked herself so many times. She pushed her curls back from her face and made a decision. 'How well do you know the Dove Cottage archive?'

Dan looked surprised. Whatever he'd been expecting, she thought, that hadn't been it. 'I've done some research there, when I was doing the linguistic comparisons between De Quincey's early work and Wordsworth's prose. It's a vast archive. More than fifty thousand items, or something like that.'

'So many that it's never really been definitively catalogued. Anyway, they're about to open a new library and study centre, so a lot of the material has been boxed up waiting for the move. More or less inaccessible to anyone needing to study it.' Jane paused, shaking off the last traces of doubt.

'So,' she continued, 'I wanted to look over some family letters and, typically, what I needed was packed away. But I've known Anthony Catto, the centre director, since I was at school. I worked there a couple of summers when I was an undergraduate. So I persuaded Anthony to let me go foraging. And in among all the stuff that I expected to find, I came across something that I'd never seen referred to anywhere in the literature.'

'Dramatic pause,' Dan said drily. 'Come on, Jane, you're killing me here.'

'It had been tucked into the wrong envelope, along with the letter that should have been there. I don't expect anyone had even noticed it. The letter it was with is of no particular significance, you see. It probably hadn't been touched for years.'

'Jane,' Dan said loudly.

She closed her eyes for a moment, summoning the image from her memory. 'It was a letter from Mary Wordsworth to one of her sons. John, I presume, since she refers to children but not a wife and John was a widower. "My beloved son, I trust you and the children are in good health. I have found this day troubling matter in your father's hand. It may surprise you that, in spite of the close confidence between us, I was in ignorance of this while he lived, and wish heartily I had remained in that state. You will easily see the need for secrecy while your father lived, and he left me no instructions concerning its disposition. Since it closely touches you, and may be the occasion of more pain, I wish to leave to you the decision as to what should be done. I will convey the matter to you by a faithful hand. You must do as you see fit."' Jane opened her eyes and looked seriously at Dan. 'You see what that could mean?'

Dan frowned. 'It could mean almost anything, Jane,' he said gently.

'Well, no, Dan. William and Mary had an extraordinarily intimate marriage. They didn't have secrets from each other. Nevertheless, they were good at keeping secrets as a family. Look how long it was before the world got to know about William's affair with Annette Vallon and their illegitimate daughter. Whole generations went by and not a whisper of scandal emerged.'

'OK, OK, I grant you that. But all the same . . .'

Jane swept on regardless. 'For William to have kept something from his wife, it must have been a really big deal. Life and death sort of stuff. That's one point. The other is the bit about how this matter closely touches the son. Now, John was married to Isabella Christian Curwen, who was the daughter of Henry Christian Curwen. And he was Fletcher Christian's cousin. By the time of Wordsworth's death, Isabella was dead. And the marriage had been a pretty miserable one for the most part. She was a spoiled little rich girl who enjoyed poor health. And I mean enjoyed. John had already suffered plenty at the hands of the Christian Curwens. I've racked my brains to come up with an alternative, but the only thing I can think of that explains both the secrecy and the possible occasion of pain for John is if I'm right and Fletcher not only came back but also told William the whole story.'

'It's still pretty tenuous,' Dan said. 'I mean, it could have been something discreditable about Isabella that William had found out about.'

Jane looked disappointed. 'See, I told you it was just a bee in my bonnet,' she said shakily, trying to make light of it.

'No, don't get me wrong. I think it's more than that. Whatever Mary was referring to, it's something nobody else has dealt with and that in itself is interesting from a scholarly point of view. I think you need to follow this up. And soon, Jane.'

'I've sat on it for more than a year now, Dan. It'll wait till I have some time to pursue it properly through the new archive.' She drained her coffee and pulled her coat round her, preparing to leave.

'You think so?'

'Why wouldn't it?'

'Jane, you're the one who pointed out the bog body had what sounded like South Sea tattoos. What if that body does turn out to be Fletcher Christian? After we spoke the other day, I did some basic research online. And one of the things I read was that Fletcher was supposed to have set up as a smuggler after he came back. That's exactly the sort of career that could lead to a mysterious death out on the fells. It really could be him. And if it is, the whole world and his wife will be all over every Lakeland archive. And it'll be too late. Somebody else will have stolen your dream.' He gripped her hand tightly. 'You need to move fast. And you need help. Help with expertise. And that would be me.'

'I knew I could place my trust in you, Willy,' he said. 'My brother spoke of your kindness in defending me against those calumnies published against me in the public prints.' Indeed, I had written to the Editor of the Weekly Entertainer denouncing the pack of lies that had been published under my old friend's name, as a personal kindness to his brother Edward. 'How came you to be here?' I asked him. He said it was a long tale & one that he would be happy to share with me. 'There have been vile lies spread about me & I would have the truth told. I can think of no man better fitted to render my story fit for the public than you, my old friend.' I will confess I found myself astonished at the notion of becoming his amanuensis, but the more I pondered, the more it seemed to me a fitting subject for verse. The composition of my long Poem on my life has given me a taste for the epic over the lyric, & epic this tale will surely be, encompassing as it must the best and worst of man's nature.

6

Jake Hartnell paused for a moment in the warm shade under the corrugated portico of Koutras's mini-market, hefting the heavy plastic bags in one hand. It had been three weeks since he'd left England, three weeks since he'd heard a news broadcast or read anything beyond a casually glimpsed headline in a British newspaper. The sun might have darkened his olive skin to the point where he could almost pass for a southern Mediterranean native, but he knew differently. Catching sight of the familiar mastheads, he felt a sudden unexpected stab of homesickness.

He crossed the narrow road and dumped the shopping in the back of the open 4x4, then walked back to the rack of foreign-language newspapers. He reckoned the papers would be a few days out of date, but cast adrift as far as he was, it made no odds. He pulled *The Times* and the *Guardian* out of their slots and went back into the chill air conditioning to pay the extortionate prices the overseas editions commanded, then set off on the short drive back with a curious lightening of the spirit.

When Caroline Kerr had invited him to escape from

London to her place on Crete, he'd imagined a sump-tuous villa complete with terrace and olive grove, in spite of her use of the qualifier 'little'. After all, her London home was a three-storey house five minutes' walk from Hampstead Heath, exquisitely furnished with the sort of antiques that quietly stated their viewer was in the presence of money old enough to have taste as well. Besides, people of her class never boasted about what they had. Their 'little' places in the country were generally massive Georgian rec-tories or cottages whose sizes had been trebled over the passage of time. So his expectations had been high.

The twenty-minute drive from the airport across the burnt red and dusty sage green of the Akrotiri peninsula had promised little, but when the turquoise sea came into view, his heart had lifted. Caroline had barrelled the 4x4 down a steep road past a tiny white chapel carved into a rock escarpment to a half-moon beach dominated by a wooden taverna with tables spread over the sand. She'd stopped abruptly behind the taverna to pick up her keys. Jake had looked around, appreciatively noting the presence of several imposing houses in the hinterland of the bay, wondering which would play host to his new life in the sun.

To his surprise, Caroline had driven past the houses, up a track by a small concrete boat slip to a trio of cottages perched on a narrow ridge overlooking the bay and the wider sea beyond. 'Here we are,' she'd said with a tone of deep satisfaction. Jake could hardly hide his disappointment as he followed her across a small paved patio into the tiny interior. He hadn't walked away from his life for this, he heard himself curse inside his head. The door opened straight into a small living room, furnished with a couple of armchairs, a plain table with four dining chairs and an expensive sound system. Along one wall was a rudimentary kitchen – sink, fridge, oven, hob, two cupboards and a work surface. The cool tiled floor was bare of rugs. On a shelf above an open fireplace a group of small Minoan figures clustered. They were the only decoration in the room. Caroline made a soft noise of satisfaction. She crossed the room in a few strides and opened one of the two doors leading off. 'This is the bedroom,' she said. 'Just dump the bags in there.'

It was another plain room, dominated by a wide, carved wooden bedstead. A mosquito net hung from the ceiling. The only other furniture was a simple wardrobe. All that lifted it above the most basic back-packer accommodation was a pair of magnificent silk Bokhara rugs, one on either side of the bed. Christ, he thought, this was a scant step above bloody peasant life. Jake had dropped their suitcases on the floor and returned to the living room. Caroline gestured to the other door. 'The bathroom,' she said. 'A little better than primitive Greek, I think you'll find.'

Curious, he'd opened the door. He knew from Caroline's London house that she was serious about her ablutions, but he'd experienced Greek plumbing before and had no high hopes. To his astonishment, he found himself in a smaller replica of the Highgate master bathroom. Marble floors, a deep bathtub, a two-person shower cubicle, twin washbasins; all the luxury modern design could provide. 'Bloody hell,' he said, backing out. 'How did you manage that?'

Caroline tossed her dark blonde hair away from her face in a familiar gesture of indifference. 'Contacts, darling, contacts.' She walked into the bedroom and unfastened her suitcase. 'Clean clothes, then a very big drink.'

Sounded good to Jake. 'It's wonderfully simple,' he said, following her lead and raking through his case for some shorts. 'But how on earth do we work here?'

Misunderstanding, Caroline laughed. 'I know. It's so tempting. The sea, the beach, the taverna. It's hard, but I have to remind myself that the only way I can justify spending two months a year here is to keep the wheels turning.'

'No, I meant practically. You don't have a computer, a fax, a phone line as far as I can see.'

Caroline straightened up, shorts and T-shirt in her hand. 'Honestly, Jake, you're so twentieth century sometimes. Laptop, Blackberry, wireless internet connection – that's all I need. I get the auction catalogues online, and if there's anything I want to bid for, I do it by phone. And I have good contacts locally who keep an eye out for anything they think might interest me. Believe me, there's some extraordinary stuff to be had over here. Wonderful illuminated texts from the monasteries, beautiful sheet music from the Middle Ages that is so lovely one wants to weep. I promise you won't be disappointed with what we find on this trip. It never fails to astonish me. Reminds me of the sheer joy of having this wonderful stuff passing through my hands. You'll see.'

'I thought they were pretty strict about antiquities not leaving the country?' Jake asked idly as he stripped off jeans sticky from the plane and the drive.

'They are. But there are always ways,' she said, her tone repressing further questions.

He'd realised by now what she meant by that. For someone whose principal business lay in the buying and selling of bits of paper – holograph letters, manuscripts ancient and modern, illuminated sheet music – it was easy to send irregularly acquired material back to the UK. As long as the envelope looked like an innocuous piece of business post – a brochure for a villa, say, or a prospectus for a new commercial development – nobody in the Greek or British post office was going to look twice at it. 'In a dozen years of doing this, I've only lost one item in the mail,' Caroline had told him matter-of-factly the first time they'd visited the main post office in Chania. 'And it wasn't especially valuable. People only take an interest if you start dressing it up as recorded delivery and insuring it. Otherwise, it gets taken for granted.'

Their days had quickly assumed a pattern. They'd sleep late then Jake would drive up to Horafakia for fresh bread, fruit and yoghurt. Breakfast on the terrace, then down to the beach for a swim. Sometimes they'd go into Chania so Caroline could meet one of her Greek contacts who would occasionally produce some piece of work that would take his breath away; otherwise, Caroline would write emails and make phone calls while Jake read auction catalogues or lounged in the sun with a book. From time to time, they would immerse themselves in a manuscript, discussing the hand of the scribe, the likely origins and, finally, its potential value. He was pleasantly surprised by how much he was learning from Caroline. Lunch at the taverna was followed by sex and sleep then drinks and backgammon. In the evenings, they'd drive out for dinner. The day would end with another bout of sexual activity. Jake was gradually beginning to understand why Caroline preferred younger lovers; men of her own age, he'd been led to believe, generally didn't have the stamina to meet her demands. Not that he minded. He enjoyed sex and she was an enthusiastic and imaginative partner.

What he did mind was the worm of boredom that was working its way to the surface of his mind more and more frequently. Like most men in their late twenties, he'd fantasised about a life like this. Sun, sea, sex and a sugar momma to pay for it all. Caroline was a sardonically amusing companion, never clingy, seldom anything other than equable in temper and openhanded with her knowledge. But still dissatisfaction niggled at Jake.

It wasn't that he felt guilty. He'd convinced himself he was right not to tell Jane the whole truth about Caroline. It would only hurt her. Instead, he'd explained that there were good practical reasons why he and Jane should loosen the bonds of their relationship – he'd have to travel for work, he'd be away in Greece for a couple of months, it wouldn't be fair on Jane to hang around waiting for him. He'd said that Caroline was in her early forties, but had omitted to mention her lean, lithe frame, her shapely legs, her swatch of dark blonde hair or her dancing green eyes. Or that sex with Caroline had been a breathtaking adventure, right from the first cocaine-fuelled fuck at Tom D'Arblay's party. The party Jane had had to miss because she was giving a paper at some stupid bloody symposium in Cardiff.

He'd thought it was a one-shag stand. Nobody had been more surprised than he when Caroline had texted him the next day to suggest they meet for a drink. Over cocktails in a chic Soho bar, Caroline had been bright and brilliant, showing him an autograph letter from John Keats that she'd bought only that afternoon. Then she'd put a proposition to him. She was tired of being a one-woman band. She wanted an associate in her business buying and selling rare documents. He was, she said, the one she wanted. He knew enough of the technical aspect of what they would be buying and selling to avoid the pitfalls of obvious forgeries and faked provenances. He was clearly smart and ambitious. 'And you're a pretty good fuck too,' she'd added, smiling wickedly over the rim of her glass.

She'd given him a week to think it over. He'd made his decision by the next morning. His boss had been furious, Jane had been appalled at his abandoning the supposed purity of museum life for the cut-throat world of collectors and high rollers, and his father had warned him about what happens when beautiful women get bored. None of it had mattered. For the first time in a long time, Jake was having fun. Crete had merely seemed the icing on the cake.

Until reality had replaced the fantasy and he found himself bored for the first time since the age of thirteen.

Jake drew up outside the cottage. He ran his hands through his thick dark hair, wondering whether Caroline would read the meaning in the newspapers. He grabbed the shopping and added the contents of his bags to the food already arranged on the patio table. Caroline emerged with a jug of freshly squeezed juice just as he slumped into a chair, clutching the papers like a shield in front of his chest.

A smile quirked one corner of her mouth. 'Well done, Jake,' she said, filling the tumblers.

'What?'

'You held out longer than anybody else I've ever brought here. Three weeks and two days. That's a record.' She leaned over and kissed him, rumpling his hair with one hand and running the other over the front of his shorts.

'You don't mind?' Jake said, wrong-footed.

'Why would I mind? I'm not an ostrich. I'm not here to escape.' She slid elegantly into her chair and tipped her sunglasses from her hair to cover her eyes. 'I'm here because I love it and it's possible for me to be here without fucking up my life or my business. The only reason I don't have you buy a paper every morning from Koutras is that I read the bloody things online, sweetie.'

They settled into their papers, Jake smarting at Caroline's condescension. He was beginning to wonder how seriously she took his expertise; too often, he was left feeling like a gigolo, appreciated only for his bedroom skills and not for the quality of his mind. He was only half taking in what he was reading, but when his eyes stumbled over a familiar name he stopped short and returned to the beginning of the story. 'Fuck me,' he breathed softly.

Caroline glanced up. 'I rather thought I had,' she teased. 'What is it, darling?'

Jake shook his head. 'Nothing, really.' He passed the paper across the table, pointing to the story. 'It's just that I know the place where it happened.'

Caroline skimmed the story. 'Fellhead,' she said, her voice clipped and her face unreadable. 'Would that be where the lovely Jane hails from?'

Neither of them had spoken much of their past by tacit agreement, but Jake had mentioned spending time in the Lakes with Jane when Caroline had been thinking of buying a bundle of Robert Southey's letters. 'That's right,' he said. Then he grinned. 'I hope she's seen that story.'

'Why? Because Fellhead doesn't hit the headlines often?'

'No . . .' He leaned across and pointed to the penultimate paragraph. 'Because she'll be convinced this is evidence of one of her hare-brained theories.'

'I don't understand,' Caroline said in a tone that indicated this was seldom her chosen state.

'The black tattoos. They're the sort that sailors used to get in the South Seas back in the old days when sailing ships put in at the islands to take on stores and trade with the natives,' Jake explained. 'For example, most of the sailors on the *Bounty* had tattoos done while they were in Tahiti collecting the breadfruit they were supposed to be bringing home.'

'What an arcane piece of knowledge.'

'Jane lectured me so often on her pet theory that it stuck.' Jake leaned back in his chair, pleased to be in the driving seat for once. 'She believes that Fletcher Christian didn't die on Pitcairn. That he came back to the Lakes where he was sheltered by his family. It's a rumour that's been going the rounds up there for the best part of two hundred years.'

'Amusing,' said Caroline. 'And amazing how urban legends sprang up even before the urban sprawl itself.'

He grinned, sharing her enjoyment. 'But Jane has taken it one step further. That's the hare-brained part. She's convinced that, if Christian came home, he would have been burning to tell his story, to set the record straight.'

'She's probably right,' Caroline said, languidly reaching for her cigarettes and lighting up. 'In his shoes, who wouldn't want to get their side of the story out there?'

'Well, Jane believes that he looked up his old schoolfriend William Wordsworth and told him his version of events. And that William wrote it all down as a long narrative poem, which of course he could never publish without dire consequences for himself and for the entire Christian family.'

Caroline was sitting up straight now, yanking her sunglasses off and fixing him with a hard stare. 'Fletcher Christian was at school with Wordsworth?' she demanded.

'Apparently. Jane says that part of the story is incontrovertible fact. But the rest of it is rumour, gossip and Jane's fantasy.'

'Jake, do you have any idea what such a poem would be worth, supposing it really existed?' Suddenly, the cloak of Crete had fallen back to reveal the sharp London dealer that he had first met.

He frowned, uneasy and wrong-footed. 'I'd never given it any thought. A hundred thousand?'

Caroline shook her head in disbelief. 'At least ten times that. Probably more. I'd estimate between one and two million, depending on how long the poem is.'

Jake whistled. 'Pity it's not for real,' he said firmly.

73

Caroline stared at him with an unreadable expression. 'How do you know it's not for real?'

Jake spluttered. 'There's no evidence that it exists. That it ever existed. Just Jane's crazy idea.'

'That would be the same Jane who is a Wordsworth scholar?' Caroline said, acid behind the sweetness.

'Yes, but . . .'

'So she presumably knows what she's talking about.'

'You can't be taking this seriously,' Jake protested, anger simmering below the surface as he felt himself being dismissed yet again.

'You're at the start of your career in this business, Jake. Can you afford not to take it seriously?'

I told him I was willing to consider his request favourably, except that I feared there would be unpleasant consequences if I were to publish such an account. 'You are a wanted man & if I were to claim for my Poem the name of truth, I would be tarred with the same brush. Harbouring a known felon is an offence against His Majesty and I should be loath to deprive my wife of a husband and my children of a father even to defend the honour of an old friend such as you. Further, it would incite a manhunt against you in this place where you feel most safe.' This was not a concern that had occurred to my friend, but he was quick to see its force. 'It is not for myself that I care what is said, but for my family,' he said. At length, we agreed that if I were to forge a Poem from his tale nobody should be made privy to it until we both were dead. Thus would we protect ourselves and clear his reputation in one fell swoop.

7

Professor Maggie Elliott looked over the rimless glasses perched on the end of her nose. 'It seems to me, Jane, there are two discrete elements here. One is the letter from Mary Wordsworth which alludes to something that, as far as we can tell, has not been elucidated by any other scholar. The second is the discovery of a body in the Lake District which may or may not have tattoos typical of the South Sea Islands during the period of the mutiny on the *Bounty*. Would you agree with that analysis?'

Jane shifted slightly in her seat. 'Well, yes.'

'But you have it in mind that these two elements could be inextricably woven together? Based on little more than a rumour you heard as a child?'

'A rumour that has persisted for the best part of two hundred years,' Jane said, a cast of stubbornness settling on her face.

'But a rumour nonetheless.'

Jane hated the way Professor Elliott assumed the pedantry of an Oxbridge don in spite of having acquired all three of her degrees at redbrick universities. Given her age, she should be a laid-back egalitarian, not some fogey acting twenty years older than her age and several gradations above her class. 'A rumour that is backed by a significant amount of circumstantial evidence,' she said, determined not to be worn down. 'As I outlined to you. And there is one other detail . . .'

Professor Elliott raised her eyebrows interrogatively. 'Yes?'

'The notebooks of Samuel Taylor Coleridge are in the British Museum and one of them contains the entry: "Adventures of Christian, the mutineer". The same notebook he was using during the period when he composed *The Ancient Mariner*. And when you read the poem in that light, it's not hard to spot links to the *Bounty*'s voyage.'

'Such as?'

'The terrible storms they endured going round the Cape. The way they were driven south towards the ice before making it through into the South Seas. And the albatross. It's a matter of record that the *Bounty*'s crew shot and ate albatross during their voyage. As far as I know, there was no superstition attached to killing those particular birds at that time. But for his poem to work, Coleridge had to invent a metaphor for sin. And killing a beautiful wandering bird suited his romantic soul right down to the ground.' Jane's hands wove a sensuous pattern in the air as she described the bird. 'However, what we also know from contemporaneous accounts is that it was Wordsworth who came up with the idea of the albatross on one of their walks together. I don't think it's reaching to suggest that the notion had already been planted in his mind by what he knew of the *Bounty*.'

Professor Elliott shook her head. 'Your timing's wrong, surely. Coleridge was working on *The Ancient Mariner* when he and Wordsworth were in Dorset. It's much too early for Fletcher Christian to have been back in England. And certainly there's no reason to suppose he was in Dorset.'

Jane nodded. 'I'm not suggesting Wordsworth knew the story at first hand from Fletcher at that point. But I think it's indicative of an existing interest in the mutiny. And in Edward Christian he had the perfect source to satisfy his curiosity. Edward would almost certainly have heard about the killing of the albatross from the mutineers who were brought back or from Bligh's accounts. It's exactly the sort of detail that would have struck Wordsworth. And if William had already shown an interest in the mutiny, all the more reason why Edward would send Fletcher to him when he finally came home.'

Professor Elliott gave a smile that was hard not to take as condescension. 'That is even more tenuous a theory than this putative concatenation of body and letter. What leads you to the belief that there is some urgency attached to the exegesis of the letter?'

In the three hours since she had left Dan, Jane had taken the opportunity to marshal her arguments. 'It's not just the body that makes the matter more urgent. The Jerwood Centre is about to open at the Wordsworth Trust. Sooner rather than later, every scrap of paper in that archive is going to be scrutinised, and it's likely that whoever comes across that letter from Mary will know enough about what they're looking at to realise it needs to be followed up. I found that letter. I want to be the one who gets on the trail of whatever it means.'

Professor Elliott sighed. 'This can scarcely be news to you, Jane. You say you encountered this letter a year ago. Why did you not pursue it earlier? During the long vacation, say? Why wait till term has begun and you have a teaching load?'

Jane could feel anger rising and tried to keep her voice level. 'Maggie, it may have escaped your notice, but I don't earn enough from my teaching here to support myself. I spent a large part of the summer working behind a bar and the rest of it trying to turn my thesis into a book for which I have miraculously got a publishing contract. But even supposing I had had the time to follow this up, much of the Wordsworth archive has been inaccessible because of the renovations and building work. I couldn't have done anything about it even if I had wanted to. Yes, the body does add urgency in my mind, but it's far from the only consideration.'

Her department head smiled, this time without any air of patronage. 'I do appreciate that, Jane. Believe me, if I could find a way to pay you and your fellow teaching assistants more, I would do it. I fully understand the negative impact it has on your research. And in spite of the conclusion you appear to have leapt to, I do not discount the potential significance of the bog body. If it proves to be that of Fletcher Christian, or indeed any other of the *Bounty* crewmen, it would increase exponentially the chances of there being a manuscript such as you posit.' She pulled her computer keyboard towards her and flashed Jane a look over the top of her glasses. 'Strange though it may seem to you, I do remember the excitement of academic discovery. It hasn't been entirely subsumed by the weight of departmental administration.' She clicked her mouse and studied the screen. 'You're teaching two seminars a week, and you're supervising three students, is that right?'

'That's right. But –'

Professor Elliott raised a finger to demand silence as she navigated her way around the departmental timetable. 'Let me see,' she drawled.

'Dan Seabourne has volunteered to take over my teaching load for a couple of weeks, provided we can rejig the timetable so the two seminars are on the same day.' Jane risked interrupting the process.

Eyebrows raised across the desk. 'Really? How unlike him to burden himself with more work.'

Jane grinned. 'He's not as lazy as he sometimes looks. It's just that he hasn't quite figured out where he's going next, workwise.'

Professor Elliott harrumphed. 'And you're confident he has the expertise in your area to manage the work?'

'I think so. They're undergraduate seminars. It's not that hard to stay one step ahead of the group. Not these days, with seminars the size lectures used to be,' Jane added with a tang of acerbity.

'Again, not something over which I have a deal of control,' Professor Elliott said. She studied the screen again. 'That should be manageable. Very well. Mr Seabourne it is. I'll email him to make sure he knows when and where he is supposed to be. You have –' she glanced at the timetable again – 'two weeks and three days before you need to present yourself for duty. I trust that will be long enough.'

Jane got to her feet. 'If I've not started to make some headway by then, it's not going to be susceptible to easy unravelling.'

'And if you have?'

Jane reached for her bag. 'Then I might be back here begging.'

Professor Elliott gave her a sharp look. 'I do hope not. I don't want your record looking like that of someone who is not committed to the department. One never knows when cuts will be demanded.'

It was, Jane thought as she walked down the dingy corridor, the nearest she was ever likely to get to a wholehearted endorsement from Maggie Elliott. It wasn't exactly an enthusiastic encouragement to get cracking and find what she was looking for, but it was a damn sight better than nothing.

Dusk had already fallen over the towering fells and dark waters of the Lake District when the hearse pulled up at the discreet rear entrance of Keswick Memorial Hospital. The doors swung open to reveal a black body bag on a hospital trolley, a porter at one end. River Wilde supervised the loading of the precious cargo into the hearse then arranged to meet the undertaker's men back at the funeral parlour.

We make a pretty strange cortege, she thought to herself as she eased the bulk of her Land Rover out of its car park space and into the wake of the hearse. Talk about the odd couple. A body with no one to mourn it and a forensic anthropologist who wants to steal all its secrets. A limo and a Landie. Hell, I could just have loaded the body in the back and not bothered the guys from Gibson's.

It would have been much simpler to have left the body *in situ* at the hospital, but the administration had been adamant that their mortuary was for the use of the recently dead, not those who had been in the ground long before the hospital had even been dreamed of. She had reminded them that they had already agreed to rent her time on their equipment, which would mean bringing the body back, 'like a large and inconvenient parcel,' but they were not to be moved. Unlike Pirate Peat, as she had privately dubbed him. She wondered if that was the sort of human touch the TV team would appreciate.

She was feeling pretty pleased with herself. An hour before, Phil Toner had called to say he had decided to go ahead with the project. A researcher would be with her in the morning to discuss the schedule and arrange filming. Not only that, but they'd also accepted her figures at face value and agreed to the fee she'd suggested. She pulled a rueful face. 'You sold yourself too cheap, girl,' she muttered under her breath. But at least she would be able to afford all the techniques required to paint the fullest picture possible of her mystery man. It was an unusual luxury, since the practical side of her job normally involved the minimum required to identify human remains. Mostly, her work was about bringing closure to the living; the relatives of soldiers, of civilians lost in massacres, of victims of natural catastrophe, of climbers lost on mountains, of bodies buried in shallow graves. Identity was all. This, however, would be a different matter altogether. This was about unravelling one man's story. Identification would be a bonus.

She followed the hearse into the car park behind the imposing Victorian villa that housed Gibson's Funeral Services and waited patiently while the men shifted the body on to a trolley then wheeled it inside to the embalming room. According to Andrew Gibson, the thirty-something great-great-grandson of the first Gibson, it had been installed when the house had been built in 1884 and little had changed since except for the installation of more modern plumbing. The walls were white, brick-shaped tiles, the faint craquelure of age lending them warmth. The embalming tables were solid mahogany, their original ceramic liners replaced with stainless steel. The counter-tops and the cabinets were all of the same wood. Through their glass doors she could see beakers and measuring columns that could have dated from the same era. It wasn't hard to imagine men in wing collars and frock coats going about their business with the dead inside these four walls. River had loved this place the minute she'd clapped eyes on it. She just knew the TV team were going to feel the same. It would, she hoped, feel like a Sherlock Holmes drama, only for real.

The men loaded their burden on to one of the tables. River slowly unzipped the bag and exposed the body to the air. She gazed down at the stained skin, the wizened limbs and the dark hair and tried to conjure up a picture of what he must have looked like in life. Once those legs had carried him over the tracks of the fells; once, she wouldn't mind betting, they had held his balance on the pitching deck of a sailing ship. Those arms had raised sail, climbed rigging, spliced ropes. They had held other warm bodies. That mouth had kissed as well as eaten, spoken as well as drunk. He had been a living, breathing human, just like her. Now it was her job to make him come alive all over again.

Three hundred miles away, Jane was wolfing a generous bowl of spaghetti in Trattoria Guido with Dan and Harry. The restaurant was Dan's discovery; he'd found it tucked away in an alley off a side street near the university. It looked as if nothing had changed inside since the 1970s – checked red-and-white table-cloths, guttered candles stuck in Chianti bottles, badly executed murals of Sorrento all gave it that time-warp feel. The menu, too, had been untouched by culinary fashion. A diner would look in vain for balsamic vinegar, sundried tomatoes, mozzarella di bufala or rocket. Here, the staples were spaghetti, penne and tagliatelle, the favoured sauces Bolognese, carbonara, arrabbiata and marinara. But the food was tasty, the portions vast and the prices low, so it had clung to its clientele of office workers and the kind of students who favoured content over form. Jane ate there at least twice a week.

Harry spoke through a mouthful of lasagne. 'Can't believe Missy Elliott swallowed your tale, Jane. From what Dan's said about her, I thought she was tough as old boots.'

'She is,' Dan said. 'But she's smart enough to want to be on board if Jane turns out to be on the money. So, Jane, what's our plan of action?'

'Start at the beginning,' she said. 'You're teaching tomorrow and I'm going back to the Lakes to talk to

Anthony Catto at the Wordsworth Trust to see if any other uncatalogued material has turned up lately. Meanwhile you can have a damn good look at the Wordsworth family tree and check out John's descendants. The last thing we know about whatever it was that Mary found among William's papers is that she sent it to John. For all I know, somebody in the family could have been sitting on it for the last hundred and fifty years.'

'As if,' Harry muttered.

'Harry, this is a family that managed to keep William's French lover and their illegitimate daughter secret for a hundred and twenty years,' Jane pointed out. 'There is no other poet in English literary history who made such a fetish out of the creation of his own image, and his family went along with that one hundred per cent. Nothing was ever said or done to contradict William's picture of himself, even when that meant turning a blind eye to the most glaring omissions. *The Prelude* is an astonishing poetic achievement, but it's also an early example of outrageous spin doctoring. It was Dorian Grey in reverse – the more time stripped William of his youth and powers, the more glossy *The Prelude* became.'

'She's right, you know,' Dan said, filling up their glasses with Guido's strong red wine that came to table without a label. 'Wordsworth's compulsive remaking of his life is one of the reasons why I think Jane might really be on to something. Of all the writers I can think of, Wordsworth is probably the only one capable of writing a major work only to decide nobody gets to see it because the circumstances of its composition reflect badly on him.'

'Even so, you'd think somebody down the years would have been tempted to cash in on it, if it exists.' Harry pushed his plate away, defeated by the final slab of pasta and meat.

'Not this family,' Jane said. 'Reputation, reputation, reputation. It should be carved on their coat of arms.'

'And you're the woman to break the silence, Jane,' Dan said confidently. 'Now, where are we going to celebrate your mission?'

'I was going to go home and pack.'

Dan made a dismissive noise. 'Jane, Jane, what are we going to do with you?'

'You're getting middle-aged,' Harry confirmed. 'Dan's right, we should go out on the razz.'

Jane groaned. 'Oh, all right. But I'm not dancing till dawn like the last time. I'm going to turn into a pumpkin at midnight, and that is a promise.'

Three hours later, they were leaving a Soho pub, en route to a nearby club, tipsy but in control. The same could not be said of Geno Marley, whose senses quickened to alert when he heard the front door of the Marshpool Farm flat whisper open.

Tenille's luck had just run out.

My friend fears for his safety, as who would not in his position. If he is taken, he will be hanged. Little doubt attends that. Although many years have passed since the sensational case of the mutiny on the Bounty & although few think of Captain Bligh now Admiral Nelson's name is on the lips of all, there are still many who would smile even as the hangman slipped his noose over that tanned & sinewy neck. 'Are we safe here from prying eyes?' he asked. I told him that the garden at Dove Cottage is left to my exclusive use when I am working. There is what we call the New Door that gives on to the passageway, but none comes through it when they know I am at work. The garden itself is protected from the idle curiosity of passers-by with its thicket of rambling roses & honeysuckle. We are as isolate here as if we were on the very summit of Helvellyn.

8

The banging, Jane slowly realised, was coming from outside her head. She growled in her throat as she tried to force her eyelids open. 'Slapper,' she berated herself, realising she'd fallen into bed without bothering to take off her make-up. She rubbed her lashes free of mascara and groaned. She pushed herself into a sitting position, wishing immediately that she hadn't done so. Her stomach roiled and an acid burp joined the staleness in her mouth in an evil brew. There was a pain in her sinuses and, inexplicably, her legs ached when she tried to move them.

Somehow, she dragged herself out of bed and lurched for the door, snatching at her dressing gown as she passed. She wrestled with the arms, calling, 'OK, OK, I'm coming,' to whoever was trying to break her door down. The sound of her own raised voice made her wince. Jane unfastened the locks and chain securing the door and yanked it open. 'What the hell . . .' she began, but found herself addressing empty air as Tenille pushed past her and dived into the front room. Jane rubbed a hand over her face. It didn't make anything clearer. With a sigh, she closed the door and followed Tenille.

Jane leaned in the doorway for support and took in the picture of frightened misery curled in the bean bag. 'Before you open your mouth, Tenille, I need to tell you that I have the hangover from hell. So this better be good.'

Tenille shivered and pushed a knuckle into her mouth. Jane could see her teeth biting down hard on it. It took her a moment to figure it out in her messed-up state, but eventually she realised the child was fighting tears with every ounce of strength she possessed. That was shock enough to restore Jane to something approximating a normal state of awareness. In all the time she'd known Tenille, she'd seen her angry, frustrated, smarting under injustice, defiant and outraged. She'd never seen her anywhere near the verge of tears. She'd also never seen her look so young. Her eyes were wide, but the rest of her face seemed to have shrunk round the bones. The prettiness that threatened future beauty was in abeyance, replaced with a taut fragility.

Jane crossed the room and squatted down next to Tenille. She put a cautious arm round her shoulder. Physical contact wasn't something they did usually, but she'd worried needlessly. Tenille slumped against her, body rigid. Jane said nothing, just let her free hand rhythmically stroke the girl's arm. Then suddenly the barriers broke. Tenille burrowed into her side like a lamb butting up against its mother and the crying began. It started as a quiet weeping, then rose to a desperate, gulping sobbing that shook them both under its force.

Jane felt completely at a loss. She couldn't remember any adolescent trauma that had reduced her to this state. She'd shed her share of tears, but never in this abandoned, helpless way. She found herself mouthing the traditional platitudes – 'there, there,' and 'it's OK, Tenille, you're OK with me.' But they seemed helpless against this tide of anguish.

At last, the terrible sobs subsided and Tenille pulled away, wiping her eyes and nose with the back of her hand. Her eyelids were swollen and she was breathing hard through her mouth. 'I'm sorry,' she said thickly.

'It's OK. That's what friends are for,' Jane said, despising herself for finding nothing but cliché. 'You want to tell me what all that was about?'

Tenille looked away. 'You was out last night,' she said accusingly. 'I came round, but you was out.'

'I went clubbing with some friends,' Jane said.

'So I went back down the flat. I didn't want to, because I knew he'd be there, but you was out so I didn't have no choice.'

'Who was there?' Jane wondered if the drink had induced short-term memory loss. She seemed to be missing crucial logical steps in the conversation.

'Geno.' Tenille spat the word as if trying to rid her mouth of a bad taste.

'Sharon's boyfriend?' The cold hand of apprehension took hold of Jane's chest.

'Sharon's fucking bastard boyfriend.'

Oh shit, oh no, oh shit. 'Wasn't Sharon there?'

'Sharon's on nights. She says he has to stay over to make sure nothing bad happens to me.' She gave a bitter laugh. 'She's too fucking stupid to see he's the bad thing waiting to happen.'

Jane rubbed her back. 'Has he been . . . bothering you?'

'He looks at me. You know?'

Jane knew. 'What else?' She dreaded the answer.

'He's said things, when Sharon's out the room. How he likes sweet young flesh, that sort of shit talk. Man, I *knew* he was just waiting his time till she was on nights.'

'What happened, Tenille?'

She began picking compulsively at the zip on her jacket. 'First couple of nights, he was pissed and passed out on the sofa. But last night he was waiting. Soon as I came through the door, there he was, standing in the doorway, undoing his trousers.' She shuddered. 'Told me it was time I tasted some real loving.' Her lip curled in contempt. 'Bastard. I tried to get back out the door, but he was too fast. He grabbed my arm and dragged me into the living room and threw me down on the sofa.' She shook her head, as if to shake off the memory. 'Then he got his cock out. Man, I never been so scared my whole life. I thought for sure he was going to rape me. Then I realise he wants me to blow him. Just the fucking idea made me want to throw up. So I grabbed the lamp off the table and I smashed him over the head with it.'

Jane felt her heart contract in fear and pity. 'You did the right thing, Tenille.'

'I didn't hit him hard enough. I should have fucking killed him. But he was just stunned, like. So I jumped up and ran for my room. I pulled the drawers and the bed across the door so's he couldn't get in. I was shaking, man, fucking shaking. The next thing is he's hammering on the door and screaming like a fucking animal. Jane, I didn't know what to do. He was like a crazy man. The door was shaking, I thought he was going to break it down.' She gave a shaky laugh. 'Then I got salvation.'

'What happened?'

'You know that asshole lives next door to us? Big fat greasy biker geezer?'

Jane nodded. 'I've seen him. Ugly bastard, right?'

'Ugly and mean. Next thing I know, he's at the front door, telling Geno to keep the noise down or else he'll break the fucking door down and rip Geno's liver out. And suddenly it all goes quiet. Last thing I hear is Geno standing outside my door, saying, "You can't stay in there forever, bitch." I nearly pissed myself. I tell you, I never closed my eyes all night. I waited till I heard Sharon come home, then I was out the door and down here. Man, I was praying you were home.'

'You did the right thing, Tenille.' Jane gathered her woolly thoughts around her. She was going to have to do something about this. Tenille couldn't be left at the mercy of Sharon's sick bastard boyfriend. 'You can stay here for now,' she said. 'I'm supposed to be going away today for a couple of weeks, but I'll get this sorted before I go.'

Tenille looked incredulous. 'You? Whatchu gonna do? Geno's not going to listen to you. And there's no point telling Sharon, she'll just twist it round so it's my fault, like usual.'

Jane got to her feet. Tenille might be the street-wise one of the pair of them, but Jane knew something the girl didn't. It might just be estate gossip, but she had a feeling it was more than that. And if she was right, it would give her a weapon that would make Geno head for the hills faster than a speeding bullock. Jane straightened her shoulders, trying to look like someone who could take care of business. 'Trust me, Tenille. I'm going to fix this.'

Jake slipped off his sandals and let the cool marble work its magic. He felt overheated, which was crazy, given the pitch of the air conditioning inside Chania airport. He suspected the dark blue, grey and white décor was meant to be soothing, but it wasn't helping him feel any less out of sorts. Funny to think that only the day before he'd been indulging himself with dreams of home. But now that he was in the departure lounge with a ticket for London in his pocket, he felt a curious mixture of apprehension coupled with determination to prove to Caroline that he could cut the mustard.

It had all happened so fast. Within minutes of their initial conversation, Caroline had been online, searching the bucket shops for a plane ticket for him. When he'd tried to ask her what she had in mind, she'd shushed him with an impatient, 'We'll talk, Jake. Now let me sort this out.'

Long minutes had passed before she exclaimed, 'Perfect.' She clicked the wireless mouse a couple of times then sat back, a smile of satisfaction neatly in place. 'There you go, Jake,' she said, turning the screen to face him. Apparently, he was now booked on a flight from Chania to Athens, with an onward connection to Heathrow. The following day.

'You're not coming too?'

Caroline gave him a puzzled look. 'This is your

show, Jake. I'd only cramp your style. You surely don't think Jane is going to be thrilled to see you if I'm hanging on your arm?'

'I don't understand what you want me to do, Caroline.' He tried to sound casual, but it came out petulant.

'It's very simple. You've just opened up the possibility of a fascinating and valuable find. I want you to track it down. And if you can't manage that yourself, I want you to be glued to the side of the person who does.'

He pushed his hair back from his face in a gesture of exasperation. 'But, Caroline, we've no evidence that the bloody thing exists.'

'According to you, Jane seems to think so,' she said, sweet reason in a sundress.

'It's just a crazy theory.'

'Believe me, I've made some great finds chasing wilder geese. Look at it this way. Jane is in a unique position. She's a Wordsworth scholar. And she comes from Fellhead. Now, in my experience, serious scholars don't get worked up about things like this unless there is some spectacularly good reason. Bear in mind, Jane may not have told you everything she knows.'

Doubt chased surprise across Jake's handsome face. 'Why would she hold back? Are you saying she didn't trust me?'

Caroline chuckled. 'When academics have something they think might give them an edge, they trust no one. Sweetie, no matter how much Jane loved you, you can bet your bottom dollar that if she had knowledge that might be parlayed into professional stardom she'd have hugged it to her bosom. And this body in the bog could be the catalyst that gets things moving in a more urgent way.'

'This is insane,' Jake said.

'No, Jake, this is business. If you seriously want to make a career of this, you're going to have to be prepared to exploit your contacts and find ways to make sure that when something good turns up, you're standing at the shoulder of whoever has their sticky hands on it.'

'I get that,' he said, feeling patronised and belittled but unable to find a way through to asserting himself. 'What I don't get is what you expect me to do. In practical terms.'

Caroline exhaled a thin stream of smoke. 'Go and see Jane. Mend as many of your fences as you need to get alongside her. Be contrite. Tell her you read the story in the paper and it made you realise you were wrong not to take her theories seriously. Persuade her that she is the one and only person who can track down this bloody manuscript, and make her do it. That's what I want you to do.' She turned her head to look out across the bay, as close to irritation as he'd ever seen her.

'I don't think she'll be very pleased to see me,' he muttered.

'Of course she won't. You walked out on her. But you'll do what it takes to get back in her good books, Jake.'

'What do you mean, "what it takes"?'

'Do I have to spell it out? Tell her you want to find this manuscript to spite me, if that's what works.' She smiled serenely. 'I'll leave it up to you.'

'It won't be easy.'

'Use your charm, Jake. There's not much point in having it otherwise, is there?'

As he remembered her words, fresh determination surged through Jake. He'd show Caroline he could be much more than a toyboy. He would make her take him seriously, whatever it took.

The shower had helped a little but Jane still felt raw and tender. She made them both coffee, swallowing a couple of painkillers while she waited for the kettle to boil. She wasn't sure if what she was planning was the right thing, but she couldn't see any alternative and she wanted to be as close to firing on all cylinders as she could manage. She took the mugs through and perched on the edge of her bed. 'There's someone I've got to go and see,' she said. 'I want you to wait here.'

'Who you going to see?' Tenille demanded. Having unburdened herself, her usual demeanour seemed to be reasserting itself.

'Someone I think will be able to help.' Jane hoped her tone would head off further questions.

Tenille stared into her coffee. 'My dad,' she said expressionlessly.

Jane tried to hide her surprise. Not long after Tenille had started hanging round with her, Jane had fallen into conversation at the bus stop with one of her neighbours, a young mother from a couple of doors down. 'It's none of my business,' the woman had said, 'but I noticed that Tenille hanging round your place. You want to watch yourself there.'

'Why is that?' Jane had bristled. 'She seems like a bright kid.'

'She's bright, all right. But it's her old man you want to worry about.'

Jane frowned. 'I think you're mixing her up with someone else. She hasn't got a dad. She says she doesn't know who her father is. Her mother always refused to tell her, and Sharon says she's got no idea.'

The woman gave a contemptuous little snort. 'If Tenille doesn't know, she's the only one. Everybody else round here knows the Hammer is her dad.'

Jane felt her eyes widen in shock. 'John Hampton?'

'That's right. He's always kept an eye out, but from a distance, like. Sharon doesn't want her to know, see? I mean, you can see why, can't you?'

Jane could certainly see why. She'd learned very early on that John 'Hammer' Hampton was the criminal equivalent of the mayor of Marshpool Farm. He was a serious gangsta, not some teenage wannabe. Drugs, sex and violence were his stock in trade and there was no doubting his grip on the illegal activities on the estate. Jane had heard stories of punishment beatings meted out to those who thought they could freelance on the wrong side of the law without giving the Hammer his due.

And now, here was Tenille openly acknowledging something Jane had thought was deeply buried. 'You know about your dad?' Jane said, stalling for time to get her head round this.

'That he's the Hammer?' Jane nodded. Tenille shrugged. 'I've sort of known for years. Somebody at school told me. I didn't believe them at first. I didn't want to, I suppose. But one day when Sharon was out, I went through her things. And stuffed right down the back of one of her drawers, I found a photo of my mum with the Hammer. He had his arm round her. They was smiling into each other's faces, like they was in love or something. And then I knew for sure.' She took a deep breath. 'He's never said a word to me, like. He's always walked straight past me without a look. I figured he don't want to know.'

'Or else he wants to protect you,' Jane said, reaching for a gloss that might give Tenille a more positive image of her father. 'He must have enemies. By not letting on to you, it's like he's saying, "I could give a shit", which means you're a less attractive target to someone who wants to get at him.'

Tenille looked sceptical. 'Or else he just don't want anything to do with his bastard now the baby mother's gone. It's not like he hasn't had his pick of other women since my mum died. He's probably forgotten all about her by now.'

She was probably right, Jane thought wearily. But right now, talking to the Hammer was the only thing she could imagine restoring Tenille to safety. It wasn't a comfortable thought. Her skin crawled with apprehension and revulsion. The things she'd heard laid at the Hammer's door were not calculated to inspire a desire to spend time in his company. 'We'll see about that,' she said, half to herself.

'You gonna talk to him about Geno?' Tenille looked at her with incredulity.

'Of course I am.' Jane finished her coffee and stood up.

'Respect,' Tenille said, sounding surprised at herself. 'You're pretty spicy for a white girl.'

Or pretty stupid. 'Stay here till I get back. Don't let anybody else in, OK?'

'You know where to find him?' Tenille asked.

'I've got a tongue in my head. I can ask.'

'No need. This time of the morning, he'll be at home. D Block, far end. Flat 87.'

Jane acknowledged the information with a nod and grabbed her coat. 'Don't worry, Tenille. We'll get Geno sorted out.'

We are agreed that he will return in three days when we are both free from encumbrance or obligation. I will confess that I am eager to hear his story. So much has been written and said about the destiny of this ship but only one of the principals has been heard from. It is certain that my friend's account will provide us with much fresh insight into the mutiny itself & solve the mystery of what happened subsequent to the Bounty, & to those who took her. Aside from my friend, I think there is no man living on these islands who has an inkling of the fate of the Bounty after she sailed away from Otaheite with her crew of mutineers & Natives. I am eager to comprehend these events & to translate them into a Poem. I am limbered up for such a long work with my great Poem. It will be a remarkable undertaking.

9

Jane closed the front door behind her and paused, taking a deep breath. She was probably mad to do this. Whatever the unwritten rules were, she was almost certainly breaking an unconscionable number of them by turning up unannounced on the Hammer's doorstep to tell him it was time to take care of his unacknowledged daughter. But Tenille didn't have anyone else to look out for her. There was so much promise there, Jane knew she couldn't just walk away and leave the child to sink or swim.

She turned up her collar against the wind and made her way across the estate to D Block, the tallest of the eight L-shaped buildings that comprised Marshpool Farm. It stood at the north side of the estate, a couple of storeys higher than the other blocks. To her surprise, the far entrance lobby was free from rubbish and graffiti. There was even the faint smell of pine disinfectant. She thought she'd chance the lift since she was going to the eighth floor. Not only did it arrive when summoned, but its interior could not have been cleaner if it had been in one of the towering office blocks at Canary Wharf. If she needed evidence of the power of John Hampton, it was here before her eyes.

Flat 87 was opposite the lift. The door was painted a deep burgundy, in sharp contrast to the scruffy grey-blue of the other doors on the landing. Vertical blinds on the windows obscured the interior. Jane squared her shoulders and pressed the doorbell. For a long moment, nothing happened. Then the door swung open, revealing a massive mixed-race man in his early twenties dressed only in a pair of jogging pants. His broad torso could have served as a living diagram in an anatomy class, the muscles large and well defined. He glared down at her. 'Wassup?' he demanded in a mid-Atlantic drawl.

'I need to see John Hampton,' she said, her voice half an octave higher than normal, her accent scarily middle-class even to her ears.

The man looked amused. 'He's not expecting you.' He began to close the door.

Jane put out a hand to stop him, knowing she didn't have a cat in hell's chance against the power of his shoulders but making the gesture anyway. 'I do need to see him,' she said. 'It's a family matter.'

He gave her a disbelieving look. 'I don't think so.'

'Please, just tell him Jane Gresham needs to see him about a family matter. I'll wait.'

'You might be here for a long time, Jane Gresham.' He pushed gently against the door and she dropped her hand. She was banking on the woman at the bus stop having told the truth when she said the Hammer kept an eye on Tenille. If that were true, he could not fail to know about Jane's place in her life. It might be enough to gain her admission.

She paced to and fro between the door and the lift for what felt like a very long time but was probably only a couple of minutes. When she heard the door open, she whirled around to find the same young man beckoning her. 'Your lucky day,' he said. 'Mr Hampton's a very busy man, but he can give you five minutes.'

'That's all I'll need.' She followed him into the flat, whose interior was unlike any other she'd seen on Marshpool Farm. The thick carpet in the hall matched the burgundy of the front door, and the pale walls were decorated with framed photographs of performance cars. The man gestured to her to enter the living room, then closed the door behind her. The room smelt faintly of sandalwood. Sitting opposite her on a cream leather sofa beneath a huge gilt-framed reproduction of one of Jack Vettriano's *film noir* paintings was a short, square black man wearing blue jeans and a white T-shirt. His head was as bald as a bowling ball, his brown eyes deep-set like finger holes. Jane had never been this close to John Hampton, but she'd seen him in the distance. It didn't prepare her for his charisma. Afterwards, she couldn't have described the room; his presence dominated her consciousness. She understood at once how John Hampton had come to wield the power he did.

'Dr Jane Gresham,' he said, his voice a bass rumble. 'What brings an English teacher to my door speaking of family?'

'I want to talk to you about Tenille,' she said, trying not to show how unnerved she felt. 'May I sit down?'

He waved towards a matching armchair in the corner. 'Be my guest. Tenille?' he said, making a show of racking his brains. 'One of the kids on the estate, right?'

'People say she's your daughter.'

'People say a lot of things, Dr Gresham. A lot of them are bullshit.' His face was impassive, his body still.

'It's true she doesn't take after you in looks,' Jane said. 'But I suspect she's inherited your ambition. And your toughness. And your intelligence.'

'Flattery won't get you child support, if that's what you're after.'

'There's more than one kind of child support, Mr Hampton. And right now, Tenille needs something from you.' She couldn't quite believe her nerve.

He sighed and rotated his head, as if loosening a stiffness in his neck. 'You're bold, I'll give you that. But you're confusing me with someone who gives a shit.'

Jane pressed on regardless. While she was still in the room, she had a fighting chance to break through his apparent indifference. 'Her aunt has a boyfriend called Geno Marley. He's been sniffing around Tenille. And last night he tried to rape her.' Now she sensed she had his full attention, though she could not have said quite what had changed.

'I don't understand why you're telling me this, Dr Gresham. This Marley character isn't one of my people.'

'Tenille is, though. And a word from you would take him out of her life.'

'And why should I do that?'

Jane shrugged. 'If she's your daughter, the answer's obvious. And if she's not, well, it would be the right thing to do anyway, wouldn't it?'

'You think I'm some kind of social worker? Here to solve people's problems?'

She sensed he was playing with her, but she didn't know how to enter his game. She got to her feet. There was nothing to be gained by staying. 'You must do what you think best,' she said. 'Now, if you'll excuse me, I have things to do.'

He nodded. 'I'll have a word, Dr Gresham. I don't like scumbags who molest young girls any more than you do. You can tell Tenille she'll be safe.'

'Thank you.' She turned to go, then paused, her hand on the door. 'Whoever Tenille's father is, he should be proud of her. She's remarkable.'

'Goodbye, Dr Gresham. I don't expect we'll meet again,' he said. He sounded so much like a Bond villain that the spell broke.

Jane grinned. 'You never know,' she said.

When she emerged from the flat, she felt elated. In spite of the Hammer's feigned indifference, she was certain that she had achieved what she'd set out to. She could leave for Fellhead with a clear conscience, secure in the knowledge that nothing bad was going to happen to Tenille.

One of the best things about living and working in Carlisle was the stunning scenery on her doorstep, River thought. She'd discovered it was hard to drive for long in any direction without finding herself in a landscape of breathtaking beauty, whether it was the bleak rolling uplands of Northumberland, with Hadrian's Wall the crossbeam to the Pennine spine, or the grandeur of the Lake District National Park with its fells, forests and moody waters. She'd grown up near Cambridge in a landscape of unrelenting flatness that exhibited a limited range of variety. Up here in the north, the changing seasons were somehow nearer the surface, with every day bringing some subtle alteration to the world around her. It was, she thought, a landscape as susceptible to analysis for its history as the human body itself. Recently, she'd joined a group of university staff who went hillwalking every Sunday, and only the previous week she'd been brought up short by a casual comment from one of her fellow walkers. As they'd made their way up the eastern side of Great Gable, he'd remarked that if Wordsworth were to return to England now, he'd find more changes in his native Lakes than he would in the quadrangles of his Cambridge college.

'We think of the landscape as unchanging, but we're wrong,' he'd said. 'Here, everywhere we look we see the hand – or rather, the foot of man. Look at the erosion on these paths. Look at the roads,' he added, waving his hand in the general direction of Buttermere and Derwent Water where the sun could be seen glinting on the metal roofs of cars. 'Choked with traffic every decent summer's day. In Wordsworth's time, there were meandering drover's tracks, not roads carved out of hillsides like chunks cut off a cheese. And they were mostly empty. This landscape tells the history of the last two hundred years more clearly than any urban sprawl.'

'Not to mention the history of the tearoom,' another colleague had commented darkly. 'I'm surprised there isn't one waiting for us on the top of Great Gable.'

River had tucked the initial idea away for further consideration and this morning, as she drove out of

Carlisle on the old Roman road towards Bothel, she reflected on it again. Nearly two thousand years had passed since this road had been built by legionaries miles from their home, forced to eat unfamiliar food and accustom themselves to the often hellish winters of the northernmost part of the empire. She wondered how much of what she was seeing now would have awakened memories in their ghosts. Perhaps the skyline, perhaps the colours. But not much else.

She loved the place names too, with their echoes of another wave of invaders. The Vikings had left their mark on the places they occupied with suffixes – Ireby, Branthwaite, Whitrigg. And there were other wonderful names whose origins she knew nothing of – Blennerhasset, Dubwath and Bewaldeth. Driving from Carlisle to Keswick wasn't just pretty, it was poetry in motion.

She turned left on to the winding road that led between the forested massif of Skiddaw and the long finger of Bassenthwaite. All around her, the trees were changing colour. On the hills, the bracken was turning brown against rough upland grass that the summer rains had left a more vivid green than usual. The lake spangled dark sapphire in the autumn sun and River felt lucky not only to be alive but to be moving through nature at her most glamorous.

She wondered how it had been for Pirate Peat on his last journey on the hill above Coniston Water. With luck, the palaeobotanists might be able to tell her what time of year he had died. But what none of them would ever know was whether he had made that final trip by day or night, in sunlight, rain or mist. Had he been alive to the beauty that surrounded him, or was he one of those who seem unmoved by their surroundings? Was this his home, or was he merely passing through? That at least was something she would probably be able to answer eventually. And once they had established how old the body was, she would be able to track down contemporary drawings and paintings that might reveal something of what her cadaver had seen when he had walked these hills. All of this would only enrich the TV programme, as well as satisfying her own urge for knowledge.

Her speculations dissipated into the ether once she hit the outskirts of Keswick and had to concentrate on getting where she was going. She pulled into the visitors' slot in the police station car park and hurried inside, composing herself in her professional demeanour for her meeting with DCI Rigston. She was almost sorry that they wouldn't be working together; she'd liked him when he'd first briefed her, something which hadn't happened too often in her encounters with police officers.

The civilian on the front desk directed her to the canteen, where she found Rigston tucking into a bacon roll. He got to his feet immediately and shook hands, wiping his fingers with a paper napkin first. 'Can I get you something to eat? Early call-out, I missed breakfast,' he said, gesturing apologetically at his plate.

'Don't mind me, I'm fine,' River said, sliding into the seat opposite him. 'I'm sorry to interrupt your meal, but this won't take long. I thought you'd like to know that my preliminary investigations lead me to believe this body is well outside your remit.'

Rigston grinned, showing a row of even white teeth. 'Thought as much,' he said. 'But I'm glad to have it formally confirmed all the same. Do you know how long he's been in there?'

'Hard to be precise at this stage. But, ballpark, I'd say somewhere between 1785 and 1815. That's a very rough guesstimate,' she added hastily. 'Don't hold me to it. I'll have a better answer once we've completed the work-up.'

'You're giving him the full monte, then?' Rigston looked mildly surprised.

'All the bells and whistles. And the best of it is, I've got someone else to pay for it.' As she spoke, she watched him eat. You could tell a lot about someone by the way they ate. Ewan Rigston took small bites, chewing carefully with his mouth closed before he swallowed. He paused between mouthfuls, considering his next point of attack. So, not the kind of man who charged at things like a bull at a gate. Measured, thoughtful, and maybe a little bit repressed, she thought.

'How did you manage that?'

'Northern TV's going to film the whole process. They're making a documentary series about my Pirate Peat.'

'Good for you. Maybe I could get them to sponsor my armed robbery investigation,' he added wryly. 'But what's with the "Pirate Peat"?'

'They like a nice catchy tag. We found him in a bog, hence the "Peat" part. And his tattoos are typical of a sailor, so I let my fancy run away with me. Besides, it sounds better than Seaman Peat.'

'You're right about that. Good luck with it.'

'Thanks. Would you like me to keep you posted?'

He nodded. 'That would be great. In fact . . .' He

hesitated briefly, then said very quickly, 'I don't suppose you'd fancy meeting up for a drink?'

It wasn't an idea that had so much as crossed River's mind until that moment. But the more she thought about it, the more she liked it. She smiled. 'Yes, actually, I think I would. And you can give me the benefit of your expertise.'

'How so?'

'Well . . .' And she broke off with an embarrassed laugh. 'I just realised I don't know your first name.'

He laughed with her. 'It's Ewan. So does that mean I get to ask you where your name comes from?'

River winced. 'Hippie parents.'

'Must be hard to be taken seriously with a name like that. I have to admit I thought somebody was taking the piss.'

'No kidding.' She flashed him a smile that didn't make it as far as her eyes. 'But hey, it breaks the ice.' The smile was gone. 'And I do expect to be taken seriously.'

Her determination not to be discounted prompted the image of his daughter, the twelve-year-old Rigston saw less and less frequently as her own concerns had become more pressing than the need to see a father who hadn't lived under the same roof for five years. Like Marnie, River Wilde had the air of someone with something to prove and an absolute determination to succeed. He reminded himself this woman wasn't a child, no matter how young she seemed. She was accustomed to sights he hoped his daughter would never have to negotiate. 'Naturally,' he said. 'I wouldn't dream of doing otherwise.' His expression was friendly and open. River felt herself relax again.

'So why do you need the benefit of my expertise?' he continued.

'Because if he hadn't been dead for such a long time, I think he definitely would be one for you. I won't know for sure till we've done the full body X-ray and CAT scan, but, at this point, I'm inclined to think our Pirate Peat did not die from natural causes. I think somebody caved his head in.'

For Tenille, being left alone in Jane's flat was almost worth the reason for the boon. Jane had come back cheerful from her meeting with the Hammer, but had said little about it except that she was convinced Tenille would have no more trouble with Geno. 'Huh,' Tenille snorted.

'I understand why you might feel dubious,' Jane had said. 'But my gut feeling is that the Hammer doesn't say things he doesn't mean. Now, I'm sorry, but I've got to go, Tenille. I've got a train to catch. I'm going to be away for a couple of weeks. You can hang out here for the rest of the day if you want, just close the door behind you when you leave, OK?'

'Yeah, OK. Can I use your computer?'

Jane pondered for a second or two then nodded agreement. 'But you have to go home tonight. I don't want you holing up here indefinitely. Promise?'

Tenille had made a pretence of sulkiness, but she'd promised. She would check out the flat later and, if Geno was there, she'd simply come back to Jane's. She had the key, and knowing Jane was gone, she had the freedom to treat the place as her own for a fortnight. One way or another, things would be sorted out by then, she told herself. No matter what Jane thought, she had no conviction that the Hammer would deal with Geno. He wasn't the sort to take orders from any woman, never mind a middle-class white one.

Tenille waited patiently while Jane packed a bag with clothes and books, then as soon as she left, she headed into the study. She sat down and her finger hovered over the power switch. She felt too weird and too wired to go online. She'd taught herself over the past few years to think of herself as alone in the world, a single particle spinning through the constellations of other people's lives. Since her mum had died, she hadn't allowed herself to feel like she belonged anywhere. Sharon didn't want her, she knew that. Her aunt was acting out of obligation, not love. Without her mum, Tenille was disconnected from the world, unstrung and free. She'd tried to make herself believe that was the best way to be, and mostly she succeeded. When first she'd been told that the Hammer was her real father, that self-contained part of herself had not wanted to believe it. She couldn't have put words round it at the time, but it was something to do with not wanting that kind of connection with anyone because to be connected was somehow to render herself vulnerable.

What had made her feel almost comfortable with the idea was the recognition that, even if he was her father, the Hammer wanted nothing to do with her. He had never acknowledged her existence, far less any relationship between them. He had never done any of the things that even the most hopeless of absent fathers occasionally managed. Never turned up on Christmas Eve with an armful of badly wrapped, expensive but inappropriate presents. Never slipped in to the back row of a school nativity play. Never taken her to a movie or McDonald's. The long and short of it was that he'd never shown the slightest interest in her.

And that made it all the more unlikely that he'd do anything to defend her from Geno. After all, what would it say about him if he did? It would be as good as shouting from the top of D Block that she was his daughter. He might suddenly decide he wanted to start doing the rest of the things that a father was supposed to do, like making sure she went to school and all that shit. Tenille really didn't think she wanted that pressure in her life.

On the other hand, she sure as hell didn't want Geno in her life either. And if the Hammer didn't do something about it, she wasn't sure how she was going to manage that. It wasn't like she knew anybody who would weigh in against Geno, and she couldn't afford to hire any of the local thugs to sort him out. She swore under her breath and turned on the computer, determined not to think any more about it.

I set this down as it was told to me, in the words of my friend:

I had sailed with Lieutenant Bligh before I signed on the Bounty and found him a man whose moods were impossible to predict. When all was going well with the voyage, he would be charm itself. I had reason to know this more than most, for on that first voyage he kept me close, often inviting me to dine with him in his cabin. But if anything chanced to go wrong on board ship, he was choleric and intemperate, always seeking around to cast the blame on another. Never was any occasion of blame laid at his own door. He was also jealous of his position, demanding as of right that respect which a captain needs must earn. Bligh squandered his opportunities to command the good opinion of the men by reason of his vitriol. Sailors are not known for their nicety of expression, but even below decks in the most vile conditions I have never heard language so foul as Bligh would pour out in his expressions of scorn and rage. But he was a fine navigator, and I knew that I could learn much at his side, and so I was willing to forgo my misgivings & to accompany him again, most particularly on such a long voyage.

10

The air even tasted different, Jane thought as she swung down the platform at Oxenholme. She caught sight of her father near the exit and waved cheerily. Allan Gresham raised his hand slightly in response, the small gesture of a modest man more at home on the fell with his Herdwick sheep than he would ever be where people congregated.

Jane dropped her bag and threw her arms around him, brushing a kiss against his rough cheek. 'Thanks for coming, Dad,' she said.

'You can't rely on the buses,' he said, picking up her bag with a surprised grunt as he felt the weight. 'What've you got in here? Gold bricks?'

'I wish. It's books, papers. A few clothes.' Jane fell into step beside him as they made for his Land Rover in the car park.

Once they were clear of the station lights and their faces were obscured by early evening darkness, Allan cleared his throat. 'You're not in any kind of trouble, are you?'

'Why would I be in trouble?' Jane's voice betrayed astonishment.

Allan hefted her bag into the back of the Land Rover and gave a helpless shrug, hands spread at his sides. 'I don't know. It's just . . . It's the middle of term. You've got a job to do. Students to teach. I didn't think you could up sticks with no warning.'

'I haven't, Dad. This is official. Study leave. Something's come up that I need to pursue right away, and my boss has given me a couple of weeks off.'

They climbed aboard and Allan started the engine. He raised his voice to be heard above the rhythmic grunt of the diesel. 'I thought you did dead poets? How can that be urgent?'

'It's the body in the bog, Dad,' Jane said.

He chuckled. 'Fletcher Christian, eh? I wondered how long it would take you to convince yourself this was your man.'

'It might not be him,' Jane protested. 'I never said it was. And chances are it's got nothing to do with him or the *Bounty*. But it's given me a peg to hang my theory on, and that's good enough to buy me some time to look properly into something I turned up last summer.'

'You've always had a talent for persuasion,' Allan said, resigned echoes of old conflicts in his tone. 'So if this is your man, how did he end up dead in a Cumberland bog?'

'I haven't a clue. And to be honest, that's what interests me least. I'll leave that to the historians.'

Her father nodded. 'Any road, I'm glad there's no trouble.' He snatched a quick sidelong glance at her. 'We cannot help worrying about you, all the way down there.'

It was, she knew, a coded way of asking about Jake.

The familiar familial habit of talking about things without actually mentioning them. 'I'm all right, Dad. What can't be cured maun be endured. And I'm good at enduring.'

'Some folks can't tell the difference between sugar and shite, right enough.' They fell silent, an easy quiet broken only by the swish of the wipers on the windscreen.

'How's Gabriel?' Jane asked as they turned off for Fellhead.

'He's grand,' her father said proudly. 'A big strong babby. Started crawling. Your mother said to Diane, "Now your life's really over."' He chuckled. 'I mind when you got going. You would set your heart on getting somewhere and nothing would stop you. Funny, you were that different from Matthew. He was into everything. You couldn't take your eyes off him. But he never had that single-minded determination you had, even when you were tiny. So I reckon we'll get a taste of what Gabriel's going to be like now he's off.'

Jane knew the story. It was one of many that always made Matthew scowl. 'It'll be nice to see Gabriel. They change so quickly when they're that small. Does he still look like Granddad Trevithick?'

'Aye. Your mother says it's only because he's bald and round in the face, but I reckon she's only saying that to keep Diane's mum happy. She reckons he looks like her brother at the same age. He'll end up looking like himself, whatever.'

'I wonder if he'll get the Gresham curls?' She reached over and rumpled her father's thick hair.

'He won't thank us if he does. It's all right for lasses,

117

but us lads don't like looking as if we've spent all day at the hairdressers.'

Jane peered out of the window as they reached the outskirts of the village. Every cottage was imprinted on her memory. She could have picked any of them out of an identity parade. Most were picture perfect, but there was always the odd one whose owner either didn't care or couldn't afford to keep it in good repair. Locals dreaded the death of those inhabitants more than any other because the houses always went to outsiders who were taken with the romance of having a holiday cottage in the Lakes and loved the idea of a bargain they could remake in their own images. Their wallets had pushed even semi-derelict properties out of the reach of most of those who had to subsist on Lakeland wages. Jane's heart sank at the sight of a new For Sale sign. 'What happened to Miss Forsyth?' she asked.

'She had another stroke. Couldn't manage the house any more so she's gone into a home in Keswick,' her father said succinctly as he swung the Land Rover into the narrow lane that led up to their farmhouse on the edge of the village.

'So I suppose that'll be another holiday cottage,' Jane sighed. In the short span of her life, she'd seen almost a third of the homes in the village change hands from families who could track their ancestors back hundreds of years to incomers who did their shopping in distant supermarkets and had no interest in village life except as a curiosity pickled in aspic.

'I don't think anybody round here's got the money for it,' Allan agreed. 'Mind, the house by the Post Office, the couple that bought that live here year round. She does something with computers and he publishes a magazine for ramblers.' He shook his head. 'Doesn't feel like proper jobs to me, but at least they're not just weekenders.'

Allan pulled off into the gateway leading into their yard and parked by the lambing shed. The low farmhouse seemed to crouch against the hillside, its weathered stone blending seamlessly into the landscape. Buttery yellow light spilled out of the kitchen windows, their outline blurred in the heavy drizzle. They hurried through the rain to the back door, shaking themselves like dogs when they were inside the flagged hallway. The glorious aroma of lamb combined with rosemary and garlic wafted round them in a welcoming miasma.

Judy Gresham appeared in the kitchen doorway, wiping her hands on her jeans. 'Jane,' she exclaimed, satisfaction written on her face. In spite of the hard life of a hill farmer's wife, Judy wore her years lightly. She looked more like a woman in her forties than her mid-fifties, her dark brown hair as thick and luxuriant as it had been when Jane had loved to wind it round her fingers as a child. Jane relished the look of surprise on the faces of university friends she'd brought back here when they met her mother. Her father was exactly what they expected – weather-beaten face, stocky frame dressed in overalls over jeans and plaid shirts. But her mother confounded them. Instead of an apple-cheeked woman in pleated skirt and apron stirring jam for the WI stall to the tune of 'Jerusalem', they were confronted with a slender, well-kempt woman in jeans and stylish shirts, never seen in public without make-up, earrings and nail varnish. The features in her oval face were small and neat; Jane wished she'd inherited those rather than her father's deep-set eyes, wide cheekbones and very definite nose. Beside her mother, Jane always felt a big and frumpish disappointment. That was her projection, however; Judy had never indicated by word or look that she was anything other than delighted in her daughter's appearance.

Now she folded Jane in a tight embrace then held her at arms' length for a critical scrutiny. 'You're a sight for sore eyes,' she said. 'It feels like ages since you were home.'

'It's only been a few weeks, Mum,' Jane protested.

'Months, more like.' Her mother turned into the kitchen, confident daughter and husband would follow. The scrubbed pine table where the family had eaten countless meals was laid for dinner, water glasses gleaming in the soft light. 'Perfect timing,' Judy continued. 'The joint's just ready. Sit yourselves down.'

Five minutes in the house and London felt like a foreign country, Jane thought as she watched her mother pile roast potatoes and parsnips round the thick slices of lamb. No matter how hard she tried to convince herself otherwise, this was where she belonged. This was where she felt most alive. Impossible to imagine that only that morning she'd been confronting a London gangsta in his own living room. If she told her parents, their mouths would fall open in shock, their eyes agleam with concern and incomprehension. *And they'd be right*, she thought, reaching for the plate and setting it down in front of herself.

A couple of melting mouthfuls into the lamb, Jane

heard the back door open. 'Only me,' her brother's voice called from the hall through the rustle of an outdoor jacket being removed.

Judy looked faintly guilty. 'Matthew, what a lovely surprise,' she said as her son walked in, pushing damp curls away from his forehead.

Matthew Gresham took in the scene and gave a bitter little smile. 'Very nice,' he said. 'I brought that magazine Diane said you wanted,' he said to Judy, tossing a rolled-up copy of a gardening monthly on the table as he dragged a chair back and plonked himself down like a sulky child. Jane watched it uncurl, waiting for the other shoe to drop. 'What are you doing home in the middle of the week in the middle of term?' he said, his voice deceptively pleasant. 'You blotted your copybook, Sis?'

'Study leave,' Jane said. 'It's good to see you, Matthew,' she added, trying to appear pleasant.

'All right for some,' Matthew said. He sniffed the air. 'Nice bit of lamb. You been slaughtering, Dad? I'll look forward to something more exciting than pasta arrabbiata for Sunday lunch.'

Judy's lips tightened but she said nothing. Jane wondered how differently her brother might have turned out if her mother hadn't been so willing to let him rule the roost as a child.

'Your mother makes very good pasta,' her father said. 'You can't beat home-made tagliatelle. And it takes a lot more time to prepare than a joint. Which you'd know if you ever turned a hand in the kitchen.'

Matthew flicked his eyebrows upwards. 'So what's this study leave all about, then? Time out to mend a broken heart?'

Jane shook her head, a rictus smile plastered on her face. 'I see the charm and diplomacy is still a work in progress. No, Matthew, this is nothing to do with Jake. There's some documentation I need to look for up here and my professor agrees with me that I need to do it sooner rather than later.'

'Documentation you need to look for? You're not still banging on about Wordsworth's lost masterpiece?' Matthew stretched across and picked a fragment of lamb from the serving plate, popping it into his mouth with a murmur of appreciation. Then suddenly he snorted with laughter. 'Oh, I get it. You've convinced your gullible boss that the body in the bog is – ta da! – none other than Fletcher Christian.' His face soured again. 'God, you've got it so easy down there. Fancy a few days in the Lakes with a bit of home cooking? I know, come up with some daft notion and sweet-talk the world into dancing to your tune.'

'Give it a rest, Matthew,' Allan said. 'Your sister's not in the door five minutes.'

'And it's not as if you've got much to complain about,' Judy said brightly. 'A beautiful baby boy, a lovely wife and a good job. There's millions would be happy with your lot.'

'So is that it, Jane?' Matthew continued relentlessly, ignoring his mother. 'You're going to waltz back in here and find Willie's epic on the *Bounty* and make your fortune?'

Jane swallowed her half-chewed mouthful and glared at her brother. 'I'm pursuing a line of research. But if I do find anything, it won't be me getting rich, it'll be Wordsworth's heirs. Or whoever has title to whatever it is I find.'

Matthew looked scornful. 'Let's not be naïve here, Sis. OK, you're the only person in the world who believes in the magic manuscript. But if you do find it, it'll be the making of you. A brilliant career, all off the back of the Lakes.'

'And how do you think people would make a living round here if it wasn't for heritage tourism?' Jane countered. 'There's other parts of England just as beautiful, but they don't have anything like the tourist income we have. The history of literary connections with the Lake District is one of the main reasons people come here. Whether it's Wordsworth, Beatrix Potter, Ruskin or Arthur Ransome. Their legacy has given back much more than they ever took out of the area.'

'But this? This won't be something that generates money and jobs in the tourism industry, will it? This is not going to help create jobs for the kids I teach and their families. It'll be a handful of outsiders getting rich.' He shook his head. 'I never thought you'd be one of the ones treating this place like a cash cow.'

'There's a long and noble tradition of that, Matthew. Wordsworth and his friends were a part of it too. Do you despise them as well?' There was an edge to Jane's voice now. She knew it would be enough to make Matthew back down.

He threw his hands up in surrender. 'You've always got an answer, Jane.' He pushed his chair back, the feet screeching on the stone-flagged floor. 'I better be getting back. I've got lessons to prepare. Nearest I'm likely to get to study leave.' He stood up. 'How long are you here for?'

'A couple of weeks. When's the best time to catch Diane on Saturday?'

Matthew shrugged. 'Pretty much any time, if it's raining. Which it looks like it's set on for the next few days.'

'Tell her I'll drop in. I'm dying to see Gabriel.'

'Sure you can spare the time to play aunties and nephews? I mean, you are supposed to be studying, right?'

'Grow up, Matthew,' Allan said wearily.

Matthew snorted. 'I'm not the one playing hunt the metaphorical slipper, Dad. If anybody needs to catch the boat from Fantasy Island, it's Jane. Wake up and smell the coffee, Sis. There's no pot of gold at the end of the rainbow. Time to join the rest of us in the real world.'

Modifications were made to the Bounty before she set sail for the South Seas so that she could accommodate our cargo of breadfruit on our return voyage. On account of this, conditions were exceeding cramped for all on board, for officers as much as for the common seamen. Such close quarters always breed squabbling among the men, and it was impossible for we officers to hold ourselves aloof from the petty disputes that can fester on board ship. But that was as nothing compared to the tyranny of Bligh. He was a martinet with the men and no less so with the officers. For the most part, I was fortunate enough to be excluded from this general treatment. Bligh still seemed desirous of my good opinion and had me to dine in his cabin whenever I was not on watch. I confess I felt discomfort from the first at being singled out thus. I did not wish the men to think I was allied with Bligh. Nor was I easy in my mind as to the nature of his affection for me.

11

Damp mist held the heavy tang of the polluted city close to the ground. It clawed at throats, making smokers cough harder, and shrouded heads in street-light haloes. The glow from windows was romanti-cised by the fog, but it was fooling no one. The pavements were quiet; it wasn't the sort of evening to tempt people away from their own TVs.

Tenille stretched and checked the clock on the PC. Just after ten. It was time to make a move. Part of her wanted to stay here, snug in the cocoon of Jane's flat, isolated in a place where she could pretend her life was different from its ungentle reality. But another part of her wanted to test the mettle of Jane and her alleged father. She gathered her stuff together and trudged towards the door. She took a last look around, checking the door key was still in her pocket, then stepped out into the night. After the warmth of the flat, the clammy cold made her shiver as she hurried along the gallery to the stairs. She had just begun to climb the two flights to her floor when she heard a low boom. The fog muffled it, making it impossible to divine its direction or identify its source. But unexplained noises were hardly an unusual event on Marshpool Farm, and it barely registered on her consciousness.

Heading towards the final turn of the stairs, Tenille realised there were footsteps coming down the steps towards her. The footsteps of someone big and confident, judging by the sound. Instinctively, she dodged to one side, making room for whoever it was to pass. Round here, making room could sometimes mean the difference between getting home in one piece or not.

She rounded the stairs and came face to face with John Hampton moving quickly down. A confusion of feelings hit her: apprehension, anxiety and curiosity. If he was surprised to see her, he didn't show it. He didn't even break step, merely glancing briefly at her, his face blank of expression. As he passed her, he said softly, 'Not a good time to go home, Tenille.'

She stopped short and stared after him. A shoot of happiness blossomed inside her. He'd done it. He'd done it for her. Tenille grinned and ran up the few remaining steps, eager for the first time to see Geno. She didn't think he'd be keen to hit on her any time soon.

The door to the flat was slightly ajar; she pushed it open and walked in. There was a strange smell, like fireworks. The hall was in darkness, except for a thin sliver of light outlining the living-room door. Tenille pushed it open, eager expectancy drawing a smile on her face.

The sight that confronted her was not what she had anticipated. Where she expected to see Geno curled in an agonised ball on the sofa, all that was recognisably his were his trousers.

The top half of his body was unrecognisable.

Mangled meat jumbled with chewed-up fabric. Tatters of skin hung like macabre decorations from his head and neck. Blood, hair and flesh were spattered over the sofa and the wall behind it. Inside the room, the stink was different. Shit, gunpowder and something metallic bit at Tenille's throat. She could feel her gorge rising but the gruesome remains on the sofa still held her with a terrible fascination. It was as if her mind had split in half. Part of her was rejoicing in the knowledge she was safe. The other part was wondering why she wasn't screaming.

. Tenille took a step forward, almost tripping over something lying on the worn carpet. In her shocked daze, she bent down and picked it up. The wooden butt of the sawn-off shotgun felt warm in her hand. Her other hand ran absently over the smooth metal of the barrels. This had been her friend. This had bought her salvation. This had been her father's chosen tool.

The thought of John Hampton cracked the shell. The horror of what was spread before her hit like the slam of a door. She threw the gun from her, appalled and shaking. Her prints were on the gun now. Dimly she recognised from dozens of TV shows how this would look. She had to do something. It wasn't enough to wipe the gun. She knew that, however clever her father might be, there would be microscopic traces. She'd watched enough episodes of *Forensic Files* to understand that neither she nor her father was safe.

Forcing her eyes away from Geno, Tenille tried to control herself, dragging a shuddering breath into her lungs. She had to do something. But what? She had to get out of the room so she could think straight.

Tenille stumbled back into the hall and squatted on her haunches, head in hands. There had to be something she could do to make sure her father was in the clear for this. He'd come to her rescue when she'd needed him. Now she felt the need for some comparable gesture. A recognition that she appreciated what he'd done for her.

She racked her brains, recalling the true crimes she'd watched unfold on late-night satellite TV. Every night, another death. Every death, another investigation. Tips and hints for those with the brains enough to grasp their significance and heads sufficiently cool to put them into practice.

Her face cleared. Fire, the great cleanser. It wouldn't disguise the fact that Geno had been blown away by a sawn-off before the fire had started. But a good enough fire would clear up any traces that she or her father might have left at the scene of the crime. Tenille got to her feet. All she needed now was something to make sure the blaze caught a good hold. She wished she lived in one of those houses where they had a garden shed full of stuff that would go up like a Roman candle. Cans of petrol for the lawnmower. Gas bottles for the barbecue. That sort of thing.

Tenille went through to the kitchen and opened the cupboard under the sink. Bleach, fabric conditioner, all-purpose cleaner. Totally useless. She banged the door shut and went through to her aunt's room. Perfume was alcohol, that would give off fumes that would help a fire, she thought. She grabbed the few bottles off Sharon's dressing table, then noticed an economy-sized bottle of nail varnish remover. That would burn, she was sure of it. Tenille added it to her haul. She was about to return to the living room when she noticed a canister in a half-open drawer. She yanked it out and helped herself to a pressurised can of lighter fluid.

At the living-room door, she closed her eyes momentarily, trying to steady herself. 'Get a hold of yourself, girl,' she said loudly, driving herself back into the room. This time, she tried not to look at Geno. She crossed to the sofa where she emptied out all of the bottles. The sweet sickly aromas rose around her, blotting out the smells of violent death. Then she pushed the nozzle of the lighter fluid can hard against the wooden arm of the sofa. The liquid gas emerged, spreading over the scarred veneer and soaking into the surrounding fabric as it evaporated. The harsh oily smell of the butane made Tenille wrinkle her nose and turn her face away. She let the whole contents of the canister escape before throwing it on the floor.

Now all she had to do was light the fucking thing. Where was the bastard's cigarette lighter? Her earlier exultation had subsided now; she had started to grasp the finality of his death and the almost casual way it had been meted out. However grateful she was to her father, she couldn't keep fooling herself that this was a good thing. She really didn't want to look at Geno.

Tenille sidestepped the feet sticking out from the sofa, kicking the gun nearer as she did so. That sofa was going to go up like a torch. Sharon had bought it off some dodgy second-hand shop, there was no way it was going to be anything other than a fire-trap. She looked down at the cluttered end table next to Geno. The tumbler he'd been drinking from had been shattered by stray shot, and his cigarettes and lighter were covered in glass shards and rum. Tenille reached out for the lighter and grimaced as the sticky spirit coated her fingers. She backed towards the door and wondered what to do next. She didn't want to be too close to the sofa when she lit the flame. But she had to be close enough to get the fire going.

'Stop messing,' she scolded herself. She took a step back towards the sofa and ignited the lighter. It seemed to burn with a higher flame than usual. At arm's length, she reached out towards the soaked upholstery. She was still inches away when there was a sudden whoosh and a sheet of flame ran over the area she'd saturated. At once, the flames started to lick over the cushions towards Geno.

Tenille jumped back nervously, ready for flight. But she wanted to be sure this wasn't just a flash in the pan, that it would really burn the way she needed it to. Within seconds, she had her answer. Tongues of flame spread quickly over the cheap synthetic material, melting it as they went, sending spirals of greasy black smoke upwards.

Time to get the fuck out, Tenille told herself, turning on her heel and making for the door. She slammed it shut behind her, then took off down the gallery towards the stairs. Thank Christ she had Jane's door key. She could hole up there, wash her clothes in Jane's machine and claim she'd never been near the flat all night. Jane would have to back her up, because she didn't know about the key. As far as she knew, Tenille had no way of getting back in once she'd left.

Tenille reached the top of the stairs and turned for

one last look. The only difference from usual was that the light showing through the curtains was more orange. She wondered if she should call the fire brigade. She didn't want the fire to spread, to maybe claim other lives. That would be the worst thing that could happen. But if she made the call, it would put her in the frame; 999 calls were, she knew, recorded and saved.

The curtains stirred. Soon they'd go up too and somebody would see what was going on. They'd call the fire brigade. Tenille turned on her heel and set off down the stairs at a run. It would be all right. Somebody would see.

What she didn't know was that somebody already had.

When I speak thus, it is not to assign impure motives to Bligh. He never attempted the crime of sodomy on my person, nor did I ever hear that he had such inclinations towards any other. No, it is rather that, having chosen me as his protégé, the man took my affection towards any other as a personal slight. One of my fellow officers on this voyage was a distant kinsman, Peter Heywood, whose family had shown mine kindness when we were forced to remove to the Isle of Man. It was my duty as well as my pleasure to take this young man under my care, and Bligh chastised me often for this. 'Sirrah, the boy must find his own way,' he was wont to say. He seemed not to comprehend that my care for Heywood was identical to his adoption of myself as his personal charge. His vanity could not countenance what he took to be my preference for the company of another. These matters came to a head in a most miserable fashion in Otaheite.

12

As she emerged from the farmyard on her mountain bike, Jane took a deep breath, savouring the aroma of the autumn morning. It was a glorious day, surprisingly mild for the time of year. The night's rain had left a sparkle in the air, brightening the turning leaves and deepening the greys and greens of the landscape. The sun was climbing behind Helvellyn, casting a golden halo round the summit. She turned to look upwards at the great bluff of Langmere Fell, its craggy outcroppings dark against the sky. She could see her father's sheep, pale grey and cream blurs against the bracken and scrubby grass of the high moorland where they grazed. A grin spread across her face and she shed the last of the city. This was where she belonged.

She turned the bike downhill and freewheeled into the village, a journey she had made more times than she could count. As always, the sudden opening out of the view caught at her heart, the light glinting on the tail of Thirlmere, the pikes and crags rising beyond in tight contours to the skyline. What must it have been like for Fletcher Christian, she wondered, coming home to this after the South Seas? Would his spirit have risen with joy and relief at being enclosed by his familiar mountains, their muted colours the palette of his youth? Or would he have yearned for the lush tropics with their improbable colours? Would the cold and damp have made his bones ache for that hotter southern sun? Would the women have seemed pallid and uninteresting after the exotic beauty who had given him a son? Would he have felt that he had come home, or would this have seemed merely a different kind of prison from Pitcairn?

Whatever his story, it couldn't have failed to fire William Wordsworth's imagination. In her mind's eye, she conjured up a picture of the poet sitting in his garden at Dove Cottage, head bent over the intractable lines of *The Prelude*, that long narrative of his early life whose writing and rewriting occupied him for the best part of fifty years. So much elided, so much glossed over. While it had the appearance of candid revelation, the biographers had demonstrated that it was in fact a construct that stripped William's early life of anything personally scandalous or politically questionable. That didn't detract from its value as poetry, but it cast serious doubts on its worth as biography. Which, paradoxically, made Jane feel all the more strongly that there was merit to her theory. The absence of direct written evidence in William's published work, given so much else that was absent, did not mean the events she pictured had not taken place.

Jane pedalled on down Langmere Fell, the busy water of the Lang Burn chattering on her left as it cascaded brimful towards Thirlmere. As she slowed down for the junction with the main road by Town

Head, she wondered if, when they'd met again, William had recognised the prodigal immediately. Bligh's description of the twenty-three-year-old at the beginning of the voyage stuck in her mind. He stood five feet nine inches tall, above average height for the time. He had a noticeably dark complexion, which would have been darkened further by years of exposure to the sea winds and the strong sun of the southern oceans. According to Bligh, he'd been 'strong made' though slightly bow-legged. She imagined him as a sort of Caravaggio figure, a chiaroscuro of light and shade at the captain's table, his dark eyes glinting in candlelight. Striking, distinctive-looking. She didn't think it would have taken the observant poet long to connect the apparent stranger with the spirited boy he'd known in his youth. It must have rocked him to his foundations. Just when he'd smoothed over his own slightly disreputable past and reinvented himself as the poet with moral authority, here was one of the most notorious figures in recent history standing before him, claiming the obligations of friendship. It was nothing if not dramatic. At least William would probably have been spared a witness to his discomfiture; their reunion would certainly have been a private encounter, since Fletcher could hardly have hazarded anything else.

Jane passed the turning for Grasmere and rounded the curve in the road. Now she could see the signs for Dove Cottage and the Wordsworth Museum. At least it wouldn't be too busy today, she thought. Not like high summer, when tourists crammed into the tiny rooms where the Wordsworth family had lived their cramped, sociable lives. William would have regarded it as nothing less than his due; he had never really doubted his genius, fretting only that the world was a little behind him in that respect.

Jane parked her bike then entered the pretty café with its pine chairs and tables. Anthony Catto was sitting in a corner reading the morning paper. He looked more like an ageing rocker than a museum curator, with his long silver hair pulled back in a ponytail and his oblong designer glasses perched on his nose. He was wearing what Jane had come to recognise as his working uniform – work boots, faded jeans, denim shirt and a brown leather waistcoat whose pockets were always bulging with the reminders he constantly scribbled for himself then promptly consigned to what he referred to as 'the working files'. But in spite of his appearance, there was nobody alive who knew more about the life and work of William Wordsworth and his family. His adult life had been a quest for information about the poet and his world that bordered on the fanatical. More than that, there was none of the jealous guarding of his knowledge that Jane had found so depressingly prevalent in academic life. Anthony was generous to a fault with his erudition. Some might have said generous to the point of boredom; Jane would not have been one of them.

'Morning, Anthony,' she called as she headed for the table.

He looked up, his craggy face creasing into a smile. 'Jane, my dear,' he said, his voice rich and plummy as Jack Horner's pudding. 'How lovely to see you.' He unfolded his lanky height from the chair and extended a hand. Jane took his warm dry palm in her chilled one and shook it. 'My, but you're cold,' he exclaimed.

'I cycled down from Fellhead. It felt mild when I started out, but it ended up a bit colder than I expected,' she admitted ruefully.

'City life's making you soft. You're losing that Lakeland hardiness,' he said, pouring her a coffee.

'No, that's bred in the bone. It'll take more than a bit of cold to see me off.' Jane sipped her coffee appreciatively.

'Well, Jane, I'm most intrigued by this letter of Mary's. After we spoke, I tracked it down, right where you told me it would be.' He shook his head, mouth twisted into an expression of disapproval. 'Extraordinary that nobody came across it before. Well, I say extraordinary. But there are still far too many items in the archive that still haven't been fully catalogued.'

'And it was tucked inside the wrong envelope. Do you think it refers to a poem?'

He tugged at his earlobe. 'Mary is annoyingly non-specific, isn't she? It could be a letter, it could be notes for a poem, or it could be a poem itself. Or indeed, all three. Tell me why you think it might be a poem.'

'I think Fletcher Christian came back,' Jane said abruptly. She felt as if she'd been telling this story in one form or another for days. But she knew she would have to earn Anthony's help so she prepared to give it a new spin.

Anthony's smile bordered on the indulgent. 'Ah, that old Lakeland chestnut. Still, though somewhat implausible, it's not beyond the bounds of possibility.'

'I'm glad you think so. Now, I believe he left Pitcairn

somewhere around 1793 or 1794. Certainly before the children were old enough to have any memory of him. It's hard to know how long he took to get back to England. Whether he made his escape on a whaler or managed to sail all the way to South America in one of the jolly boats, he would still have had to make his way across to the Atlantic and work his passage back, probably as an ordinary seaman. All of that would have taken time. Years, perhaps.'

Anthony nodded. 'Agreed.'

'Now, even though he knew he'd probably been convicted of mutiny in his absence, he had no reason to suppose that anyone outside the seafaring establishment would know anything about it. He wasn't to know that Bligh's phenomenal voyage had turned the mutiny into the eighteenth-century equivalent of *I'm a Celebrity, Get Me Out of Here*. It must have been a hell of a shock when he discovered he was notorious.'

Anthony frowned. 'He was a bright chap, your Mr Christian, wasn't he?'

'By all accounts, yes. Why do you ask?'

'It would have made a certain sense for him to have remained overseas while he communicated with someone at home he could trust. If for no other reason than to make arrangements for his return.'

Jane nodded. 'Perfect sense.'

'And that might well explain the curious incident of William's letter to the *Weekly Entertainer*,' Anthony said. 'You know about the letter, of course?'

'William wrote to the paper to repudiate a pamphlet purportedly written by Fletcher describing his post-*Bounty* adventures. I've seen the pamphlet and it's the most preposterous rubbish.'

'But it had clearly gained sufficient currency with the public at large for William to rise above the parapet to denounce it as spurious. Not only is it the only reference in his writings to the mutiny, but it's also the only letter he ever sent to a newspaper that was signed with his own name rather than a pseudonym. Doesn't he say something along the lines of having the best authority for his assertion? Which might suggest that Edward Christian knew exactly where his brother was, or at least knew enough to persuade William to state categorically that the pamphlet was a farrago of lies.' Anthony leaned back in his chair, satisfied with his rationale. 'So far, so logical. But how do we get from this point to the putative poem?'

Jane smiled. 'It's all a question of timing. I think Fletcher stayed away until the *Bounty* was old news. I think he came back around 1804.'

'Why then, specifically?'

'By then, England was at war with France and every sailor's mind was focused on Napoleon. Nelson, not Bligh, was the naval hero on everyone's lips. It had been ten years since Fletcher had escaped from Pitcairn and I'd guess he was pretty bitter and frustrated that Bligh had robbed him of that time at home. He must have desperately wanted to put his side of the story. Wouldn't you?'

'Absolutely.' Anthony rubbed his chin. 'I see now where you're going with this. By 1804, William was not only a poet of some reputation, he had also shifted his interest from short lyric poetry to the epic. He was working on *The Prelude*. He was probably *dreaming* in iambic pentameter. He was in precisely the right creative place to deal with the material.'

'Right. And what could be more natural than Fletcher turning to William? Who better to tell his side of the story than someone he'd known since boyhood?'

'Imagine how disappointed Fletcher must have been when he realised William was never going to publish it.' Anthony smiled at her, his grey eyes crinkling at the corners. 'Jane, you've spun a very pretty web out of next to nothing. How do you propose to anchor it more firmly to reality?'

Jane grinned. 'Well, in an ideal world, Anthony, we'd open one of your boxes and find William's notes and the completed poem.'

'Failing that?'

'I need to find John's reply to Mary. That might give me some clues where to start looking for whatever it was William didn't want anyone to see.'

Anthony pursed his lips. 'I don't recall ever reading anything of that nature.'

And you would if you had, Jane thought. She still remembered once asking Anthony if he knew when the back door to Dove Cottage had been built. Without hesitation, he had replied, 'It must have been in or around March 1804. Dorothy refers in a letter that month to it having been installed.' If John's letter to his mother was in the archives, Anthony would know. 'That's a pity,' she said.

Anthony raised an admonitory finger. 'But there are a couple of boxes of family letters that have not been fully catalogued. They've been sitting at the back of a cupboard for years. We only found them when we were packing up the archive for the transfer to the new centre. Deborah took a quick look through and they were from after William's death, so there seemed little urgency about getting to them. You're very welcome to take a pass through them yourself.' Never one to hang around, he drained his coffee cup and stood up expectantly. 'There is a price, of course,' he added as they walked back to the kitchen.

Jane felt a slight tingle of surprise. It wasn't like Anthony to be so direct about the trading of favours. He was normally far too much the diplomat. 'Of course,' she said.

'You have to express undying admiration for our new Jerwood Centre,' he said, turning back to show her an impish smile.

'I think I can just about afford that,' she said, following him out of the café.

We arrived in Otaheite on the 25th day of October 1788 after a long and treacherous voyage. We had failed to breach the Horn, so had to turn back and make our voyage the long way round by way of the Cape of Good Hope. The men were exhausted and sick, notwithstanding Lieutenant Bligh's insistence that they dance every day on deck to maintain good physical condition. Otaheite seemed to all like a paradise on earth rich in everything a man could desire. I considered myself fortunate in that I was sent to build a camp ashore, where I was to supervise the collection of the breadfruit whose transportation was the very purpose of our voyage. Among the men I chose to accompany me was young Peter Heywood, in part because I thought him safer under my care than on board under a captain who would not hesitate to make him victim to his vindictive spirit. As I look back upon it now, I believe I may have chosen the wrong path.

13

Tenille surfaced from sleep in a panic, not remembering for a moment why the light was coming from the wrong direction. She thrashed free of the unfamiliar duvet in the strange bed, looking wildly round as she struggled for her bearings. Then the night before piled in on her, memories tumbling over each other in a kaleidoscope of horror. Sleep had left her sticky-eyed and sweaty, the tormented dreams like a bad taste in her mouth.

She tumbled out of bed and ran for the bathroom, just making it in time to throw up in the toilet. She lay huddled on the floor, shuddering at the unwanted images playing behind her eyes. Geno's blood, Geno's shredded flesh, Geno's clothes ripped to rags. She wasn't sorry he was dead; her teenage vision of the world admitted few shades of grey and, as far as she was concerned, he had been scum. But she was sorry she'd had to see what was left of him after her father had made him pay what was due.

She heaved herself to her feet like an old woman and shuffled into the kitchen. Somehow, the scouring of her stomach had left her hungry. All there was in the fridge was a chunk of cheddar cheese, a carton of orange juice, half a jar of mayonnaise and the remains of a bunch of spring onions. No milk, no Coke. 'Useless,' she muttered to herself, opening cupboards. A packet of oatcakes. Pasta, rice, tinned tomatoes, kidney beans and lentils, a few packs of instant Chinese noodles. Coffee, Earl Grey tea, drinking chocolate. A box of breakfast cereal, the kind that was all dried fruit and grains. Grumbling under her breath, Tenille grabbed the cereal and tipped some into a bowl. She poured orange juice over it and took it back to the living room.

She switched on the radio and tuned it to the local talk radio station. She needed to find out what they were saying about Geno's death. She climbed back into bed with her food and chewed miserably while she waited for the news bulletin.

First up was some political bollocks. Why did the announcers always sound so cheerful, she wondered. Who were they trying to kid? Did they think people wouldn't notice the crap if they made it sound like they were telling you you'd won the lottery? The relentless good spirits continued to the second item. 'Police have launched a murder inquiry following a serious fire in a flat on the notorious Marshpool Farm Estate in Bow. The body of a man was discovered by the fire crew attending the blaze. Detective Inspector Donna Blair, who is leading the inquiry, has appealed for witnesses.' A new voice spoke. 'We believe that the victim may have been shot and the fire set to cover the crime,' she said, her tone blankly official. 'We would appeal for anyone who saw anything suspicious in or around

G Block of Marshpool Farm Estate between ten and eleven yesterday evening to come forward.'

Tenille made a derisive noise. Fat chance. Nobody was going to grass up the Hammer, not if they wanted to live to see their next birthday. The announcer moved on to the next story and she tuned out the sound of his voice. There had been no surprises in the news item. She knew from watching forensic documentaries that the fire wouldn't have disguised the fact that Geno had been blown away first. But, hopefully, it would have destroyed any traces that would lead back to her father.

She ought to think about putting in an appearance. Sharon wouldn't be too worried once the police had told her there was only one body in the fire. She'd just assume Tenille had come back late and, finding the place crawling with cops and firemen, she'd done as any Marshpool Farm resident would in the circumstances and gone to ground. But she'd better not leave it too long. She decided she'd monitor the news until late afternoon, then she'd turn up, claiming she'd been sleeping at a friend's house, too frightened to show her face. That should cover it.

A couple of hours later, she was interrupted in the middle of an online conversation about Keats' 'Ode on a Grecian Urn' by a knock at the door. 'Fuck,' she muttered. On silent feet she made for the door, jumping nervously as the caller knocked again, this time more loudly and for longer. Tenille edged towards the door, then inched up to the spyhole. She risked a quick look.

Her mouth fell open in surprise. The last person she expected to see standing outside Jane's door was that scumbag Jake Hartnell. It had been ages since he'd fucked off. Jane hadn't said much about it, but Tenille had read the misery in her face when she talked about him going off to Greece. Now it looked as though Greece hadn't worked out and the useless wanker was back. Well, she was sure as hell not going to open up for him. Nor did she have any intention of letting Jane know he'd come knocking.

The letter box rattled and Tenille pressed herself back against the wall, holding her breath. 'Jane?' he called out. Like that would have made Jane come running, Tenille thought contemptuously. She heard him sigh, then the flap clattered shut. She stayed put, wanting to make sure he was gone before she made a break for the study. Long seconds passed, then the letter box banged back and a sheet torn from a notebook fell to the mat. Tenille counted to sixty, then bent down to pick up the paper. She shook her head in exasperated disbelief as she read it. *Dear Jane, I just got back from Crete and came straight round to see you, but you weren't in. I've missed you and I want to see you. I'll give you a ring later. Hope we can meet for a drink or dinner. Love, Jake.*

Love, Tenille thought. Adults could be so stupid. You didn't have to be a genius to know Jake's stupid note had no chance of getting a result. The way he'd upset Jane, he'd need to splash out on the entire contents of a flower shop before she'd maybe think about letting him buy her a bottle of champagne. At least, he would if Jane had any sense. Which Tenille seriously doubted where Jake was concerned. She screwed the paper up into a ball and tossed it into the bin as she went back to her chat room. No way was she going to give Jane the chance to make a fool of herself over Jake again.

It was the least she could do in return for Jane sorting Geno.

Jake turned away and walked briskly down the bleak gallery, frustrated at Jane's absence, wondering where she was. He was sure this wasn't one of her days for the Viking, nor did she teach today either. She should have been home. It never occurred to him that it was unreasonable to expect that her life would still run to the rhythms that had driven it when he had been part of it.

He took the stairs at a run, trying not to think about why they stank of acrid smoke instead of piss, and hurried back to where he'd parked the car. To his relief, Caroline's Audi was still there, apparently untouched. He knew Marshpool Farm well enough to realise that broad daylight was no guarantee of a smart car's safety. Nor were the two police cars parked nearby. Once inside, he locked the doors and pondered his next move. He was going to have to work at getting back in with Jane again. Face to face, one to one was the best way to achieve that. The Viking was out of the question; Harry would be there at her side, ready to put the shaft in. Harry had never liked him. The university was no better a prospect. There, she'd be flanked by colleagues, friends, students, all convenient shields to hide behind. And the library was a bad idea. Too easy for her to take refuge in the silence.

One thing was certain. He couldn't hang around the estate, staking out her flat like some seedy private eye. He'd attract far too much attention from the sort of people who wouldn't hesitate to do whatever it took to part him from car, wallet and mobile phone. Not to mention the police, who would be interested in anyone driving a car like the Audi around the Marshpool.

At last, because he couldn't think of anything else to do, he called the university. If she had changed her schedule and was teaching today, it would be a lot easier to keep watch for her there. Then he could follow her and choose his moment.

When he was finally connected to the English Department secretary, she put him on hold while she made enquiries. Jake drummed his fingers impatiently against the wheel as he tried not to listen to the tinny whine of Sting's voice. What possessed the people who chose the music to fill callers' ears, he wondered. Why couldn't they choose something calm and soothing so the person hanging endlessly on the line would have their homicidal urges eased rather than exacerbated? He was profoundly grateful when the music stopped abruptly and the woman's voice came back on the line. 'You're out of luck,' she said. 'Jane Gresham isn't teaching today. In fact, she has a leave of absence. She won't be back in the department for two weeks.'

'Leave of absence? Why? Is there some family crisis or something?'

'All I can tell you is what's in the system. "Leave of absence for purposes of study", that's all it says here. If you want to leave a message, I can put it in her pigeonhole.'

'No, thanks all the same. I appreciate your help.' Jake ended the call with a quickening of his heart.

Study leave, in the middle of term. That could only be because something unforeseen and urgent had cropped up.

Something like a body in a bog, perhaps.

Detective Inspector Donna Blair frowned at the forensic report. 'Are you sure?' she said.

'I'm sure,' the fingerprint technician said. 'Your boys brought in the remains of a sawn-off shotgun from the scene. The stock was too badly charred for prints, but we got lucky with the barrel. Even though fire boils off the water content, if it's not too intense, the fat deposits remain on the metal. We tried Sudan Black . . .'

'Spare me the details,' Donna said.

The technician shrugged. 'It's all in the report. We got a couple of prints. They don't match anyone in the database, but they do match the elimination prints we took from Tenille Cole's bedroom.'

Donna shook her head, depressed at the thought. 'It fits. We've also got a witness who has her leaving the flat about five minutes before the fire was reported. OK, thanks.'

Chip off the old block, Donna thought as she ran downstairs to the interview room. The Hammer's daughter seemed to be following in her old man's footsteps. The media were going to love this. There would be a feeding frenzy the minute they twigged the prime suspect was a pretty teenager with the kind of lurid background that was a gift to journalistic spin. No matter that the Hammer had taken no part in her upbringing; the connection would be enough to transform Tenille Cole into the kind of cold-blooded killer that would chill the hearts of readers all too ready to demonise any section of the population that wasn't identifiably them.

Donna took a detour into the ladies' toilet where she locked herself into a cubicle. If their prime suspect was the killer, there weren't too many likely motives floating around. The obvious one was the one most calculated to piss Sharon Cole right off. Donna wanted to be ready for the fall-out. Sitting down on the toilet, she closed her eyes, breathing deeply. She cleared her mind, picturing waves breaking on a winter beach, until she could feel her shoulders lowering.

Moments later, she was striding down the hall towards the interview room. Sharon Cole's head snapped up as soon as Donna entered the room. Her eyes were red-rimmed, but she held herself erect in her chair. 'What're you keeping me here for?' she demanded. 'I'm the victim here.'

Donna understood the emotions hiding behind Sharon's bravado. She had a gift for empathy. But while most cops who shared that knack used it to get alongside their target, coaxing information from them, Donna had a different approach. She used her understanding to dive under their guard and go straight for their vulnerabilities. The more uncomfortable she felt, the more she knew she was unsettling her opponent. Come a certain point and they would crack open for her. Her forensic skill at dissecting witnesses and suspects made her colleagues regard her with wariness. She didn't care. She got the results and that was what counted. Taking bastards off the streets, that's what she was there for, not social work.

Donna waited till she was seated opposite Sharon before she opened her mouth. 'Don't give me that victim routine, Sharon. You're guilty as hell and you know it.'

Confusion wriggled across Sharon's face. This wasn't how she expected to be treated, not after the solicitude she'd experienced at the hands of the officers who had brought her in. 'I was at work all night. Ask anybody, they'll tell you.'

'You might not have blown Geno to kingdom come. You might not have fired your own flat. But you're responsible for what went down there last night.' Donna could feel Sharon's anger. What she wanted was unease, but she wasn't there yet.

'That's bullshit. You saying I hired some hitman? Why would I do a thing like that? I loved Geno.'

Donna rolled her eyes. 'Oh please, spare me that. All you were to each other was a convenient shag. Though, come to think of it, some people in your shoes would have considered hiring a button man.'

'What do you mean, "in my shoes"?'

Now the unease was there. Time for Donna to make her move. 'A woman whose man is playing around on her with her thirteen-year-old niece,' Donna said. 'Some women –'

'Wait a fucking minute,' Sharon yelped, interrupting. 'What the fuck are you saying? You saying Geno was messing with Tenille?' She tried to look contemptuous, but the quiver in her curled lip told another story.

'I can't think of any other reason why Tenille would blow the bastard away, can you?'

Sharon's eyes widened and she pulled her lips back,

hissing through her teeth. 'You're crazy, bitch. Tenille wouldn't do a thing like that.'

'I don't think I'm crazy,' Donna said. 'Tenille's fingerprints are on the gun. Tenille was seen running away from the flat only minutes before the alarm was raised. And she's not been seen since. Doesn't look good for the kid, Sharon.'

Sharon twitched, her eyes cutting to Donna, fear showing through the cracks. 'No way was Geno a paedo. It was me he wanted. You're just trying to get me riled up. I don't believe you.'

Donna shrugged. 'Like I care. Right now, Tenille is my number one suspect. And you're going to tell me where I can find her.'

'Think again, bitch. Why would I help you fit her up for murder?'

The defiance was only skin deep, Donna knew. It wouldn't take much to puncture it. She leaned forward and fixed her fierce blue eyes on Sharon's watery brown ones. 'Because if you don't, I'll start working on the assumption that you knew Geno was abusing Tenille and you put the kid up to killing him. To protect herself and to take revenge for your hurt pride. And I'll make sure Tenille and her brief know that's the way I'm thinking. It'll take some of the heat off her and turn it right on you, Sharon.'

Sharon glowered. 'Even if I knew where Tenille was, I wouldn't tell you, bitch. No way Geno was messing with her, and if I'd have thought that, I wouldn't have left it to Tenille to handle it.'

'No? Who would you have gone to? Her father?'

Sharon looked away. 'She hasn't got a father.'

'That's not what they say on the Marshpool. They

say the Hammer is her dad.' Donna let the words hang for a moment. 'In fact, that might be a better way to go. I could go to the Hammer and suggest that the best way to protect his daughter is to maintain that her Auntie Sharon put her up to it. I'm sure the Hammer wouldn't have any problem finding some luckless sod to admit he supplied the gun to you, Sharon. I'm thinking the Hammer is going to care more about his kid than he is about you.'

Sharon pulled her cigarettes out of her pocket. Donna batted the pack from her fingers. 'No smoking in here,' she said. 'Besides, you'll need more than a nicotine hit to protect you from the Hammer. Where is she, Sharon?'

Sharon flashed her a glare of pure loathing then looked away. 'I don't know where she is, and that's the truth.'

'Friends. Homies. Who does she hang with?'

Sharon sighed. 'She's a loner. She doesn't fit in. She hangs out at the library.'

Donna snorted. 'Gimme a break. You expect me to believe the Hammer's kid spends her free time in the reference room?'

'We're not all stupid scum, you know,' Sharon flared up. 'Tenille's a bright girl. Wants to make something of herself.'

'That's not what the school says. Her attendance record sucks, and you know it.'

Sharon made a sharp sound of irritation. 'Maybe so. But that girl could show her teachers a thing or two.'

'And she learns all this at the library?' Donna said, her tone dripping disbelief.

'Some teachers got more sense than the ones at that school,' Sharon said. 'There's a woman lives on the estate. She teaches at the university. Tenille goes round her flat sometimes.'

Donna's interest quickened as she sensed truth. 'Name and address,' she demanded, reaching for pen and paper.

Sharon shrugged. 'I don't know. She lives in our block, I think. But I don't know where.'

'You're telling me Tenille was spending all this time with a strange woman in her flat and you don't know where it is?' Donna faked belligerent outrage. She knew there was nothing unusual in Sharon's behaviour, not on the Marshpool where a depressing number of parents had no clue where their kids were at any given hour of the day or night.

'It's better than hanging around the estate smoking drugs and drinking cans,' Sharon said combatively. 'All I know about this woman is she's called Jane and she's a teacher at the university.'

'Which one?'

Sharon looked baffled. 'Just, the university.'

Donna pushed her chair back, the legs shrieking on the vinyl tiles. 'I'm going to check this out. You better not be lying to me, Sharon. Far as I'm concerned, till I talk to Tenille you're still in the frame.'

'You can't do this,' Sharon protested, getting to her feet. 'I want to go.'

Donna jumped up and rounded the table with breathtaking speed. Toe to toe with Sharon, so close she could smell the cooking fat in her hair, she held the other woman's eyes. 'Don't make me arrest you, Sharon. I can have you banged up here on suspicion of conspiracy to commit murder and arson so fast your eyes will water. Now, be a good girl and sit down.'

Sharon backed away from her. The chair caught the back of her knees and she fell clumsily on to the hard seat.

Donna smiled. 'I'll have someone bring you a cup of tea.' She headed for the door. *Gotcha, Tenille.*

Our work, though tedious, was easy enough. Our mission was to collect eight hundred breadfruit plants, and this we had achieved in a mere two weeks. But to have set sail for home at that point would have been near suicidal. No captain with any regard for his ship or his cargo would attempt to cross the Pacific in the rainy season, nor would he have any prospect of clearing the Endeavour Straits in the teeth of the head-on prevailing winds. And so we were of necessity confined on Otaheite until the 4th day of April in the following year. This was in truth no hardship for officers nor men. The natives were hospitable, the women generous with their favours, the food good and plentiful, the climate most delightful. We learned to speak the native tongue and they called me Titreano, the nearest they could come to pronouncing my family name. I formed many friendships, among them Mauatua, who later became my wife and whom I christened Isabella, for my cousin Isabella Curwen. For my part, the separation from Bligh was only an added benefit to a life that was the most pleasurable I had ever known.

14

At first glance, it didn't look like much. Half a dozen archive boxes, that was all. But Jane knew better. Inside each of those boxes would be a drift of brittle paper, some of it untouched for a generation or more. Letters in assorted hands, crabbed or copperplate; scrawled notes and fragments in faded ink; indecipherable drafts complete with crossings-out and revisions; it was all lying chaotic in wait to strain her eyes and the limits of her knowledge.

Anthony had promised her there was no other uncatalogued material in the Trust's ownership. 'Of course, there is a considerable amount of other Wordsworth material out there in the wild, but we have no way of knowing definitively what there is and who owns it,' he said. Seeing Jane's glum expression, he smiled. 'Don't be downhearted. We do have so much more than anybody else. And let's not lose sight of the fact that it was here you found your first clue.'

Jane's smile was bleak as a Fellhead winter. 'I'll hold that thought,' she said, hefting the first box on to the table in the study cubicle Anthony had assigned to her. 'Bloody family. You think they ever threw a bit of paper away?'

'It's a good strategy for hiding the things you don't want people to know,' Anthony said, shifting a stack of books on to the floor to make more work space for Jane. 'You present the impression of candour by virtue of the sheer volume of what is available. And because there is so much of it, nobody thinks to question what might not be there. It's only when skeletons like Annette Vallon come tumbling out of the cupboard that we realise how much we've bought the party line.' He smiled. 'But even the most efficient of systems is only as good as the humans applying it. And every now and again, something slips through the net. Like Mary's letter. If that takes you where you think it might, you will go down in the annals of literary scholarship.'

Jane shrugged. 'That's not why I'm doing it.'

'I know that.' Anthony's eyes twinkled as his smile broadened. 'What you want is to read it, isn't it?'

'Yes. The mutiny on the *Bounty*, it's an extraordinary story. And if I'm right, William came to it at the pinnacle of his powers. I want to see what he made of it.' She spread her hands wide. 'It's right in the middle of my speciality. William's personality and poetic gift brought to bear on a story that was still dynamite. And the hiddenness of it all, so typical of the man.'

'It's a thought, isn't it? That imagination working on such powerful raw material. It's possible it might have been the best thing he ever wrote.'

Jane shivered. 'Don't, Anthony. I can't afford to let myself think like that. I might be wrong. I might be right and it might not exist any longer. I've got to try to keep my feet on the ground.'

'I understand. Good luck, Jane. I'll be around all day if you need me. Either in the office or in the museum.'

He slipped out of the cubicle, leaving Jane to her papers. She took the lid off the first box and looked inside. A stack of brown envelopes and cardboard folders filled it to the brim. Someone had at least taken the minimum steps to preserve this material even if they hadn't actually catalogued it. With a sigh, Jane took the first envelope out of the box and began her tedious task.

DI Donna Blair glanced over her shoulder, checking that the patrol car with its complement of uniforms was parking behind her. She knew her male counterparts would be sneering at her behind her back for refusing to knock on doors on the Marshpool without back-up from the boys in blue, but she didn't give a toss. Besides, none of them would be any happier than she was about venturing into the badlands anything less than mob-handed. The only difference was that the blokes would find some excuse to jack up the putative threat level. Like a totally made-up tip from one of their snouts that the villain they were looking for was tooled up. Donna couldn't be arsed with that sort of bull-shit game-playing. Maybe that was what pissed them off most, she thought as she got out of the car, pulling at the bottom of her tailored jacket so it sat properly.

Detective Sergeant Liam Chappel trailed in her

wake as she walked over to the four uniformed consta-
bles, his hollow-cheeked face as cheerful as a wet
weekend in Walthamstow. 'Nothing dramatic, lads,'
Donna said, the sharpness in her voice betraying the
tension they all felt. It had taken her several hours
to get a name and address out of the council housing
offices and the delay had done nothing to improve
her frame of mind. A series of petty bureaucrats had
tried to block her with bollocks about data protection,
but she had pointed out that the electoral roll was in
the public domain and would provide her with all the
information she needed. 'I'm just asking you to make
my life a little bit easier by looking at your rent rolls,'
she'd growled. 'We both get our wages out of the
same pot, we're supposed to be on the same side.'
Eventually she had prevailed, though not without
expending more energy than some jumped-up town
hall jobsworth merited.

Donna brandished the printout she'd finally
extracted from the grumbling council official. 'This is
not your usual Marshpool takedown. Jane Gresham
is not some chav scrubber. She's a respectable citizen.
She even has a job, which makes her about as common
round here as a school prize for perfect attendance.
So we are going to knock Ms Gresham's door and
have a reasonable conversation with her about the
whereabouts of Tenille Cole, not kick her door in.'

'And if she turns out to be one of them radical
feminist lesbian civil libertarians who doesn't want to
invite us in for a polite chat?' DS Chappel asked.

'Then we'll kick her door in,' Donna said, turning
away from him and gazing up at the monolithic
concrete cliff looming above her. 'OK, lads, bring the

ram.' She led the way. 'Anyone want to offer odds on the lift working?'

It was odd, Tenille thought, that something that seemed so desirable when it was rationed lost its charm when it was the only thing on offer. Normally, she never tired of hanging out in chat rooms and talking to like-minded people about the things that interested her. But today, with unfettered access and nothing to distract her, the internet palled as never before. She quite fancied watching TV, if only for the local news. Except that the TV was in the living room and could probably be seen flickering through the nets Jane had up at the window that gave on to the walkway. That would be a dead giveaway that the flat was occupied if anybody came looking.

In the end, she'd taken the bean bag and the radio through to the study and kept the volume down low while she sprawled on the floor trying to hang on to enough concentration to read. But it was hard to settle. Anxiety gnawed at her and the more she tried to tell herself everything was chill, the harder it was to believe it.

It was almost a relief when she heard a tattoo of knocks on the front door. Tenille froze, eyes wide and hands grasping her book in a white-knuckle grip. More knocks, then a woman's voice. 'Miss Gresham? This is the police. Open up, please.' A silence that seemed to stretch to infinity.

Then the clatter of the letter box. The same voice, more clearly now. 'Miss Gresham, I must warn you that if you don't open the door willingly, we will have to force an entry.'

Tenille's tongue seemed to swell in her mouth, cleaving to the hard palate. Fear stabbed at her bladder, making her want to piss. What the fuck? They shouldn't be mouthing off about breaking Jane's door down. Even if they'd made the connection between her and Jane, it wasn't witnesses they came looking for with a battering ram.

Before she could take the next logical step, there were more knocks on the door, accompanied by shouting this time. Then a sudden stillness, broken by the unmistakable rasp of the mad Irishwoman next door. 'Jesus, Mary and Joseph, what in the name of God are youse making all this racket for?' The usual coda of a phlegm-laden cough concluded her question.

'And you are?'

'I'm Noreen Gallagher. I'm the one who was trying to have a wee sleep in front of the telly until you lot started waking the dead.'

'We're looking for Jane Gresham,' the woman cop said. Tenille screwed up her eyes in concentration, desperate not to miss a word.

'You'll not find her here now, will you,' Noreen said contemptuously.

'This is her flat, isn't it?'

'Of course it's her bloody flat. But she's not in it. She's away home to the Lake District for a couple of weeks. She went off yesterday morning. She knocked to tell me she was going. Big rucksack on her back and all. So you'll not find Jane Gresham here. What are youse after Jane for, anyway?'

'That's police business, Mrs Gallagher. Is anybody else staying in Miss Gresham's flat?'

Noreen hawked expressively. 'Not since she got rid of that boyfriend of hers. Useless lump. I told her, you deserve better than that. But the young ones won't be told, will they? They have to make their own mistakes.'

'You're sure there's nobody else who has a key?'

Noreen sniffed so loudly Tenille could hear the catarrh rattle. 'Believe you me, if there was anybody in there, I'd know. These walls are so thin you can hear a mouse fart.'

A pause. Then the woman cop weighed in again. 'Do you know Tenille Cole?'

'I know Tenille. She's all right. She's not got a mouth on her like some of those black bitches.'

'Have you seen Tenille today?'

'I'm just after telling youse, Jane's away. Jesus, what would Tenille be doing round here when Jane's away?'

'She doesn't have a key to the flat?'

Noreen coughed long and hard. 'Jane's not daft. She keeps an eye out for Tenille, but she wouldn't do something that stupid. I'm telling youse, I've never seen or heard Tenille round the flat without Jane. Oh, wait a minute,' she said, realisation pumping excitement into her voice. 'Don't tell me youse are looking to blame Tenille for shooting that swaggering darkie her auntie was living over the brush with?'

'I can't discuss police business, Mrs Gallagher.' The woman cop knew how to stand her ground, that much was obvious.

'It's funny, you don't look stupid,' Noreen said. 'Looks can be deceiving, though. All I'll tell you is that you'll end up making a right arse of yourself if you go down that road. There's plenty round here that would murder you as soon as look at you, but Tenille's not one of them. Now, be on your way and stop wasting my time.'

There was a murmur of voices then Noreen Gallagher's rose above them in a full-blooded yell. 'Youse are not breaking that door down. What the hell are youse playing at? I'm telling you, there's nobody in there. Jane Gresham's a respectable woman, she's got valuables in that flat. I'm not going to stand by while you break her door down for no good reason, then leave it standing wide open for the toerags round here to strip it to the bare walls. Not to mention that she's the kind who knows lawyers who would sue the pants off of youse for doing it.'

'Step away from the door.' A man's voice this time. 'I don't want to have to arrest you, love.'

'It's all right, Sergeant.' The woman cop was back in the driving seat. 'Mrs Gallagher has a point. Here's what we're going to do, Mrs Gallagher. I'm going to leave an officer here to watch Miss Gresham's flat, and we are going to make contact with her and clear this matter up. Now, do you know where in the Lake District she's gone?'

'I've no idea. It's where her family lives. Some village, not the town. That's all I know. They'll know at her work, won't they?'

'We'll try that. Thanks very much, Mrs Gallagher.'

'Next time, you could be a bit quieter.' She hacked her way out of earshot. Tenille could hear the tail end of her explosive cough through the wall.

Fuck, fuck, fuck, Tenille thought. What now? She couldn't stay here, that was for sure. And with a cop outside the door, she couldn't get out either. She was, she thought, totally fucked.

Jane yawned and stretched her back, stiff from hours of poring over some of the most tedious written material she'd ever encountered. Her eyes were smarting from deciphering an assortment of handwriting dating back a hundred and fifty years. There were family letters, scraps of travelogue, even instructions to a builder for the erection of a milking parlour at some unspecified farm. But nothing so far in William Wordsworth's own hand, nor anything connected with Mary Wordsworth's enigmatic letter. Nothing but desperately dull, mundane matters related by those who had none of the prosodic gifts of the poet or his diarist sister Dorothy.

Jane looked at her watch. She'd give it another quarter of an hour, then she'd see whether a cup of coffee could revive her enough to continue. With a sigh, she reached into the third box and pulled out a cardboard folder containing half a dozen sheets of yellowing paper with the familiar brown spots of foxing. They were covered in a tight slanting script which Jane recognised as that of William's eldest son John. All of the letters seemed to be addressed to his brother Willy, written on various dates in the summer and autumn of 1850, mere months after William's death. The first three contained only routine family news with nothing of note. But as she began the fourth sheet, she realised this was something different. It appeared to be the second page of a letter and, as Jane read it, she felt her face flush and sweat break out along her hairline.

At first she could scarcely believe her eyes. She wondered almost whether the intensity of her desire had somehow brought into being the very thing she sought. But it was no illusion. The more she read it, the clearer it was to Jane that what she held in her hands was another brick in the wall.

Her fingers shaking, she slid the brittle sheet into a transparent plastic envelope. She stared long and hard at it for a few minutes, then stood up on almost steady legs. She needed to find Anthony.

. . . which you will understand is a matter lying close to my heart. I have no wish to speak ill of the dead, but the latter years of my marriage to Isabella brought more grief than joy to all of us. I cannot see that I should be expected to countenance more shame & misery brought to my door because of my connection to that unfortunate family. Our Father's words remained unknown & unsuspected during his lifetime, & I see no benefit to any of us in changing that state. In short, I have followed our Mother's directions & done as I see fit. I have instructed Dorcas to take it back from my house forthwith & to insure that no eye should be cast on it again. I vouchsafe that, as I write, it is no longer in existence. Nothing would be served by any other end except the besmirching of our Father's name, as I trust you will concur. Let us speak no more of it. I pray God that you are all in good health & expect to see you before the month's end.

Your loving Brother John

15

Anthony held the plastic sleeve by the corners and
frowned in concentration. Jane bit her lip and waited
for the verdict. Time stretched till he put it down on
his desk, fiddled with his ponytail then finally dragged
his eyes back to hers. 'Do you want to call Jake, or
shall I?' he asked.

His words sent a frisson of shock through Jane's
stomach. 'Jake?'

'It needs to be authenticated. As indeed does Mary's
letter. On the face of it, you seem to have uncovered
another supporting element for your theory, but before
we can be certain that this is not some elaborate hoax,
the documents must be examined.' He smiled. 'It gives
young Jake the perfect excuse to come and visit us.
Not that I imagine he needs an excuse.'

A confusion of embarrassment and foolishness
swept over Jane. It was thanks to Anthony that she
and Jake had met in the first place. He'd been
summoned to Dove Cottage to authenticate a bundle
of letters that had been offered for sale to the Trust.
Because of her particular interest in Wordsworth,
Anthony had brought him through to the café to meet

her. Anthony hadn't exactly played Cupid; he would have shivered with horror at the mere idea of being thought to have such base motives. But he had invited them both for dinner with him and his wife Deborah and if not exactly the midwife, he had certainly been present at the birth of their interest in each other. 'It wouldn't be appropriate to ask Jake,' she stalled, trying to find a way to tell Anthony it was over without making them both uncomfortable.

Anthony's eyebrows rose as he reached the right answer. 'Ah,' he said. 'Does that mean you two are no longer stepping out together?'

Jane felt her cheeks flush. 'We're not seeing each other any more, but that's neither here nor there as far as the letters are concerned. Jake's the wrong person for the job because he's left the museum.'

'Really? I hadn't heard.'

Jane was too fond of Anthony to point out that the depths of Lakeland was hardly gossip central. 'He's gone off to work for a woman called Caroline Kerr. She's a –'

'Dealer,' Anthony said, a world of disdain in the single word. 'I know Caroline Kerr. I have conducted business with her. Not from choice, you understand, but because she has been in possession of something we wanted rather badly. She had a suspiciously fine estimate of how much we wanted it and how much we were prepared to pay, and she took us to the last penny available.' His mouth twisted in distaste. 'Bright woman, and passionate about her field, but I didn't like her style. Well, what a disappointment Jake has turned out to be on all fronts. I'm sorry, Jane.'

She managed a weak smile. 'Given that he's gone

to the dark side, it's probably for the best, Anthony. I'm sure the museum can provide you with someone at least as well qualified.'

'Oh, no doubt,' he said, impatient to move on, away from the awkwardness. 'And I will set matters in train at once. But let us assume for now that both documents are what they purport to be. This really is rather a find, Jane. At the very least, it does not contradict your theory. And there is this telling sentence: "I cannot see that I should be expected to countenance more shame and misery brought to my door because of my connection to that unfortunate family." That does seem to point ineluctably towards the Christian Curwens. I can't think of any other family of whom John would speak in such terms. He was very bitter about Isabella, even after her death.'

'You couldn't make this stuff up, could you?' Jane said. 'Some historians think Fletcher Christian was in love with Isabella Curwen, and that's the reason he named his Tahitian wife Isabella. But for whatever reason, she chose his cousin John and he went off to sea. Then Fletcher comes back after the *Bounty*, is probably protected by John Christian Curwen and Isabella, then confides in William, who writes the story but keeps it hidden. Then fifteen years later, his son marries Isabella's daughter. It's like a Barbara Cartland novel.'

'It's another connection that strengthens your theory, though. If William had been remotely tempted to publish later in life, the connection to his son would have been a powerful brake.' He picked the letter up again. 'The question we really have to ask is whether this takes us any further forward.'

171

'It would if I knew who Dorcas was.'

Anthony looked faintly surprised. 'Sorry, I thought you realised.'

Jane groaned. 'No, Anthony, I don't have your encyclopaedic knowledge of the *dramatis personae*. I have no idea who Dorcas is.'

'Dorcas was taken on as a maid at Dove Cottage after the long-serving Janet died in 1847.' Anthony frowned. 'Dorcas Mason, that was her name. It can't have been a very jolly time to have been employed by the Wordsworths. William plunged into grief by the death of his favourite child, Dora; sister Dorothy becoming more and more tyrannical; then Isabella's death and all the attendant issues around the grand-children. That's probably why she didn't stay very long.'

'When did she leave?'

'That I will need to check.' He reached for his mouse and began to click, glancing up at her with a twinkle. 'You see, I'm not entirely the fount of all knowledge, Jane.' He paused for a second, typed something on his keyboard then clicked the mouse again. 'Here we go. Letter from Mary Wordsworth to her friend Isabella Fenwick, August 1851. A year and four months after William's death. "We are to lose our loyal and hard-working Dorcas, who is to be married before the month's end. She will make a fine wife and deserves a share of happiness after enduring this grieving household with such forbearance." There you go, Jane. Now you know all I know about Dorcas Mason.'

'Unfortunately, it doesn't really give us any clue as to what she might have done with the manuscript after John handed it back to her.' Jane sighed. 'It's so frustrating.'

'I suppose it depends on how literally she took John's instructions. She might have taken it back to Mary, but that would have been going against John's wishes. She might have taken his words to mean she should destroy it. But she had been part of that household for three years – long enough to have been indoctrinated with the notion of William's godlike standing in the world of letters. It's possible she couldn't bring herself to do anything other than preserve his words. She may have kept it, Jane. Kept it and never showed it to a living soul, in accordance with John's wishes.'

Jane leaned forward in her chair. 'If Dorcas kept it, surely it would have surfaced by now?'

'One would imagine so. But it's possible it was passed on to her descendants with other papers that have never been properly examined. Or that it was impressed upon whoever inherited it that it didn't belong to the family and must be held in trust.' Anthony shrugged. 'We've had papers handed over to us that had been sitting in deed boxes for three or four generations.'

'I'd like to think it might have survived,' Jane said wistfully. 'But it's not likely, is it?'

'It's possible, and that's enough. Jane, you need to start tracking down Dorcas Mason's descendants. You can't afford to pass up the chance, however slim it might appear.' Anthony pushed back from his desk, the castors of his chair rumbling on the wood floor.

Jane nodded, knowing he was right. 'I haven't the faintest idea where to start. I don't know anything about genealogy.'

'The County Record Office at Carlisle has all the old parish records. Births, marriages and deaths. And then there's the censuses. And St Catherine's House in London. You're a trained researcher, Jane, it's not beyond your capabilities.'

'I'm working with a colleague, he's still in London. He could get cracking there while I make a start up here,' Jane said, her expression lightening at the thought.

'There you go.' Anthony stood up. 'Now, be off with you. I need to make arrangements for these documents to be authenticated.'

By the time she emerged from Anthony's office, the blue skies had disappeared behind a low muffle of cloud. Large drops of rain splattered on the ground, leaving marks like scattered handfuls of coins on the ground. She ran for the café, pulling out her mobile and calling her mother. Martyrdom had never been Jane's strong point. No way was she cycling home in this.

There's no middle way with teenage despair. Either it vanishes like a chalk mark in a rainstorm or it acquires the immovable weight of a granite slab. With Tenille, it was the former. Within minutes of plunging into the depths with the realisation that her chances of escape from Jane's flat were minuscule, she was developing a plan to put into action if the slenderest of opportunities presented themselves.

The most important thing was to put some distance between herself and the Marshpool. Let the dust settle while she came up with a way to get out from under. The only place she could think of where she might find shelter was with Jane in Fellhead. So the first priority was to figure out how to get there. She had some money, but she wasn't daft enough to consider taking the train or the express bus. If the cops were looking to put her in the frame, they'd have spread her description and maybe even her picture around. Every cop would be looking for her, and the bus and train stations were where they'd look. Hitching was out of the question for the same reason. That only left local buses. She had to plot a route that would take her from London to Fellhead by hopping from town to town.

Tenille logged on and found a journey planner site for motorists where she asked for a route avoiding motorways. That would give her an idea of the waypoints she should be aiming for. She printed out the map of the route and circled the towns she needed to get through. Then she started to hit the bus company websites. It was achingly tedious stuff, but eventually she had printed out a list of local bus timetables that more or less linked together to get her to Fellhead. It would take a couple of days, but she was pretty sure she could make it.

It didn't do to take chances, though. She wasn't going to make it easy for them. She needed to change her appearance, just in case any eagle-eyed smartass was looking to make a name for themselves. She looked at herself critically in the mirror. Chopping off her dreads would be a start. But she could do, *had* to do better than that. In tight clothes, there was no mistaking her gender. But in the baggy threads that were the uniform of young black rappers, she could pass for a boy, easy. Anybody with their eyes peeled for a teenage girl wasn't going to look past the slouch and the style. They just wouldn't see her under the camouflage. Especially since the last thing most people wanted was to make eye contact with a young black male. The stereotyping sometimes had its advantages.

She wondered whether Jane's wardrobe might provide her with the right disguise. Jane wasn't big, but she was both taller and broader than Tenille. A quick search revealed she was out of luck. Nothing with the right logos, nothing any street rapper would be seen dead in. And crucially, no big bulky jacket to keep out the weather and prying eyes alike.

Tenille went through to the bathroom and raked around in the wall-mounted cabinet till she found a pair of nail scissors. Then she carefully snipped away at her hair, leaving tight little spirals all over her scalp where the dredds had been. The face in the mirror was a stranger to her; losing the frame of hair emphasised her good bones and her full lips. She could pass for an adolescent boy, she thought. She certainly didn't look like Tenille any more. She scooped up the hair from the sink and crept back to the study. She wasn't about to leave a big clue for the cops. She reached across the desk and cracked open the window, then she let her shorn locks fly out into the chill darkening air. She watched them spiralling earthwards, imagining them scattered on the ground below like strange hairy caterpillars.

Next, she tiptoed through to the kitchen. She knew where Jane kept what she needed. Under the sink she found a hammer and, in the drawer, a torch. She took them with her and stashed them in her backpack.

Tenille stared out into the empty evening. All she could do right now was done. And she was still trapped, still with no way out. Deflated, she slumped in the chair and wondered how the hell she was going to get to a place where she could put her plan into action. She'd been sitting staring gloomily at the bus timetables for about ten minutes when she almost started out of the chair. The sudden sound of knocking on the wall completely freaked her out. What the hell was mad Noreen Gallagher up to? There was a swift tattoo of half a dozen knocks, then a pause, then another short salvo. Then silence.

Which was broken by the unmistakable sound of Mrs Gallagher's front door opening. Tenille heard the familiar raucous throat-clearing of Jane's neighbour, then, 'You must be freezing your bollocks off out there. You might as well come in and get a drop of tea.' Her voice sounded grudging enough to be genuine.

Tenille crept into the hallway, the better to hear what was going on. She heard the reply clearly, although the officer spoke more quietly than Mrs Gallagher. 'That's very kind of you, ma'am, but I have to stay at my post.'

A thick, gurgling snort of laughter. 'Anybody would think you were guarding the crown jewels, son. Listen, you heard what I told your boss. These walls are so thin, there's no way anybody could be in there without me hearing. If Tenille turns up, you'll hear her knocking the door. Or, if she does have a key, you'll hear the door opening. There's no privacy on the Marshpool, believe me. Besides, you've no chance of catching her, standing out there like a lemon. The minute she comes on the landing, she's going to see you, looming up there like a big palooka. And she'll be off, like a greyhound that's seen the hare. Whereas, if you're sitting in my living room, you'll hear her and you'll be able to sneak up and take her by surprise.' Tenille could picture Mrs Gallagher, arms folded across her skinny chest, cigarette jammed in the corner of her mouth, a look of sly certainty on her face.

And she could hear the indecision in the cop's voice. 'You think?'

'I know. Listen, I can tell you when they've had beans for their tea next door. Come on, come away in. The kettle's boiled, it'll not take me a minute to mash you a nice cup of tea.'

Tenille heard the heavy tread of the police officer as he crossed the threshold and walked into Mrs Gallagher's living room. She heard the clatter of the front door closing. She heard the rumble and murmur of conversation. She didn't know why Mrs Gallagher was intent on giving her a chance, but she knew she was going to take it.

Tenille crept back to the living room for her jacket and her backpack then tiptoed to the door. She eased it open a crack and listened. Nothing she wasn't expecting to hear. She inched the door back until there was just room to slip around it. Then she put the key in the lock and turned it so the tongue slid back into its housing. She gently pulled the door to, then let the lock return, sliding her key free. She turned on her heel and moved out along the gallery, taking each step as gently as if she were walking on bubbles.

The next part of her plan required darkness, which was at least an hour away. But that was OK. The

Marshpool was her ground. She would have no trouble keeping out of sight until then. The hard part was over with. She'd be cruising now.

That I would have to pay for my pleasures ashore became clear to me as soon as we embarked on our return voyage. From the first, Bligh found fault with every task I performed in the course of my duties. He attacked me verbally in front of the men, humiliating me and accusing me of the most absurd actions. And yet he expected me still to attend him in his cabin and listen to him hold forth upon the slights cast upon him by all and sundry. He would also use these occasions to castigate me for my failings. I tried to endure this most heinous treatment with equanimity, but I could not forbear such treatment forever. When at last he accused me of harbouring unnatural feelings towards Peter Heywood and of acting upon those feelings on Otaheite, I was unable to contain myself and spoke most intemperately to him. His response was that I should hold my tongue or spend the rest of the voyage in the brig. I was cut to the quick by his high-handedness and reduced to near despair by his behaviour towards me.

16

By the time Judy arrived at Dove Cottage, Jane's natural enthusiasm had reasserted itself. As they drove home, the bike stowed in the back of the car, Jane told her mother what she'd found.

'I'm not sure I follow all the ins and outs,' Judy said. 'But from what you're saying, you think your idea might really be true? That Fletcher Christian came back and told his story to Wordsworth?'

Jane pulled a face. 'I've no proof, as such. But the circumstantial evidence just keeps getting stronger.'

'That must be exciting for you,' Judy said. 'I suppose it's quite a big thing in your world, this manuscript?'

'It would be a sensation, Mum. Imagine, being able to read a Wordsworth poem that's hardly been seen since it was first written two hundred years ago.'

Judy laughed. 'Don't expect me to read it. I've always thought he was a boring bugger.'

'Well, he made our way of life possible,' Jane said.

Judy flashed her a surprised glance. 'How do you reckon that, then?'

'He made the Lake District fashionable, popular. People came here because of him.'

'Thank you, William, for the tourists, with their litter and their exhaust fumes and their path erosion,' her mother said, acid in her voice.

'Well, yes. But also thank you, William, for the sheep.'

Judy looked incredulous. 'What's he got to do with the sheep?'

'If Beatrix Potter hadn't come here on her holidays and fallen in love with the Herdwicks and made them her life's big project, they would probably have died out, and what would we be farming then? And what would the landscape look like? It wouldn't be open country like it is now, with smart Herdwicks that don't wander from the fell they were born on. It would be fenced off into fields, like the Cheviots, to keep in the stupid sheep. What Dad calls the lesser breeds. So, while I dislike being overrun by townie tourists as much as you do, I'll take that as the price of the sheep and the landscape.'

'Point taken,' Judy said, knowing from long experience that there was no arguing with her daughter's passion for the land. She sometimes thought Jane was as hefted to Langmere Fell as the sheep themselves. 'Thank you, William, for the sheep. So what's your next step? Have you got to look for more papers?'

Jane shook her head. 'I've been through all the uncatalogued material. I couldn't find anything else. No, what I've got to do now is find out whether Dorcas Mason has any living descendants and go and talk to them to see if they know anything about the manuscript. I need to get Dan to go to the Family Records Centre in London and I need to start dredging the parish records up here.'

'You need to talk to Barbara Field.'

'Bossy Barbara Field, the chairwoman of the WI?'

'How many Barbara Fields do you think there are round here?' Judy said drily. 'Yes, bossy Barbara Field from the WI. It's her hobby, family history. She gives talks on it to other WIs. Tells people how to go about finding stuff out. Matthew's doing a project on family trees with the kids and he got a lot of his info off Barbara. She's very helpful, you know.' Judy drew to a halt in the farmyard. 'Leave the bike till the rain stops,' she said, opening the car door and running for shelter.

Jane ran after her, shaking her head like a wet dog as she entered the house. 'Maybe I'll give her a ring.'

'I'll call her now. No time like the present.' Judy tossed her waxed jacket on its peg and went through to the farm office. Jane followed her nose to the kitchen, savouring the aroma of some rich meat stew.

Her father looked up from his copy of *Farming Today*. 'Good day?'

'Better than good. I found another brick in the wall. A letter that backs up my theory.'

'Good for you. If you find this poem, is it going to make you rich?'

Jane shook her head, a wry smile twisting her mouth up at one corner. 'I shouldn't think so. What it will do is make me famous in academic circles. It'll fast-track me on the career I want.' She registered the faint look of disappointment in her father's eyes. 'Was there a particular reason for you asking?'

Allan rubbed his palm against his cheek. 'Cock-eyed optimism,' he said. 'A bit of money never goes amiss on a farm, you know that. I just thought, with you saying last night that it would be priceless, there might be a few bob in it.'

'There will be, but not for me. Whoever can establish legal title to it, they're the ones who'll get rich. Sorry. But if I do find it, there'll be a book contract, maybe some newspaper articles.' She reached out and covered her father's work-worn hand with hers. 'I'd be happy to share it.'

Allan shook his head. 'I wouldn't take money you'd worked for. A windfall, now that would be different. But I won't have you working for my benefit. We're doing fine, your mum and me. Don't worry about us.'

Before she could reply, Judy bustled briskly into the kitchen. 'That's that sorted, then. Bossy Barbara's expecting you round at hers at eight o'clock.'

Jane rolled her eyes. 'You're too good to me.'

Judy patted her on the head as she made for the stove. 'And it's beef olives for dinner.'

'You can tell she doesn't want you to go back to London,' Allan said.

'That makes two of us,' Jane said, heading for the door. 'I need to call Dan.' She settled down at the cluttered desk in the office. 'Hi, Dan,' she said. 'I've got good news and bad news.'

He groaned. 'Give me the bad news first.'

'You've been researching the wrong family tree. Sorry, I wasted your time having you chase up the Wordsworths.'

'You say that like there's another family tree I should be researching,' he said warily. 'What happened? Did you find something?' Jane explained what she'd discovered, reading the letter over the phone. 'But that's terrific,' he said when she reached the end. 'It's not conclusive, I know, but it indicates there's definitely something there worth chasing. Even if it's not the *Bounty* poem, it could be something else that's just as significant in the field. So you want me to start on Dorcas Mason and her family?' he asked.

'That would be a big help. I'm going to do what I can up here – Anthony says there's a lot available in Carlisle, and Mum's got me hooked up with one of her cronies who apparently is the bee's knees when it comes to family history. Between us, we should be able to come up with something to have a crack at.'

'It'll be a slog, but it'll be worth it if we turn something up.'

'I've never been to the Family Records Centre, have you?' Jane said anxiously.

'No. But family history's such a huge thing these days, I bet they've got it all streamlined and user-friendly. Leave it to me, I'll get it sorted.'

'I appreciate this.'

'No, I'm the one who should be grateful to you for letting me in on it.'

'How did the seminar go today?'

Dan groaned histrionically. 'You're right, Damien Joplin is a pain in the arse.' He went on to give her an account of the seminar he'd taught for her that afternoon. By the end of his recital, they were both giggling, mimicking students and their less than perceptive responses to *Lyrical Ballads*. 'You're not missing a thing,' Dan concluded.

'Sounds like it. OK, we'll talk again soon.' They wound up the call and Jane sat for a moment, staring out of the window at the valley below. Never mind the money, never mind the fame. What she wanted was to hold that manuscript in her hands and read it.

River traced an outline on the CAT scan with a pensive finger. She'd spent the day with the film crew, who were her new best friends, moving Pirate Peat back to the hospital, supervising the full-body X-rays and CAT scan before escorting him back to Gibson's funeral parlour. Everything had taken twice as long as it should have because of the demands of filming, but she didn't much mind. The advantages provided by their money far outweighed the inconveniences this far. But she'd agreed to get together with Ewan Rigston for a drink, and there hadn't been enough time to head back to her office and drop off the films and pictures before meeting him in Keswick at seven.

So instead she'd found a quiet corner in the hotel bar they'd fixed on as a rendezvous and had spread the CAT pictures across the table. Truth to tell, this was probably the least informative process she would subject the body to, but even so, she had learned a little more about her man. She couldn't help wondering if Ewan Rigston would be as much of a challenge to unravel.

It had been a while since River had been drawn to the idea of any relationship other than the purely professional. Bitter experience had taught her that most men were either turned off by what she did or inappropriately turned on by it. Neither response was what she craved. She had no strong conviction that Ewan Rigston would be different, but she wasn't about to dismiss him out of hand either. She took a thoughtful sip of her tomato juice and gave herself a mental shake, returning her thoughts to the images in front of her.

She was studying what seemed to be a depressed skull fracture when Rigston pulled out the chair opposite hers. 'I'm not interrupting, am I?' he said, his brow furrowed in apology. 'I know I'm a bit early. I can sit up at the bar till you're ready, if you've still got work to do.'

'No, I was just passing the time,' she replied, somewhat surprised at how pleased she was to see him. 'I'm early too.'

'You ready for another one?' He indicated the lacy dregs of scarlet trailing down the glass.

'Yes, thanks.' She handed it to him.

'Virgin or bloody?'

'Virgin. I'm driving.'

He nodded and crossed to the bar. He was a substantial man, no denying that; broad shoulders and strong thighs that his off-the-peg suit did nothing to disguise, a large head with a close-cropped fringe of hair round the bald dome, big hands that dwarfed the slender tumbler. She imagined he would have been handy on the rugby field. He probably had ten years on her, but he was still winning the race where muscle lurches headlong towards fat. She suspected his size made him wary with women, nervous of hurting them unintentionally. An unexpected bolt of desire hit her. She wanted to break down that presumed gentleness, wanted to get down and dirty with him. 'Get a grip,' she scolded herself softly.

By the time he returned with her tomato juice and a pint of bitter for himself, she had herself under control, though still wondering where that moment had come from. She accepted her drink and shuffled her papers together.

'That our bog body?' Rigston asked.

'The same. We just did the full-body X-rays and CAT scans. It confirmed what I thought when we spoke before.' She pulled out an X-ray. 'Look –' She ran her finger round the area in question. 'Definitely a skull fracture. It seems to have been caused by a blunt instrument, rounded end, probably a bit less than five centimetres in diameter. If I had to hazard a guess, given the time and place, I'd go for the knob of a walking stick or something similar.'

Rigston stroked an eyebrow, his face the impassive mask of someone trained not to give anything away. 'Suspicious death.'

River shrugged. 'I'd say so. Murder. Or maybe he was trying to rob someone who turned on him?'

'We'll never know.' Rigston took a deep drink of his beer.

'But we already know quite a few other things,' River said. She pointed to the seams where the bones of the skull came together. 'Look at the sutures. They gradually fuse as we age. I can tell from this that our man was around forty, give or take a few years either side.' She flicked through her pile, pulling out another X-ray and a couple of CAT scan sections. 'And we also know that he was shot in the shoulder in his mid-twenties.' She pointed to the shoulder blade, where an irregular circle looked puckered and uneven compared to the smooth bone surrounding it. 'Classic penetrating injury.'

'You can date it that precisely?' Rigston looked impressed.

'The skeleton rebuilds itself. Bones regenerate. Different bones take different lengths of time to heal. Ribs are quick, the femur takes longer, the skull even more time. A wound like this in a flat plane of bone like the scapula will take years and will never heal completely because of the extent of the damage. It probably ached in the winter. I'd say he took this bullet ten to fifteen years before he died.'

'You seem pretty sure about it being a gunshot wound.'

River grinned. 'Elementary, my dear Rigston.' She pointed to a couple of flecks on the X-ray round the edge of the damaged bone. 'Metal fragments. Back then, bullets were made of lead and its alloys. Soft metal, snagged on the bone as it went through.' He smiled and she felt inordinately pleased with herself.

'Impressive,' he said. 'What else?'

She spread her hands. 'That's it for now. But there's a lot more to come.'

'Like what?'

She flashed him a suspicious look. 'You really want to know? Or are you just humouring me?'

Rigston shook his head, amusement crinkling the skin round his pale blue eyes. 'I'm interested. I know what happens at a post mortem, but I've got next to no idea about what you actually do. And I'm not a man who enjoys ignorance.'

River gave him a shrewd look of assessment. Her first instinct was that his interest was genuine intellectual curiosity, not prurience. She decided to trust herself. 'Well, we'll be doing a post mortem, but not the sort you're accustomed to seeing, with the big Y-incision. What I'll be aiming for is minimal invasion. So most of the internal investigation will be done by camera – like with a laparoscopy. I'll take tissue core samples from anything that's left of the major organs, like a keyhole biopsy.'

'Why do you do it that way?'

'It preserves the integrity of the body. Something like this will probably end up in a museum or a university. It helps if I don't completely trash it in the process of finding out what it can tell us.' She tipped her glass towards him. 'In a few years' time, your Home Office pathologists will be doing more work like this. They've already done the first virtual post mortem at Leicester. Apart from anything else, it helps assuage the religious sensibilities of Jews and Muslims.'

Rigston grinned. 'Not to mention the sensibilities of the coppers who have to attend post mortems. No more picking the rookies off the floor when the smell hits them.'

River acknowledged this with a nod. 'Did you know that how we smell when we're dead depends on what we eat? Humans and pigs smell sweet, dogs are rancid and horses are sour. It's all to do with the levels of nitrogen.'

He pulled a face. 'I don't know that I'd call it sweet.'

'But poets do. They talk about the sweet smell of decay.'

'I don't read much poetry,' Rigston said. 'I don't think many cops do. It's not got much to do with the nitty gritty of what we do.'

'Or with what I do. There's nothing poetic about sucking out the contents of a stomach or a bowel.'

'You have to do that?' Rigston seemed intrigued

rather than disgusted. River was glad her instincts seemed to have been on the money so far.

'We do. Especially in a case like this, where the stomach contents will probably be well preserved. And the lower part of the gastro-intestinal tract could well contain seeds and vegetable fibre that will tell us even more about his diet. One of my colleagues once found a whole Brussels sprout on its way out.'

Rigston did look disgusted this time. 'Now that's too much information,' he said, squirming in his seat. 'Can we get back to the scientific stuff?'

'Wimp,' River said lightly. 'OK. We'll hope and pray there's enough soft tissue left for us to take muscle samples and maybe even brain tissue samples to do toxicology and DNA testing. And then we get to the really interesting stuff. The teeth will tell us where he was living when they were formed. We'll know if he was UK born, and if so, which part of the UK. The bone will tell us if he's been living else-where in the world in the previous ten to fifteen years.' She grinned triumphantly.

He cracked a huge smile, revealing his own regular white teeth. 'That's bloody amazing,' he said. 'And you can tell what diseases he's had?'

She shrugged. 'Some. Not as many as we would like. I can tell you already that he didn't have syphilis. No pitting of the bones. So our sailor was either astonishingly clean living or lucky.'

Rigston took a long drink. 'I envy you,' he said.

'Why?'

'What you do, it's real detection. Most of what I do is just a case of figuring out which of the local villains is most likely to have committed whatever stupid bloody crime has landed on my desk. Contrary to all the books and TV shows, I almost never get to pull together all the different elements of a case to make a complete jigsaw. When I joined up, I thought I'd get to use my brain.' He sighed. 'Trouble is, most villains haven't got the brains God gave a Herdwick.'

'That must be depressing.'

'It is. So let's not talk about it any more.' He drained his pint and pushed back in his chair. She felt a moment's disappointment. Was this it? The first man in months who hadn't wondered why a nice girl like her was messing around with old cadavers, and he wasn't even sticking around for a second drink? 'Are you in a hurry to get back to Carlisle, or do you fancy a curry?' Rigston asked.

River's stomach fluttered in a way that had nothing to do with food. 'Only if we don't talk shop. Yours or mine.'

He grinned. 'It's a deal.'

That night, I lay awake considering the import of Bligh's words. It was clear to me that if I did not endure his iniquitous and unwarranted treatment, I would be forced to suffer a different sort of torture. Neither alternative seemed tolerable to me. Tossing and turning thus, I recalled the evening I spent in the company of my brother Charles at Spithead. We were aboard Bounty awaiting orders to sail, and Charles was returning from Madras as ship's surgeon in the employ of the East India Co. I hired a small boat and boarded his vessel, the Middlesex, as she was still sailing. In the course of a fine evening's talk, my brother confessed to me that there had been a mutiny on the voyage home and that he had been one of the officers in the case. The captain had provoked such unrest and unhappiness among his men that at last an officer held a loaded pistol to his breast. Four officers, including my brother, attempted to wrest command from him, but failed in the attempt. When we spoke, my brother had still no notion of what punishment might await him. But his mutiny was on a private ship and his only punishment was to be barred from serving with the East India Company for two years. Strange, is it not, that my brother got off so lightly for the same offence for which they would yet hang me if they could lay hands on me.

17

A darker shape within the shadow of a stairwell stirred. Night kept its secrets remarkably well on the Marshpool Farm Estate, mostly because half of the streetlamps were out of action. Some had burned out naturally; more had been disabled because, unlike legitimate merchants, the retailers of the Marshpool preferred the cover of darkness for their transactions. It didn't matter whether they were selling drugs, smuggled booze and fags, stolen DVD players or their bodies; the process was helped along by an absence of light. There was no denying it made life easier for Tenille that evening. If anyone noticed her flitting from one end of the estate to the other, they didn't let on, either to her or to the police.

Tenille cautiously made her way to the far end of the Marshpool, where a decrepit row of lock-up garages marked the boundary between the estate and the rest of the world. A low parapet shielded the flat roofs from anyone in the car park below. She crossed behind the garages and squeezed into a narrow gap between their back walls and the high wooden fences of the private houses beyond. About fifty yards along, she came to a section of fence that was sturdier than its neighbours. One of the more enterprising of the estate's burglars had screwed small blocks of wood to the fence, creating a rudimentary set of footholds. It was an easy way into a suburban garden, which in turn led to its fellows and beyond.

But Tenille had discovered some time ago it was also a possible route to the roofs of the lock-ups. She liked to sit on the roof on sunny days, basking in the warmth as she read in peace. The roof was fragile, though; she had learned to be careful to make sure there was a joist underfoot as she crossed roofing felt that had grown brittle with age. Tonight, she planned to turn that to her advantage.

It was pitch black in the gap and Tenille had to find her way by touch. When she reached the section she was looking for, she leaned in to the fence, gripping the higher wood blocks with her fingers as she launched herself upwards. A short scramble and she was sitting astride the top of the fence, nine feet above the path. Gingerly, she manoeuvred herself into a crouch, one hand on the fence to keep her from falling. With infinite slowness, she inched the other hand towards the roof of the garage. As soon as she felt the rough roof covering, she pushed herself upright, allowing herself to fall towards the roof. Both hands on the roof, she kicked off with all her strength from the fence and pulled herself up and across the gap, twisting so she landed lying along the edge of the roof.

Tenille exhaled noisily. She'd made it so far. Now for the hard part. From up here, there was nothing visible to mark where one garage ended and another began. But she knew there were ten of them. The one she wanted was third from the end where she'd entered the gap. It was hard to be certain, but she thought she needed to be about another six feet to her left to be sure she was in the right place. Tenille inched along the edge of the roof, not caring about damaging her clothes. She wouldn't be needing them much longer. When she judged she was in the right place, she eased her backpack off and took out the hammer.

One blow cracked the elderly felt; the second smashed through it. Tenille used the claw of the hammer to pull back enough of the brittle material to allow her to hammer a hole in the plasterboard of the ceiling. She shone the torch through the gap she'd made and allowed herself a snort of relief. She'd guessed right. She was directly above the lock-up where Junior B and his brother kept their stash. She could see cardboard boxes stacked along the walls, some of them already opened, the torch beam gleaming on the plastic bags that contained the stock for Junior B's market stall.

It didn't take long to make the hole big enough for her to get through, though Tenille was careful to keep it as quiet as possible. Even though most people on the Marshpool had made a career of seeing and hearing no evil, there were still certain unexpected noises that might provoke further investigation. Once she was sure she could get through and back out again, Tenille dropped her backpack through the hole. It landed on a stack of boxes a few feet below her. It was, she thought, safe to go.

Within ten minutes, she had kitted herself out in

baggy trousers, a polo shirt, a baggy overshirt, a water-proof jacket and a baseball cap, all covered with the right logos to make her pass for a cool dude. All of them fake, of course. She had also grabbed a change of trousers and a couple of T-shirts and stuffed them into her backpack. Sorted. All she had to do now was get out of there.

Stacking the boxes into a high enough pile was harder than she had bargained for. It seemed to take ages, and it was heavy work. By the time she'd constructed a pyramid she could climb up, she was breathing heavily and sweating. All that kept her going was the desperate desire not to be caught.

Finally, almost an hour after she'd entered the lock-up, she was back on the roof. She lowered herself down as far as she could and dropped the remaining six feet to the ground, every bone in her body juddering as she hit the unforgiving cement. She pulled her bus schedule out of her pocket. She had to get to Victoria in time for the last bus to Oxford. A piece of piss, she thought, changing her walk to a swagger as she stepped out into the night. She was on her way.

Barbara Field's cottage was a monument to the flora of the English countryside. Roses rampaged over her three-piece suite, clematis climbed and curled over her curtains and the wallpaper boasted more bunches of wildflowers than the average Mothering Sunday could muster. Dried flower arrangements were every-where and the walls displayed framed cross-stitch samplers of cottage gardens. Jane thought there should probably be an Observer Field Guide to Barbara's living room. Barbara had greeted her with, 'We'll just have a cup of tea and you can tell me what you're looking for. Then we'll go through to the office and see what we can dig out.' Predictably, the cup had been floral too – a hedgerow scene of primroses and cowslips.

Barbara had listened attentively as Jane had explained what she hoped to find, nodding occasionally in an exaggerated way that made Jane feel very young and very stupid. But then, Bossy Barbara, as Jane had dubbed her in early childhood, had always made her feel very young and very stupid. There was something about the perfection of a hairstyle that looked as solid as a motorbike helmet and a permanently starched white blouse that never seemed to accumulate stains from gravy, ink or garden, which felt deliberately calculated to leave everyone else on the back foot, Jane thought. 'Well, that all sounds perfectly straightforward to me,' Barbara said briskly at the end of the recital. 'Let's go and see what the magic box of tricks has to show us,' she added, reminding Jane of her habit of dubbing everything with absurd circumlocutions. She shooed Jane out of the room and down the hall to what Jane vaguely remembered had been referred to as 'the family room' in her youth. It had always baffled her, since Barbara and Brian Field were themselves childless. It was, she supposed, as odd as Barbara's fascination with genealogy, given that her own genes would perish with her.

The room had been transformed into a surprisingly plain office. It contained a desk with a computer, a worktable with three chairs and a portable TV on a small trolley. Instead of the samplers, the walls here were covered with family trees, elaborately drawn in fine calligraphy. 'My inner sanctum,' Barbara said with satisfaction. 'Brian has his potting shed, I have my little shrine to our ancestors.' She drew one of the worktable chairs across to the desk and settled it at an angle to her own office chair. 'Now, let's see what the information superhighway has to tell us about Dorcas Mason.'

Her fingers ran across the keys with an agility that surprised Jane, more accustomed to her mother's two-fingered forays into the farm accounts. 'You're very good at this,' Jane said.

Barbara smirked. 'I like to think I've always made the best of everything I've turned my hand to. You young people write us all off as soon as we collect our bus passes, but there's many a fine tune played on an old fiddle.'

Jane gritted her teeth and smiled. 'I wouldn't be so daft as to underestimate you, Mrs Field.'

Barbara went straight to her 'Favourites' menu and clicked on 'County Records'. As she clicked and typed, she talked Jane through it. 'When I started building our family trees, it meant trailing round parish churches and looking through the records. But now most of the parish records are held centrally at county records offices, and you can access them for a small fee. Census records are online, and so are wills from 1858, when the Court of Probate was established. And of course, there are the Mormons.'

'The Mormons?' Jane tried to sound polite rather than baffled by what seemed a complete non sequitur.

'They've got a vast genealogical database. I think the idea is to baptise the dead . . .' Barbara's voice trailed off, distracted by the commands she was typing into a search engine. 'Now, Dorcas Mason, you said?'

'That's right.'

'Do we have any idea when she was born?'

'She was working as a maid for the Wordsworth family in 1847, so she must have been at least fourteen by then. So, sometime before 1833.'

'Let's start searching at 1800, then,' Barbara said, typing in the dates and clicking the mouse with a flourish. Seconds passed, then a message appeared on the screen: *1 matches found. Please enter your password to access.*

Barbara looked pointedly at Jane. It took her a moment to realise she was supposed to turn away while Barbara entered her personal password. When she looked back at the screen, it showed details extracted from the parish records. Dorcas Mason had been born on 5th April 1831 at Sheepfold Cottage, Cockermouth, in the parish of Brigham to Thomas and Jean Mason. Her father had been described as a farrier, and she had been baptised three weeks later. Barbara turned a triumphant smile on Jane. 'The miracle of modern technology,' she announced, as if it were entirely her invention. 'I'll print it out for you.'

'That's terrific,' Jane said, her spirits rising at this first official trace of the woman who had carried off William's mysterious manuscript. 'And it's very helpful. But I'm actually more interested in what happened to her later. She supposedly left the Wordsworth household in 1851 to get married. Will there be records of any marriage and children? Of her death?'

'Of course, my dear.' Barbara turned back to the screen and entered the search requirements. This time, the wait was slightly longer. And the message less satisfying: *0 matches found*. Jane's heart sank. It felt as if Dorcas had been within reach, only to have been snatched away again.

'How very annoying,' Barbara said.

'Surely she can't just have disappeared?'

'Well, no. By this point in time, society was quite well regulated. People didn't get married and give birth without records of it. Either she was married and had her family in a parish whose records aren't on the online database – which does happen more often than I would like.' Barbara made it sound as if this oversight was a personal slight. 'Or else she married outside the county and moved away.'

'How would I find out which it was?'

Barbara sucked air over her teeth. 'Well, you see, the way you're going about this is rather unusual. Normally, people are working backwards. They know roughly where they're going because each document provides them with clues for where to look next. Working forward is a different thing altogether, because we have no idea where to start. If she didn't marry a local man, your Dorcas could have ended up anywhere in the country. Even in Scotland.' Barbara pronounced the word as if she were speaking of the distant reaches of the galaxy.

'So what's my next step?' Jane tried to keep the impatience from her voice.

'I'd suggest the County Records Office in Carlisle. They've got the hard copies of all the registers. If Dorcas has slipped through the net online, the certificates will still be there. Failing that, you're going to have to start trawling through the records of births, marriages and deaths at the Family Records Centre, down in Islington in London. You can get professional researchers to do that for you. It doesn't come cheap, but they are very efficient.'

'I've got that in hand already. One of my colleagues is going to make the searches in London. What about her will? Would that be online?'

'It depends when she died. Before 1870, women had no entitlement to own property so they couldn't make a will. After that, only married women could make wills, and even then they could only leave property settled on them for their separate and personal use.' Barbara patted her on the arm. 'And I don't think a serving maid would be in that position, do you, Jane?'

'Probably not. But there might have been something . . .' Jane's voice tailed off miserably.

'If there were, it would be in her married name. And since we don't know what that is, we're stuck.' Barbara signed off from the internet with an air of finality. 'I think the best thing is to hope your colleague strikes it lucky at St Catherine's House.'

Jane recognised dismissal when she saw it. 'Thanks, Mrs Field. You've been a big help.' Three minutes later, she was climbing the lane back home, determined not to be defeated. Dorcas Mason's descendants were out there somewhere. Between them, she and Dan were going to track them down. And when they did, they were going to find out what the Wordsworths had been so determined to keep hidden.

*   *   *

203

'Bloody rain. Bloody country,' Jake Hartnell yelled in exasperation. 'Who the hell drives around in a tractor at ten o'clock at bloody night? All because I miss one fucking road sign and end up on the road to nowhere.'

Oblivious to his frustration, the tractor continued to crawl along at twenty miles an hour. The road was too winding for Jake to risk overtaking so he kept creeping closer to the tractor only to pull back when its muddy spray obscured his windscreen yet again. What might have been mildly amusing on the Akrotiri peninsula was infuriating in the dark in the middle of the Lake District. 'God, but this is the pits,' he complained. 'What are you doing here, Jane? I'd have thought you'd be glad to get away from this godforsaken hellhole, not run back at every opportunity. Jesus Christ, how could I be so fucking stupid, talking this up to Caroline? I've more chance of finding the crew of the bloody *Marie Celeste* than you have of finding Wordsworth's lost masterpiece. Bloody tractor.'

After a couple of miles, the tractor finally turned off and Jake roared past. Within minutes, he was on the outskirts of Keswick. 'Thank Christ,' he said. He made a couple of passes round the small confines of the town centre before settling on what looked like the most civilised of the hotels. He drove through a narrow archway into a cobbled yard which was surprisingly full. He finally found a space in a far corner and squeezed the Audi in between a people carrier and a Range Rover with an alarming collection of scratches and dents.

There was nobody on reception, though the bar seemed still to be doing a brisk trade. Wearily, Jake rang the bell on the desk. As he waited, he idly flicked through a display of local attractions. *Dear God, a pencil museum,* he thought. What hope was there for him in a place whose prime wet-weather attraction appeared to be an entire museum dedicated to the insertion of graphite into wood?

At last, a matronly woman emerged and greeted him with a beaming smile. 'Sorry to keep you. How can I help you, sir?' she said cheerily.

Jake wondered briefly what medication she was on and whether she could spare any. 'Have you a room available?'

The woman looked doubtful. 'Is it just for the one night?' She opened a fat ledger and ran a finger down the page.

I wish. 'I'll be here for a few nights,' he said. 'I'm not sure yet.'

The plump finger halted. 'We've got one single left,' she said. 'I can let you have four nights.'

'That'll do nicely,' he said, praying that would be long enough to settle things with Jane. He took out his wallet and presented his company credit card. 'Has it got internet access?' he said, with no hope of a positive response.

'You can plug into the phone if you want analog access, but there's a wireless LAN area just off the Derwent Bar,' she said, as nonchalant as if he'd asked whether they had running water. 'Now, do you need something to eat? The kitchen's closed, but I can rustle you up some soup and a sandwich if you'd like?'

'That would be wonderful,' he said, meaning it. 'And is there any chance of a copy of the local paper?'

Less than an hour later, he was lying back on his bed, stomach full of ham sandwich, leek and potato soup and Theakston's best bitter. 'It's actually called the *Keswick Reminder*,' he said to Caroline, who sounded remarkably perky considering it was past one in the morning on Crete.

'How fabulously Victorian,' she said. 'Do they still have the fatstock prices on the front page?'

He chuckled. 'Not quite.'

'Still, if one is marooned out there in the sticks, I expect it does contain all one needs,' Caroline said. 'So have you learned any more about this body in the bog?'

'There's a lot more local colour, but not much detail about the body itself. I suppose the forensic anthropologist hadn't had much time for tests by the time the paper went to press.'

'Pity. So have you made contact with Jane yet?'

'I've only just got here, and they go to bed early in these parts,' Jake protested. 'Besides, I thought I'd check out the lie of the land first. See if I can have a chat with this Dr Wilde, the forensic anthropologist. Maybe she can narrow down the age of the body.'

He heard Caroline sigh. 'The body's not the thing, Jake. It's Jane's manuscript that we're interested in. You need to win her over as soon as you can.'

'It's not as simple as it would have been in London,' he said. 'It won't be so easy to get her on her own. And I need to talk to her face to face, one to one. If I turn up at Cold Comfort Farm, I'll have her dad glaring at me and her mum plying me with home baking laced with arsenic.'

'So what do you propose?'

It was Jake's turn to sigh. 'I'm going to have to act like some bloody silly spy. Find a vantage point where

I can watch the farm, follow her when she goes out and hope she ends up somewhere I can speak to her.'

Caroline's voice was rich with laughter. 'Oh God, I'd love to be a fly on the wall. Jake auditioning for the cloak and dagger.'

'I'll keep you posted,' he said, resentful at her apparent lack of confidence in him.

'Do. I expect great things of you, Jake. Sweet dreams.'

And she was gone. *Sweet dreams*, he thought, bouncing experimentally on the overly soft mattress. *As if.*

A waning moon hung low over the car park, turning the remaining leaves on the overhanging trees into ragged tatters. River shivered as the damp night chill invaded the hotel hallway through the door Ewan Rigston held open for her. 'Brrr,' she said, passing him. 'Nothing like the Lakeland air to make that warm glow disappear.'

'It doesn't tempt you to a moonlight stroll round Derwent Water, then?' he teased, falling into step beside her.

'You're not serious?'

He laughed. 'I'm not dressed for it. And even if I was, I wouldn't pick a night like this.' He sniffed the air and pointed up at a mass of cloud shouldering its way over Castlerigg Fell. 'It's going to rain.'

'Better call it a night, then. I wouldn't want anything to spoil it.'-They'd reached her Land Rover and River turned to face him, suddenly uncertain of what she wanted. 'I had a great evening, Ewan.'

He inclined his head. 'Me too. I can't remember the last time I enjoyed myself so much.'

His face was in shadow and she couldn't read it. 'We could do it again some time?'

'I'd like that. You could give me an update on Pirate Peat.'

She felt a twinge of disappointment. 'If you like.'

He leaned against the Land Rover. 'You know what the locals are saying?'

'About Pirate Peat? No, what?'

'They're saying Fletcher Christian can finally be laid to rest.'

River frowned. 'Fletcher Christian? As in the mutiny on the *Bounty*? What's that got to do with our cadaver?'

'He was a local lad, Fletcher. And the word round here has always been that he made it back home afterwards. Some say he was a smuggler up on the Solway Firth. And some reckon his family on the Isle of Man took him in.' He shrugged. 'Who knows?'

River was intrigued. She mentally reviewed what she knew about her cadaver and set it against the little she knew about the *Bounty* story. 'I suppose it's possible. Pirate Peat had been to the South Seas, no question of that. But I'd have to do some research. Check out dates and such.' She grinned. 'Now that would really excite my TV guys. I'll have to tell them in the morning.' She stood on tiptoe and kissed Rigston on the cheek. 'Thank you for that.'

Before she could move away, he pulled her close. 'Thank you for this evening,' he said, his voice low and dark. Then his mouth was firm against hers, the fine sandpaper of his stubble sending a shiver through her that had nothing to do with the cold. Her lips parted and her tongue darted against his. Heat spread downwards from her belly and her hands found their way under his jacket. When they separated, they were both breathing heavily. 'I'm sorry,' he gasped. 'I didn't mean . . .'

She slid her hand round to the front of his trousers and ran her fingers over the hard outline of his penis. 'Oh, I think you did,' she murmured. 'It takes forty-six minutes to get to my place. How long to yours?'

Two hundred and fifty miles away, a coach lumbered through the outskirts of Oxford. The passengers were an ill-assorted bunch: a minor civil servant who had spent the evening after work at the cinema with a colleague; a handful of students returning from an indie gig in Shepherd's Bush; three Australian back-packers on the next stage of their world tour; a scatter of couples and singles coming home from an evening out in the big city. Some dozed, some read, some chattered, some stared through their own reflection at the shops and houses that lined the bus route through Headington towards the narrow thoroughfare of St Clements.

The young black kid slouched in a seat halfway up the bus hadn't merited a second glance from anyone. The peak of a baseball cap cast most of the face in shadow, a sanction against the sort of insolent stare that might have awakened a twitch of apprehension among fellow passengers.

Tenille shifted in her seat and checked the time. The bus was running on schedule. She had no idea what kind of place Oxford was, except there were a lot of students and old buildings. But she figured it couldn't be that hard to find a quiet corner to doss down in. She didn't care if she didn't get much sleep. She'd be on buses all day, she could nap then. Besides, every time she nodded off, she risked those nightmare images of Geno coming back to haunt her. Sleep really didn't matter. What mattered was staying out of the way of the cops. And she had no doubt she could manage that.

She wondered whether they were looking for her outside the Marshpool yet. She wondered whether they'd been in touch with Jane yet.

But not for a second did she wonder whether she was doing the right thing.

The memory of my brother's story planted a seed in my head that, no matter how I tried to dislodge it, would not budge. The _Middlesex_ mutiny had failed because there was an insufficient appetite for mutiny among the common sailors. But I was willing to wager that Bligh had damned few supporters among the men. Too many of them had endured his vile tongue and his petty martinet ways. I resolved then and there that if my treatment at Bligh's hands should become intolerable, I would seek my brother's solution and accept the consequences, whatever they might be. The following day, the final grain of sand was added to the mountain that was already oppressing me. Bligh accused me in front of the men of being a common thief then punished the whole crew for my alleged crime of stealing his cocoa-nuts. I know not what a stronger man would have done in such a circumstance. I know only that I could no longer bear the weight of his volatility, his vanity and his viciousness.

18

A single road ran through Fellhead. Unless a driver was determined to twist and wind up the side of Langmere Fell and over a difficult, narrow mountain pass, there was only one logical way in and out of the village. Jake set his alarm for six, and by quarter to seven he was at the Fellhead road end, worn out by the previous day's travelling and feeling aggrieved that Keswick had been unable to supply him with a takeaway carton of decent coffee to kickstart his brain. A thin drizzle fell relentlessly, cutting visibility and leaching colour from the landscape. Low cloud covered the fell tops and lowland sheep huddled miserably against stone walls and trees.

He didn't want to drive into the village; there were a few residents who might just recognise him from the previous visits he'd made with Jane. And he certainly had no desire to bump into Judy Gresham popping into the village store. Whatever Jane had said about the ending of their relationship, it wouldn't have painted him in the sort of light that would endear him to a parent. Instead, he parked in a gravelled area twenty yards up from the road junction, a place where walkers could leave their cars convenient for the footpath that climbed up Langmere Fell.

There was more traffic on the narrow road than Jake had expected and he had a couple of false alarms; one Land Rover looked much like another at a distance. But just after eight, his patience was rewarded. Red Fiestas like the one Judy drove were less common and when one emerged from the village to speed down the road towards him, Jake pulled the brim of his baseball cap further over his eyes and squinted out from under it. As the car drew level, he recognised Jane's profile. He waited till she had turned north on the main road, then he slipped into gear and after her.

The road towards Thirlmere followed the arrow-straight line of the old Roman road, so Jake hung well back. At least the weather meant Jane had her lights on, so it was easy to keep her in sight. He was oblivious to the misty beauty of the lake on his left and the ghostly outlines of trees on his right as he drove, focused only on the red tail-lights up ahead. He didn't even notice the signs announcing roadworks ahead. Jane's car disappeared round a long shallow bend and, as he swung round behind her, he saw disaster ahead. The lights controlling the single-lane traffic through the roadworks turned from amber to red just as Jane shot through. He was tempted to jam his foot down and go for it, but at the last minute he ran out of nerve and slammed the brakes on, slewing to a stop just as headlights approached from the opposite direction. Heart pounding, he clenched the steering wheel. Christ, that had been close.

Jake wiped sweat from his upper lip and waited

impatiently for the light to change. He glanced down at the map to confirm what he already thought. There wasn't anywhere for Jane to turn off, not till she got to the head of the lake. On one side was water, on the other the steep wooded lower slopes of Helvellyn. If he stepped on it, he might just catch her. As the light changed from amber to green, he shot forward and raced up the road. But by the time he reached the point where decisions had to be made there was still no sign of the Fiesta. Here, Jane could either have carried on into Keswick or forked right towards the main drag leading to the M6 and anywhere. Jake hesitated for a moment then gambled on the road to what he considered civilisation. His superior speed and road-holding might just be enough to catch her. And if he didn't, he could always double back to Keswick and cruise the car parks.

A mile later, he rounded a bend and almost went into the back of a tractor ambling along between the low stone walls bordering the road. Time to give up the chase. Frustrated beyond words, he took advantage of the next gateway to make a seven-point turn and head back to Keswick. Half an hour's searching later, he was forced to admit defeat.

There wasn't much point in going back to the road end. When Jane returned, she would be going home, back to the protective bosom of her family. And he couldn't think of any other way to cross her path. At least he could be fairly certain Jane hadn't come up with any documentary evidence to support her theory, otherwise she would have been spending her time with Anthony Catto at Dove Cottage.

At that thought, his brain made one of those

unfathomable leaps that scientists call inspiration and priests divine intervention. When he and Jane had been together, they'd spent a week in Barcelona. To save on luggage, they had taken only his laptop. She had loaded her email software on to his machine and he had never removed it. It should still be there, complete with stored password. He could raid her account without her ever knowing. He had no doubt whatsoever that there would be a trail. These days, there was always something in the mail.

River pulled on a white lab coat over the clothes she had been wearing the previous day. In spite of only having had a couple of hours' sleep, she felt as if her brain cells were sparking like metal under a welding torch. Good sex would do that every time, she thought, stretching her arms out above her head and enjoying the feeling of well-being that surged through her. It had been the best fun she'd had in a long time.

There had been nothing awkward about waking up together either. They hadn't spoken much, it was true – she'd been too eager to get online to see what basic information she could gather about Fletcher Christian, and he'd been happy to let her use his computer. It had all felt very relaxed, very natural. She had no idea where it was going. But for now, she was more than happy to make the journey.

River fastened her coat, grabbed a clipboard with her notes and hurried through to the funeral parlour's embalming room where Pirate Peat lay in wait for her, his body exposed under the glare of fluorescent strips and TV arc lamps. As she entered, she gauged her audience. Two students taking their masters degrees in Forensic Anthropology, one other from Archaeological Sciences and one palaeobotanist. And to one side, a cameraman, sound woman and a director. 'Before we begin,' she said, looking at the students, 'I'm going to apologise to you in advance. Some of what I'm going to go through today will be simplistic in the extreme. That's because I have to pitch it at a TV audience who don't have the advantage of your undergraduate degrees. After we're done with the filming, we can sit down and go over what we've looked at with a little more scientific rigour. But please watch carefully what I'm doing and take notes where you need to. Are you all happy with that?'

They nodded and grunted assent. 'We'll need you all to sign a release,' the director chipped in, 'authorising us to use your images in the final programme.'

'Will there be a fee?' one of the male students asked slightly mutinously.

'Just being here should be fee enough for you,' River said. 'This is not an opportunity that comes along very often. I can say with some degree of certainty that you'll be the only two masters students in the country who'll be getting such a hands-on experience with a bog body this year. So just be grateful we're not charging you for the favour.' She turned to the director. 'Before we get started, I wanted to run something past you. I'm told there's a rumour buzzing round the town that this could be the body of Fletcher Christian.'

'Who's Fletcher Christian?' the director asked.

River tried not to roll her eyes. 'The guy who led the mutiny on the *Bounty*.'

'What? Like in the Mel Gibson film?'

'That's right.'

The director looked at her as if she was mad. 'So how did he end up in a bog on Langmere Fell? I mean, that was in the South Pacific, right?'

'Right. But apparently he was from round here. And there was a rumour that he made it back to the Lakes.'

'Cool.' The director looked vaguely impressed.

'I was wondering if we could incorporate the speculation into what we're doing? Wouldn't that make it a better sell to the viewers?'

'I suppose so. I'll need to run it past Phil, though. He's the boss.'

River tried to curb her impatience. 'I've already done a little bit of research online this morning. Why don't we just proceed as if we're going to go down that path? I can make reference to it as I work. Then if Phil decides against it, you can always edit it out. How does that sound?'

The director spread his hands. 'Why not? Anything to make a dead body sexier.'

River allowed herself the smile of a woman who knows what sexy really means. 'Are we ready?'

The sound woman stared down at her dials and muttered, 'Up to speed.' The cameraman looked through his eyepiece and said, 'Rolling.'

River stared down at the body. 'Even a body as old as this one gives us a wealth of information. Our bodies encode our personal identity. They tell the world what has been done to them and what they have done to themselves. Even the most superficial examination can tell us something.' She pointed as she spoke. 'The skull, the pubic synthesis, the joint degeneration – all this conspires to tell us our man was around forty years old.'

She looked up at the students. 'This body was found in Carts Moss, a boggy area towards the base of Langmere Fell. That's unusual enough in itself to generate local interest. But when the word spread about these tattoos . . .' She paused to indicate the dark shading on the chestnut-coloured skin, then looked up again and continued: '. . . a completely different level of interest was aroused.'

She ran her hand gently over the remains on the table. 'Forensic anthropology is all about identity. Who was this person? What happened to them while they were alive? And what impact did that have on how they died? Most of what we do is solid scientific fact. But like the archaeologists, we also have to rely on other evidence, some of it anecdotal, some of it social, because the science is meaningless without a context. And when it comes to anecdotal evidence, we've already got an intriguing possibility right here. Could this be the body of a Cumbrian called Fletcher Christian who sailed away in the *Bounty* on a voyage to the South Seas where he led a mutiny against his captain? Certainly that's what some locals believe. As we make our journey towards discovering all this body has to tell us, let's bear in mind the possibility that we might just be able to identify this body very precisely even though it's been in the ground for a couple of hundred years.'

She turned to the whiteboard set behind her. 'And cut,' the director said. 'We need to change our camera position, River. So we can see what you're writing.'

A few minutes later, everything was ready again. River took a blue marker pen and started to make a list on the right-hand side of the board. She headed it *Fletcher Christian*. Below, she wrote a list based on what she'd garnered from her swift sweep of the internet.

Born 25/9/1764 Moorland Close, nr Cockermouth, Cumbria
Male
Height: 175 cm
Hair: very dark brown
Dark complexion
Strong made
Star tattoo on left breast
Tattooed in South Sea Island style – buttocks completely coloured black, probably with decoration lines round the upper border
Slightly bow-legged
Very sweaty, particularly in the hands – ?primary hyperhidrosis?
One version of his death on Pitcairn refers to him being shot in the shoulder.

She stood back and surveyed what she had written. 'It's not much, I know, but we're lucky in that it does give us some concrete physical evidence to go on.'

River turned back to the body. 'Well, we know our body is male. We also know that its age is consistent with it being Mr Christian. And he does have long dark hair. That will have been darkened by exposure to the peat, but we can conduct tests to establish more clearly its original colour.' She took a tape measure from her pocket and stretched it out alongside the body. 'A hundred and seventy centimetres. Apparently five centimetres shorter than our man. Any comments?'

The female forensic anthropologist said, 'We all lose height as we age. And we can't be certain how accurate the initial measurement was. So it doesn't exclude this being him.'

'Correct,' River said. 'Sadly, we can't make any estimate as to his weight because we don't have any idea how much soft tissue has been leached away by the acid in the peat. We've got very little left and certainly not enough to make even a reasonable guess. He does look quite broad in the shoulder, however. So, again, we have nothing to contradict our wild hypothesis. The other disappointment because of the lack of soft tissue is that we've no way of knowing whether our cadaver suffered from any disorder of the sympathetic nervous system that would lead to hyperhidrosis. Now, let's take a look at his leg bones. Anyone have anything to say?'

They crowded round the table. The director took the opportunity to rearrange his crew to capture a new angle. The same student spoke again. 'The leg bones look pretty straight to me. I wouldn't have thought he was bow-legged.'

'I don't agree,' her opposite number said. 'Look at the knees. The medial femoral-tibial joint is worn down on both legs. If he started out as mildly bow-legged, over the years that would have put stress on the inside of the knee joint and caused this kind of arthritic presentation. Especially if he led a physically active life.'

220

'The arthritis could have nothing to do with being bow-legged,' the female student protested. 'It could be simple wear and tear, particularly if he was over-weight.'

'I don't think there were many fat sailors around in the eighteenth century,' the young man countered. 'The food was crap and the work was hard. And besides, he's pretty young at forty to have that level of joint degeneration.'

'I'm inclined to agree with you,' River said. 'Again, we can't exclude Mr Christian on the basis of our findings. At this point, then, all we can say is nothing we've seen with our eye contradicts the possibility. And we have one piece of non-invasive evidence that does give some weight to our idea.' Reaching beneath the table, she pulled out the X-ray and CAT scan images of the cadaver's shoulder. While she waited for the camera to set up on the portable light-box she'd had the students bring down from Carlisle, she ran through what she had already told Ewan Rigston about the injury to the shoulder blade. Then she ran through it twice more for the camera. By the end of that recital, she was beginning to feel bored with herself. Time to move swiftly on.

'What we're going to be doing for the rest of this session is taking samples. We'll be taking teeth for stable isotope analysis to find out where he was living when they were formed. More teeth so we can age him more precisely. A bone sample from the femur for stable isotope analysis to see where he'd been in the last ten to fifteen years of his life. We'll be analysing them back at the university with the mass spectrom-eter. We'll also be taking hair and nail samples to check for toxicology and different food substances. And the contents of the gastro-intestinal tract so the palaeobotanists can have their fun. We'll try to find enough soft muscle tissue to use for DNA and toxicology. And when we've done all that, we'll have a much better idea of this man's identity. Whether he's Fletcher Christian or not, he can't hide from us.'

River looked straight down the barrel of the camera. 'And when we know more about who he is, maybe we'll even have some idea of who killed him.'

The events of that fateful night have been described by several of those present. My brother Edward has shown me those accounts and I find them accurate by and large as to the facts of the matter, though necessarily faulty when it comes to imputing thoughts and motives. You may easily satisfy yourself as to the true course of events from their stories. What I must say most clearly and strongly in my own defence is that I had no intention that Lieutenant Bligh and his companions should perish or be forced to endure the trials of that terrible voyage across the Pacific in an open boat. There was land within easy reach when we cast them off from Bounty. A navigator of Bligh's stature and with his knowledge of those waters must have known he could easily make landfall then and there. There was no need but Bligh's overweening vanity for them to be afflicted with such a torment as he forced them to endure. He became a hero as a result, but he could have killed them all in the doing of it. And that is the measure of the man.

19

DI Donna Blair dealt with the final allegedly urgent piece of paper on her desk and looked out across the incident room. 'Kumar,' she shouted.

The young PC who was supposed to be tracking down Jane Gresham looked up apprehensively. 'Yes, ma'am?'

'In here.' Donna drummed her fingers on her desk as she waited for him to scramble into her office. 'Have we got Jane Gresham yet?'

'No, ma'am. I finally tracked down her workplace. She works at the Centre for Editing Lives and Letters, Queen Mary University of London, but the only address they've got for her is the Marshpool. The girl I spoke to says Gresham's off somewhere on study leave, she thinks her boss might know where. So the boss is going to call me back.' .

'Christ. I've still got a bloody uniform on the door. This is costing money we haven't got. You know how it works in an investigation like this – we're not high profile, so we don't get the budget.'

'Surely the kid would have shown up by now if she was planning on hiding out there?' PC Kumar was still fresh enough to the job to think he would earn Brownie points by making obvious suggestions to his boss.

Donna rolled her eyes. 'And maybe she's been hiding out somewhere else on the estate, waiting till the heat dies down and she can get to her safe house.' She sighed. 'Stick with it. Have you tried going through the phone book for the Lake District to see if there are any Greshams listed?'

'I was going to, but then the woman at the university said study leave, so I thought maybe the neighbour got it wrong.' As soon as the words were out of his mouth, PC Kumar knew his mistake.

'I'm the one who's paid to think,' Donna said. 'While you're waiting for Jane Gresham's boss to call you back, get started on the phone book. I expect there's only a few dozen Greshams in the region. And before you get stuck in, get me the media centre, or whatever the press office is called this week. Now it's beginning to look like she might have done a runner, it's time to get the kid's face out there.' Kumar retreated and Donna scowled at his back. It wasn't him she was pissed off with. What really pissed her off was being outsmarted by a thirteen-year-old. If anyone doubted Tenille Cole's parentage, here was their answer.

She raked through her drawer till she found some nicotine gum. She didn't want to talk to the Hammer, but she had a nasty feeling that it was going to come down to that. Not that the prospect frightened her; it was the thought of another pointless fencing match that would take the case no further forward that she dreaded. But there was no getting away from it. This was a murder inquiry and in these days of cold case squads, it could be professional suicide to leave any stone unturned, as several of her senior colleagues had been finding out lately.

Please let Kumar find Jane Gresham, she thought. *And please let Jane Gresham know where we can find Tenille.*

Matthew smiled at his pupils, a genuine smile that transformed the sulk his face had become in repose these days. It pointed up his resemblance to his sister, whose more optimistic take on life had given a sunnier cast to her features. It was a smile his son saw more than anyone else, and his pupils had learned to relax under its warmth. 'You've all done really well,' he said, the praise sincere. He'd been pleasantly surprised by how far everyone had managed to trace back their family trees and the detail they'd managed to acquire. The executions varied, admittedly. A couple were computer-generated, complete with scanned-in photographs; both produced by the children of incomers whose parents worked in IT. But even Jonathan Bramley, whose handwriting still made Matthew despair, had made a decent attempt at making his family tree look as it should.

'This is going to make a very impressive centrepiece for our end-of-term display,' Matthew continued. 'So we've got plenty of time to see if we can go even further back into history. What we're also going to be doing is looking in more detail at the sort of lives our ancestors led – what their living conditions were like, what sorts of jobs they did, what their family relationships were.'

He smiled again. 'But before we get into that, I

want Sam and Jonathan to come up here with their family trees.'

The two boys eyed each other as they walked to the front of the class. Sam looked wary, Jonathan surly. Sam's project was beautifully laid out, clear and informative. Jonathan's looked even more wanting alongside it, but it was clear enough for Matthew's purposes. 'Have you two looked at each other's work?' Matthew asked, squatting down so he was on a level with both boys.

Both shook their heads. 'OK. Now, turn around to face the class and hold them up so we can all see them.' Matthew paused while they did as they were asked. 'The first thing we notice with these two family trees is that both Sam and Jonathan can trace their descent back several generations. That's because they both come from families that are local. It's only been in the last thirty years or so that people have become so mobile. Before that, most people stayed pretty close to the place where they'd been born. If they moved more than twenty miles or so, it was generally because of the need to find work. My grandfather, for example, moved from Cornwall to Cumbria because he was a miner and the tin mines in Cornwall were closing. But he heard there was work here mining slate and so he left his home and his family and came to Cumbria. He married a local girl, and so he stayed.

'Sam and Jonathan come from a long line of Cumbrians. And if we look back in time six generations,' Matthew said, standing behind the boys and running his finger back up the branches, 'we find something very interesting indeed. Here's Sam's great-great-great-great-grandfather, Arthur Clewlow. And here's Jonathan's great-great-great-grandmother May Bramley. And her name before she was married was May Clewlow. And then if we look one branch higher up the tree, we can see that Jonathan and Sam's family come from a common root – the marriage between Arnold Clewlow and Dorcas Mayson in August 1851.' He rumpled their hair.

'So if the body in the bog is Sam Clewlow's monkey ancestor, Jonathan, I guess he's made a monkey of you too.'

Jane rubbed her eyes, but they felt just as gritty and tired when she opened them again. There was no question about it, parish registers had never been compiled with an eye to legibility. Crabbed scrawls vied with minuscule script, curlicues confused her and abbreviations puzzled her. Even with the aid of a magnifying glass, it was a struggle to make sense of the entries. She didn't envy the poor sods charged with the data entry of the records that had already been made available online. It also made her wonder just how accurate those online records were. She was accustomed to reading old manuscripts, but there were some entries she'd had to give up on, others that were barely decipherable and yet more whose interpretation was debatable. Had a weaver in Ambleside in 1851 really called his son Endocrine? She thought not, but could imagine no other word that fitted the scribble.

The task Jane had set herself was wearisome and far less entertaining than her usual research. Generally when she was pursuing her scholarly interests, she would come across interesting little asides and byways that provided some leaven in the lump. But the County Records Office was all lump.

Jane sighed and turned back to another dusty volume. She sincerely hoped Dan was having more success than she was.

Jake sat cross-legged on the bed, his laptop open before him. The dial-up connection via the phone point was tediously slow compared to wireless access, but he wanted privacy for his piracy. He booted up Jane's email program and was pleased to see that, as he'd suspected, she'd left her password stored on the dial-up screen. He hesitated for a moment. What he was planning was about as shabby as it got. And Jake didn't like to think of himself as shabby. But he had his future to consider. Frankly, a little shabbiness was neither here nor there if that was all that stood between him and the literary find of the century.

That was all the argument he needed to overcome his scruples. Jane's inbox contained a stack of emails that had been read and saved as new; Jake knew from experience that these were emails that she had either not yet answered or else was keeping close to hand for easy reference. There was only one unread message in the box, and as soon as Jake saw the sender's name, his curiosity burned harder. If Anthony Catto was writing to Jane, it was most likely something to do with her research. But if he read it before Jane, she would realise someone had hacked her account. And nobody but he had her account details. That realisation would scupper any chance he had of getting her on his side.

The alternative was to open it and then delete it.

If it was important, he could always fake an email from Jane to Anthony asking him to resend it. Before he could have second thoughts, he opened the email.

Dear Jane,
I've been in touch this morning with the document team at the British Library and they've agreed to examine the letters with a view to authentication and attribution. Well done you for finding them and for understanding their potential significance.

After our conversation yesterday, I remembered something that does loosely tie in to your hypothesis. WW wrote in 1841 re the Windermere area: 'So much was this region considered out of the way until a late period that persons who had fled from justice used often to resort thither for concealment, and some were so bold as not infrequently to make excursions from the place of their retreat for the purpose of committing fresh offences.' It seems a rather curious thing for him to say unless he had some personal knowledge, don't you think?

Let me know how you fare with Dorcas.
Best Wishes
Anthony

'Son of a bitch,' Jake said softly. So she had found something after all. Something that gave support to her Fletcher Christian theory.

Eager now, he called up Jane's sent mail. The last item in the box was addressed to Dan Seabourne. He remembered Dan – his smart repartee, his groomed good looks and his thinly-shrouded dislike of Jake. Dan had always been close to Jane. If she was going to confide in any of her colleagues, he would be the one. Impatiently, he opened the email and knew he'd struck gold. Jane referred to a letter from Mary Wordsworth about some mysterious material in William's hand. She'd also included a copy of a letter from their son John. Supposedly to help Dan in searching for Dorcas Mason's descendants at Family Records. Hastily, Jake copied both emails and forwarded them to his own mailbox. Then he composed a quick note to Anthony Catto, posing as Jane, claiming to have accidentally deleted Anthony's message and asking him to send it again. His final act was to delete copies of what he'd sent. A computer expert would doubtless be able to recover what he'd done, but he didn't imagine his laptop would ever attract the interest of one of those. He'd done enough to cover his tracks, he was convinced.

He closed down Jane's account then opened his own email, checking the forwarded messages had arrived safely in his mailbox. Then he reached for his mobile and called Caroline. 'I know what she's got,' he announced without preamble when she answered the phone.

'She told you?'

'Not exactly. I hacked into her email.'

'So is it good?'

Jake ran through what he had uncovered. 'There *was* definitely something,' he concluded. 'Whether it's still around is a different story. But as long as I can get alongside her, we can let Jane do the legwork.'

'I don't think so,' Caroline said slowly. 'No reason why we shouldn't try to steal a march on her. By all means, carry on with our original plan. It won't hurt to know exactly where Jane is up to. But if we can get to Dorcas's descendants ahead of Jane, so much the better.'

'How are we going to do that?'

'We'll hire a professional to search the records in London.' Caroline was brisk and businesslike.

'Where would we find one of those?'

'I know a probate lawyer at Lincoln's Inn. He's always having to track down stuff like that. You've no idea how people lie when there's money at stake. So where is she now?'

'I don't know. I tried to follow her this morning but I lost her thanks to some roadworks.'

'Never mind. At least you've got something to show for the day. I'll call you as soon as I hear anything from London. And good luck with Jane, darling. Do what you have to do.'

The rain that drizzled relentlessly over the Lake District was also soaking Derbyshire. Tenille was oblivious to it. Her backpack was a pillow between her head and the rain-spattered window of the bus that dawdled up from Ashbourne to Buxton. It was her fourth bus of the day and she was weary to her bones.

Oxford hadn't had much to offer in the way of shelter. Because there were people on the city centre streets well into the small hours, there were also police officers patrolling. The few possible places she spotted in the area round the bus station were already occupied by people she didn't want to doss down next to, even if they'd been willing to share. She didn't want to go too far from the bus station either, in case she couldn't find her way back for the early bus that would take her on the next leg of her journey. She'd ended up in an alley behind a restaurant, squeezed in between two dumpsters that stank of rotting food. Her sleep had been fitful because she was so cramped that she kept waking with pins and needles in her legs. The night had seemed to go on forever.

By the time Tenille dragged herself back to the bus station, she was seriously questioning the wisdom of her plan. Maybe she should just head for the nearest cop shop and hand herself in. It couldn't be more uncomfortable than last night. But by the time she'd breakfasted on a bacon butty and a can of Coke, her resolve had reasserted itself. She'd climbed on board the 7.22 to Banbury, determined to make it to Fellhead. She wasn't sure what Jane would be able to do. But Jane was the only adult in her world that she trusted to be able to do something. And besides, it was Jane who had got her into this mess. It was Jane's job to get her out of it.

I had often mused about what sort of captain I would make should I ever be fortunate enough to become master of my own ship. And I confess that many times on the outward voyage I had considered how differently I would run the ship from my captain. Putting these notions into practice proved to be no mean feat. I knew I would have to master those gestures that would indicate to the men that their welfare was at my heart, that I deserved their respect and that I was worthy of command. I wanted to enforce discipline without autocracy, and so from the very start I encouraged the men to hold meetings to discuss how we should proceed. On the second day after the mutiny, I ordered the royals to be cut up and sewn into uniforms for the crew, giving up my own officer's kit to provide a blue edging. I believed that this would impress the natives, but also that it would engender a spirit of comradeship and orderliness among my crew. I also supervised the division of the goods and chattels of those who had left with Bligh. In short, I tried to be the man I would have liked to serve under.

20

Matthew couldn't hide his pleasure at Jane's absence when he arrived at the farm with Gabriel for their regular Friday teatime visit. With Jane not there, he was deferred to, his opinion seldom challenged, his presence welcomed gratefully as if he were bestowing a precious gift. Which, of course, he believed without reservation that he was.

And so he enjoyed bringing Gabriel for tea with his grandparents. Naturally, they fussed over the baby, but Matthew regarded that as releasing him from any tedious aspect of Gabriel's care. He loved his son, no question of that. He simply wasn't very keen on the practical application of that love, particularly where it pertained to the changing of nappies and the preparing of feeds.

'Jane gone back to London, then?' he said, almost as soon as he'd settled Gabriel on the ragrug on the kitchen floor with a clutch of toys around him. 'I thought she'd soon get bored back here.'

'She's anything but bored,' Judy said. 'She's making real progress. She found a letter at the Jerwood Centre yesterday and she went off first thing to the County Records Office at Carlisle to try and track down some woman who worked for the Wordsworths.'

'Waste of time,' Matthew scoffed. 'But that's academia for you. Any will-o'-the-wisp that catches their attention and they're off, grant application in hand, desperate to talk it up.'

'Jane's not like that,' Judy said, sitting down on the floor beside Gabriel and tickling his tummy. Gabriel gurgled and laughed, squirming under her fingers. 'She really believes in what she's doing.'

Matthew rolled his eyes. 'She should try working in the real world for a week, see how she liked that. Doing what I do would have her on her knees in a day.'

Allan Gresham walked into the kitchen in time to hear his son's words. He didn't have to be told who he was referring to. 'Jane does work in the real world, Matthew. She serves behind a bar, she teaches students. She's never gone a summer without having a job. And on top of that, she does her own work. You can't accuse your sister of sitting back and taking handouts.'

'Maybe not. But she gets to do exactly what she wants. Always has. She doesn't have responsibilities like I have.'

Allan said nothing. He had learned to ignore his son's perennial discontent. Engaging with it only re-inforced it. He walked across the kitchen and put the kettle on as Jane walked in. Her face lit up when she saw her nephew waving legs and arms in the air. 'Hello, Gabriel,' she said, crossing straight to where her mother was playing with him. She

236

squatted down and held out a finger for him to grasp. 'God, he's gorgeous,' she said. Her voice changed to the register people adopt with babies. 'You are gorgeous, aren't you, Mr Man?'

'And hello to you too, Jane,' Matthew said.

'Did you have a good day?' her mother asked, stepping into her familiar role as buffer zone before Jane could respond.

Jane sat back on her heels. 'Disappointing. It's bizarre. It's as if this woman disappears into thin air. I've got the birth certificate, I've seen the letter from Mary saying she was leaving in 1851 to get married, but there's no trace of the marriage certificate. I searched all the registers up to the end of 1853, but not a sign. And no death recorded either. Dorcas Mason vanished without trace.'

Matthew hid his surprise at a name he'd seen only that day. 'Who?' he said.

Jane picked up her nephew and got to her feet, smiling into his face. 'Dorcas Mason. She worked as a maid for the Wordsworths.'

'Why are you interested in a maid? Was old Willie having a bit of hanky panky with the serving girls?'

Jane glared at him. 'Even if he hadn't been a devoted and faithful husband, by the time she came to work for the family I think he was well past being interested.'

'So what's the big deal about Dorcas what's-her-name?' Matthew persisted, pretending uncertainty.

'Mary Wordsworth found some sort of manuscript after William's death. Whatever it was, it upset her. She sent it to her son John because she said it touched him and his family. John was married to Isabella Christian Curwen, the daughter of Fletcher Christian's cousin.'

'So you think this manuscript is your fantasy poem?'

'I don't know. But it might be.'

'Interesting.' Matthew accepted a mug of tea from his father. 'And where does Dorcas come in?'

'Dorcas brought the manuscript to John, who didn't want it in his house, not after the grief Isabella had brought him. So he told her to dispose of it. And that's the last we ever hear of it.'

Matthew's eyebrows rose. 'So she either used it for kindling or hung on to it, is that what you're saying?'

Jane nodded. 'If it survived, it's been a well-kept family secret. Always supposing they know what it is they've got.'

'Anybody mind if I turn on the TV for the news?' Allan said, hand poised over the remote control for the portable that sat on the kitchen worktop.

'No, go ahead,' Jane said absently, her mind still on her work. 'I don't honestly have high hopes, but I can't just leave it like this. I have to try and find out what happened to Dorcas.'

Matthew began to say something but his mother spoke over him. 'Of course you do. Will you go back to Carlisle next week?'

'No point, I've looked through all the relevant material. My only hope now is that Dan can find something at Family Records.'

The news came on in the background, the volume loud enough to be heard but not loud enough to disrupt conversation. 'That's where you live,' Allan exclaimed, reaching for the volume button on the remote. 'Marshpool Farm Estate.'

All eyes swung round to the TV set, where the newsreader was giving the camera her best serious stare. '. . . two nights ago. Police are anxious to trace the whereabouts of a thirteen-year-old girl who had been living with her aunt in the flat where the murder took place.' The screen changed and a school photograph filled the screen. Jane gasped. 'Oh my God,' she said.

The newsreader continued: 'Tenille Cole has not been seen since fire ripped through the sixth-floor flat where the murdered man, Geno Marley, was found.' The screen changed to the talking head of a police detective framed against the familiar grey concrete of the Marshpool. 'We are very anxious to trace Tenille,' he said. 'She has not been seen since the shooting and the fire and we are extremely concerned for her welfare. We would urge her or anyone who knows where she is to come forward.'

Back to the newsreader. 'The government has announced new measures to deal with . . .' Allan muted the sound and turned to Jane. Her face was white and she clutched Gabriel so tightly that he had begun to whimper.

'For Christ's sake,' Matthew said, standing up and reaching for his son. 'You're scaring him.'

Jane handed Gabriel over without a word, her eyes wide and her teeth biting her lower lip. Judy took one look at her and hurried to her side, putting her arms around her. 'Are you all right?'

'That's London for you,' Matthew said. 'If it's not

239

suicide bombers, it's murderers. You're not safe even in your own home.'

Allan shook his head. 'Thank God you were up here, Jane.'

Jane let her mother hug her. 'I knew it was bad, where you live,' her mother said, her voice heavy with self-reproach. 'We should never have let you take that flat. We'll have to see what we can do about getting you somewhere else to live.'

Jane disengaged herself, patting her mother on the shoulder. 'It's not like that, Mum. Someone like me, I'm not at risk. This kind of thing, it's contained. It's people dealing with their own. Their lives, their world – it doesn't touch mine.'

'So why are you acting like you've just seen a ghost?' Matthew asked, for once not unkindly. 'What are you not telling us, Jane?'

She visibly pulled herself together. 'I know Tenille, that's all.'

'That black girl in the photo? You know her?' Her father sounded bewildered, as if an alien world had reached out and touched his own. 'How do you know someone like that?'

'You mean because she's black or because she's a teenager?' Jane asked, showing a rare irritation with her father.

'Because she's mixed up with a murder, your father means,' Judy the peacemaker said. 'And it's a good question. How do you know a lass who's wanted by the police in connection with a murder?'

'She's not wanted by the police like you make it sound. They're concerned about her,' Jane said defensively.

'Which is what they always say when they've got a suspect on the run,' Matthew pointed out. 'So how do you know her?'

'She lives in the same block as me. We got talking one day and I discovered that she loves poetry. She lives with her aunt who doesn't give a toss about her and she doesn't get much encouragement at school so she comes round to my flat to borrow books and talk about poetry.' Jane shook her head. 'I can't believe this.'

'You're saying she's the one black kid on your sink estate who's managed to keep her hands clean?' Matthew sounded incredulous.

'Oh please, spare me the parochial prejudice,' Jane said, exasperated. 'There are a lot of perfectly decent people, black and white, who live on the Marshpool. Frankly, given the lack of opportunities she's had, I think it's a miracle Tenille has turned out as well as she has.'

'What? The target of a nationwide police hunt?' Matthew snorted with derision. 'She's obviously got a whole other side to her life that you don't know about.'

'This is nothing to do with Tenille,' Jane said impatiently. 'The murdered man, Geno Marley, he's her aunt's boyfriend. Whatever trouble he brought in his wake, it's nothing to do with Tenille.' Jane turned away abruptly, not wanting her mother to see her face. Judy had always had a knack for spotting lies. 'I'm going upstairs. I want to check this story out online, see what I can find out.'

'Jane . . .' her mother said fruitlessly as she left. Judy looked helplessly at Allan. 'We can't let her go

241

back there. It's bad enough worrying about her being blown up, without this.'

'I don't see how we can stop her. She's a grown woman, Judy, she makes her own choices.'

'Hasn't she always?' Matthew stood up and handed his son to Judy. 'I need to be getting back,' he said, gathering together the baby paraphernalia that accompanied him everywhere he took his son and packing it into his buggy. 'Oh, and I'm off to Hadrian's Wall with the kids tomorrow. Diane said she'd definitely be home in the morning if Jane wants to come down for coffee. Maybe you could pass the message on when she's finished trawling the London underworld?'

But as he pushed his son downhill towards the village, it was not murder that occupied his thoughts. Dorcas Mason's name had been a bolt from the blue. He'd have to check when he got home, but he was pretty sure he knew exactly where he could lay hands on Dorcas Mason's descendants. If he helped Jane find her precious manuscript, he'd share in the glory. And it would put an end to her paranoid complaints that he was obsessed with getting at her. Deep down he was as tired of their constant fencing and bickering as Jane was. This could be his big chance to show he was a good brother after all. One she'd never be able to twist to show him in a bad light. The sunny smile lit Matthew's eyes again and he began to hum softly under his breath as he walked.

The bus to Lancaster had been late, and Tenille had missed the connection that would have taken her to

Kendal, the gateway to the Lake District. She had found a burger bar near the bus station where she was trying to spin out a cheeseburger and a Coke for as long as possible. But the skinny lad behind the counter kept staring at her. At first she wondered whether he'd rumbled her disguise, but as time crawled by and she had the chance to check out the rest of the clientele, she realised it was more likely because she was the only black teenager in the place. She'd always known that outside London there weren't so many black people, but that hadn't prepared her for feeling this conspicuous.

If she stuck out like a sore thumb somewhere like the burger bar, she realised that sleeping rough was going to be an even tougher option than she'd thought. This was the kind of small city where the cops would know their regulars, and they'd know her for an outsider right away. If the cops in London had spread the word that she was on the run, it wouldn't take even a dumb provincial cop long to suss her out.

Tenille stared down at the table. She'd been kidding herself that this was some kind of an adventure. But it wasn't. It was lonely and scary and, no matter how hard she tried to forget it, Geno was dead. He was dead because of her.

All her life, her dad had been on the outside. She'd told herself she didn't care, that she was fine without him. But now he was on the inside, and she couldn't separate the confusion of feelings that created. Sure, she was proud that he'd shown her respect by dealing with the threat against her. But the other side of that pride was a horror at what he'd done and how he'd done it, leaving Geno for her to find like that. And now she was on the run because of something she hadn't asked for.

Tenille felt a lump in her throat, like there was a piece of burger bun stuck there, refusing to go down. Everything was all fucked up. She was tired and miserable and she was probably in more danger out on the road than she had ever been from Geno. It wasn't fair. She shouldn't have to be taking care of herself like this. Other people didn't have this shit to deal with.

She rubbed her eyes, determined not to burst into tears under the harsh lights of a burger bar. She had to get a grip. Find something to calm herself down. She closed her eyes and summoned up the words.

My heart aches, and a drowsy numbness pains
My sense, as though of hemlock I had drunk . . .

That was the way to go, she thought with relief. Let the words wash over her. Let them be the focus of her mind. Keats and Shelley, Coleridge and Byron. They would help her make it through the night. She wasn't alone. She could get through this.

An hour's drive away, Jane sat in front of her laptop, her head in her hands. Her mother had called her down for dinner, but she had made the excuse of an upset stomach. Judy hadn't questioned Jane's claim of a dodgy chicken sandwich in Carlisle; it played too neatly into her innate mistrust of any food that hadn't been prepared by a card-carrying member of the WI.

There had been no sandwich, but Jane felt sick nonetheless. Her stomach had lurched at the news-reader's words and, as they had sunk in, nausea had crept over her. Geno Marley was dead. Murdered. Shotgunned to death, according to one of the websites she'd accessed. Blasted into oblivion only hours after she'd alerted John Hampton to the threat the man posed to his daughter. It couldn't be a coincidence.

This wasn't what she'd wanted or expected. She'd thought Hampton or his muscle would have warned Geno off. Maybe roughed him up a bit to make their point. She hadn't bargained for so extreme a response. She had blundered into a world whose rules she didn't comprehend. She'd tried to prevent a crime, not cause one. And now she had blood on her hands, a man's life on her conscience. Nothing in her past had prepared her for that weight.

Her first reaction had been to call the police. But as soon as she considered that, she knew it wasn't an option. There was Tenille to consider. Why the police were after her was a mystery to Jane. Where was she? What had she done to make them so eager to find her? Bloody Matthew had been right. They didn't issue appeals like that for the innocent. Somehow, Tenille was caught up in this. Jane couldn't under-stand how, but she knew in her bones that going to the police would not help her friend.

Besides, she had no proof that John Hampton had killed Geno. If the cops started questioning him, he'd know who had put his name in the frame. Her big fear, now that Tenille's name was in the public domain, was that the Hammer would consider Jane a poten-tial weak link in the chain. He didn't know anything about her; he might not trust her to stay away from the police. Given what she now knew him to be capable of, Jane didn't think he'd hesitate to extract what he considered to be appropriate vengeance on her. And she didn't want to die.

Jane shivered in spite of the comfortable warmth of her bedroom. She had saved Tenille. She just hadn't bargained on the price of salvation.

There was an exhilaration and an intoxication in being free men upon an ocean that scarce an Englishman had ever seen. But these feelings were tempered by the burden upon me of finding a safe haven for my crew. The men who had supported me deserved to live their lives without threat of discovery, and to go back to Otaheite would have placed that liberty at risk. Every captain sailing in those waters knew it for a good, safe anchorage and too many ships put in there for it to provide a safe hiding place for so many of us. Even if the natives could have been persuaded to hide us, someone would have betrayed us by accident or intent. I spent many hours in the captain's cabin, poring over Bligh's maps and charts in my attempts to find a sanctuary place. My choice at last alighted on Toobouai, three hundred and fifty miles south of Otaheite. There we made landfall on 24th May. I had expected another island para-dise. I could not have been more mistaken.

21

For once, waking in her own bed failed to lift Jane's bleak mood. She'd slept badly, waking every hour in a thrash of tangled bedclothes and bad dreams. Images of Tenille, of blood and fire and smoke chased chaotic montages of her family and friends through the endless concrete galleries of the Marshpool. Guilt churned her stomach. Her eyes ached and her head felt thick and useless. But in spite of her expectations, the smell of frying bacon wafting up the stairs provoked a sharp stab of appetite. She hated herself all the more for her hunger.

Jane dragged herself out of bed and into the bath-room. What was it about her parents' generation? Nobody over fifty had a decent shower. What she wanted was a cleansing cascade of scalding water, not this feeble sprinkling. She understood that her desire was as much for the symbolic as the actual, but the knowledge didn't make the experience any more satisfying.

Before she went downstairs, she decided to check her email one more time for a message from Tenille. There was nothing from her, but Dan had sent her a late-night email.

Hi, Toots

How are you doing? I wish I had some better news for you, but I'm afraid it's a no-no. I spent most of today at the Family Records Centre, but I wasn't able to make any progress on Dorcas Mason. I found the birth certificate that you already have, but after that, nothing. It's as if she walked out of the Wordsworth house into oblivion. The only thing I can think of is that she was marrying someone from overseas. That would explain her disappearance from the records. Maybe she met a sailor and went off to live in France or Spain? I'm more than willing to go back on Monday and search some more, but, to be perfectly honest, the records here are not that difficult to work through and I'm really not sure where/how else I could usefully search.

    Talk to you soon,
    Love and hugs,
    Danny Boy

'Bugger,' Jane said loudly. She'd been pinning her hopes on Dan, but he'd had no more luck than she had. Logically, she knew there was nowhere obvious left to look. But a core of obstinacy in her refused to let her give up. 'I'll think of something,' she muttered.

When she walked into the kitchen, she found her mother was frying sausages; a covered dish of bacon was sitting on the Aga. Judy looked over her shoulder to give her daughter the practised scrutiny of a parent. 'You look terrible,' she said.

'Dan drew a blank with Family Records.'

Judy swung round, her eyes concerned. 'Oh, Jane, pet, I'm so sorry. I know you'd set your heart on this.'

Allan walked in as she was speaking. 'Morning,' he said, kicking off his boots at the kitchen door.

'Jane's had bad news,' Judy said as she expertly divided the breakfast between three warm plates.

'About that lass on the TV?' Allan's face darkened in a frown.

'No, about her project,' Judy said, her voice almost drowned in the rush of water from the tap as Allan scrubbed his hands. 'Dan can't find any trace of that Dorcas woman.'

He glanced over at Jane. 'Why not put the word out locally what you're looking for, maybe someone will come up with something.' It was a long speech for her father.

'That's a really good idea,' Jane said. 'I can get Bossy Barbara on to it, see what she can dig up through her local history contacts. I bet she's on some obsessive Cumbrian genealogy weblist. Meanwhile, I thought I'd go out walking this morning. See if a stride up the fell can cheer me up.'

'Oh, that reminds me. Matthew said Diane was going to be in this morning, if you fancied a coffee,' Judy said.

'Is Matthew going to be there?'

'No, he's taken some of the older kids across to Hadrian's Wall for the day. He's good about that, organising trips.'

With a gaggle of parents to do the hard work, Jane thought cynically. 'I'll pop in on her, then. Leave the walk for this afternoon.'

'Aye, I think you'd be wise,' Allan said. 'Those clouds should lift by the end of the morning. Should be a bonny afternoon.'

Jane gave her father a grateful look. 'You're full of good ideas this morning. A bonny afternoon on Langmere Fell's just what I need.'

Jake woke to a dull and inescapable pressure inside his head. He was sweating stickily and his mouth tasted rank as a ditch. Groggily, he squinted at the red digits of the clock radio by the bed and groaned. Too late to even think about staking out Fellhead. He let his head fall back on the pillow and wondered what on earth had seemed so attractive about drinking the night away with a visiting rugby team. He didn't even like rugby. He coughed and instantly regretted it. He wanted to lie immobile in the dark for the rest of his life. Which, if he was lucky, would not be too long.

His body had other ideas. Within minutes of each other, rebelling stomach and bowels had him lurching for the bathroom. After his second trip, he started to feel that it might just be possible to continue living. He dragged himself into the shower and leaned against the wall while the water poured down.

Half an hour later, he'd made it as far as getting dressed and booting up his computer. The brightness of the screen seemed inhumane, but he persevered and managed to get online. He groaned again when he saw an email from Caroline. He really didn't want to be harangued this morning, not even virtually. But he opened it anyway, because he couldn't not.

251

Good morning, Jake. I tried calling you on your mobile, but it was switched off. I presume you're hot on Jane's trail or talking to a forensic anthropologist. Anyway. Here are the search results from Family Records. As you will see, our chap has done a very thorough job. That's the joy of professional researchers – they have the imagination to try alternate spellings for an era where literacy was still pretty hit and miss. As you'll see, by the time she got married, Ms Mason had become officially Mayson. You can get started right away on tracking down the whereabouts of the current generation. Let me know how you get on.

Talk to you soon.
Caroline xxx

Attached to the email was a document that outlined the family tree of Dorcas Ma(y)son. She had married a man from Yorkshire and had three children before her husband died prematurely. She had obviously then returned to her native Cockermouth, since that was where her death in 1887 and the marriages of her children had been registered. Flicking through to the end, Jake saw she had several direct descendants. His heart sank. This was going to be no fun whatsoever. But it would be worth it in the long run, he told himself. Well worth it.

He decided to check Jane's email while he was online. If she had made any headway, he wanted to know about it before he wasted time on leads she'd already blown out. When he opened Dan's email, he was expecting to find the same ream of results that Caroline had sent him. He was pleasantly surprised to read that Dan had failed. 'Dan to a T,' he muttered. 'Too lazy or stupid to check any other spelling.'

Finally, he dialled Caroline's mobile.

'Jake, good to hear from you,' she said cheerily.

'I got your email,' he said. 'Impressive research.'

'I thought so. It really gives you something to get your teeth into.'

'That's true. But I still think it would be better to hitch a ride on Jane's coat-tails if I can.' *Anything to buy myself some time. I don't have to tell Caroline I know Jane's going nowhere fast.* Silence on the other end of the phone. 'People will see her motives as being purer somehow. She might get further that way.'

Caroline chuckled. 'I think you spent too long in the public sector, Jake. Money is what makes the world go round. Wave enough money under their noses and they'll be happy to sell their granny, never mind a few bits of mouldy old paper. This is a windfall you're offering them, and they're going to be bloody delighted at the prospect of an unexpected wedge landing in their bank accounts. No, you go for it. We're ahead of the game at this point, let's make the most of our advantage. The dice are rolling in our favour. I'm starting to get a good feeling about this, darling. I expect great things of you. Oh, and if you get the chance to make overtures to Jane, you should go for it. But if that doesn't work out, at least you've still got her email.'

'Yeah, yeah,' Jake said. 'I'm on top of things.' Spying on his ex-girlfriend and keeping the results from his current one made him feel curiously powerful. They might think they could discount him, but he would show them who was really the player in this game. 'I'll talk to you later.'

'Mmm. Think of me swimming in the bay. It's a glorious day here, you need to get yourself back as soon as possible before the weather breaks.'

The line went dead. Jake stared at the phone. Offhand, dismissive, indulgent – that had been her tone. It was time for him to assert himself against these women.

Motherhood suited Diane, Jane thought, watching her sister-in-law settle Gabriel in his baby bouncer for a nap. When she'd been working in the bank, she'd been a high-octane kind of woman, filled with energy that had to find an outlet either in ambition at work or in projects around the home. She'd refitted their kitchen almost single-handed, only calling on help from Allan when a job really needed two pairs of hands. She'd had the good sense not to involve the famously clumsy Matthew in any practical sphere.

She had ventured into parenthood with the same determination for success, but somehow the process had mellowed her. She had lost her sense of frenetic urgency, taking things at a calm, measured pace and apparently finding the time at last to smell the flowers. As Gabriel's eyelids flickered then shuttered his eyes, she sat back on her heels and smiled. 'Now we can talk like adults,' she said.

'He's really good,' Jane said. 'I don't think I've ever seen a calmer baby.'

'You should hear him when he wants attention at

three in the morning. Or when he's hungry,' Diane said. 'Nothing calm about that.' She got to her feet and settled on the opposite end of the sofa to Jane. 'But in general, yes, he's great. I just wish he'd start sleeping through the night. I can't tell you what I'd give for eight hours' uninterrupted sleep.'

'So I take it you're not planning on another one any time soon?' Jane teased.

Diane looked at her seriously. 'I'm not planning on another one at all.'

'Really? It was that grim?'

Diane gave her a level stare. Never one for beating about the bush, she said, 'People think that being an only child's some kind of handicap. Well, I was an only child and I don't feel like I've missed out. To be honest, Jane, I've spent too long watching you and Matt tearing lumps out of each other to want to be a spectator to that sort of warfare on a daily basis.'

Jane was long past being offended by Diane's candour, accepting it was as much part of her personality as her generosity and loyalty. 'We're not that bad,' she said.

'For the spectator, you are.'

'I'm sorry. I just wish he wasn't so resentful all the time with me. After all, he's got the perfect life – he's got you and Gabriel, he's in Fellhead, living in a beautiful house at a peppercorn rent because it goes with his job, which is one he loves. I'm the one stuck in a scummy council flat working two jobs to keep body and soul together so I can have half a chance at the career I want.'

Diane grinned. 'He's not good at counting his blessings, is he? But he's a good man at heart, you know.

The kids think the world of him, and kids are good judges.'

Jane really didn't want to get into this with Diane. She had never talked about the way Matthew had tormented her as a child and she wasn't about to break her silence with his wife. But she knew that whatever face he presented to Diane and the world, there was a mean streak in Matthew that she didn't believe he'd grown out of. 'I believe you,' was the white lie she chose.

'So how's your project going?' Diane asked, seeing it was time to change the subject. 'Matt said you'd hit a snag but you were hopeful of getting some information from London.'

Jane pushed her hair back from her temples. 'I thought I was getting somewhere, but the wheels just came off.' She fiddled with the fringe of one of the appliqué cushions Diane had made for the sofa. 'Do you mind if we leave it at that? Just talking about it depresses me.'

'I am sorry, Jane.' Diane reached across and patted her hand in a curiously impersonal way, as if her mind was already racing to the next subject. She jumped to her feet. 'I tell you what, let's be really naughty and have a drink.'

'It's only half past eleven,' Jane protested weakly.

'Yeah, but I've been up since six so it feels a lot later. Come on, let's be bad girls. The sun's shining and I've got a bottle of Pimms in the kitchen.' Diane snatched Jane's hand and pulled her up from the sofa. 'I don't think you've had nearly enough fun since you and that shit Jake split up.'

Jane let herself be led through to the big kitchen

at the back of the house. The substantial four-bedroomed house would have been out of the price range of most locals, but Matthew and Diane had been the beneficiaries of one of those English eccentrics who had fallen in love with the Lake District. Back in the 1970s, the local authority had decided to sell off the remaining village schoolhouses to the highest bidder. Richard Grace, a Londoner who'd made a fortune in property development before buying the biggest house in Fellhead for a weekend retreat, had decided his village would best maintain its high educational standards if it could attract dynamic head teachers. So he'd bought the school-house and set up a trust that made it available to the head teacher at a peppercorn rent. As property prices had soared over the intervening years, it had proved a powerful sweetener. And now her brother lived in the house Jane had always fantasised about in-habiting. And still he wasn't satisfied. 'I love this view,' she said, gazing out of the window towards the craggy ridge of Langmere Fell.

'It's glorious,' Diane agreed, pulling a cucumber and a lemon from the fridge. 'Oh, damn, I forgot the jug. Be a love and get the big crystal jug out of the dining-room cabinet, would you?'

'No problem.' Jane crossed the hall to the dining room, which looked out on a wall of dense foliage, a felony compounded by walls panelled in dark wood. Even on the brightest summer day it was a dark and murky place. No wonder the family never ate there. Instead, Matthew had colonised it, turning it into a sort of school annexe, strictly for marking and lesson preparation and not to be confused with the study

257

he'd made of the fourth bedroom, where he retreated to surf the internet and play computer games. *Lucky bastard*, Jane thought as she snapped the light on and glanced at the spread of papers covering the long table.

She carried on towards the tall glass display cabinet where the best glasses were on show, but as her brain registered what she'd seen, Jane broke stride and almost stumbled. She grabbed at a heavy oak chair to steady herself and gazed down at an array of family trees executed in childish hands. Some had managed to find large sheets of paper, a couple had used wallpaper offcuts, others had Sellotaped A4 sheets together in a mosaic that accommodated the shape of their families. Two were set conspicuously to one side, drawing Jane's eyes inexorably.

One had been drawn with some style, photographs attached to the lower branches. The other was scrawled, the linking lines wavering and uneven. But as Jane backtracked down the ancestors of Sam Clewlow and Jonathan Bramley, she understood immediately why Matthew had set them apart.

Jonathan and Sam had a common ancestor back at the turn of the nineteenth century. Dorcas Mayson had married at the age of twenty and had borne three children. Sam's line sprang from her firstborn son, Jonathan's from her youngest child, the only daughter.

Jane could scarcely believe what she was looking at. The spelling was different, but well within the boundaries of nineteenth-century variation. It had to be her Dorcas. There couldn't be two of them born and married in the same year. Here was the crucial evidence she needed for her next step, evidence of Dorcas Mason's line of descent. Not only had Matthew known about this, he had deliberately kept silent. How could he do that to her? And more importantly, what was he planning to do about it?

Rage burning in her heart, Jane stormed out of the dining room and into the kitchen. Diane looked up, then did a double take as she saw Jane's expression. Jane struggled to keep control, then lost it. 'What the fuck is Matthew playing at?' she demanded.

Having trouble in penetrating the lagoon, we stood off and sent one of the ship's boats towards the shore. Our first attempt at landing on the island was greeted by a war canoe whose crew attempted to swamp our boat and were only driven off by gunfire. On the second day, we contrived to sail the ship inside the lagoon. The natives came in droves to look. Their canoes crowded close, the warriors chanting and blowing their conch shells, a terrifying sight in their scarlet and white war livery that tested our nerve. None of the natives could be inveigled to extend us overtures of friendship in spite of our being able to make ourselves understood in the Otaheitian dialect. The scent of battle was in the air. I set night watches and by morning, the number of canoes was too great to count. Three days after we had made landfall, a double canoe containing eighteen women and paddled by a dozen men arrived alongside. We took this to be an overture of friendship. But the true state of affairs was that it was the Trojan Horse of the natives.

22

Jake knew there was something about him women liked. Maybe it was because he genuinely took more pleasure in their company than that of men. Or maybe there was about him the promise of an easy ride, a man who was not going to challenge or demand but simply settle for a quiet life. Whatever it was, he knew he traded on it and that it earned him the ill-disguised contempt of his father. He also knew that it was misleading. Underneath that charm he harboured a ruthlessness that he seldom had to call on but which he had no reluctance whatsoever to engage when he needed it. He didn't think he'd need it today, however. Even hung over, he thought his charms would be enough to win over a seventy-three-year-old widow.

According to the information Caroline's researcher had come up with, Edith Clewlow lived at Lark Cottage, Langmere Stile. Her husband David, the great-great-grandson of Dorcas Mason and Arnold Clewlow, had died in 1998 and the 2001 census listed Edith as the only occupant of the cottage. Jake had chosen Edith as his first target by reasoning that inheritance generally passed down through primogeniture in the male line. It didn't hurt that he also knew where Langmere Stile was. In his bleary state, any little helped. He wasn't thrilled that getting there involved driving through Fellhead, but he wasn't planning on stopping.

The sun felt cruelly bright as he set off. Sunglasses didn't seem to help, and he could feel his dull headache intensifying as he wound his way up the side of the fell. Fellhead itself was quiet. The only pedestrians he passed were hikers making their way to the start of the steep path that led precipitously to the ridge. A mile further on, he came to the straggle of cottages that was Langmere Stile. Four low dwellings huddled by the roadside, all looking as if they needed more love and attention than their occupants were prepared to lavish on them. Exposed on the barren side of the fell just above the tree line with an untrammelled view of an old quarry, they were too miserable even on a sunny day to appeal to the weekend commuters. Jake assumed they had originally been built for the quarry workers who were probably grateful for a roof over their head.

He slowed as he approached, checking the names of the cottages. Bluebell, Crocus, Daffodil and Hyacinth. Somebody had had a sense of humour, he thought. But no Lark Cottage. Frustrated, Jake looked around, as if another cottage might be hiding somewhere in the bare landscape. Up ahead, the road made a sharp right-hand bend, at the edge of which he could see a section of stone gable.

Rounding the corner, he discovered a single-storey stone cottage, its paintwork fresh, its small garden neatly tended. Unlike its neighbours, Lark Cottage had a view down to Langmere itself and across to Helvellyn. Jake pulled the Audi on to the verge beyond the cottage and walked back. He shoved his sunglasses into his shirt pocket and tried to arrange his face into an open, friendly expression.

The woman who answered the door looked older than her years. Jake's own grandmother was in her late seventies and she looked as if she could give Edith Clewlow a good ten years. Narrow-shouldered and bent over with the tell-tale hump of osteoporosis, the woman thrust her face towards him. Pallid wrinkled skin hung loose on her small-boned face. Her silver hair was cut short and styled as simply as a child's. But the blue eyes behind her large varifocals were lively and her expression was one of intelligent suspicion.

'Mrs Clewlow?' Jake said.

'Aye. Do I know you, young man?'

He smiled. 'No, Mrs Clewlow. My name is Jake Hartnell. I wondered if you might be able to spare me a few minutes of your time?'

'Not if you're selling something. I've already got double glazing and I like my kitchen the way it is. And any work that needs doing, my grandson Frank does for me.'

'That's very commendable of him. But I'm not selling anything. In fact, it's quite the opposite. What I wanted to discuss could possibly be of benefit to you.' He tried for the reassuring look.

'It's not timeshare, is it? Only, I don't do foreign holidays. Not since Mavis Twiby had such a terrible experience when she broke her hip in Greece. You take your life in your hands abroad, you know. Being young, you probably don't think it matters, but it does. Especially with all this terrorism.'

'It's not timeshare, Mrs Clewlow. I want to speak to you about one of your ancestors.'

Her head drew back and her eyebrows climbed. 'My ancestors? You're the second person to ask about my ancestors lately. Well, the third, I suppose, really, if you count our Sam.'

Jake felt a spasm in his chest at her words. How could he have been beaten to the draw like this? He was so sure he was ahead of Jane. 'Someone else?' he said. It was an effort to keep his voice level.

'Aye. Our Sam, my great-grandson, that is – he's been doing a project at school about family history. He's a lovely lad, Sam, a credit to his mum and dad. Always got time for his old great-gran as well, not just when he wants to pick my brain about his family tree. Any road, it seems he's done a right good job of it. The headmaster said as much this morning. Rang me up special to talk to me about it. He said I'd been a right good help to Sam and he wanted to thank me personally.'

Jake's brain was racing. 'You mean Matthew Gresham?'

'Aye, that's right. You know Mr Gresham?'

Jake nodded. 'I do. I know his sister Jane better, but I've met Matthew a few times.' What the hell was going on here? Had Jane managed to overcome Matthew's antagonism towards her enough to enlist his help?

Edith's air of suspicion had completely dissipated in the face of such evidence of Jake's bona fides. 'You'd better come in, then. I can't be standing for too long,

I've got chronic back pain, you know. And nothing they give me does a bit of good,' she continued as she ushered him into a bewilderingly cluttered but preternaturally clean living room. Nothing seemed to have been left in its virgin state. A transparent plastic runner covered the carpet on the route from door to armchairs. The armchairs themselves had loose covers underneath antimacassars, arm protectors and throws to shield the loose covers. Photo frames were adorned with the bows florists garnish bouquets with; the very book Edith was reading was encased in a Mylar sleeve. The room had the chemical tang of furniture polish and air freshener. Jake was amazed he hadn't been asked to remove his shoes at the door and put on one of those white suits forensic scientists wear. 'Doctors,' Edith continued as she dropped into the armchair nearest the fireplace. She closed in on herself like a hedgehog. 'What do they know? Give you one set of pills and, before you know it, you can't move your arms because they react with one of the pills you're already on. Blood pressure pills, cholesterol pills, heart tablets. Shake me and I'd rattle. I don't know what I'd do without my family around me. Take a seat, young man, don't be standing there like Piffy.'

Jake perched gingerly on the edge of an armchair. 'Thank you. I appreciate you taking the time to talk to me.'

Edith snorted. 'At my age, time's there to be filled. When I was young, there were never enough hours in the day. Now, breakfast to bedtime can feel like forever. I've got plenty of time to spare for a chat, lad. So, what is it about my ancestors that could interest somebody like you enough to come all the

265

way up to Langmere Stile? Because you're not from around here, are you?'

Jake shook his head. 'I live in London. I'm a specialist in old manuscripts. I used to work at the British Library, but now I work privately as a broker between buyers and sellers.'

Edith looked puzzled. 'I don't understand. What's that got to do with me and my family?'

'It's actually your late husband's family that I'm interested in. Well, one member of his family, to be precise. His great-great-grandmother Dorcas. Did he ever mention her?'

Edith frowned. 'Not that I recall. Surely she'd have been in her grave long before he was born?'

'More than forty years before. But you know how it is with families – sometimes the old stories get passed down the generations.'

Edith rubbed her chin between thumb and forefinger. 'I don't recall any stories from that long ago. And it's not that my memory's going. My body might be falling to bits but I've still got all my chairs at home.' Edith tapped the side of her head to make her point. 'I don't think I ever heard anything further back than his great-uncle Eddie getting a medal in the First World War. Much good it did him; he got himself killed in action at the second battle of Ypres. But Dorcas? I never heard tales about her. The only way I even know her name is that it's in the family Bible. I had to look it all up for our Sam. That's why it's fresh in my mind, like.'

Jake's hopes flickered into life again. If she had a family Bible, she might also have family papers. 'You've got the family Bible?'

'Aye. It's falling to bits now, but it's been in the family since 1747.'

'That's a fascinating thing to have. Are there other family papers too?'

Edith laughed. 'You make us sound like royalty. Folk like us don't have family papers, lad. We could barely read and write back in the old days. Nay, the only thing I've got from David's family is the old Bible. Why would you think we'd have family papers that would interest the likes of you?'

'I wondered if Dorcas had left any papers. A diary, maybe. Or something similar.'

'But why? What makes you think that?' Edith gave an incredulous little laugh. 'What's so special about Dorcas Clewlow?'

Jake spread his hands in an attempt to diminish the significance of his interest. 'It was a long shot. The interesting thing about Dorcas is that before she married Arnold Clewlow she was a maidservant to the Wordsworth family. She was working there in the last years of William Wordsworth's life and stayed on for a while after he died.'

Edith seemed to pull herself more erect. 'William Wordsworth, you say? Well, cover me in feathers and call me a bird of paradise. Who'd have thought it? Fancy me marrying into history and not even knowing it.'

'So you see why I'm interested in anything Dorcas might have left behind. There are plenty of scholars and collectors willing to pay good money for anything connected to Wordsworth. I came across Dorcas's name in some family letters and thought it was worth a try. But I can see I've wasted your time.' Jake made to stand up.

'Nay, you've cost me nowt. But even if I could be more help, I couldn't let something like that go out of the family. I tell you what I'll do, I'll mention it to Frank when he comes in tomorrow morning. He's a fine lad, our Frank. Comes in every morning to make sure I've made it through the night. I'll get him to ask around the family, see if anybody's ever heard anything.'

'That would be helpful.' Jake fished in his wallet for a business card. 'You can reach me on my mobile,' he said. 'I'll call you right back, save on your phone bill.'

'Don't hold your breath,' Edith said, struggling out of her chair. 'They say we've got long memories in these parts. In my experience, that only covers grudges.' She smiled. 'And there's plenty of them round here.'

Jake trudged back to the car, trying not to feel too downcast. On the positive side, it seemed as if Dorcas's past was a secret history as far as her family was concerned. Which meant someone somewhere might have a little treasure trove whose contents had never been thoroughly explored. The more he thought about it, the less he liked the idea of Edith Clewlow spreading the word round the family. He didn't doubt that the younger generation would have more of an eye for the main chance and less concern with keeping things in the family if those things turned out to be a potential goldmine. Talking to them directly would be better than having Edith bend their ears about hanging on to their heirlooms. He wondered about calling her later to suggest she keep his visit to herself. Would it have any effect, or would it just make her suspicious? He kicked out at a clump of grass, angry with himself for not handling Edith more effectively.

As he reached the car, he realised his hangover seemed to be improving. What he needed was some exercise to see it off once and for all. Then he could decide whether to bother any more old biddies today or whether to have another crack at making contact with Jane. He reached into the car for the Ordnance Survey map and spread it out on the roof. Studying his position, he realised that the road had brought him within a mile of Carts Moss. One of the hundreds of footpaths crisscrossing the Lake District crossed the road about quarter of a mile ahead. From there, it was only a mile or so to the moorland where the body in the bog had been found. It would, he thought, be interesting to see the putative last resting place of Fletcher Christian. He grabbed his backpack and set off.

Half an hour later, he was standing on the margins of a strange landscape. On a long plateau of moorland, human hands had joined with the weather to carve the peat hags into curious shapes, tussocks of grass like sprawling islands in a black morass. Puddles of brown water seemed to ooze from the ground and a faint smell of decay hung in the air. It was, Jake thought, a pretty dismal place to meet one's end. How different had it been all those years before when a man had met his death as he walked these hills? He would never know. If the dead man was truly Fletcher Christian, it was a bathetic end to a dramatic life.

The place was depressing Jake, so he struck off up the hill at an angle. Fifteen minutes later, he found himself rounding the broad flank of Langmere Fell, a perfect Lakeland vista opening up before him. To his surprise, he was looking down at Fellhead. And there was the Gresham family farm. Reaching into his backpack, he pulled out his binoculars.

He swept them over the village and, as he reached the lane leading to the farm, he was astonished to see Jane walking up the road. 'Bugger,' he said aloud. 'Missed you again.' He watched as she climbed the hill, her familiar movements tugging at his memory and reminding him of the good times. They'd walked these hills together a couple of times and he'd marvelled at her strength and agility. It shouldn't have come as a surprise after the sexual energy they'd shared, but it had taken him aback to realise she could leave him standing on the fells.

As she turned into the farm gate, another figure swam into his field of observation, sweeping Jane into a hug. Jake was taken aback. He fiddled with the focus wheel, as if that would somehow alter the identity of the person he was looking at. 'What the fuck?'

What was she playing at? Had she rumbled him? Was she indulging in an elaborate charade to piss him about? Jake lowered the binoculars and chewed at the skin round his thumbnail. He had a bad feeling about this. A very bad feeling indeed.

We gave the women gifts and were civil towards them. The five men who boarded with the women were like jackdaws. They tried to steal whatever they could, and I myself thwarted a native in an attempt to steal our compass card. I sent him on his way with stripes from the cat, and his companions followed rapidly. We rejoiced at their departure, but all the while another party had cut away the marker buoy for an anchor. I fired my musket at them and ordered the crew to fire a four-pounder loaded with grapeshot. As they fled, I decided to press home our advantage and we made for shore in our ships' boats. They hurled stones at us; we fired our muskets at them till they fled. We killed eleven without loss on our side. The men christened the anchorage Bloody Bay. And yet, I liked the look of the place and thought it sufficiently out of the way to provide a haven for us. But the murmurings of the crew against Toobouai were such that I decided we should return to Otaheite for some little time.

23

It was a lot harder than it sounded, this hillwalking shit, Tenille thought as she laboured up another steep incline. She reckoned she was pretty fit, but agility and speed didn't count for much on these punishing ascents. And the descents were almost worse. It felt as if someone had injected a red-hot iron rod through the middle of her thighs. She had found a new respect in her heart for Wordsworth, who had tramped miles over these hills as if it was nothing more than a stroll in the park.

Of course, Wordsworth had only had poetry to worry about. He wasn't on the run from the cops, skint and sleep-deprived, scared and stained with travel. Tenille pulled the map out of her pocket again and tried to match the weird lines and blue patches to the landscape she was looking at. The Ordnance Survey map was as unfamiliar to her as the hills and dales around her. She'd bought it at the bus station in Kendal when she'd realised that there wasn't a bus to Fellhead on a Saturday. One of the drivers had told her that the Keswick bus would drop her at the road end, but she'd decided against that. She'd already figured out that black stood out round here like a pig's head in a halal butcher's. People would remember a black kid getting off the bus and, if the cops had figured out where Jane was, somebody might just make the right connection. So she'd bought the map and puzzled over it. It was like trying to solve one of those IQ tests they'd made her do at primary school. What was the difference between a path, a footpath and a bridleway, for Chrissake? And did it matter?

Eventually she worked out that if she got off the bus at Dove Cottage, like all the tourists on the Wordsworth trail, she could take a footpath over Grasmere Common that would bring her out on the right side of Langmere Fell. Then she could cut straight down the hill to Fellhead and safety. She could find somewhere to hide out until she could make for the farm under cover of darkness.

It was, she thought, a good plan. She was mostly just grateful to be away from Lancaster. Thinking about what had happened there sent a shiver through her. She'd thought she was sorted when, after a lot of wandering around, she'd come upon a small park near the city centre. It had been almost midnight when she'd found a bench that was surrounded on three sides by a high hedge, like a little secret bower. Although she was cold and still hungry in spite of the burger, she'd curled into a ball and fallen straight into oblivion.

She wasn't sure what had woken her, but when her startled eyes jerked open, she saw a man silhouetted against the smudge of light from the distant streetlights. He was short and stocky and smelled of drink. Tenille had panicked, pushing herself against the back of the bench, already calculating the chances of escape. Not good, not at this point. 'You working, son?' the man demanded, his northern accent thickened with alcohol.

It took her a moment to process his words; she had forgotten that she had gone to sleep a boy. She knew about such things, of course, but it had never occurred to her that she might be prey to sexual advances in her assumed role. What the hell was she supposed to do now? 'No,' she said, trying to deepen and roughen her voice. 'I was sleeping, all right?'

The man grunted. 'You wouldn't be here if you weren't working. What's wrong? You don't fancy me?' He reached forward and she heard the unmistakable sound of a zip opening. She couldn't see his face, couldn't gauge how serious he was. 'Take a look at this.'

The faint blur of his penis emerged against his jeans. Tenille scrambled back, feet on the seat of the bench, half-crouched and ready to spring when the opportunity presented itself. She could feel the sweat of panic running down her spine, smell its rancid edge. The man thrust his groin towards her. 'Come on, you little prick teaser, all I want's a fucking blow job, I'll pay you, for fuck's sake.' He reached for her head but she dodged him, almost losing her balance.

Then his hand was between her legs, clutching tightly through the fabric of her trousers. Suddenly he let go and leapt backwards. 'You little fucker,' he shouted. 'You're a fucking bitch. You trying to make an arse out of me or what?'

He was zipping himself up now, her chance to get away. As she powered off the bench and tried to pass him, he threw a punch at her. It caught her a glancing blow on the shoulder, but it wasn't enough to stop her. She raced into the dark, a harsh sob escaping from her throat as she dived into the tangled branches of a clump of rhododendrons. She fought her way to the heart of the thicket and curled into a ball, pulse racing and breath ragged, tears pricking her eyes. Calm was a long time in returning, but eventually she managed to doze off again.

Her rest had been broken and shallow. Every night sound was enough to penetrate her sleep and most were sufficient to rouse her. By the time light began to creep into the sky, Tenille had been more than ready to shake the dust of Lancaster off her feet. An early bus had brought her to Kendal then to the local service which had brought her to the revelation that was the Lake District. She'd seen Jane's photographs, she'd read about it in poems and books, but nothing had prepared her for this. She'd always felt some degree of doubt that a landscape could stir the deepest emotions. Tenille had seldom been outside London, and then only to seaside resorts like Southend and Clacton. Her own limited experience had provided her eyes and heart with nothing inspirational to inhabit. But as beauty unrolled before her, mile after mile, she began to have a glimmer of understanding of the passion that could come simply from being alive in a place like this. She found herself growing eager to leave the confines of the bus, to strike out into the countryside and take it into herself. It was enough to make her forget how tired, hungry and dirty she was.

But now, a couple of hours later, the first exhilaration of beauty was past and she was feeling the miles in her legs. She found a flat rock and sat down to rest, marvelling yet again at how empty this place was. Grasmere had been busy with tourists, but once she was about ten minutes' walk from the village, it was as if she'd left humanity behind. Tenille had never had so much space to herself. She'd only passed two other people on their way down. They'd been upon her before she had time to take evasive action and she'd been astonished when they'd smiled at her and said, 'Grand day for it, isn't it?'

She'd ducked her head in reply, unsure what the deal was in situations like this. How was she supposed to respond? If she spoke, would they take that as an invitation to conversation? But they were already past her, boots crunching on the loose stones at the edge of the path. Now, she was alone again, apart from the odd bird circling overhead. Tenille studied the map and tried to figure out where she was. Gradually, she began to make correlations between the representation and the reality. There was a small rise ahead of her. Once she breasted that, she should be able to see Fellhead below her.

She stuffed the map back into her backpack. She was hot now and wished she had had enough money left to buy some water and something to eat. But she was down to her last few quid and she hadn't wanted to spend it. She'd passed a stream earlier and had thought about drinking from it, but she'd been scared it wouldn't be clean. There could be a dead sheep further upstream for all she knew. There was a reason why they put chemicals in the water before they let you drink it.

Wearily, Tenille got to her feet and set off to

scramble up the short incline that would bring her a view of Fellhead and Jane's home. As she rounded a rocky outcropping at the summit, she saw a figure standing on the path a short distance below her. He had binoculars to his eyes and he was staring down into the valley. She stopped, reluctant to draw attention to herself.

The man took the binoculars away from his eyes and Tenille gasped. She wasn't the only person who had followed Jane back to the Lake District. But what the hell was Jake doing, spying on his ex-girlfriend?

Jane strode up the hill, fizzing with a mixture of anger and delight. Diane had of course sprung to Matthew's defence. His class assignment had been under way well before Jane had arrived back home. There was no reason why he should remember one name out of hundreds that featured in the family tree project. Obviously, Matthew had separated out those two cases in particular because they had a common ancestor. If he'd intended to keep this information from her, why would he have left the papers lying on the table for anyone to see? Jane was paranoid. Matthew would never deliberately try to scupper her research and it was horrible of Jane to suggest that he was planning to usurp her work. How could she even think her own brother would go behind her back and try to discover the missing manuscript for himself?

In one sense, Diane was right. It should be unthinkable. But where Matthew was concerned, Jane found it all too easy to imagine her brother hugging his knowledge to himself then taking advantage of it to conduct his own search. If he wasn't planning a double-cross, why keep the knowledge about Dorcas Mason to himself?

Jane had tried not to vent her fury on Diane, but it had seeped out round the edges. The Pimms had failed to materialise and Jane had insisted on copying the relevant family trees before she left. It was true that the children had concentrated on their direct lines of descent. But with the material she had gleaned from Matthew's pupils' efforts, she could go back to Barbara Field and see whether they could trace all Dorcas's extant descendants. Then she could start the slow process of interviewing them to see what she could discover.

Even this positive thought wasn't enough to restore Jane's even temper. But the sight that greeted her when she turned into the farmyard put Matthew's duplicity out of her mind for the time being. Sitting on the bench that stood against the farmhouse wall, head back and basking in the sunshine, was the last person she expected to see. She stopped in her tracks.

'Dan! What on earth are you doing here?' Jane said.

Dan straightened up and grinned. 'Two heads are better than one, even when they're butting against a brick wall,' he said. 'I thought we could brainstorm together, see if we could figure out a plan of action since I've let you down.' He got to his feet and they met in the middle of the yard, arms round each other in a warm hug. Jane suddenly felt restored. Maybe her brother was a useless waste of space, but she had friends who loved her enough to put themselves out for her.

'So where's the car?' Jane asked.

'I left it down at the village pub. I didn't want to presume on your parents' hospitality so I booked in there.'

'Idiot. Of course you're staying here. We'll unbook you as soon as we've had lunch.' They walked to the farmhouse, Dan's arm over Jane's shoulders. 'You didn't let me down, you know. I'm just grateful you tried. I am so pleased to see you,' she said. 'Especially right now. You're never going to believe what I just found.'

Dan's eyes widened, his handsome face sharpened with shock. 'Not the manuscript?'

Jane snorted scornfully. 'No such luck. No, I found out why you didn't have any luck with Family Records.'

'What do you mean?'

She stopped in mid-stride and produced her copies of Sam and Jonathan's family trees. 'Because somebody couldn't spell.' She pointed to the line on the family tree. 'Mayson, not Mason.'

Dan looked astonished. 'But that's fantastic, Jane. How did you find that out?'

Briefly, she outlined Matthew's treachery.

'I can't believe it,' he said, his face tight with anger, sharp lines cutting either side of his mouth.

'Believe it. But I've got what I need. It'll be easy to fill in any blanks now.'

Dan spread his arms wide then pulled her into a hug. 'Perfect timing, as it turns out. Now I'm here, we can start doing the interviews together.'

'Can you stick around?' Then Jane frowned. 'But isn't this your weekend for the hospice?'

Dan raised an eyebrow. 'Fancy you remembering that. Yes, I should be there, reading to the dying. But I thought the living were more important. I got Seb to cover for me. He owed me a weekend anyway. So everything worked out perfectly.'

'Except that Harry's not here,' Jane said, pushing open the farmhouse door.

Dan gave her his naughty little boy look, head down, eyes looking up from under his brows. 'I didn't actually tell Harry I was coming. He thinks you're chasing rainbows and, frankly, I could do without being scathed this week. Anyway, he's gone off to Yorkshire for some war game. They're re-enacting the battle of Marston Moor. Again.' He rolled his eyes. 'Who knows, maybe it'll come out different this time.'

'Honestly, Dan, you love a good conspiracy, don't you?' Jane led the way into the kitchen, where Judy was trying to make sense of a pile of invoices at the table. 'Mum, this is my friend Dan.'

'We've already introduced ourselves,' Judy said. She pushed the papers together and stood up. 'Come and sit down, Dan. I was just waiting for Jane to get back to dish up the dinner.' Over her shoulder, she said to Jane, 'Your dad's gone over to Borrowdale to look at a ram. He wants some new blood in the herd. So it's just the three of us.' She took a pie from the oven and put it on the table, followed by a dish of roast potatoes and another of mashed swede.

'Wow,' Dan said. 'Do you eat this well at every meal?'

'Yup,' Jane said, serving up the pie to Dan and herself. 'My mother tries to bribe me to stay by feeding me up.'

Dan tasted the steak pie. 'Oh God, Mrs Gresham, this is heaven on a plate.'

'Thank you, Dan, it's always a pleasure to have a guest who appreciates his food. You'll be stopping, I take it?' Judy smiled encouragingly.

Dan nodded, chewing frantically before he spoke. 'If that's all right. I was going to go back tomorrow, but now . . . well, I can stick around for a few days to help Jane.'

'We've got interviews to do.' Jane smiled grimly. 'I've managed to make some progress where I least expected to. It turns out Matthew knew all along where to find Dorcas Mason's descendants. He just didn't bother telling me. Diane asked me to get something from the dining room, and there it was, sitting on the dining table. Two substantial chunks of Dorcas Mason's family tree. Courtesy of Matthew's class who are doing a project on genealogy,' she said, her voice clipped to a sharp edge.

'What wonderful luck, love,' her mother said, the warmth of her voice belying the anxiety in her eyes. 'And how nice of Matthew to sort them out to show you.'

Jane sighed deeply. 'Whatever,' she said. 'But I need to go and see Bossy Barbara again. What I've got isn't complete and I think she'll be able to help me fill in the gaps. I'll give her a ring after lunch and see when she's free.'

'Be still, my beating heart,' Dan said.

'I'm so glad you're here,' Jane said. 'At least now I get the chance to show you some of the countryside. We can go up on the fell and I'll show you my dad's sheep.'

Dan looked down at his designer trainers. 'Whoopee. I can hardly wait.'

'You can borrow a pair of wellies. You'll love it,' Jane said.

'And then can we go and look at Dove Cottage?'

Jane nodded happily. 'Yes, we can. And if you're a very good boy, I'll introduce you to Anthony Catto, the greatest living expert on Wordsworth.'

Dan pretended to look afraid. 'Great. Now I can be exposed for the literary fraud I am.'

Jane laughed. 'Don't worry, he won't eat you. I promise you, Dan, you're going to have a visit you won't forget in a hurry.'

We made landfall in Matavai Bay on Otaheite on 6th June. I was apprehensive about our reception but necessity lends us the abilities we need to survive. I discovered to my surprise that I could lie with such conviction that I would be believed by the natives. I recalled that Bligh had convinced the natives that Captain Cook was still alive & sailing the Pacific yet so I told Chief Teina that I was there under orders from Cook himself to acquire the necessities for founding a new settlement which Bligh had gone ahead with Cook to make a start on. We acquired from the natives 312 pigs, 38 goats, 8 dozen fowls, a bull & a cow. In addition, nine native women elected to join our party, including my own Isabella. Also, eight men & ten boys. Thus we set sail again for Toobouai, where we arrived on 26th June. This time, to my surprise we found an apparent welcome.

24

'Stop the car, I'm going to be sick.' There was no arguing with the urgency in Dan's voice. Jane pulled on to the narrow grass verge, hitting the hazard lights as the car drew to a halt. Even before she had completely stopped, Dan had the passenger door open and he was stumbling out of the car. Almost immediately Jane heard him retch and cough. She leaned across the passenger seat and, by the dim light of the car's interior lamp, she could see him bent double and heaving.

'Are you OK?' she asked, realising as she said it how fatuous a question it was.

'Oh God,' he panted, staggering upright and leaning against the car. 'I thought one of those mussels tasted funny.'

'God, Dan, I'm so sorry.'

'Not your fault,' he groaned, falling back into his seat. 'Can't blame you if the fucking chef can't tell when his seafood's off.'

She handed him her water bottle. 'Have a drink.'

Dan took a couple of sips and shuddered. 'Sorry.' He wiped his face with the back of his hand. 'Christ, I feel like shit.'

'You need to go to bed. I'll drop you back at the farm then I'll go and see Barbara by myself.'

'But I want to hear what she has to say,' he protested feebly.

'You'll hear all about it in the morning. Trust me, you don't want to be in Barbara's house if you've got an upset stomach. It's a shrine to air freshener. I swear the only time she gets aroused is when she sees an advert for a new product. "Make your home smell forest fresh with a battery-operated fan-assisted air-purifying gel," and she's slavering. One breath in there and you'll be heaving. No, best if you take care of yourself. It'll be nice and quiet – Mum and Dad have gone out to a silver wedding do in Grasmere, they won't be back till late.'

'No, I don't want to go back to the farm. Take me to the pub, I'll stay there instead. They'll have an *en suite* room. I don't want to be disturbing everybody, getting up in the night to be sick or whatever. And I don't want to feel self-conscious and embarrassed. Take me to the pub, Jane.'

'Don't be daft, Dan. You don't want to be staying at the pub. It's too noisy, you'd get no peace. It'll be fine, nobody's going to make you feel embarrassed about being ill.'

His face crumpled. 'It's not about you or your parents. It's me. I just feel self-conscious, I'd rather be in the pub.'

'No. You're not going there.' Jane was adamant, her face firmly set. 'I've got a better idea. We've got a holiday let up the hill. It's empty just now. You can stay there. You'll have all the peace and quiet you need and you can make as much noise as you want.

I don't think the sheep will mind. And your bag's in the boot already from when we picked it up after lunch.'

'OK, I haven't got the strength to argue,' Dan said weakly, pulling the door closed and winding the window down. 'Promise me you'll drive slowly.'

Jane set off at little-old-lady speed, driving through Fellhead and up the lane past the farm, trying to ignore Dan's groans. Half a mile further up the Langmere Fell, she pulled into a narrow driveway. 'This is it,' she said.

Dan followed her into a squat stone building whose single storey was divided into a bedroom, living room, kitchen and bathroom. He made straight for the bathroom while Jane turned on the heating, made up the bed and unlocked the small cupboard where Judy kept a stock of teabags, coffee sachets, sugar and toilet rolls. She knocked on the bathroom door when she was done. 'I'll see you in the morning,' she said.

'Thanks,' Dan groaned. 'I'm sorry.'

It was a fine evening so Jane dropped the car off at the farm and walked back down to Fellhead. Barbara was waiting for her, whisking her straight through to the nerve centre of her genealogy project. 'No wonder we couldn't find her if she got married in Yorkshire,' she said, making it sound as if Dorcas had moved to Tahiti. 'Not to mention the incorrect spelling. But with this much to go on, it should be a piece of Black Forest gateau. Now, let's get started.'

It was almost ten when Jane emerged, clutching a sheaf of computer print-outs. A skein of low cloud had obscured the moon while she'd been with Barbara, turning the night gloomy. A stranger would have struggled to negotiate the lane up to the farm, but sure-footed in the darkness Jane made her way along the familiar route without a second thought.

Thanks to Barbara, she now had a full family tree for Dorcas. Perhaps in the morning she could go through it with Dan, assessing which of the surviving family members was most likely to have the manuscript. It would be helpful to have another pair of eyes on the closely printed material. And, selfishly, she was glad to have someone around to occupy her. Since Dan had arrived, she realised, she hadn't thought once about Geno Marley's murder.

Rigston's dream incorporated the strains of Jan Hammer's 'Crockett's Theme'. It took a few seconds for him to realise the sound was real, that his mobile was ringing. He struggled up from sleep, reaching for the phone on the bedside table. 'Sorry,' he mumbled, rubbing his eyes with his other hand. 'DI Rigston,' he said. There was a pause, during which he pushed himself upright. 'Why me? Can't this wait till the morning?' he sighed. 'OK, let me get a pen.' He swung his legs over the edge of the bed and walked naked to his leather jacket. He wrestled a pen and notebook from the inside pocket and sat down on the end of the bed. 'OK, let me have the details . . . How are you spelling that? OK . . . Uh huh, I'll call DI Blair . . . Right . . . Fellhead? It's going to take me a good hour to get over there. OK, tell the Super I'm on my way.' He ended the call and made a rueful face at River.

'I'm really sorry, love. I've got to go out.'

She squirmed down the bed and stroked his back.

'Don't worry, I get it. In your job, there's no such thing as off duty.'

He shivered at her touch then dialled the number the duty officer had given him. 'DI Blair?' he said when the call was answered. 'This is DI Rigston in Keswick.'

'You're going to check on Jane Gresham for me, is that right?' The woman sounded harassed.

'Happy to oblige. I'm presuming there's no reason to suppose this . . .' Rigston checked his notes '. . . Tenille Cole is going to cut up rough?'

'Your guess is as good as mine. She's got no form, but she's got connections.'

'Connections?'

'Her dad runs the Marshpool – one of our charm schools for criminals. He's a hard man. A serious villain. Word is she doesn't have direct dealings with him, but given that she's wanted for blowing a man away with a sawn-off shotgun then firing the flat to cover her tracks, I'd say the word is well off the mark.'

Rigston felt a chill that was nothing to do with the temperature in his bedroom. 'You think there's any chance she'll be tooled up now?'

'No. I think she panicked and ran. I don't think she'd be headed for Jane Gresham if she had the security of a gun.'

'And you don't think her dad's up here keeping an eye out for her?'

Donna Blair laughed. 'Not his style.'

Rigston felt uneasy, but he was prepared to take the word of someone whose sharp end was a lot more jagged than his. 'OK. I'm going out there now.

I'll keep you posted.' He ended the call and turned to River. 'I'll be back as soon as I can.'

'"Tooled up?" Did I hear right?' River said, her grey eyes troubled.

'Apparently not,' Rigston said. He pulled a rugby shirt over his head. 'Let's hope the Met got this one right, eh?'

The cloud was his friend, reducing both visibility and the desire to stand around enjoying the night sky. He'd only seen a few people coming and going from the pub in the past hour and he was damn sure they hadn't even noticed his car, never mind that there was a driver at the wheel. He'd been prepared to move out if he'd been spotted. Risks were for fools and he was no fool. Besides, there would be other opportunities to deal with the obstacle she'd become. Unsuspecting victims were the easiest to pick off; he knew that from experience. But he'd been lucky. Nobody had seen him, least of all the one person he was interested in.

She'd come walking out of the house without a sideways glance, as if she had too much on her mind to pay attention to anything outside herself. He'd waited for her to enter the lane before he'd started the engine, giving her a full minute's head start, steeling himself for what he had planned. He crept slowly down the village street from his vantage point, then turned into the lane.

The full beam of the headlights picked her out, a black silhouette against the hedgerow. He took a deep breath and dropped down into second. The engine screaming, he slammed his foot hard on the accelerator and aimed for Jane.

*   *   *

289

The roads were quiet. By nine on a Saturday in the Lakes, most people were either home in front of the telly or ensconced where they planned to spend the rest of the evening. As Rigston drove he picked over his grievance at being dragged from his bed. Other people's villains. The last thing he needed. At least the female DI from the Met had had the decency to warn him there was media interest in this one.

He couldn't help thinking about his own daughter. Not so far off the age of this murder suspect. He wanted to believe that sort of thing couldn't happen on his patch but he knew it wasn't true. He thought of Dewsbury. Quiet little town in the middle of West Yorkshire. A place where nothing much ever happened. Yet within the space of a couple of months, the cops in Dewsbury had to deal with a teenage girl abducting a five-year-old and hanging him from a bloody tree, and a suicide bomber blowing up a tube train in London. Used to be that sort of thing only happened in big cities with a seething underclass. But he knew the poison was spreading and he feared for his own child.

And this particular teenager wasn't without resources. A gangster father in the shadows wasn't a negligible consideration. In a world made small by motorways and electronic communication, crime wasn't a prisoner of its own patch any longer. A man could be eating dinner in London while the hit he'd ordered on his mobile was taking place in Manchester. Or, Rigston supposed, in the Lakes. It wasn't a comforting thought.

Rigston swung the wheel round and turned into

the lane leading to the Greshams' farm. He saw a distant set of tail-lights disappear up ahead, then he braked suddenly as he saw a body sprawled by the side of the road.

Rigston pulled up and jumped out of his 4x4, calling out, 'I'm a police officer. Are you all right?' Nothing. Not a sound, not a movement. Rigston hurried forward, slicing the body into segments of dark and light as he passed in front of the headlamps.

As he crouched down to examine it, the body pushed itself up on one elbow. A young woman looked up at him, mud smeared down one side of her face. Her eyes were wide with shock, her hair tangled with leaves. 'Were you chasing that mad bastard?' she gasped.

'No, all I saw were some tail-lights. What happened?' He reached out a hand to steady the woman as she got to her feet.

'A car. Coming up the hill way too fast.' She shook her head, as if to clear it. 'And then . . .' She frowned, looking incredulous. 'I know this sounds crazy, but it was like he steered straight at me. I had to dive into the hedge.' She rubbed her shoulder. 'I think there's a bit of wall in there too.'

'Probably a drunk,' Rigston said. 'Did you get a look at the car? Make? Registration?'

'No. I was dazzled by his headlights. And then I was in the hedge.' She brushed herself down.

'With no ID, there's not much point in me calling it in,' Rigston said with a sharp exhalation of irritation.

'At least I'm still in one piece.'

'Have you far to go?'

'No.' The woman gestured to her left. 'I live in the farm just ahead.'

Rigston frowned. 'Are you Jane Gresham?'

She took a step away from him. 'How do you know my name?'

'A lucky guess. I was on my way to see you, Ms Gresham. Why don't you hop in for the last few yards?'

She folded her arms across her chest in a defensive gesture. 'You'll excuse me, but how do I know you're who you say you are?' She looked as if she was barely holding herself together.

'You're wise to be cautious.' Rigston took out his photo ID and held it low in the beam of his headlights so she could see it clearly. 'I hoped we might have a word?'

'It's gone ten o'clock,' Jane said. 'Won't this wait till morning? I mean, I was nearly run over a minute ago.'

'I'm afraid not, it's a serious matter.' Interesting, he thought, that she didn't immediately ask what it was about. And that she wanted to procrastinate.

A few minutes later, he followed Jane into a cosy farm kitchen. In the light, he could see she was attractive in a dark, strong-featured way. It was a face you wouldn't forget in a hurry, with its deep-set eyes, firm mouth and a nose that was definite without being too big. She threw her filthy jacket over a chair and went to the sink, rubbing her fingers through her hair to dislodge leaves and twigs. 'Give me a minute,' she said, running the taps and washing her face and hands. Then she leaned against the Aga, her arms folded over her chest, her face pale. 'Is this about Tenille?'

'Now why would you think that?'

'We do get TV up here, Chief Inspector. I saw the appeal for anyone who'd seen Tenille to come forward.

And I can't think of any other reason why a senior police officer would be demanding to talk to me at this time on a Saturday night.' She glared at him.

'Have you seen Tenille Cole since Wednesday evening?'

Jane shook her head. 'I came up here on Wednesday. So no, I haven't seen her.'

'Have you heard from her? An email, perhaps? A text, a phone call?'

'I'm sorry to disappoint you. No, I've heard nothing at all from Tenille. Which is not surprising, I don't think she's ever emailed me or texted me or phoned me as long as I've known her. You can check my laptop if you don't believe me.'

'I don't think that'll be necessary at this point. How does she usually make contact?' Rigston asked.

'She turns up on my doorstep.'

'How would you characterise your relationship with Tenille Cole?'

'I suppose I'd call myself her mentor. And her friend.'

'Her mentor? In what sense?'

Jane sighed. 'I know it's hard for people like you to believe this about a black teenager, but Tenille loves poetry. She doesn't just love it, she grasps what it's about. She has an understanding of the Romantic poets that would shame most English students. That happens to be my subject area. So mostly she hangs out at my flat and reads poetry and literary criticism, and sometimes we talk about what she's been reading.'

'You talk about poetry?'

'And criticism.' Jane's smile was condescending. Ewan thought it was a deliberate attempt to rile him.

'And you don't think that's odd?'

'It's very odd. But that's the way it is. Nothing unhealthy. Nothing depraved. Nothing criminal.'

Rigston shook his head, baffled. 'You talk about her personal life?'

'Very little. She comes to my flat to get away from the rest of her life. She tries to leave it at the door.'

'So you don't know why she might have shot . . .' Rigston glanced at his notes. 'Geno Marley?'

'Tenille did not shoot Geno Marley,' Jane said with a familiar degree of conviction that depressed Rigston. He had seen too many people make that tragic mistake.

'How do you know that?' he asked mildly.

'Because it's not who she is. She doesn't run with the wannabe gangstas and the aspiring baby mothers. She despises that life.'

'According to what I've been told, her father's right at the heart of that life.'

Jane shook her head impatiently. 'Tenille doesn't have a father. At least, not one she's aware of. She's been brought up by her aunt. Her mother's dead. She's never had a dad in her life.'

'So the name John Hampton doesn't mean anything to you?'

'Of course it does. I live on the Marshpool.'

'Were you aware that he's Tenille's father?'

'I've heard gossip to that effect. But I've never seen him so much as acknowledge her in passing.' Jane looked away, her expression sad. 'Tenille says she doesn't have a father. I'm inclined to take her word for it.'

Rigston switched tack, hoping to catch Jane on the back foot. 'Is she here, Ms Gresham?'

Jane looked up, shocked. 'Of course not. She wouldn't have the faintest idea how to find this place.'

'Then you won't mind if I take a look around?'

Jane looked baffled and angry. 'You people,' she said bitterly. 'If I say no, you'll think I have something to hide. If I say yes, I'll feel insulted and invaded.' Her head came up and she looked Rigston straight in the eye. 'Fine. Look all you want.' It was a direct gaze that told Rigston he was wasting his time. Still, it didn't do to be seen to back down.

'Thank you,' he said.

She shrugged. 'You're only doing your job. I've got nothing to hide.'

I had dreamed of Toobouai as our new Eden, a small paradise for those of us who had weathered the worst of storms. I took advantage of the apparent new-found friendliness of the natives & negotiated land for a fort with the natives & relations were good at first. But factions grew within the crew. There were not enough Otaheitian women to go around & the native women would only be taken by force, which practice I could not approve. Some of the men wished to return to Otaheite, others simply to flout my authority because they thought they were their own masters now, not understanding the need for leadership to provide unity of purpose until a colony could be properly established. In the end, I decided we should go back to Otaheite to allow those who wished to disembark. But while we were yet making our preparations to leave, it came to all out war with the Toobouaian natives & it became clear to me that we could never return there as settlers. I was bitterly disappointed & could not but see this failure as my responsibility.

25

Tenille shivered in the sharp gust of wind that swirled into the gap in the rock formation where she had taken shelter late in the afternoon. After she'd seen Jake on the hillside, she'd scrambled up the fell away from the path, scrunching down among the brown fronds of bracken till he had finally walked out of sight. Damp and cold, she'd headed cautiously in his wake and stood where he'd been standing.

There was one farm in his line of sight, and she reasoned that it must be Jane's home. Who else would he be spying on, after all? She supposed she ought to be grateful to him. She'd been uncertain how she was going to find it. She didn't want to break cover and ask anyone for directions. And although she was pretty sure she would recognise the place from Jane's photographs, she wasn't sure how many farms would be scattered around Fellhead.

Once she'd spotted the farm, the next problem was how to get to it. She frowned at the map. The obvious way was to carry on along the path till she came to the road that led down into Fellhead. Then she would have to walk through the village and up the lane to the Greshams' farm. If she was going to do that safely, she'd need to wait for darkness to fall and she'd have no way of knowing who was in the farmhouse. Making contact with Jane without anyone else knowing would be difficult.

The alternative was to strike out over open country, cutting down the hill at an angle that would bring her out above the farm. She could see a rocky outcropping that might give her enough cover to keep watch and wait till she could be sure of getting Jane on her own. Unappetising though her route looked from here, it was the only sensible option.

She'd set off down the slope, realising within minutes that this was a lot harder than walking the paths. The ground was uneven, tussocks of coarse cottongrass and heather threatening her ankles. Every now and then she would step unwittingly into boggy peat that threatened to pull the shoes from her feet. It was slow going, and the afternoon had worn away by the time she reached the rocks she'd set as her target. To her relief, there was a narrow cleft in the outcropping on the side facing the farm and she squeezed into it. The ground was fairly dry, being protected by an overhang, so she sat down with a deep sigh of relief. She couldn't remember ever having been so tired. All that kept her awake were the sharp pangs of hunger that made her stomach grumble.

Tenille was surprised by the sprawl of the farm and its outbuildings. When she thought of farms, she thought of thatched cottages surrounded by fields, maybe with an occasional charming stone barn thrown in. But here, three sides of the farmyard were flanked by buildings. The farmhouse itself was a sturdy two-storey building that took up most of the width of the side facing the gate. The two longer sides were occupied by an assortment of outbuildings, ranging from a long low shed with metal panelled walls and a corrugated plastic roof to a variety of squat stone buildings. She had no idea what they were all used for.

The first sign of life was the arrival of a Land Rover which pulled over to one side of the yard. A man got out of the driver's seat, followed by two black-and-white dogs. The dogs disappeared into a wooden hut near the big shed and the man went into the house. Half an hour later, he came back out again, loaded a couple of hay bales into the Land Rover and drove off with the dogs. He returned twenty minutes later.

Just before seven, a dark green 4x4 pulled into the yard. A man and woman came out of the house and got into the back seat before it drove off again. Jane's parents, she assumed. But still no sign of Jane herself. Tenille was starting to fret. What if Jane wasn't here? What if she was off with her mates, having a night out and staying over? What if she'd had to go somewhere else for her research project? Tenille didn't know what to do. She felt faint with hunger and her mouth was so dry she didn't think she'd be able to speak.

A little after eight, the yard lights came on to reveal a red Fiesta driving into the yard. Tenille jumped to her feet with delight when she saw Jane emerge from the driver's seat. But instead of making for the house, Jane walked back out of the gate, turning down the hill towards Fellhead.

Dejected, Tenille slumped against the rock. She

blinked back tears. She'd come so far in every sense, but she had practically exhausted her reserves. She knew there was no way she could endure a night on the fell in the open. She made a deal with herself. If Jane wasn't home by midnight, she'd creep down to the farm and find somewhere she could sleep. How hard could that be?

Time dragged by. Tenille found things to be amazed by: the quiet that fell like a blanket with the dark; the carpet of stars entirely alien to one brought up in the light pollution of London; the way the air changed its smell as it grew more chill; but most of all that she didn't find all this strangeness scary. How did Jane endure the noise and the stink and the perpetual neon of London when she'd grown up with this?

Just after ten, a different 4x4 drove in. And hallelujah, there was Jane. The man driving it got out and followed Jane into the house. Minutes went by, then lights started going on and off all over the house. What the fuck was going on?

After darkness had returned to the house except for one window, the door opened and the man came out again. He went from building to building, entering each one then finally returning to the house. Tenille had enough street smarts to understand exactly what was going on. The man might be alone and without a uniform, but she knew a police search when she saw one. She folded her arms across her chest, hugging her shoulders. They knew about Jane. She'd known deep down they'd get there eventually, but part of her had wanted to believe Jane would be her safe haven.

What was worse was that Jane knew about her.

Well, she knew the police version. Tenille had no expectation of a fair crack of the whip from the cops. She didn't know if there was any evidence against her, but whether there was or not, she was connected to the flat and she would be high on any suspect list. They might pretend they only wanted her as a witness, but she knew it would be more, much more than that. And if they got their claws into her, she was fucked. She couldn't grass up her dad, no way. Not because she was afraid of him, but because he had proved that he was her dad in the sense that counted. He had protected her; she would do the same for him because nobody else in her whole life had ever done that for her.

Except for Jane, of course. But much as Tenille loved and respected Jane, she knew they were different breeds. Not because of the colour of their skin but because the lives they'd led had brought them to diverse understandings of the way the world worked. Jane truly hadn't known when she'd gone to the Hammer how it would end. Tenille had known there would be violence, though. Extreme violence. And she'd done nothing to stop it. So although it was Jane who'd sown the seed of Geno's destruction, it was Tenille who could have stopped it. And she knew her friend well enough to know that Jane would nevertheless take the burden of guilt on herself.

So she owed Jane too. She had to protect Jane just like she had to protect her dad. And that meant not falling into the hands of the cops. Just as well she hadn't already gone down to the farm to find a hiding place for the night.

After what felt like a long time, the man returned

to the farmhouse. A few minutes later, he re-emerged, got into the 4x4 and drove off towards Fellhead. Tenille watched the swathe of light from his headlamps as he turned right at the junction and headed down towards the main road. He was really gone.

That left Jane.

It took much longer than Tenille had expected to get down to the farm. Nothing in her past had trained her for negotiating treacherous terrain in the dark. Tenille lost her footing several times, twice ending up flat on her back. By the time she made it to the corner of the farmhouse, her trousers were soaked and there was a long streak of black mud down one sleeve. She stuck her head round the corner of the building, trying to make out the sensor for the yard lights. She eventually spotted it, set to one side of the door. This was the kind of thing she did know about. She reckoned that if she stayed hard against the wall, she would clear the inside edge of the arc covered by the sensor. There was only one way to find out.

Tenille crept round the corner, face to the wall. She inched along, past a pair of darkened windows, past the door, to the edge of the uncurtained window that cast an oblong of yellow light on the pitted concrete of the yard. She risked a quick peek. It was the kitchen. One of those cooking ranges that they had in posh houses on the telly, the end of a kitchen table. But no sign of Jane.

She ducked under the window and straightened up at the far end. This time, her swift glance was rewarded. Jane sat at the dining table, a sheaf of papers in front of her and a glass of wine to hand. There was no sign of anyone else in the room. Tenille took a deep breath and stepped in front of the window. She tapped hard on the glass.

Jane's head shot up and she stared at the window. Tenille moved right up to the glass. Jane's mouth widened in shock and she leapt to her feet, almost knocking over her chair in her haste. She disappeared through the kitchen door. Moments later, the outside door opened. As she stepped out, the yard lights sizzled into life. Tenille stood awkwardly, head cocked to one side, unsure of her reception.

'Tenille?' Jane sounded wary. 'Is that you?'

Tenille pulled the baseball cap from her head. 'Yeah. I had to cut my hair.' Of all the ways to start the conversation that she'd been rehearsing all day, that hadn't even featured in the long list.

'What the hell are you doing here? The police are looking for you.'

Tenille felt her bottom lip trembling. She'd been holding herself together for so long and now she just couldn't do it any longer. Tears sprang from her eyes. 'Can I come in? I'm freezing,' she said piteously, her whole body shivering.

'Of course, come on. Look at you, you're soaking.' Jane hugged Tenille to her then hustled her into the kitchen. 'Wait there, I'll get you some dry trousers.' She returned a few minutes later with a pair of fleecy sweatpants. 'Get these on. Stand over by the Aga where it's warm.'

Tenille was too exhausted to do anything other than what she was told. The heat from the Aga felt blissful. She pulled off wet trainers and changed her trousers. Meanwhile, Jane had taken a brick of home-made soup from the freezer and was zapping it in the microwave. She kept glancing at Tenille as if she had a million questions, but she said nothing.

'I legged it,' Tenille said once her teeth had stopped chattering.

'So I gathered,' Jane said, busying herself getting a bowl and spoon on the table. 'I had the local police round here earlier.'

'I know, I was watching.'

Jane raised her eyebrows. 'The cops in London sent them. But I already knew about Geno from the news. Come on, sit down and eat this soup. Then we can talk properly. My parents won't be back for an hour or so.'

The first bowl of soup barely touched the sides. As Jane ladled out a second helping, Tenille said, 'Got any bread?'

Jane fetched a couple of rolls and some butter and watched while they disappeared at record speed. 'You were ready for that,' she said when Tenille finished.

'I haven't eaten since last night. And I did a lot of walking today. I made it over the hills from Grasmere and I didn't get lost once. I tell you, you need a map up there. I nearly got all turned around a couple of times before I figured out which hill was which. Like, I dunno how Wordsworth and them managed all that walking around without maps.' She wiped her mouth with the back of her hand. 'That was great. Thanks, Jane.'

'You're welcome. But you have to tell me what's been going on.'

Tenille hunched her thin shoulders and sighed. 'My dad blew Geno away. I found him lying dead in the flat. I wasn't, like, thinking straight, I just wanted to make sure he didn't get caught for it so I set fire to the flat. I tried to hide out in your flat, but the cops came calling and I knew it was only a matter of time before they found me there so I did one.' Her mouth twitched in a grimace. 'I didn't have anybody else to go to. So I came here.' She gave a quick up and under look. 'You're not, like, angry with me, are you?'

'I'm not angry, no. I'm concerned. Like I said, the police were round here earlier –'

'Did you tell them about going to my dad?' Tenille interrupted.

Jane shook her head. 'No. I wanted to wait till I'd had the chance to talk to you. But they are seriously looking for you. They searched the place and they asked for the key to my flat so they can get in and look for you there. I told them there was no point, but they wouldn't take no for an answer. You're going to have to give yourself up, Tenille. This is not just going to go away.'

Tenille glowered defiance at Jane. 'Sure it'll go away. It's just a black waster that's been killed. A week or two goes by and nobody will give a shit.'

'Maybe not in the normal way of things. But it's not like you can stay on the run forever. You're thirteen, not twenty-three. And as soon as you resurface, they're going to be coming for you.' Jane sounded exasperated.

'I know that,' Tenille said, all sulky teenager. 'But maybe they'll get another suspect. Take the heat off me, then I can come back.'

'That's not going to happen while they're concentrating on finding you. Tenille, you're going to have to tell them the truth. Actually, we're both going to have to tell them the truth. You have to tell them about Geno and I have to tell them about going to your dad.'

'They won't believe us,' Tenille said dully.

'Why wouldn't they? Your dad makes a far more credible suspect than you. He's got a reputation and, I presume, a record to match.'

'Yeah, but I think I left my fingerprints on the gun.'

Jane looked at her in horror. 'You *think* you left your fingerprints on the gun? How the fuck did that happen?'

Defensive, Tenille said, 'I picked it up, all right? And I didn't wipe it off afterwards. I forgot. I was in a state. Maybe it burned up in the fire, but if it didn't, they're not going to believe it wasn't me.'

'Tenille, they're a lot more likely to believe it was your dad.'

She shook her head stubbornly. 'I'm not grassing him up. And neither are you.' She gave Jane a calculating look. 'So, are you going to hide me or what?'

Jane looked thunderstruck. 'Hide you?'

'Yeah, hide me. Just till the fuss dies down and we can figure out what we're going to say.'

'I can't hide you here. The cops have already searched it once.'

'All the more reason why they won't search it again. They've looked, I'm not here.'

Jane shook her head. 'This is a bad idea, Tenille. Look, why don't you sleep here tonight and in the morning we'll go to the police and tell them the truth.'

'The truth isn't going to work. We've got to come up with something better than the truth. My dad stood by me, I've got to stand by him.'

'He killed a man, Tenille.'

Tenille looked away. 'No. Geno was trash, he deserved what he got. You think I'm the first kid he messed with? You think I'd have been the last? No. My dad did a good thing and I'm not going to send him to jail for it.' She pushed the chair back from the table. 'You won't help me, fine. I'll just go back on the road again. I made it this long, I can make it a bit longer.'

Jane grabbed her by the wrist. 'Wait. You're not leaving.'

'I'm not staying either if all you're going to do is dob me in.' Tenille wrenched her arm free from Jane's grip, her expression wounded. 'You say you're my friend. But you're not. You're just the same as all the other whiteys. When it comes right to it, you just the same. I should have stuck with my dad. He knows what to do with grasses.' Tears started to her eyes and she brushed them away impatiently. 'Fuck you, Jane. Fuck you.'

On June 22nd, we reached Matavai Bay once again. There, we divided all that was practical to take from the ship in equal proportions. Sixteen men elected to leave the ship, eight chose to remain with me. My heart was heaviest when I bade farewell to Peter Heywood. But it was right for him to leave us. He was not implicated directly in the mutiny & I believed he would not suffer unduly for staying with me. Under cover of darkness, I went ashore to take my final leave of him. I could not go in the light of day, for I was too ashamed of the unravelling of the lies I had told Chief Teina to look him in the eye. We walked together along the sandy beach, Peter & I, & I asked that he explain to my brother the truth of what had transpired between Bligh & myself. I had not until then acquainted him with Bligh's foul accusation, & his horror convinced me that I had been right to mutiny rather than have our names besmirched by Bligh's baseless calumnies.

26

Derwent Water sparkled silver and blue in the sunshine. A few dinghies were already cutting through the water, the angles of their sails indicating the strength of the breeze that ruffled the lake's surface. But Jake had no eyes for beauty that morning. England and this task had made him jaded and faded in a matter of days. He relished nothing that lay ahead of him – neither further encounters with the elderly nor a potentially bruising reunion with Jane.

At least he could postpone that while Dan Seabourne was hanging around the place. Jake had never warmed to Dan and Harry, finding their constant flirting both unnecessary and embarrassing. He suspected the lack of warmth was mutual and he didn't anticipate Dan's presence lending any help to his attempts to get alongside Jane.

His worries about Dan's presence extended beyond the purely personal, however. As far as Jake knew from his reading of Jane's email, Dan had failed so far in his searches at the Family Records Centre. Where Caroline's researcher had come up with a wealth of material, Dan had drawn a blank.

Or so his email had said. If it had been the truth, Dan's arrival in Fellhead made little sense. Why would he have come all the way from London if he had truly nothing to report? Jake's flesh goosepimpled as the only explanation he could imagine crystallised in his mind. If Jane had realised her email had been hacked, she could have texted Dan or phoned him and told him not to send his results. And maybe even to go one better and send an e-lie to fake him out. If she was aware of the hack, she had to suspect it was him. And if she suspected him of such a shit's trick, there was no way he was going to get anywhere near her research.

He'd just have to find another route to what he wanted. Jake picked up a pebble and threw it as far out into the water as he could. It plopped, then the ripples spread, merging with the tiny waves created by the wind to disappear almost immediately. *Sunk without trace. Whatever it takes, that's not going to be me.*

'You look terrible,' Jane said, taking in Dan's grey pallor and sweaty skin. 'That mussel really did for you, didn't it?'

'I've never liked shellfish,' Judy said. 'When you think what they feed on, it doesn't make you want to put them in your mouth. Can I get you a cup of tea, Dan? Or something to eat? We had our breakfast a while ago, I hope you don't mind us not waiting for you, but Jane said better let you sleep.'

'She was right,' Dan said, his voice thin and colourless. 'I don't think I could face eating anything, but a cup of tea would be a gift from the gods. I thought the fresh air would do me good, walking down from the cottage.' He sighed then squeezed his eyes shut. 'But I can't remember the last time I felt this rough.' Judy reached across and patted his hand, then put the kettle on.

'I got rescued by a cop last night.' Jane tried to sound breezy and nonchalant. It felt a bit like whistling in the dark.

Dan's eyes widened in surprise. 'What?'

'I was walking back from Bossy Barbara's when some drunk driver nearly ran me over. Mum reckons it must have been Billy West from over the hill. The local teenage tearaway driver. I was picking myself out of the hedge when a detective inspector from the local nick turned up.' Jane fiddled with the fringe of a table mat, meeting no one's eye.

'Just by chance? Or was he chasing the drunk driver?'

'That's what I thought at first. But no. That was just coincidence. He was on his way to see whether I knew anything about Tenille's whereabouts. And then he decided he needed to search the place while he was here. So his bosses could report back to Scotland Yard that they'd done the job properly, I suppose.'

'I still don't understand,' Judy said, pouring boiling water into the teapot. 'I mean, why run away if you've got nothing to hide?'

'I imagine because she believes she won't get a fair crack of the whip from them. You think they'd be pointing the finger at her quite so quickly if she was a nice respectable white middle-class girl from Hampstead? I don't think so. And that'll be why she's run.'

Dan shook his head. 'Poor kid. So they thought she might be hanging out with you?'

Jane shrugged. 'I don't think so. Not seriously. I think the inspector was just going through the motions. What he really wanted to know was if I'd heard anything from her. Email, text, whatever.'

'And have you?' Dan asked.

Don't lie unless you have to. 'I'll tell you exactly what I told them: No, I haven't heard from Tenille at all.'

'I still can't get over the rush to judgement about Tenille. I mean, she's a nerdy black kid, right? It's not like she runs with the gangs or anything. Or is there something you've not been telling me?'

Jane waited till her mother had gone through to the pantry, then said softly, 'Her real dad's the gangsta who runs the Marshpool. He doesn't acknowledge her as his daughter but everybody knows. Including, it seems, the police.'

'Ah,' Dan said.

'"Ah," is right. But it still doesn't make Tenille guilty of anything except being scared.'

'Busy night, then. Are you OK? Did you hurt yourself?'

'I bruised my shoulder, that's all. It was scary. Like he was coming straight at me. Lucky I knew the road better than the lunatic behind the wheel. I only had a split second, but I knew where to jump.'

'Thank God for that. Bloody teenagers, getting their kicks out of scaring people. So, how did you get on with Bossy Barbara?'

Jane pulled the sheaf of papers in front of her. 'More family trees than you can shake a stick at.' As Judy came back in with a leg of lamb, Jane said,

'Bossy Barbara came up trumps, Mum. Thanks for putting me on to her.'

'I'm glad, love. We all want you to do well, you know.'

While Judy busied herself with the meat, Jane passed some of the papers to Dan. 'I thought we could go through them, put them in order of likelihood based on the primogeniture principle.'

Dan looked at her as if she'd suggested going down to the village to catch a small child to spit-roast for lunch. 'I don't think I could read without throwing up. Actually, I was thinking of going back up to the cottage to crash out. If that's OK with your mum.'

'Of course, I wasn't thinking. You could stay up there till you go back, if you like.'

Jane tried to hide her relief. It wasn't that she wanted to be rid of Dan for himself. But after the night before, she needed freedom of action without anyone asking where she was going or what she was doing.

Dan swallowed a mouthful of tea and shuddered slightly. 'Maybe I could manage some toast,' he said without confidence.

While Judy fussed around him, Jane began to sort through the information she'd been given by Barbara Field. She began to sift it into piles, making notes as she went. It was a slow and complicated process and she soon came to realise that it was easier to accomplish with one than two. She glanced up at Dan, tentatively munching toast with strawberry jam while Judy watched him anxiously. 'Oh, and I thought I might try to talk to the forensic anthropologist who's dealing with the bog body. Suggest she might want to get some DNA samples from Fletcher Christian's direct descendants to see if it's a match.'

Dan stood up. 'Good idea. I think I'll head down to the pub to pick up my car. Then I'm going back to bed.'

'I'll drop you off on the way to church, if you like,' Judy said.

'It's OK,' he said. 'I think I need the fresh air.' He pulled Jane into his arms in a tight hug. 'I'll be better by the morning. Then we can start doing the interviews.'

She kissed his stubbled cheek. 'Thank you. I'll work on the list.' She walked as far as the farm gate with him, waving him off as he walked slowly down the hill. But instead of heading back to the kitchen table, Jane crossed the yard and cut between the long barn and the shearing shed.

She emerged into a small field with a square stone building in the corner furthest from the house. A line of oblong frosted-glass windows ran around it two courses of stone below the eaves, almost like a decorative border. The metal door was painted a dull green, fastened with a strong lock. Her father had renovated it a dozen years ago when EU regulations had made it impossible for him to slaughter his own sheep for sale to the local butchers. The old slaughterhouse was further up the fell and Allan had converted it into a holiday let called Shepherd's Cott, an occasion of much mirth in the village pub. But Allan still wanted somewhere he could butcher his own meat for his family's consumption, so he'd transformed the tumbledown outhouse, providing it with running water and electric light. He'd even added a tiny toilet and shower cubicle to avoid trailing blood and guts into the house.

Jane walked across the field, pausing apparently to enjoy the view, but in reality to check she was unobserved. As sure as she could be that the coast was clear, she quickly unlocked the door and slipped inside, softly calling, 'It's me,' as she did so.

Tenille was sitting on one of the stone benches, insulated from the cold by the sleeping bag Jane had dug out of the cellar the night before. A book was carelessly thrown down beside her and her eyes were wide with fear. Seeing it was Jane, she pulled her earphones out, allowing the unmistakable sound of hip-hop to leak out tinnily into the still air. 'All right?' she said.

'I'm fine. How about you? Did you get much sleep?'

Tenille shrugged one shoulder. 'Yeah. Took me a while to, like, settle. But once I was off, man, I was out for the count.' She managed a lop-sided version of her usual grin. 'Mus' be that country air, huh?'

'Have you got enough to eat?'

Tenille gestured at the scones and the sausage rolls Jane had filched from her mother's freezer. 'I ate all the apples. So it's a bit monotonous, know what I mean? But it's OK.'

'I'll get you some stuff tomorrow in Keswick. My mum knows to the last tin of tomatoes what's in her cupboards and her fridge, I don't want her to notice there's anything missing and start wondering what's going on. Is there anything in particular you'd like?'

Again the half-shrug. 'Chocolate biscuits? Crisps? Like, maybe some sandwiches? Not tuna or prawn, though, I don't like fish much. A toothbrush would be good too. Oh, and batteries for this,' she added, gesturing to the MP3 player.

'I'll see what I can do.' Jane perched on the bench beside Tenille. 'You thought any more about going to the police?'

Tenille shook her head, obstinate to the core. 'It's not going to happen, Jane. There's no way I can live with myself and do that.'

'You can't live here forever either.' Before Tenille could interrupt, Jane held up a hand to stop her. 'And I don't mean because I'm going to tell you to go. I just mean that it's a limited option. I have to go back to London in just over a week and I can't leave you here to fend for yourself. Besides,' she grinned, 'my dad might want to slaughter a sheep one of these days.'

'Yech.' Tenille looked disgusted. 'I just about managed to stop thinking about what goes on in here and you have to go and bring it up again. Look, it's OK, I know I can't stay here forever. But I just need time to straighten my head out without being scared every minute, OK?'

'OK.' Jane got up.

Tenille snapped her fingers and tutted in annoyance. 'Hey, with everything that's been going on, there's something I forgot. Something I meant to tell you about.'

'What?' Jane tried not to sound too apprehensive.

'Jake. He's back. And he's stalking you.'

Absolutely the last thing she'd expected Tenille to say. Shocked, Jane said, 'What do you mean? He's in Crete.'

'No, he's not. He came by the flat the day you left, when I was still there.'

'You let him in?'

'Course not.' Tenille was scornful. 'He just came to the door, I saw him through the spyhole. He shouted your name through the letter box then he fucked off.'

Jane's heart leapt at the thought that Jake had come back, and she hated that he still had the power to make her feel that way. 'That's hardly stalking me, Tenille,' she said, trying to cover her emotional reaction.

'I know that. But I saw him again yesterday, when I was trying to get here. I was on the path coming over from Grasmere. And I saw him. He was on the path above the farm, looking down through binoculars. Like he was watching for you.'

Jane's brows knitted in puzzlement. 'He was watching the farm? Why on earth would he do that?'

'Like I would know. He's a creep, Jane. You deserve better.'

'You don't know him,' she said dismissively. 'But I don't understand why he'd be spying on me. Why not just come straight to the farm?'

Tenille shrugged. 'Maybe he wanted to make sure there wasn't anybody else in the picture. Or maybe he just gets his kicks from keeping tabs on you. Like I said, he's a creep.'

'Are you sure it was him? I mean, he must have had his back to you.'

Tenille tutted again. 'Sure I'm sure. I saw him coming round to yours often enough. He's stalking you, Jane.'

Unsettled by Tenille's information, Jane shook her head. 'I don't get it.' She shook her hair away from her face as if trying to clear her head. 'I need to go. I've got work I need to get on with. You'll be OK?'

'Yeah. Don't worry about me. I'm chill.'

'You know you won't be able to have the light on after dark? Only, we can see the lights from the house.'

Tenille nodded glumly. 'I know. I guess I'll just have to get used to sleeping, right?'

'Right. Look, I'll try to come back later this evening, but no promises. It might be tomorrow. But I'll do my best.' Jane reached out and patted Tenille's hand, entirely oblivious to the echo of her own mother's behaviour. 'Try not to worry.'

Her own words sounded hollow in her ears as she made her way back to the house. *Try not to worry.* Yeah, right. Like that was an option. How long, she wondered far from idly, did they give you for harbouring a fugitive from justice? Matthew would love that. Not to mention that it would give him a free run at what she was starting to think of as her manuscript.

That thought spurred her back to the kitchen table and the records of births, marriages and deaths that she still had to plough through. She was almost finished when Judy returned from church. 'How are you getting on?' her mother asked after she'd checked the contents of the oven.

'Better than I expected. And the best news is that, if I've worked it out right, the most likely person lives just up the road.'

'That's the Lakes for you. Small world. So who is it?'

'Edith Clewlow.' Jane searched for the relevant note she'd made.

'Edith Clewlow?' Judy echoed, her face dismayed.

'You know, she lives up Langmere Stile. We used to play with her youngest grandson Jimmy.' Jane looked up and caught her mother's expression. 'What's wrong?'

Judy sat down heavily. 'She died last night. Edith Clewlow died last night.'

We left Otaheite for the last time on 23rd September. With me were Edward Young, John Adams, John Williams, William McCoy, Isaac Martin, Matthew Quintal, John Mills & William Brown. Also six native men & twelve women. My aim was to find an island free from natives, difficult of anchorage, away from sailing routes & capable of sustaining life. We travelled for some months, searching for a suitable settling place, but although we traded peaceably enough for food & water on several islands, we could not come upon a place that sufficiently matched the measures I had laid down for our home. In the end, I realised we must leave behind the archipelagos where natives roamed freely from island to island & find some remote spot with no near neighbours. After long study of Bligh's charts and maps, at last, I resolved we should make for Pitcairn.

27

Matthew stared unseeingly across the tables of bent heads in the classroom. The children were quiet, working on the arithmetic problems he'd set them. He always liked to start the week by setting a task that demanded concentration, to put a clear divide between whatever anarchy had filled their weekend and the discipline of school. He'd give them a while then work through the sums on the board before moving on to the genealogy project after the morning break.

He was still smarting from Jane's accusation at lunch the day before. 'When were you planning to tell me about Dorcas Mason?' she'd demanded the moment he walked into the kitchen.

'Today,' he said, conscious that he had the moral high ground here. 'When you mentioned her name the other night, I thought it rang a bell but I didn't want to give you false hope. So I went back home and checked through the kids' worksheets. It was too late to call you, and I was out all day yesterday.'

'You've always got an answer, haven't you?' Jane said. 'Why can't you admit it, Matthew? You were going to try to find the manuscript yourself and claim the glory.'

'I told you he'd been planning to tell you,' Diane chipped in. 'But you always think the worst of Matt.'

'That's because it's usually the right thing to think,' Jane said. 'You showed no interest in my work until I mentioned Dorcas Mason's name. All you'd done until then was take the piss. Then suddenly you wanted to know all about who she was, what her connection was to the manuscript, where she fitted in to my research. And not a word, not a hint that you might know something that would help.'

'I told you: I didn't want to raise your hopes only to dash them.' Matthew leaned across her and poured himself a glass of wine.

'Come on, Matthew. Tell the truth. You were planning to hijack my research and get the ultimate one over on me.'

'Do you have any idea how paranoid you sound?'

Allan slapped his hand flat on the table with a sound like the crack of a rock breaking off from a cliff face. 'Enough, the pair of you. If you've got a quarrel, take it somewhere else. You're both far too old to behave like this.'

And that had been the end of it as far as words were concerned. But both siblings were seething, Matthew the more so since his rare generous impulse had been so thoroughly misunderstood. He burned under Jane's contemptuous gaze and decided that, if he was going to get the kicking, he might as well commit the sin. Jane might have the academic credentials, but he had the contacts. He was the local man. He was the headmaster and people deferred to him.

Small stirrings in the classroom brought Matthew's attention back to the present. Several of the children had finished their work; the usual suspects, Matthew thought. 'OK. You've had long enough. Pencils down. Question one – who's going to give me an answer?' Sam's hand inevitably shot up in the air. 'Yes, Sam?'

'Five hundred and seventy-six, sir.'

'That's right. Anybody not get that right?' Two hands crept into the air. 'OK, Sam, come up to the board and show us your workings.' Matthew took the class through the list of problems, finishing with perfect calculation just as the bell rang for morning break. As the children scrambled to their feet and made for the door, he said, 'Sam, Jonathan? Can you stay behind for a minute.'

They drifted towards his desk, Sam trying to hide his interest and Jonathan his trepidation. Matthew laid their family trees in front of them. 'Over the weekend, I learned something very interesting. Your ancestor Dorcas Mason worked for a very important person here in Cumbria. Can you think who that might be?'

Jonathan stared mute as a heifer. But Sam was willing to hazard a guess. 'Was it Beatrix Potter?' he said.

'Your timing's a bit off there, Sam. This was when Dorcas was very young, before she married Arnold.'

Sam poked his finger in his ear while he thought. 'Was it Wordsworth, then?' he asked.

'That's right. Dorcas Mason was a maid at Dove Cottage for a few years when she was a girl. What do you think of that?'

'Cool. We can fill that in on our family trees, that she was William Wordsworth's maid,' Sam said.

Jonathan fidgeted his feet. 'Does that mean she was famous?' he mumbled.

For once, Matthew found an intervention of Jonathan's of some value. 'Well, no, not really. But she probably met some people who were very famous in their time. And that's why I was wondering if either of you have ever heard about any family papers going back to Dorcas's time. She might have kept a diary, or letters to do with her work at Dove Cottage. She might even have kept some of the papers William Wordsworth threw away – early versions of poems, or notes he didn't need to keep. Have either of you ever heard of anything like that?'

Jonathan looked blank and shook his head. Matthew was glad that there was rather less chance of the manuscript having passed down to the Bramleys. They'd probably have used it for shopping lists. But Sam's family were much more on the ball. Sam himself looked disappointed. 'I don't remember anybody ever talking about stuff like that,' he said.

'Well, maybe you could both ask when you go home tonight?' Matthew suggested gently. 'If there was anything, we could make it part of the display. That would be good, wouldn't it? Connecting our project to Cumbria's greatest son?'

Sam nodded enthusiastically. 'That would be so cool. I'll ask my dad tonight.' Then his face clouded over. 'But maybe it's not a good time.' His lower lip quivered and he clamped his mouth tightly shut.

'His great-gran died on Saturday,' Jonathan

volunteered. 'So mebbe his dad won't want to talk about the family, like.'

Matthew hid the quick flare of irritation. 'Or maybe he would understand that if there were some papers from Dorcas among her things, it would be a sort of tribute to her if we included them in the project. You can ask, can't you, Sam?'

The boy nodded bravely. 'I'll ask.'

'And you too, Jonathan. Now, off you go, enjoy what's left of break.' Matthew watched them leave. It was hard to see any common genes between those two, he thought. He hoped it was Sam who took after Dorcas. It would be heartbreaking to think of Wordsworth's great epic being used for firelighters. But in Cumbria, where men prided themselves on calling no man their master, anything was possible.

Jane had discussed their plan of action with her mother. Judy had told her that Gibson's from Keswick had already taken Edith off to the funeral parlour but that she would be returned to lie in state at the home of her granddaughter Alice. 'Do you remember Alice?' Judy had asked.

'Not really, she was quite a bit older than us.'

'She never married. Went off to college to be a librarian. She worked in Kendal for a few years, but now she's back in Keswick. Head librarian she is now. Lives up on that new estate on the Braithwaite road. She's got more room for the wake than the rest of them.'

'How do you think she'd take it if I asked whether her gran had any old papers?'

Judy gave her daughter an amused glance. 'Well, I hope you'll dress it up in prettier clothes than that.'

'I'll be diplomatic, Mum. But do you think Alice would know if Edith had any family documents?'

'Probably. But Frank's the one you need to ask. He was devoted to his gran. Went up there every morning to deliver her milk and paper and make sure she was all right. It was Frank that found her on Sunday morning; he was supposed to be picking her up for church. But she was lying dead in her chair in the living room, peaceful as if she'd just nodded off.'

'It's a pity it wasn't Jimmy who was the devoted one. I could always wind him round my little finger.' Jane smiled, remembering Jimmy's cheeky grin and his easy temperament. She'd almost had a crush on him; she'd let herself be talked out of it by her best friend who said he looked like a monkey, especially when he was hunched over his drum kit, arms flailing.

Judy pursed her lips. 'Jimmy Clewlow . . . I doubt he'll even come back for the funeral. He's hardly been seen round here since he dropped out of university to join that pop group.'

'It's not a pop group, Mum, it's a contemporary jazz quintet. And they're quite highly thought of. I've seen their CDs reviewed a couple of times.'

'Maybe so, but it's not a proper job, is it?'

'It's as much a proper job as what I do. And he probably makes rather more money than me.' The conversation had drifted off into memories of school days and talk of what her friends were doing now. But Judy hadn't told her not to go, so now they were heading off for Thistlethwaite Court and a close encounter of the Clewlow kind.

Jane was relieved to see Dan had made a full recovery from his bout of food poisoning. When she'd picked him up at the cottage, he'd been his usual self, eyes alert, head and jaw freshly shaved. 'I had an email from Anthony Catto,' she said as they drove down to the main road. 'He's dug up an interesting Wordsworth quote about fugitives from justice hiding out in the Lake District. I emailed him back and told him how we'd cracked the family tree. You never know with Anthony – he's got great resources. He might come up with something.'

'We can use all the help we can get,' Dan said. 'Now, tell me about the Clewlows.'

Childhood reminiscence preoccupied Jane on the drive to Keswick. But even if she had noticed the silver Audi that had picked up her tail at the end of the Fellhead road, she would likely have thought nothing of it. There are so few roads in the Lakes and so few passing places that it would be possible to be tailed for some time before the circumstances registered as suspicious.

Alice's house sat halfway up a cul-de-sac of identical houses which aimed for a traditional look with timber framing and stucco over half a dozen courses of grey stone. They looked marginally less out of place in the landscape than the dark red-brick executive homes that had sprung up elsewhere locally. There were three cars jammed nose to tail in the driveway and several more parked half on the kerb on either side. Jane pulled up in front of the furthest and they walked back, Jane clutching the home-baked apple cinnamon cake her mother had thrust upon her. 'You can't turn up empty-handed,' she insisted.

Jane rang the doorbell and waited. A male voice called, 'I'll get it,' and the door swung open. She could hardly believe her luck. Standing on the threshold, looking exactly as she remembered him, Jimmy Clewlow pantomimed astonishment. 'Jane Gresham,' he exclaimed. His mouth opened and closed a couple of times as he tried to find the right register for this encounter.

'I was sorry to hear about your gran,' she said. 'I just wanted to pay my respects.'

'Sure, yeah. Right, come in,' he gabbled. 'Half Fellhead's here already. But hey, I'm just . . . touched, I guess. At you. Coming like this.'

Jane nodded. 'My mum couldn't make it. She asked me to bring this.' She thrust the cake at him. 'And this is my colleague, Dan Seabourne. He's visiting at the moment.'

Jimmy's attention shifted from Jane to Dan. His expression shifted too, from confusion to sharp interest. Jimmy shook Dan's hand. Dan covered the handshake with his other hand and met Jimmy's eyes with a compassionate look. 'Sorry for your loss.'

Jimmy nodded. 'Thanks. Come on through. Everybody's in the living room. Except Gran, of course, she's in the sun room at the back. Did you want to . . . you know?' he asked Jane.

She looked embarrassed. 'It's all right . . . I'm not really into that sort of thing.' They followed him up the hall and into a low-ceilinged room that stretched the length of the house. Jimmy hadn't been exaggerating. Half of Fellhead was here, and most of them were eyeing her and Dan with curiosity.

Alice spotted a new arrival and extricated herself from the woman who ran the gift shop in Fellhead. Alice had changed surprisingly little over the years.

Her spiky brown hair was threaded with silver at the temples, but the few lines carved on her face were testament to laughter rather than dissatisfaction. She wore a simple black trouser suit and large silver earrings in the shape of a crescent moon. 'Thanks for coming,' she said automatically, her wide mouth breaking into an easy smile.

'I'm sorry for your loss. I was very fond of your gran,' Jane said truthfully.

Alice frowned slightly, as if trying to place her. 'This is Jane Gresham and her friend Dan Seabourne,' Jimmy interjected helpfully. 'You remember Jane, don't you, Alice? From Fellhead? I used to play with her and her brother Matthew up at Langmere Stile.' He held the cake up. 'She's brought a cake.'

Alice tilted her head back in acknowledgement. 'Thank you. Of course I remember you. You're in London now, aren't you?'

'That's right. I'm back for a couple of weeks to follow up on some research with Dan. Mum told me the news yesterday and I wanted to drop by and say how sorry I am.'

'That's nice that you come back home. Some people need a death in the family before they'll grace us with their presence,' she added pointedly.

Jimmy sighed with the air of a man who has heard it all before but knows better than to argue.

Jane smiled at Alice. 'Actually, we were hoping to see your gran this week.'

Alice looked puzzled. 'I didn't know you visited her. She never mentioned it.'

'No, I hadn't been yet. But I thought she might possibly be able to help us with our research.'

'Gran?' Alice sounded incredulous.

'Cool,' Jimmy said. 'What are you doing, some kind of oral history thing? Gran had a great memory, loads of stories. She'd have been just the person to talk to about that stuff.'

'You two didn't come from London to hear my gran's life story,' Alice said baldly, her expression challenging.

'No, I didn't.' Their faces were expectant, Alice's markedly less friendly. 'I don't know if you're aware of this or not but, six generations back, a member of your family worked for the Wordsworth family at Dove Cottage. She was a maid. Dorcas Mason was her name. She went on to marry your great-great-great-great-grandfather,' Jane said, ticking off the generations on her fingers.

'And you thought my gran might know something about this Dorcas woman?' Alice sounded sceptical.

'Actually, I hoped she might be able to tell me if there were any papers that had been handed down from that time. Diaries, letters, maybe even some drafts of poems that William had discarded.' Jane gave what she hoped was a propitiating smile.

Now Alice looked positively hostile. 'What is it with your family? First your brother rings her up wanting to know whether she's got any old family papers, then you show up pretending to be offering condolences but actually sniffing around to see if my gran left anything worth pawing over.'

'My brother?'

'Don't pretend you don't know. I expect you got him to make the first approach because he's the headmaster, he teaches our Sam and she'd trust him. And when that failed, you turn up here like a vulture, trying to see if we've got anything worth conning us out of.'

Jane shook her head, bewildered. Aware of the eyes turning towards her, she stuttered as she spoke. 'I've no intention of conning anyone. I'm an academic, a scholar. I'm not some con artist. All I want is to look. And I had no idea my brother had spoken to Mrs Clewlow.'

Alice snorted. 'You must think we're country bumpkins up here. Well, before you go hounding the rest of my family, here's the bottom line. My gran had nothing of value. No old papers, no valuable jewellery, no stocks and bonds. So you might as well leave now, because there's nothing for you here. Go and take your London graverobbing ways with you.'

By now, a hush had fallen on the room and all eyes were on them. 'You've got it all wrong, Ms Clewlow,' Dan said, his voice conciliatory. 'We don't want to take anything from you or your family.'

'And I don't believe you. So it's just as well there's nothing to take, isn't it? Now, I'd like you both to leave my house.'

Jimmy looked stricken, but he put out a hand and touched Jane's elbow. 'Come on,' he said softly, leading them from the room.

Jane felt the deep shock of unjust accusation. She could barely trust herself to speak. 'We're really not trying to pull a fast one,' she said as they reached the front door.

'I know that. Alice is just upset. She really loved Gran. She'll be mortified tomorrow.'

'I can't believe she got me so wrong.'

'It's like Jimmy said, she's upset. People behave oddly when they're bereaved,' Dan said.

Jimmy nodded eagerly. 'Don't worry about it. Listen, are you guys around for a while? Only, I'll be here till the funeral. I'll go spare if I have to listen to this lot till then. Do you fancy meeting up for a drink?'

Jane felt dizzy with the constant change of direction of her visit. 'OK, yeah. Call me at my parents'. They're in the book.'

Dan smiled at Jimmy. 'Great idea. Listen, I know this isn't the time or the place . . . but I really like your music.'

Jimmy looked surprised. 'Thanks. I don't often hear that up here.'

'It would be a real privilege to buy you a drink,' Dan added.

'I'll look forward to it.' Jimmy opened the door and stood there as they set off towards her car. 'Jane,' he called when she was only a few yards away. 'There are no papers. Honest.'

She looked over her shoulder at his anxious smile and knew he was telling the truth. 'Back to square one,' she muttered.

Dan glanced back at Jimmy. 'Oh, I wouldn't say that was entirely wasted. He's very cute.'

Jane rolled her eyes. 'He's straight. And you have a boyfriend.'

Dan opened the car door. 'Whatever. I think Jimmy could be very useful to us. We need to get him on our side and keep him there.'

Sharon Cole sat huddled into herself in Donna Blair's office. As soon as she'd fished the postcard out of her pocket and handed it over to the detective, Donna had taken off, holding the card by its edges, telling Sharon to sit tight till she got back. That had been almost twenty minutes ago, and Sharon was wishing she'd never bothered. She was going to be late for work at this rate, and for what? Tenille wasn't stupid. She just wanted Sharon to know she was OK. She'd assume Sharon would show it to the police. If she'd posted that card in Oxford, as sure as God made little green apples, she was planning to be out of there on the next bus or train. It wasn't going to take the cops one inch forward in their search for Tenille, and it was buggering up her day royally.

Another ten minutes passed before Donna returned. 'Thanks for bringing that in, Sharon,' she said, like they were old mates or something. 'Makes me more inclined to believe you when you say all this was nothing to do with you. And you're sure that's Tenille's handwriting?'

Sharon nodded. 'She always puts them funny little circles over her i's.'

'I'll be checking, you know. She must have done the occasional piece of written work at school.' She paused for a reaction but got none. 'As far as you're aware, does she know anybody who lives in or near Oxford?'

Sharon gave Donna an 'Are you crazy?' look. 'How would she know anybody from there? She's hardly ever been out of London, never mind to Oxford.'

'Maybe a schoolfriend who moved away?' Donna tried.

'Not that I ever heard about. I told you, she didn't have many friends. Anyway, she couldn't run to a schoolfriend. How would they hide her? They'd have family, and even crap families notice when there's another kid in the house.'

'I have to check out all the possibilities. So you don't think she'd make Oxford her destination?'

Sharon snorted. 'I doubt she even knows where Oxford is.'

Donna crossed her office and stared at her crammed shelves. She pulled something out, almost causing an avalanche of paper in the process. She slapped the road atlas on her desk and opened it up to the route planner spread. 'I know where Oxford is,' she said. 'And I know where it's on the way to.' She stabbed a finger at the map.

Sharon frowned. 'Where's that, then?' she said, looking blankly at the names of towns she'd never heard before.

'It's the Lake District, Sharon. Where Jane Gresham comes from.'

For two months, we tacked through the cold south-easterly winds & unfriendly seas of the Pacific, well south of the more hospitable waters round Otaheite & Toobouai. We were chilled to the bone, exhausted by the work of manning so great a ship with so few hands. The screaming of the wind in the rigging drove us all near to madness with its pitch and constancy. Bounty was in poor fettle by then, her deck timbers shrunk & leaking, her hull in need of caulking, her sails sadly depleted & in poor order. By the time the new year came around we were in desperate need of landfall. At last we arrived at the place where, according to the Admiralty chart, Pitcairn was to be found. But there was no sign of land. All we could see in every direction was water.

28

Jane drove back into the centre of Keswick, wondering how she was going to distract Dan so she could shop for Tenille. 'I've got a few errands to run. And we need to get current addresses for the names on the list,' she said.

'I could do that if you drop me off at the library,' Dan said. 'Normally I'm good at that sort of thing,' he added ruefully.

'It helps if you have the right spelling. Are you sure you don't mind?'

'No. And you can do me a favour – if you're anywhere near a supermarket, could you get me some ground coffee?'

'No problem. I've got some things to get for home.' They arranged to meet in a café in the town centre, then Jane escaped to the supermarket to stock up on supplies for Tenille. Luckily, it was Monday, and Judy had a regular arrangement for lunch and an afternoon of whist at a friend's house in the village. From noon, the coast would be clear for her to deliver her purchases. If her dad was around the yard, she could just leave the shopping in the car till he went back up on the fell.

In the middle of the morning, the café was crowded with women taking a break from shopping and tourists fortifying themselves for the fells. She managed to find a table right at the back by the kitchen door and ordered a mug of hot chocolate and a teacake. Comfort food, that was what she needed. Something that would still the noise in her head. So much going on, so little that made sense.

At Sunday lunch, she'd almost let herself believe that Matthew was telling the truth. Even after a lifetime of bad experiences at his hands, she still couldn't help wanting to believe he was capable of change. But when Alice Clewlow had revealed Matthew's call to Edith, Jane had been forced to accept that she was right. Matthew was her enemy in this quest. His self-righteous claim to be on her side was nothing more than another of his expedient lies designed to get him off the hook while making her look petty and paranoid.

Please God, let him not form an inkling that she was hiding Tenille. He'd shop them both to the police without a second thought. And of course, that was the next problem. What was she going to do about Tenille? She couldn't think of a way to penetrate that adamantine determination to protect the Hammer. It wasn't as if Tenille didn't understand the risks involved in her current strategy. She wasn't being stupid, just stubborn. But something had to give sooner or later. The present arrangement couldn't be more than a holding pattern till Jane could come up with the resolution that was beyond Tenille right now. It couldn't go on. Harbouring a fugitive who happened to be the daughter of a man who would apparently stop at nothing to protect her was bad enough, but lying to the police and her parents had her awake all night worrying about what was going to happen next.

And then there was Jake. What the hell was that all about? She had to believe Tenille. There was no reason for the girl to lie. She stared into her hot chocolate, as if there were answers to be found in its dark depths.

She was startled back into consciousness by the sound of the chair opposite being pulled back. But the man with his hand on the chair-back wasn't the one she was expecting. 'Mind if I join you?' Jake said.

'So you are stalking me,' Jane said, her voice surprisingly steady and cool.

Jake recoiled slightly, consternation on his face. 'What do you mean, stalking you?'

'Spying on me, following me. You should be grateful I've not called the police,' Jane said, enjoying the adrenaline rush that came with indignation.

Jake held his hands palms outwards, a gesture of surrender. 'Whoa. Can we just back up there? I came to see you, Jane. To talk to you. To tell you I made a mistake.' He looked contrite. 'Please, can I sit down? People are staring.'

Jane became aware that they had indeed become the focus of attention in the tearoom. She'd had enough of other people's stares that morning. 'Sit down if you must,' she said through tight lips.

The waitress approached, undisguised avidity on her face. 'I'll have –' Jake began before Jane cut across him.

'He's not stopping,' she said firmly. The waitress drifted off, casting a couple of backward glances as she went. 'What the hell is going on with you?' Jane demanded.

Jake sighed and stared down at the tablecloth. 'Just hear me out, please. I came back because I missed you. I realise I've been stupid. I wanted to see if there was still a chance for us. To try again.' He glanced up quickly.

'So why didn't you just call me?'

'Because it would have been too easy for you to hang up on me.'

It was hard not to be melted by his piteous expression. But Jane was determined to cling to her dignity. 'So you thought you'd spy on me instead?'

'I called the university and they said you were up here. So I thought I would come up and try to get you on your own. So yes, I guess you could call it stalking. But all it was about was getting a one-to-one with you.' He looked hangdog. 'I suppose it wasn't very bright, but I couldn't think of any other way to do it. I didn't mean to scare you.'

'I wasn't scared, Jake. Just pissed off. So what happened in Crete? Did she kick you out?'

Jake looked hurt. 'No, Jane. It's like I said. I realised I'd fucked up big time and I wanted to try to make things right between us. What we had was special. And I was stupid enough to throw it away.'

'So you're saying you woke up one morning in Crete and suddenly thought, "Oh my God, I've made a terrible mistake"?'

Jake picked up a teaspoon and fiddled with it. She remembered the feel of those long fingers on her skin and tried not to show how weak it made her feel. 'It was a bit more complicated than that.'

'So let me hear the tale.'

'I . . . uh, I saw a story in the papers. About the body in the bog. And I remembered how excited you would get, telling me your theory about Willy and Fletcher.' He met her eyes directly, without flinching or blinking. 'And I remembered how much more fun that was than any amount of messing around in Crete. So I packed my bags and came home.'

She didn't know what to think. He sounded sincere. He looked sincere. She wanted him to be sincere. But he was good at sincere. She knew that of old. She cocked her head to one side, considering. 'Did you come home for me or did you come home for first crack at the manuscript, if I managed to find it?'

'Why would I think you're even looking for it?' he asked. 'You've been talking about it for as long as I've known you. But you've never been actively hunting for it. Is that what you're doing? Have you picked up a trail? Is that why you're back here?'

'Would it make a difference if I said no? Would you suddenly lose interest?'

Jake shook his head. 'It's you I came back for, Jane. Not some pie-in-the-sky manuscript which probably doesn't even exist.'

She wanted to believe him. But he'd hurt her too badly for that to be an easy option. 'Why would I want to try again?' she said sadly. 'You hurt me, you lied to me and you left me.'

'I know I don't deserve a second chance, but I love you, Jane.'

'Are you still working for her?'

'Caroline? Yes. I don't have any option, I need a

job. But I'll be looking for other work.' He shrugged. 'I've been a fool. Jane, please give me a chance.'

It was her turn to look away, to shield her face from his probing eyes. 'I don't feel ready for this, Jake,' she said slowly. 'But maybe we can meet again if you're going to be around for a few days.' She managed a half-smile. 'Provided you stop stalking me.'

'OK. It's a deal. What about lunch?'

'I can't. I'm busy.'

'Tomorrow?'

After a little persuasion, Jane agreed to meet him at his hotel for lunch. As he got up to leave, he leaned across and kissed the top of her head. A tingle ran through her from head to toe. 'I'll see you tomorrow,' he said. Then he was gone, leaving her to wonder.

Tenille inspected the contents of the shopping bag, finally pronouncing herself satisfied. 'Thanks,' she said. 'I'll pay you back when I can.'

'No need,' Jane said. 'Call it a late birthday present. So, how are you doing?'

Tenille picked up one of the paperbacks Jane had bought in the supermarket. 'Basically I'm bored shitless. I can't tell you how much I'm looking forward to these.'

'I'll bring you some more from the house. Mine are mostly down in London, but my dad has a great collection of old detective novels, if you like those?'

'Never read any. I guess I can give them a try.'

Jane sat down on the bench next to her. 'I've been thinking,' she said. 'How would you feel if I called your dad and explained the situation to him?'

Tenille scowled. 'I don't want him thinking you're asking him to dob himself in.'

'That hadn't occurred to me.'

'Well, it should've. Just like I'm loyal to him, he's loyal to me. I don't want him to hand himself over to the Bill because of me.'

'I just thought he might have some ideas about how we get you out of this mess. He's had more dealings with the law than we have, he might come up with something. Besides, I want him to know I'm no threat to him.'

Tenille looked dubious. 'Maybe. But how would you get in touch with him? I don't have no phone number.'

'I'll think of something,' Jane said, her mind a complete blank.

'Maybe your mad next-door neighbour could get a message to him.'

'Mrs Gallagher?' Jane looked baffled. 'Why her?'

Tenille looked shifty. 'I just think she'd help, that's all. She's always been nice to me, know what I mean?'

'I'll think about it.' Jane stood up. 'OK, I need to go, Dan'll be back down from the cottage in a minute then we've got to go to Grasmere. Oh, and by the way, you were right. Jake is here. And he has been spying on me. He said he wanted to make sure he got me on my own, that's why he was watching me.'

Tenille scowled. 'I told you he was up to no good. What's he after?'

'He wants us to get back together.'

'Tell me you're not going to. You're way too good for him. I saw how upset you were when he pissed off. Nobody that really cared for you would treat you like that. I tell you, Jane, you should just tell him to piss off back to where he came from.'

Jane couldn't help smiling at Tenille's seriousness. Sometimes it was hard to remember she was only thirteen. 'I appreciate your concern. And I will be careful, I promise you.' She rubbed a hand over Tenille's nappy head. 'I'll see you later.'

Tillie Swain was next on their list. She had been Edith Clewlow's sister-in-law but, according to Judy, Tillie and Edith had never got on. Tillie considered that her brother had married beneath him, and the two branches of the family had been as distant as was possible when their homes were a scant half-dozen miles apart as the crow flies. Certainly Jane didn't remember Jimmy ever talking about his Swain cousins, and she was fairly sure none of the Swains had been at Alice Clewlow's that morning.

Tillie lived in a bungalow on the southern edge of the village, one of four that made up a little enclave set back from the main road. She'd been widowed in her early fifties when her husband Don had died in a car crash on the notorious Wrynose Pass. Since then, bitterness had settled on her in tandem with crippling arthritis. When she opened the door to Jane, bent and leaning on a stick, she looked up at her with suspicion. 'Mrs Swain?' Jane said.

'Who wants to know?'

'I'm Jane Gresham. I live up on Langmere Fell, just above Fellhead.'

'Gresham's Farm? Judy Gresham's lass?'

'That's right. And this is my colleague Dan

Seabourne. I wondered if we might have a word with you?'

'With me? What about? I'm warning you now, I've only got my pension, so there's no point coming here looking for donations for this, that and the other.'

Jane shook her head. 'It's nothing like that.'

Tillie exhaled heavily through her nose. Her eyes screwed up behind her large-framed glasses as she considered. 'You better come in, I suppose. Save letting all the heat out.'

They followed her into a small over-heated living room which smelled of talcum powder and stale biscuits. The large TV that dominated the room was showing an Australian soap opera. 'You'll have to wait a minute,' Tillie said. 'I don't want to miss the end. Brad's got Ellie pregnant and now he's going to tell her husband the baby isn't his.'

'That's going to be a heck of a shock for Jason,' Dan said, perching on the sofa and staring intently at the screen. 'They've been friends for years, him and Brad.'

Tillie's tight mouth relaxed into a smile. 'You're a fan?'

'Love it,' Dan said.

She nodded. 'It's a grand show. Never a dull moment. Reminds me of when I was young.'

Finally, the credits rolled and the anodyne music flowed. Tillie turned the sound down and turned to face them. 'Besides, it's the only company I get most days, I don't like to miss it,' she said. 'So what brings you to my door, Jane Gresham?'

Jane had been fully prepared to journey all round the houses before she got to the point of her visit.

But she was pretty sure there was no point in attempting small talk with Tillie Swain unless it centred round soap operas, a subject on which her knowledge was manifestly insufficient. And if she set Dan loose on that track, she feared she'd lose the will to live. All she could hope for was to inject a bit of drama into her own quest. 'I'm on a kind of treasure hunt.'

Tillie snorted. 'You'll find no treasure here, lass.'

Dan grinned. 'Now, Mrs Swain. You're a connoisseur of the soaps, you should know that treasure turns up in the unlikeliest of places. Just have a listen to what Jane has to say before you dismiss it out of hand.'

'I'm a Wordsworth scholar,' Jane said. 'I have reason to believe that a secret manuscript was entrusted to the care of one of the family servants. A very important manuscript. An undiscovered poem by William Wordsworth. And we're trying to track it down.'

Now she had Tillie's attention. 'Would it be worth something, then?'

'It would be worth a lot of money, yes. And it would be big news. On the TV and in the papers. Whoever found it and whoever owned it would be famous overnight.'

'That's all well and good, but why are you talking to me about some secret manuscript?'

'The servant who was given the manuscript to take care of was your great-great-grandmother, Dorcas Mason. I wondered if you knew anything about it.'

A series of emotions played across Tillie's wrinkled face. Greed, desire, frustration. 'I wish I did,' she said bitterly. 'I'd know how to spend any money that came my way.' She sighed, long and deep. 'You're wasting your time here. I never heard tell of such a thing. Not even a whisper.'

Jane recognised the truth. Wearily she stood up. 'I'm sorry to have bothered you,' she said as Dan also got to his feet.

'Life's a bugger, isn't it?' said Tillie. 'This morning, I never knew I could have been rich. And now I feel like something's been snatched out of my hand.'

'Believe me, Mrs Swain, you can't be as sorry as I am.'

Tillie made a small, contemptuous noise. 'Don't count on it. You don't know the meaning of disappointment at your age.'

But I do, Jane thought as they walked back to the car. *I so do.*

You will doubtless imagine that my heart sank at this apparent failure to locate our haven. But the opposite is the case. If I could not find Pitcairn using the best Admiralty charts & the finest navigational instruments, then neither would anyone else. But the problem remained, viz, how was I to find it if the charts were wrong, isolated as it was among thousands of square miles of empty water? Well, Cartaret first discovered Pitcairn in 1767, four years before the inestimable John Harrison was awarded the Longitude Prize. I deduced therefore that it was most likely that Cartaret got the longitude wrong. So with this in mind I set as our course a generous zigzag tack along the line of latitude. On 15th January, the island finally broke the horizon & we approached as evening drew on. But our journey was not yet complete. For two more days, we were tossed about by high seas that made landing impossible. It seemed there was only one possible landfall on the island, & when once the seas had subsided, we rowed through the foaming surf. We had come home, whether we liked it or not.

29

Jake was feeling rather more pleased with himself than he had been since he'd left Crete. His meeting with Jane had been sticky, but he'd been expecting worse. It was a pain that she'd found out about him spying on her, but he thought he'd finessed that well. He picked up his phone and called Caroline, happy he had something more interesting to report than the death of a pensioner.

'Hello, darling,' she said. 'How are things progressing?'

'I finally managed to make contact with Jane today.'

'How did it go?'

'I think I'm on the right track. I'm meeting her for lunch tomorrow.'

'Did she tell you about her progress?'

'She hasn't even told me she's on a mission yet. She's playing her cards close to her chest. But I think I can worm my way under her guard.'

'And there's always her email,' Caroline said. 'You must keep an eye on that. And what about the old dears? Did you hit any more of them today?'

'I'm going to go and see the next one this evening.

Let's hope this one lasts long enough for me to dig up any family secrets.'

'Quite. We don't want any more of them dropping dead before you've got everything out of them. Maybe you should try to persuade Jane to take you with her on her interviews now you're getting back on her good side. With her local connections and your role as money man you might get further together than apart.'

'I'll do my best.' Jake tried not to sound as lukewarm as he felt. Now that he was trying to acquire a manuscript for real rather than theorising about it, he'd come to believe that Jane's softly-softly approach wouldn't get the results she was hoping for. People needed more reason to give up their family secrets than wanting to please an academic, whether she came from the next village or not. His was a far better guarantee of results, and he didn't really want Jane around to witness it.

'Any more news on whether the mystery body really is Fletcher Christian?'

'I've not heard anything. And if there was anything to hear, I would have. News flies round here like greased lightning.'

'If that's the case, perhaps you ought to go and see the forensic anthropologist after all. She might have been approached by someone with an interest in what we're looking for, someone smart enough to realise the identity of this body might make what they have even more valuable. Let me know as soon as you have any news.' The line went dead.

Jake felt curiously flat after the call. Now, when he spoke to Caroline, there was none of the rush he'd felt at the beginning. It was as if their relationship had slipped imperceptibly into the space occupied by work rather than pleasure. The uncomfortable thing was that he now found himself wondering just how much he liked her anyway, absent the sex.

Shrugging off the thought, he turned to his laptop and got online as Jane. He'd have to be careful – he didn't want her trying to log on and finding she was blocked because she was already supposedly online. But from what he knew of her family, six o'clock was dinnertime and right now she ought to be sitting at the kitchen table eating. He went straight to the <sent mail> box and found an email to Anthony Catto. As he read, he realised he'd got away with sneak-peeking her email from Catto. It soon also became clear that Jane and Dan had managed to overcome the hurdle of the misspelled surname and had found their way to a working list of Dorcas's descendants. It was time to get close to Jane.

He closed down the computer and decided to go down to the bar for a drink before he headed out to Grasmere to talk to Tillie Swain. He perched on a stool in the half-empty bar and ordered a pint of Theakston's. The barman was in chatty mood, asking how he was enjoying his stay. Jake chatted about nothing for a bit, then said casually, 'Any more news about the body in the bog?'

The barman shook his head. 'Not that I've heard. But it just so happens that the person you need to be asking that question is in here right now.' He gestured with his head towards a corner table where a woman sat poring over a folder, her face masked by a swathe of dark brown hair. 'That's Dr Wilde.

She's the one examining the body. Like her off *Silent Witness*. They're making a TV programme about it, you know.'

'Maybe I could go over and have a chat with her.'

The barman winked. 'I'd make it quick. She's probably waiting for the local constabulary.'

'Surely they're not interested in a body that old?'

'The only body DI Rigston's interested in is hers. Word is they're stepping out.'

'Oh, right.' Jake got to his feet. 'I'll just have a chat while she's waiting.' He crossed to River's table and cleared his throat. She looked up. *Nice grey eyes*, he thought. 'Dr Wilde? My name's Jake Hartnell. Sorry to disturb you, but I was wondering if you could spare a moment to talk about the body in the bog.'

'Are you a journalist, Mr Hartnell?'

Jake shook his head. 'No. I'm a specialist in old documents. And I have a passing interest in this case.'

'Sounds intriguing. Why don't you sit down?' As Jake settled on a stool opposite her, she said, 'Why is a specialist in old documents interested in my bog body? There were no documents on my lad.'

'It's a bit complicated,' Jake said. 'I imagine you've already been asked whether this body could be Fletcher Christian?'

River laughed. 'Several times. It's getting to be a bit monotonous. The answer is, I don't know at this point. There are several interesting correspondences, but until I can do a proper DNA comparison with Christian's direct descendants, it's impossible to be certain one way or the other. But I still don't see what that has to do with a document man.'

'Well, I've heard a whisper that there might be a

351

very interesting manuscript extant whose authenticity could be established if we knew for sure whether Fletcher Christian returned to the Lake District,' Jake said.

'Very mysterious.'

'One has to be discreet in my line of work.'

River smiled. 'Mine too. So somebody's touting Mr Christian's memoirs, are they?'

Jake laughed. 'You're fishing.'

'Of course I am. It's my job, interpreting the clues. Developing theories then seeing whether they pan out. So, is that what you're chasing?'

Jake shook his head. 'I wish I could tell you. But it's all still very tentative.'

'Well, if it is Mr Christian on my table, you won't be the only one jumping for joy.'

'A ticket to the talk shows, eh?'

River shook her head. 'Not my thing. More like a ticket to tenure.' Suddenly her face lit up as she looked over Jake's shoulder. 'Hi,' she said, looking past him. Jake turned to find a tall man looming over him. He looked like the wrong person to consider messing with, and he was looking at Jake with a less than friendly expression. 'Ewan, this is Mr Hartnell. He's interested in the bog body.'

Rigston smiled. 'Who isn't? What's your interest, Mr Hartnell?'

Jake got to his feet. There was something about this man that commanded answers. He hadn't expected such presence in the local law in such a one-horse town. 'Curious as to whether it's Fletcher Christian,' he said.

'Aren't we all?' Rigston turned his attention to

River. 'Sorry to keep you waiting, last-minute problem.' Back to Jake. 'You'll have to excuse us, we've got a dinner reservation.'

River gathered her papers. 'Nice to meet you, Mr Hartnell. Let's all keep our fingers crossed.' She patted his arm as she passed him. Jake watched them go, intrigued. He would never have put them together as a couple. She looked far too unconventional, sounded far too sparky to be hanging around with a copper. He wondered idly what she'd be like in bed. Then, giving himself a mental shake, he finished his pint. He had more important things to occupy him than idle speculation about someone else's sex life. He had a meeting planned with Tillie Swain that might just change the course of both their lives.

Darkness swept in on the wings of the low cloud that had already settled over the fells. Allan Gresham came into the kitchen just before six, rubbing his hands against the damp chill. 'How do you fancy pizza and a film?' he said to Judy, Dan and Jane, who were huddled round the Aga drinking tea.

'That sounds lovely,' Judy said. 'I've only done a chicken curry, it'll be even better tomorrow.'

'Sorry, Allan, but I'm just about to set off for London,' Dan said. 'I've got to teach Jane's seminars tomorrow.'

'Which is much appreciated. What's on, Dad?' Jane asked.

'No idea.' He rummaged through the letter rack and picked out the flier from Zeffirelli's in Ambleside, which combined a pizzeria with two cinema screens. 'There you go,' he said.

Jane glanced at it. She'd already seen one film and had no desire to see the other. 'You go without me,' she said. 'I've got plenty of work to be getting on with.'

Judy tried to talk her into joining them, but Jane was adamant. She'd already realised their evening out could be a ticket to a couple of hours of freedom for Tenille since Dan was all set to leave for his whirlwind trip to London. 'I'll be back tomorrow night,' he promised.

After everyone had gone, she decided to give it twenty minutes before she headed for the slaughter shed. In the meantime, she could try to find a way to contact John Hampton. She'd been racking her brains, but she hadn't been able to come up with a better idea than Tenille's suggestion.

She got Noreen Gallagher's phone number from directory enquiries. She answered after a couple of rings. 'Mrs Gallagher?' Jane said, recognising the heavy breathing as nothing more sinister than the Irishwoman's normal respiration.

'Who is this?' her neighbour demanded.

'It's Jane Gresham from next door,' she said.

'It's all rjght, you know. I wouldn't let them break the door down. I told them you were a decent woman. I don't know what the world's coming to when the police want to do the burglars' job for them.' She paused for a liquid cough.

'I appreciate that. It's good to be able to count on your neighbours.'

'There's precious few round here I'd rely on, and that's the truth. So you can rest easy, the flat's safe and I think your pal got away safely.'

'My pal?'

'That black girl that's always round at yours. I distracted the policeman so she could give them the slip. Well, it stands to reason, doesn't it? A slip of a thing like that, she's not going to be going round murdering folk, now, is she?'

Jane was confused, but she reckoned that seeking an explanation would only confuse her further. 'I'm sure you did the right thing, Mrs Gallagher. Look, I need to ask you a big favour. And if you want to say no, that's fine.'

'Ask away. Talk's free. If I can help you out, I will.'

'I need to get a message to someone on the estate . . . John Hampton.'

There was silence save for Noreen's wheezing. 'The Hammer?' she said finally.

'It's OK. I've met him. He knows who I am.'

'That wouldn't make me sleep easier at night, I tell you that for sure. Men like that, you're better off when they don't know who you are.'

'It's all right, Mrs Gallagher. I know what I'm doing.'

She snorted noisily. 'I don't think you have any idea what you're doing. That man's trouble, make no mistake about it.'

'I promise it won't bring trouble to your door. I just need you to deliver a note asking him to call me.'

'And all I have to do is stick a note through his door? I don't have to sign it with my name or anything?'

'No, nothing like that. Just a note asking him to call Dr Gresham.'

'Because he's got a fearsome reputation on him. I wouldn't want to be crossing him.'

'You won't be crossing him. He'll be pleased to hear from me, honestly.'

Mrs Gallagher sighed noisily. 'You know where he lives?'

'D eighty-seven.'

'Go on then, give me your number. I'll do it right now, tonight. Before my cold feet get the better of me.'

Jane gave her mobile number, then repeated it to make sure. 'You're a gem, Mrs Gallagher,' she said. 'I won't forget this. It's really a big deal to me.'

'You take care of yourself now. Mixing with the likes of the Hammer isn't right for a woman like you.'

Jane finally managed to extricate herself from the conversation with a promise that she would come and see her neighbour when she got back to London. She put the phone down with a sigh of relief. She had no idea what Tenille and Mrs Gallagher had been up to, and she really didn't want to know.

A few minutes later, she opened the slaughterhouse door and shone the torch on a blinking Tenille. 'How do you fancy a couple of hours indoors? Dan's gone back to London and Mum and Dad have gone to the pictures in Ambleside. They won't be back till gone ten. You could even have a bath if you wanted.'

Tenille quickly wriggled out of the sleeping bag. 'That's baaad,' she said, grinning. 'Man, I've been losing my mind in here. It's OK in the light, but it gets dark so early. I didn't realise how fucking dark the countryside is.'

Tenille followed her back into the kitchen, making a beeline for the warmth of the Aga. 'This is so cool,' she said, looking round the kitchen. 'Man, you are so lucky having a place like this.'

'I know,' Jane said. 'Maybe you can come back again for a visit when all this has died down.'

'That'd be gold,' Tenille said.

'By the way, Mrs Gallagher is going to take a note round to your dad, asking him to call me. Let's hope he's got some bright idea about how to get you off the hook.'

Tenille scowled. 'I don't want him thinking I'm not grateful for what he did.'

'Let's not go there. Do you fancy a bath? Something hot to eat?'

'I'm all right with the shower. I don't really like baths. But something hot to drink would be great. A coffee, maybe?' She watched Jane fill the kettle and set it on the Aga. 'I never asked you. What are you doing up here anyway?'

'I'm on study leave. Some research I could only do up here.'

'Research into what? Come on, Jane, take my mind off the shit. Tell me what you're working on. You know I'm interested in all that stuff.'

Jane could see the enthusiasm in Tenille's eyes and found she couldn't deny her. She made coffee for them both, then settled down at the table to tell Tenille the whole story. She even produced the family trees to show how she'd come up with her prioritised list of people to interview. Tenille interrupted several times to ask questions that were surprisingly percipient and the time sped by under the spell of narrative. 'That's so cool,' she said when Jane reached the end of her tale. 'But you're not going to get anywhere being nice, you know.'

'What do you mean?'

'If the manuscript exists, I don't buy it that nobody in the family knows anything about Dorcas and her papers. So if it does exist, they must have been holding it secret, like some sacred thing that was trusted to them. Or else they know it doesn't really belong to them, so they're keeping quiet about it. Either way, they're not going to go, like, "Hey, Jane, we've so been waiting for somebody to come along and ask us for this." They're going to go, "Oh shit, somebody's guessed the big family secret, we better all put our heads together and throw her off the scent." Doesn't matter how nice you are to them, they're going to put the wall up.'

'You think so? You think they'd still want to keep it secret after all this time? What would be the point?'

Tenille shrugged. 'Fuck knows. But people are weird when it comes to family stuff. You know they are.'

'So what would you suggest?' Jane said frostily.

'Nothing that would appeal to you, sister,' Tenille said drily.

Before Jane could say anything more, the phone rang. She started, glanced at the clock and said, 'Oh shit, look at the time.' She grabbed the phone. 'Hello?'

'Jane? It's Jimmy. Jimmy Clewlow. It's not too late to ring, is it? I know how early farmers hit the hay.'

Distracted by the call, Jane didn't notice Tenille slip a sheet of paper under her jacket. 'No, it's fine, Jimmy. Just give me a minute, though.' Jane covered the mouthpiece. 'You need to go. Mum and Dad will be back soon.'

Tenille nodded. 'Thanks for this evening. It's been really cool. I'll see you tomorrow, yeah?' She was already on her way to the door.

'Tomorrow.' Jane sketched a wave then returned

to her call. 'Sorry, Jimmy, just had to take something off the stove before it boiled over. I'm sorry about this morning.'

'Think nothing of it. Alice is stroppy at the best of times, and this morning was a long way from the best of times. Listen, I wondered if you and your pal Dan fancied getting together for dinner tomorrow?'

'Sounds good to me. But Dan's had to go down to London. He won't be back till about eight.'

'I'll pick you up at half past eight, then. That OK with you?'

'Perfect.' They chatted for a little longer, then said their goodbyes. Jane put the phone down with a smile on her face. Two birds with one stone. A possible ally in their attempts to unlock the Clewlow family memories and a perfect excuse for avoiding the dinner invitation she felt sure Jake would issue at lunch. Things were definitely looking up.

As we explored our new home, it soon became clear that men had lived here before. There were traces of paths through the undergrowth & the shapes of gardens long overgrown on the eastern slopes. The rich red earth looked fertile & we discovered plentiful supplies of all the native plants we had learned would supply the staples of life – mulberry trees for cloth, candlenuts for light, palms for thatching, fruit & vegetables growing wild. There was abundant fresh water. In short, everything we needed was readily to hand. It would be difficult going at first, but I believed we could make something remarkable here based on hard work & liberty. Our explorations had also revealed another anchorage, on the east of the island, & we removed Bounty there and prepared to settle our new Eden. I was so overjoyed at our arrival & our prospects that I forgot that there needs must be a serpent in every Eden.

30

Riding a bike without lights in the dead of night in London would be lethal. But then, the night was never dead in London. Not like here, Tenille thought as she freewheeled down the gentle slope from Fellhead to the main road. Here, now it was cloudy and you couldn't see the stars, it was like cycling underground. Tenille imagined herself as a tube train, speeding unlit through silent tunnels, empty of people. Just her and the rats, the only other things with a pulse. She supposed there were animals out there, doing their night-time thing, stalking and killing and being killed. But their domain was outside hers, it had no relevance.

When she reached the main road, she turned right towards Grasmere. Dove Cottage was easy enough to find, right on the main road and clearly signposted. Tenille swung off the road and propped Jane's bike against the wall. She prowled round the cottage, imagining Wordsworth inside, hunched over the arm of his chair, scribbling a line then pausing for thought. It was weird to think what had been written inside those walls. There was nothing special about the house, she thought. You wouldn't look at it and think, 'Wow! Somebody special must live here.'

She walked back to the bike, thinking again how lucky it was that she'd spotted it through the open door of an outbuilding when Jane had walked her to the house. She'd thought then about borrowing it for a night ride. Anything to get out of the slaughter-house, where she was going stir crazy. She'd known there was no point in asking Jane's permission, so she'd resolved then and there to wait till after midnight before sneaking out and going for a ride. Then when Jane had told her about her quest, a whole other agenda had opened up.

So here she was at one in the morning, the only person stirring. Tenille turned off the main road and cycled silently into the village proper. And that was when she realised her plan wasn't going to be quite as straightforward as she had thought. She had no idea where Tillie Swain's bungalow might be, but she hadn't imagined it would be hard to find in a little place like this. However, her experience was London, where streets were clearly named and even on estates like the Marshpool, doors had numbers. Grasmere was another creature entirely. Sure, it was pretty. But it wasn't designed to make life easy for strangers. Some lanes had no markings at all and most houses had no number, just names. And of course, there was nobody to ask.

Finally she found a village map mounted in a glass case outside a gift shop. It was almost impossible to read, but Tenille struggled with it and eventually worked out where she was in relation to Tillie Swain's house. She cycled back to the main road and turned south. And there it was, right on the edge of the village.

No lights showed in any of the group of four bungalows. Tenille left the bike at the mouth of the close then walked down to Tillie's house, staying in the shadows as much as possible. She walked down the side of the bungalow, light on her feet as a cat. Round the back, she surveyed her options. There were patio doors, which she knew were supposed to be easy to jemmy out of their runners. But she didn't have a crowbar and she didn't want to risk the noise. That left the back door, which looked pretty solid with a mortise lock rather than a Yale. She'd learned about locks at an early age, but it had been a while and she didn't have the right tools, only a pair of tweezers and some strong wire she'd picked up in the shed where the bike had been. She could do it, but she'd rather not. Her best hope was the heavy pots that were arranged around the patio. Maybe Tillie had secreted a key under a flower pot. She wouldn't be the first.

Tenille crouched down and began to tilt the pots one by one, groping underneath for anything that felt like a key. She got lucky on the fourth pot. She pulled out a key and grinned. She rubbed it clean of dirt on her trousers and headed for the back door.

A few minutes later, she had to admit defeat. Whatever this was, it wasn't the back door key. 'Fuck it,' she muttered. The only thing left to try was the front door, exposed to any insomniac pensioner who might be sitting in the dark looking out of their window. Well, there was no help for it. She was going to have to go for it.

She crept back to the front of the bungalow and tried the key. The lock turned silently and, within seconds, she was inside the hallway, breathing in the smell of old lady. The house was dark and silent. She stepped silently down the hall and glanced in at the first room on her left. The living room. A good place to start looking. She closed the door behind her and found herself in blackness. Her hand groped for the light switch and clicked it on. If someone saw the light, they'd probably assume Tillie was having trouble sleeping. She hoped.

Quickly she scoped out the room. There was an old-fashioned sideboard against one wall and she made straight for it. Both drawers were crammed with papers. Tenille pulled out the first bundle and started going through it. Receipted bills, postcards, insurance policies, a will in a lawyer's envelope. Nothing of interest. The second drawer was equally fruitless. Why anybody needed to keep her electricity bills from the 1980s was beyond Tenille.

She took a deep breath. The bedroom was probably where an old lady would hide anything really important. But there was no way she could search in there. It wouldn't hurt to look, though.

Tenille turned off the light and moved back into the hallway. The door opposite was closed and, with infinite care, she edged it open. It was a bedroom, no question of that. But the curtains were pulled back and the bed was empty. Yet it was obviously Tillie's bedroom. All the old lady things were on the bedside table – a tumbler of water, a glasses case, a couple of books. A cardigan was tossed carelessly on a chair. Tenille felt a chill in her stomach. Where was the old lady? It wasn't like there was anywhere to go.

Never mind that, she told herself. She must have gone to stay with family. Whatever. The thing was, she wasn't here and that was a golden opportunity. Tenille pulled the curtains closed, turned on the bedroom light and started searching.

Twenty minutes later, she had to admit that she'd drawn a blank. The only papers she'd found were some letters tied in faded red ribbon along with a marriage certificate for Donald Swain and Matilda Clewlow. She glanced at her watch. It was almost two. Time to get out of here if she was going to take a look at Edith Clewlow's cottage as well. There was only the kitchen and bathroom left here, and she didn't think either of those was a place to store documents.

She turned off the light, opened the curtains again and left as silently as she'd arrived. She replaced the key and headed back for the bike. It seemed as if Tillie Swain had been telling the truth after all.

She cycled back along the quiet roads, seeing nothing except a lorry with a supermarket logo passing in the opposite direction. Even up here, people had to get their own-brand fix. It was harder work going back up the hill to Fellhead, but Tenille persisted. The village was hushed and dark, the only light coming from the one lamppost on the village green. Here, Tenille paused to consult her map and the list of names and addresses she'd helped herself to earlier. The late Edith Clewlow had lived at Langmere Stile, which according to the map was a mile up the fell. Not far, but not fun either, looking at the contour lines. With a sigh, Tenille mounted the bike again and set off up the hill. Man, she was going to be so fit when she got back to London.

She found Lark Cottage with little difficulty. This time, she wheeled the bike round the back. She expected this house to be empty, and she didn't want to risk anyone passing by and seeing the bike outside. A local would be instantly suspicious, and she wouldn't mind betting they'd be straight on the phone to the cops.

This time, she wasn't so lucky with the back door. But the kitchen window wasn't latched properly and she was able to raise the sash enough to squeeze through. She landed in the sink with a loud clatter and froze for a few seconds, holding her breath. Nothing broke the stillness.

It took much longer to search Edith Clewlow's house. She had been a hoarder to a degree that would have shamed a squirrel. Tenille wondered if the old woman had ever heard of paper recycling. There were boxes of photographs, drawers stuffed to bursting with letters and postcards, an accordion file rammed full of every official document Edith and David had received. The family Bible turned up in the bedside cabinet, on top of a stack of scribbled notes about Edith's childhood in Seatoller. Beneath that was a folder filled with newspaper clippings of her family's exploits, from local football matches to sheepdog trials and village produce shows. But nothing about William Wordsworth or Dorcas Mason.

By the time Tenille had finished, the time was nudging past four a.m. She knew she had to get out before the world around her started waking up. She'd already learned that people round here seemed to think nothing of getting up in the middle of the night and driving tractors all over the landscape. She pushed a final stack of photographs back in a carved wooden box, then left the way she'd entered.

Within fifteen minutes, she was back at the slaughterhouse, bike safely stowed. She crawled into her sleeping bag, feeling like she'd done a good night's work. OK, she hadn't found anything. But at least now, two names could be properly crossed off the list.

Jane was on her second cup of coffee when her father came into the kitchen carrying the morning post, his expression glum. He had, she knew, already been up to the high pastures to check on a wether with suspected water belly, so she said, 'What do you think, then? Are you going to have to call the vet out?'

He looked momentarily bewildered, then said, 'The wether? No, I think he's fine. The vet's coming out on Thursday anyway, so I'll get him to have a look then.'

'That's good. I thought from your expression that he'd taken a turn for the worse.'

'To tell you the honest truth, what Adam was just telling me put the wether right out of my head,' Allan said, going to the fridge and pouring himself a glass of milk.

Adam Blankenship had been delivering the post in Fellhead for as long as Jane could remember, and his van seemed to function as a magnet for all the news for miles around. 'Bad news?' Jane asked.

Allan glanced at her sideways. 'It was Tillie Swain

you went to see yesterday afternoon, wasn't it? Down Grasmere?'

'Yes. Why? Has she been complaining about me?'

Allan sat down opposite her. 'She'll not be doing any complaining now, love. She died last night.'

Jane's eyes widened in shock. 'What? She seemed fine when I saw her. Apart from her arthritis, she was quite perky.'

Allan spread his hands helplessly. 'She was old. It happens.'

'Do they know what it was?'

Allan shook his head. 'Adam didn't have much detail. Apparently, her arthritis was worst in the morning so she had a home help who came in first thing to get her up and bathed. When the woman arrived this morning, she found Tillie on the bathroom floor, cold as ice. Maybe she had a fall, maybe a stroke, maybe a heart attack.'

'Poor woman. It's not how you'd choose to go, is it? Lying on the bathroom floor feeling your life ebbing away. It doesn't bear thinking about. Dying alone must be bad enough without losing your dignity as well.'

Allan ran his thumb up and down the side of his glass. 'I don't think there's any dignity in death, however it comes. All we can do is try to live with dignity.'

There was nothing Jane could find to say to that. 'It's a bit spooky, don't you think? Two deaths in the space of a few days. That seems a lot for such a small area. Especially when they're both connected to what I'm working on.'

Allan shrugged. 'It's just coincidence. I don't know

why it happens that way, but old people often seem to die in clusters. It's like, one goes and three or four others decide to give up the ghost. I don't think there's anything peculiar in them both being from the same family. Everybody from round here's connected to everybody else. You're related to half the village one way or another, don't forget that.'

'I suppose.' Jane finished her coffee and got to her feet. 'I'd better get off. I'm going to see a couple of people in Keswick.'

'Where's your mother?'

'Picking elderberries.'

'Is it that time of year already? It goes by faster and faster.'

Jane kissed her father's cheek. 'Stop trying to pretend you're an old man.'

Allan gave her a crooked smile. 'Who says I'm pretending?'

An hour and a half later, Jane was saying goodbye to the genuine article. Eddie Fairfield was a fragile eighty-two-year-old, rheumy-eyed and leather-skinned, his silver hair streaked with yellow from the nicotine cloud of pipe smoke that shrouded him. 'I gave up when I was fifty, promised myself that, if I made it to eighty, I'd take it up again. Best thing I ever did, it's the only pleasure I get these days,' he'd said when he courteously asked Jane's permission to light up. 'I can barely walk the length of the street, and I'm damned if I can remember what I had for my tea last night. Our lass brings me in a hot meal every night, otherwise I doubt I'd remember to eat at all. My son wanted to put me in a home, but I told him, as long as I've got breath in my body, I'll stop under my own roof. Have you ever been in one of them old folks' homes?'

Jane barely had time to admit she had before he was off again. 'Load of old women staring into space. Or else they're mad as a box of frogs, thinking they're eighteen again. No man's safe from those daft old women, you know. You'd think they'd have lost interest, but not a bit of it.' He twinkled a smile at her. 'If they'd have been half as willing when they really were eighteen, they would have made a lot of young lads very happy, let me tell you.'

He'd insisted on making her weak milky coffee and had tottered through from the kitchen with a plate of chocolate digestives. 'Not often I get a visit from a bonny young lass,' he said. 'Least I can do is make you welcome.'

When she'd finally got a word in edgeways and explained the purpose of her visit, he'd grown excited. 'Aye, I heard tell of yon lass when I were a nipper,' he said, his Cumbrian dialect thickening as he travelled back into the past.

Jane felt a quiver of excitement. Was this the beginning of the end of her quest? 'Really?' she said. 'What did you hear?'

He closed his eyes. 'Let me think, now. It was my granny Beattie talked about her. She was born a Clewlow. Beatrice Clewlow, born in 1880. She was the oldest. Her mum and dad, Arthur and Annie, they had four kids: Beattie; Alice, who stopped at home and never married; Edward, who died at the second battle of Ypres, never had any kids that we know of.' He winked at her conspiratorially. 'But you never know with them French lasses, do you? And then there was Arthur Junior. Anyway, this Dorcas that you're after, she was their granny. And I reckon she was as much a one for stories as Granny Beattie.' His eyes snapped open. 'She talked about her granny Clewlow quite a bit to me and Annie, my twin. Funny, I hadn't thought about that for years.' He smiled triumphantly, pleased at his own feat of memory.

'What did she tell you about Dorcas?' Jane asked, trying not to sound as eager as she felt.

He puffed out his lips in a sigh. 'It was mostly about her later life. When she was widowed and bringing up the children. But I do remember Beattie saying her granny, that would be Dorcas, had been a trusted servant of the Wordsworth family. She said her granny had been there when William Wordsworth breathed his last, that she talked about the sadness of seeing such a noble man laid low.' He shook his head. 'That's all I can remember.'

They'd talked for a while longer, but it soon became clear that Jane had mined the seam of his remembrance to exhaustion. Eddie Fairfield had no recollection of any family papers or secret connected to Dorcas. All he retained was her claim to fame – her presence at Willy's deathbed.

It was clear that Eddie would have talked to her all day, but Jane was mindful of her lunch appointment with Jake and she finally managed to extricate herself with ten minutes to spare.

She walked down the main street with some lightness of heart. She'd made progress that morning. If nothing else, she could be sure that she was looking at the right family. And she was having lunch with

Jake. In spite of her resolve not to trust him, she couldn't help the rush of blood to the head that prospect provoked. That didn't mean she had to fall for his charms all over again.

Of course it didn't.

Our early days on Pitcairn were cruel hard. Summer was at its height & stripping our tattered ship of all that could be salvaged was hot & heavy work. Nevertheless, all hands showed equal willingness to ferry our goods ashore. At length when we had stripped her of everything we could carry off, we ran Bounty aground below a 700-foot cliff & on January 23rd, we set her alight as a safeguard against discovery. She burned clean through to the copper sheathing of her hull & finally, tossed by the waves, she sank in ten feet of water. There was nothing for it now but that we should settle our colony harmoniously. We divided the land in nine equal shares among the white men, & resolved that the natives should have no land of their own, but rather that they should labour in our service, this being more fitting to their child-like mentality. At first, we lived in rough shelters of sails & branches, but we soon demonstrated our intent by building permanent dwellings of timber. Then, as if to seal our bargain with the island, my wife Isabella gave birth to my first child, Thursday October Christian nine months after our landing. I counted myself a happy man indeed.

31

Jake was already sitting at the table when Jane walked into the restaurant. She paused on the threshold for a moment, gauging her response. Such a familiar image; the wedge of dark hair flopping over his forehead, the perfect arch of his eyebrows over the long-lashed blue eyes, the coffee-coloured birthmark on his right cheekbone that resembled the smudge left by a mother's thumb, the long straight nose and the thin lips. Sometimes she thought he looked like Sherlock Holmes would have if he'd been more interested in sensuality than intellect. Once, catching him unawares like this would have caught at her heart. But now, caution mediated her every response. She had her plan. All she had to do was carry it out.

As she approached, he looked up from the menu, caught sight of her and sprang to his feet. He stepped to kiss her cheek as she shrugged out of her coat, but she shifted sideways, leaving him lunging at the air. 'You look fantastic,' he said.

Strike one. She'd deliberately taken no special care with her appearance. Jane knew she looked OK. Not fantastic. 'Nice of you to say so,' she said, settling herself in her chair and picking up the menu. She ordered a glass of white wine from the hovering waitress then smiled at Jake. 'So how are you passing the time up here in the back of beyond?'

It clearly wasn't the opening gambit Jake was expecting. He looked disconcerted, then gathered himself and gave a half shrug. 'Well, now I've given up stalking you, I've had to make do with the pencil museum. Did you know they do a whole leaflet on pencil-sharpening techniques?'

'We enjoy our simple pleasures up here,' Jane said drily. She glanced at the menu and, when the waitress brought the drinks, she said, 'I'd just like a chicken Caesar salad, please.'

Once Jake had ordered his steak and they were left alone again, Jane said, 'And you really came all the way back from Crete to try to patch things up between us?'

Jake gave her his best hangdog look. 'I told you. I realised I'd made a mistake. I don't know if it's too late, if there's too much damage done. But I want us to give it another go.'

'OK. I accept that. But I want to take it slowly. I don't want to rush headlong into anything.'

He nodded. 'You're in the driving seat.' He smiled and her stomach lurched. 'It's enough for me to be sitting here with you. That feels like a pretty good start to me.' He raised his glass and chinked it against Jane's. 'Here's to fresh starts.'

'Fresh starts.'

'So what are you doing back home? They said at work that you were on study leave.'

Strike two. The question was too fast, too soon and too bald. Her suspicions about his motives were growing incrementally. But she managed a smile and said, 'Willy and Fletcher. I found some previously uncatalogued material in the archive at the Trust that's very suggestive.'

'Suggestive of what?' Jake was trying to sound casual, but she could see his grip tightening on the stem of his glass.

'There was definitely a manuscript of some sort that the family wanted suppressed. And there are some clues in the letters that point to Fletcher Christian. I've been talking to the descendants of the last person known to have had the manuscript and I'm confident that I've got a strong lead on it.' It was a lie, but it weighed light in the balance compared to the ones he'd once told her.

'Really? You've got a lead on a Wordsworth manuscript relating to Fletcher Christian?' His eagerness was obvious now, which was entirely reasonable in the circumstances. What came next would be crucial. 'I can help, you know.'

Strike three. For once, there was no satisfaction in being right. Knowing she'd estimated Jake correctly was a stab in the heart. Jane pushed her chair back and reached for her coat. 'I don't think so. I wondered when you showed up. It's not that I suffer from low self-esteem, but I didn't think anyone as self-obsessed as you would have made such an effort to get back with me unless there was something in it for you. Well, now I know I was right. It's not me you're interested in, it's the manuscript.'

Panic spread across Jake's face. 'You've got it all

wrong, Jane. I don't give a damn about the manuscript, not compared to you.'

'I don't believe you. I think you're here for one reason and one reason only. To make you and your precious Caroline rich. Well, it's not going to happen, not off my hard work. And I'll be telling the family who own the manuscript not to trust you either.' She got to her feet, ignoring the consternation on that face she'd once loved to distraction. She was hurting hard, but she was determined she wasn't going to backslide. 'Goodbye, Jake.'

'Jane,' he cried as she walked to the door. But he didn't follow her, and she was glad of that. It reinforced her reading of the situation. It wasn't her he wanted. It was her manuscript.

Mentally berating herself, Jane got into her mother's car and set off for the eastern edge of the town, where Eddie Fairfield's cousin Letty lived in a granny flat attached to her son's house on Chestnut Hill. He'd told her Letty was Beattie's favourite grandchild; if she'd confided more about Dorcas to anyone, it would have been Letty.

Jane drew up at the car park exit, waiting for a gap in the traffic, still chiding herself for her earlier susceptibility rather than giving herself credit for her fixity of purpose. Her internal monologue was broken when to her surprise her brother drove past. She checked the time on the car clock. Twenty to two. Matthew must have left school at lunchtime.

Jane couldn't help wondering what he was up to. The family dentist was in Ambleside, the doctor in Grasmere. It was hard to imagine what was so urgent that Matthew would leave school early to deal with it.

Except, of course, his desire to beat her to the draw.

She thought of trying to follow him, but it was already too late. Three more cars had passed before she could squeeze out into the traffic, but by then he was out of sight. Cursing under her breath, Jane swallowed her anger and set off for Letty's. At least she could be pretty sure Matthew wasn't going there, since he was heading in the opposite direction.

It didn't occur to her at that point that he might have got to Letty before her. But she hadn't even got across the threshold when she found fresh reason to curse her stupidity in taking time out to have lunch with Jake. Letty seemed bewildered by her arrival. At first, Jane thought it was simply the confusion of age. Then she realised the truth. While she had been talking to Jake, Matthew had been interviewing Letty.

'Such a nice young man,' she said. 'I promised I'd look out some papers for him. I wasn't sure where they were, you see.'

Jane nodded, trying to keep her churning emotions in check. 'These would be old family papers?'

'That's right, dear. I thought they were packed up in one of the boxes in Gavin's garage. That's my son, Gavin. This is his house, he had the flat built on so I could be near at hand but still independent. But then the minute your brother had left, I remembered I'd put some boxes of family memorabilia in the wardrobe in the spare room, and when I went to look, there they were. That was lucky, wasn't it?'

Jane's heart beat a little faster. *Calm down, chances are it's nothing to do with what you're looking for.* 'It certainly was. I wonder, might I have a look at the papers? Matthew and I are working together on this project, and it would save him coming back to check them out. Since I'm here anyway . . .?'

'Of course, dear. Come through, they're on the kitchen table.'

As she followed Letty into the kitchen, she saw her quarry at once. A pile of papers, yellow with age, was loosely bundled together and tied with string. 'There you go, dear. You have a look through that and see if it's what you're looking for. Your brother was a bit vague, he just said there might be some Wordsworth papers from my great-great-grandmother. I doubt there's anything like that there, but you're welcome to see what you can find.'

Jane sat down and slipped the string off the bundle. The first sheet was unpromising. It was a letter dated 1886, addressed to Arthur Clewlow, congratulating him on the birth of his second son, also named Arthur. Jane scanned it quickly and put it to one side. The next was a recipe for rhubarb syllabub. The next few were household accounts from 1883. She carried on regardless, scrutinising every piece of paper for clues. Letty sat next to her, carrying on a running commentary of sensational irrelevance. Jane had to resist the impulse to ask her to get out of her own kitchen.

An hour later, Jane had to admit defeat. She knew more about the domestic minutiae of the branch of the Clewlows descended from Dorcas's elder son Arthur than any human being could reasonably wish for. But there was nothing about Dorcas herself, nor any reference to any manuscript in the family's possession. Jane turned over the last sheet and shook her head. 'I'm sorry, it's not what I was hoping to find.'

'Oh dear, I've wasted your time with my silly family trivia,' Letty said, looking genuinely distressed.

'Not at all. I appreciate you taking the time and trouble to look these out for us. Is that all there is? Nothing from Dorcas herself? Maybe in the boxes in the garage . . .?'

Letty shook her head. 'I'm sorry, dear, that's all I have from the old days. Granny Beattie used to talk about her granny, how she worked for William Wordsworth and was there at his deathbed, but I don't think she had any letters from her or anything like that.'

'Never mind.' Jane felt the now-familiar crush of disappointment. 'That's just the way it goes.' She stood up. 'Thanks for your time.'

'Not at all. It's a pleasure having the company of young people. I miss that, living here. When I was living in my old house down in Braithwaite I had lovely neighbours. They had two teenage lads who were always dropping in. They loved hearing stories about what it was like in the old days. But I never see them now,' she said wistfully. 'Nobody ever just drops in up here.'

Nothing Jane could think of saying felt adequate. 'I'm sorry,' she said.

'Don't get old, dear,' Letty said sadly as she showed her to the door. 'What was that song our Gavin was always playing back in the sixties? "Hope I die before I get old," that was it. They'll be old men themselves now, I suppose.'

'Only two of them,' Jane said. 'The other two managed the trick. But I don't imagine either of them was very happy about it.'

'No, I don't imagine they were. Well, good luck, dear. I hope you find what you're looking for.'

Jane waved goodbye, weighed down by the day. At least she had dinner with Jimmy and Dan to look forward to. A couple of hours to forget about betrayal and failure.

Jake finished his coffee, still smarting at Jane's treatment. Christ, what was it with women? He'd abased himself, offered his belly like a dog acknowledging the leader of the pack. And she'd taken it into her head to walk out on him. What a bitch. If he'd been relying on her loyalty, he'd have been deep in shit with Caroline by now.

Mind you, now Jane had blown him out, it was going to be a bit harder than he'd been hoping. He pursed his lips, looking so grim the waitress veered away from his table. Bitch. He was so sure he'd reel her in. But he'd had it with waiting for table scraps from the women in his life. Soon he was going to show them who was really top dog. He'd carry on with his own plans and find the bloody manuscript on his own. And then he'd show Jane what a fool she'd been to walk out on him. He'd be damned if she ever got a sniff of William Wordsworth's missing masterpiece.

Jane debated whether or not to stop off at the schoolhouse to tell Matthew not to waste his time going back to Keswick to see Letty's papers. And to give him a piece of her mind. She decided against it. There had been enough *Sturm und Drang* already that day to last her for several weeks. Besides, the fruitless journey was the least he deserved in return for his shitty behaviour. Instead, she picked up her phone and called Dan.

'Where are you?' she asked.

'I've just got on to the M1,' he said. 'Missy Elliott snagged me on my way out of the noon seminar, I think she was checking up on me.'

'Poor you. How did the seminars go?'

'You have my undying respect for not having committed an act of violence so far this term.' They laughed. 'Seriously, though, I think they went fine. Nobody asked anything I couldn't deal with, which was my main concern. And you? How's your day been so far?'

Jane filled him in. 'To be honest, the best bit was kicking Jake into touch.'

'Good for you, girl. We'll have to celebrate tonight.'

'Speaking of which, what time do you think you'll get here?'

'Seven? Half past? Depends on the traffic. Why?'

'Jimmy Clewlow is picking us up at half past eight for dinner.'

'Just couldn't stay away, huh? That's my animal magnetism for you.'

Jane poked her tongue out at the phone. 'You're wrong, you know. You just see queer everywhere.'

'We'll see.'

'I'm going now, I'm home. See you when I see you.'

As she pulled into the yard, she noticed a strange car and wondered idly which of her mother's friends had treated themselves to a new BMW. Not, she reckoned, anyone in the farming community. Not the way agricultural profits were going these days. Heaving a deep sigh, Jane dragged herself out of the car.

She opened the kitchen door to find two strangers

sitting at the kitchen table and her mother looking like the four horsemen of the apocalypse had just stabled their mounts in the barn. 'There you are,' Judy said, relief mixing with irritation in her voice.

Jane took in the visitors, who had risen to their feet without a trace of urgency. Whoever this pair were, they were no friends of her mother. The man looked rumpled, the tightness of his suit indicating that the slump of weight round his middle was relatively recent. The woman, by contrast, looked as if she worked out every day and loved it. Her taste in clothes spoiled the effect. Sweetly feminine didn't really work with shoulders like a Soviet shot-putter. 'Jane Gresham?' asked the woman. Her London accent was evident in those few syllables. 'I'm Detective Inspector Blair. This is Detective Sergeant Chappel. We need to have a few words with you.'

Jane dumped her bag on the table. 'ID?' she said. Both officers produced warrant cards, which she made a point of inspecting. 'The Met, huh? I assume you're here about Tenille,' she said, dropping into a chair. 'Have a seat, you're frightening my mother, looming like a pair of steers in her kitchen.'

They sat down again. 'Why would you assume that?' Donna asked.

'One: I haven't committed any criminal offences lately. Two: my friend Tenille is on the run from the police who have formed the bizarre notion that she murdered a man twice her age and size in London. And three,' she added, ticking the reasons off on her fingers, 'a very charming officer from Keswick came over on Saturday night and searched the entire farm in a fruitless attempt to find her.'

'Have you heard from Tenille at all since she left London?'

'I haven't had a phone call, an email, a text or any other form of communication from Tenille since I left London, which was before this crime was committed. As I told DI Rigston on Saturday. Nothing has happened since to alter that statement,' Jane said, aware she sounded pompous, but not caring. Donna Blair did not take her eyes off her for a moment.

'Tenille's aunt received a postcard from her yesterday morning, saying she was safe and well. Would you care to guess where that postcard came from?'

Jane tried to keep her face poker straight. 'No. Guessing seems to be your strong suit, since I can't imagine anything other than a wild guess that would connect Tenille to a murder.'

'We have reason to believe Tenille intended to come to you. If you're telling the truth, then I'm "guessing" something bad has happened to keep her from you. Doesn't that concern you?' Donna leaned forward as she spoke, resting her forearms on the table.

'Of course it concerns me. This whole business concerns me. And if I had any information, I would give it to you. I'm a decent citizen, Inspector. I don't believe the police are monsters. If I seem hostile, it's because I know Tenille isn't capable of murder. She's a thirteen-year-old who, unlike many of her contemporaries, doesn't hang out with wannabe gangstas. She doesn't do drugs. As far as I know, she doesn't even drink. And while you're wasting your time and resources trying to find her, the real killer is walking around laughing at you.' Jane came to a halt, feeling flushed and hating it.

'Then you won't mind if we have a look around?'
Donna said mildly.

'Better ask my mother. It's her house.'

Donna turned to Judy. 'Have you noticed any food
going missing, Mrs Gresham?'

Judy looked astounded. 'Food?'

'If she's here, she has to eat,' Donna said.

'No, nothing like that. And I would notice, believe
you me,' Judy said indignantly.

'Fine. Do you mind if we have a look around?'

Judy looked helplessly at Jane, who nodded. 'It's
OK, Mum. I'll go with them.'

She led Donna and her sergeant through the house.
When they got to her bedroom, Donna clocked the
laptop. 'Do you mind booting up your machine?' she
said. 'I'd like to take a look at your email records.'

Saying nothing, Jane did as she was asked, going
online to make it easier for the detective. Donna spent
ten minutes checking everything obvious, including
the <recently deleted> folder. 'Thank you,' she said
when she had finished.

They trailed through the remaining rooms then
Donna asked to see the farm buildings. Jane took
great pleasure in taking them on the most disgusting
route, making sure they had to walk through mud
and sheep dung. It took more than half an hour before
they were satisfied. They didn't even notice the slaughterhouse, tucked away in the far corner of the field
behind the house. But then, she'd planned their route
to avoid any possibility of them catching a glimpse of
it. Finally, Donna grudgingly admitted that Tenille did
not appear to be on the farm.

'Don't get any daft idealistic notions in your head

about protecting the innocent,' she said as Jane walked them to the car. 'If you hear from her, tell us. Like you said, we're not monsters. If she's innocent, she's got nothing to fear.'

'I will,' Jane lied. She watched them leave, uneasy. If they'd come all the way from London to talk to her, they were taking this seriously. Would they take it seriously enough to stake out the farm? A man on the hill with a pair of night-sight binoculars would spot her late-night visits to the slaughterhouse. It was, however, a risk she was going to have to take. She couldn't abandon Tenille now. She had to keep protecting the girl at least until the Hammer got in touch.

Our little community began to have the air of an established colony, with the marking out of gardens & animal pens. We fished & farmed & our fences made good neighbours of us. Our women gave birth to children & we explored our new home. Among the many strange discoveries were stone chisels & hatchets & four idols, crude representations of men hewn roughly from stone. These stones we took for foundations for our buildings, seeing no purpose in leaving them idle. We established a governance of sorts, with decisions of import being taken by a simple majority of the white men. I myself maintained a log of daily life, in part out of habit from shipboard life, in part so that our descendants might comprehend their own beginnings. Although we saw from time to time the unmistakable silhouette of whaling ships on the horizon, none came near enough to trouble us. In short, we seemed set comfortably on course to build a brave new world on our Prospero's Isle.

32

In the end, Dan had been trapped in traffic on the M6 so Jimmy and Jane had set off together, arranging with Dan to meet at the restaurant. Jimmy's company was the perfect antidote to Jane's frustrating day. His relaxed take on life, his apparent refusal to take himself seriously and his open, humorous conversation made it impossible for her to do anything other than respond in kind.

He'd suggested an Italian restaurant in Ambleside whose owner encouraged live jazz. There was no band playing that night, but cool tenor sax spilled from the speakers as they walked in. 'I love coming back here,' Jimmy said. 'I played my first paying gig here, back when I was in the Lower Sixth. Five quid each – and frankly that was overpaying us. If he likes our music, your pal Dan should enjoy it here.'

Jane smiled. 'He's got pretty eclectic tastes.'

'Are you two an item?'

Jane couldn't restrain the laugh. 'Me and Dan? No way. Even if he was my type, it would be a waste of effort. It's not women that set Dan's pulse racing.'

'He's gay?'

'As gay as they come,' Jane said, picking up her menu, trying not to show her pleasure at Jimmy's interest in her relationship status.

After they'd ordered food and wine, Jimmy grinned at her, his brown eyes twinkling with good humour. 'It's great to see you,' he said. 'I often think about those long summer days on Langmere Fell when we were kids.'

So much for Dan's gaydar, Jane thought, happily basking in Jimmy's attention. 'We must have covered every square inch of this side of the fell, playing Treasure Island and hide and seek and Viking raiders,' Jane said. 'I always liked the way you didn't make me be the beautiful princess who had to be rescued. That's all Matthew ever wanted me to be. But you let me be a pirate or a Viking.'

Jimmy shrugged. 'Anything to make up the numbers. I always thought it was a pity we grew apart after we hit our teens.'

'It goes that way. Girls have to do their girl thing and boys have to pretend to hate us. Until we get to the point where we have to start fancying each other.'

'But that's not really about friendship either, it's about the ritual dance of rites of passage,' Jimmy said. 'Spots and sexual insecurity, that's about all I remember of those middle years at school.'

And they were off down the road of reminiscence. There were undercurrents in their conversation. Jane could feel them, though she was reluctant to acknowledge their existence. Jimmy wasn't exactly handsome, but there was something undeniably attractive about him. Something to do with his obvious intelligence, but also something open and generous. The opposite of Jake, she thought. Jake, whose face was always guarded, never quite telling the whole story, always leaving her guessing as to the real agenda.

As that thought crossed her mind, Dan arrived, looking remarkably composed for a man who'd spent hours wrestling with the traffic. Jimmy jumped to his feet, a wide grin animating his face. To Jane's surprise, the men hugged in greeting. Jimmy couldn't seem to take his eyes off Dan as drinks were ordered. At one point, Dan flicked her a knowing look. So much for her instincts. There was nothing more to Jimmy's behaviour with her than friendliness. Dan had been right. He was the one Jimmy was interested in. Jane smarted briefly, then saw the funny side. She didn't even mind being exiled to the fringes of the conversation as Jimmy and Dan talked music.

They were mid-way through their main courses when Jimmy did her job for her and brought the conversation back to where she really wanted it to be. 'So, what's this research project you're working on? The one you were hoping to talk to Gran about?'

'I'm really sorry about what happened yesterday,' Jane said. 'Alice got hold of the wrong end of the stick.'

'Something Alice has always had a talent for,' Jimmy said drily. 'I didn't read it like she did. But she'd gone off on one before I could stop her. I'm sorry she humiliated you like that. You didn't deserve it.'

'I probably wasn't being very tactful. But I genuinely didn't know my bloody brother had already spoken to Edith.' Jane sighed, shaking her head.

'Matthew up to his old tricks?'

Jane's face registered surprise. 'What do you mean?'

'Matthew was always trying to make you look bad. Especially when there were any grown-ups around. He's always had issues with Jane,' he added, turning to Dan. 'It was always obvious to me. It made me very wary of him. I figured if he could be so vicious to his own sister, it was better to stay on his good side.'

Jane blinked back tears. Finding someone else who read the situation with Matthew from her side was a novelty for her. 'I had no idea anybody else saw it. I'm so used to him managing to put me in the wrong. I fight back now, but I had to leave and come back before I could really take him on.'

'So what's Matthew trying to screw up for you this time?'

So they told him: the body in the bog, the letters, the search for Dorcas Mason, the duplicity of her brother and the scheming of Jake and Caroline. Jimmy listened, occasionally asking a question for clarification. When their recital limped to its unsatisfactory end, he whistled softly. 'No wonder you were so interested in my gran. It sounds like the obvious place to start.'

'She was the most likely person,' Dan said. 'Every interview we do now takes us further from the direct line of primogeniture.'

'I could ask around,' Jimmy offered without a pause for thought. 'Everybody's going to be here for the funerals – all our side of the family and now all Auntie Tillie's lot as well.'

Dan shook his head. 'We don't want you pissing off your family.'

Jimmy grinned. 'There are quite a few in my extended family that it would be a genuine pleasure to piss off, trust me. I'll just put a few feelers out there – the way the older generation gossip, it'll soon have better circulation than any of them have these days.'

'You've always been one of the good guys, Jimmy,' Jane said.

He shrugged, looking embarrassed. 'You guys deserve a break,' he said. 'I know that if it was some undiscovered Duke Ellington piece, I'd be desperate to hear it. I'll do whatever I can to help you out.'

It was past midnight when Jane finally made it out to the slaughterhouse. The three-way conversation had grown hilarious as the connections between them had deepened. Jane had tried not to mind too much when it became clear that Jimmy and Dan were planning to rendezvous at Shepherd's Cott after she'd been dropped off.

As she jumped down from Jimmy's people carrier, she noticed a light on in the kitchen window. She walked in to find her mother pretending she hadn't been waiting up for her chick to come home.

'I was watching something on the TV and I fancied a hot chocolate to settle me down,' Judy said defensively as soon as Jane walked in.

Jane grinned. 'Nothing to do with me being out to dinner with a man you classify as one step above a dole-ite.'

'I never said that about Jimmy.'

'As good as. He's very successful in his field, you know. Not many musicians make it work, but he seems to be.'

Judy harrumphed. 'He would say that, though, wouldn't he?'

'Mum, you can calm down. It's Dan he's interested in, not me.'

It was comical watching Judy trying to act as if this were everyday conversation in Fellhead. 'Oh,' she said at last. 'Well, fancy that.'

'I'll make myself a coffee,' Jane said, taking pity.

'At this time of night? You'll never sleep,' Judy said, relief in her voice.

'Mother, I'm twenty-five, not twelve.' And so it had gone on, the gentle bickering of two women who love without understanding each other. Judy had eventually gone to bed, leaving Jane sipping coffee and reading the parish magazine by the Aga. Jane gave her mother fifteen minutes to fall asleep, then she changed from her smart shoes into her wellies and tiptoed out of the house.

Jane crept along the wall, trying not to trigger the yard lights. Then, hugging the hedge, she made it into the field. She turned the key in the lock and inched inside the slaughterhouse. She sensed at once that the building was empty.

Panicking, she snapped on her torch and shone it round the room, caring less about possible discovery than proving her instincts wrong. But her gut had told her the truth. Tenille was gone.

But not gone in a permanent way. Her possessions were still here, scattered around the sleeping bag nest. She wouldn't have gone without her MP3 player or her books. Her backpack was missing, it was true. But her change of clothes was still here. So where the hell was she? Had she gone for a late-night stroll, imagining it would be safe at this time of night? More importantly, would she be able to find her way back in the dark?

Jane considered waiting for her to return. She would be easier in her mind if she knew the girl was safely stowed back in the slaughterhouse, even if it did make her feel as if she was acting like her own mother. And she suspected Tenille's reaction would be much the same as her own – get out of my face, leave me alone, it's none of your business. Only Tenille wouldn't hold back as Jane had done. She'd let rip and the thin thread of trust between them would be damaged again.

And what would happen then? What would happen if Tenille got sufficiently pissed off to disappear into the night for good? The cops would find her sooner or later. But, more significantly for Jane, she had sent a message out into the world for John Hampton. How would he react if he called, only to discover Jane had driven Tenille away? Or worse. What if he and Tenille had already made contact? What if he was on his way back here now with her? Jane shuddered at the possibilities unfolding in her head.

No, best to leave it. Best to head back to her own bed. Best to put everything in a box and leave it sealed up till morning. At least that way she might just get some sleep. Things were happening out there in the dark. But she didn't want to know what they were or how they would affect her. Let them get on with their own thing. All she wanted was to bury the day a mile deep in sleep.

It was totally spooky how just a few days out of

London had messed with her head, Tenille thought as she approached the outskirts of Keswick. Like, this was the sort of place she should feel secure. Somewhere with streets and shops instead of sheep and hedges. But it felt like this was a bad place for her, a place with people and traffic. Because both of those also meant cops. Being on these streets was weird and scary.

The worst bit was not knowing where she was going. The Ordnance Survey map was as much use here as a chocolate chip pan. And a bike without lights was asking for trouble on streets where occasional cars drove past. As the houses grew more dense around her, Tenille pushed the bike into an alley and set off on foot for the town centre, hugging the shadows, completely without a plan. She couldn't ask anybody, not looking like she did. She almost felt homesick for London, where she could have asked a cabbie for directions, or found an all-night internet café and googled the address.

But luck was with her. As she drew close to the town centre, streets of huddled Victorian terraces branched off on either side, their names testament to the era of their construction. Those names meant nothing to Tenille; when Sebastopol Street followed Inkerman Street and Crimea Street, it came as a huge relief. All she knew was that the serendipity had made her night.

Eddie Fairfield's house was halfway down the terrace. As she looked up at the narrow façade, her heart sank. It was way too public for a frontal assault, and she had no idea how to get round the back. She walked on to the end of the street, where she spotted a tight entryway leading between the end house and the corner shop. Tenille took a few steps into the alley and found it turned into a wide passageway running the length of the street. And, conveniently, each back gate had its wheelie bin standing sentry beside it. Enough of them had numbers painted on the sides for Tenille to figure out which house was Eddie's.

She pushed against the gate in the brick wall, pleasantly surprised when it opened easily and silently. She found herself in a small back yard, no more than a dozen square metres of concrete enclosed by brick walls and the house itself. She crept across the yard, nearly crying out loud when a cat jumped yowling on to the wall behind her. Man, she was going to have nerves of steel by the time she'd finished sorting Jane's research project out for her.

Even more surprisingly, the back door of the house was unlocked, swinging open as she depressed the handle. Tenille couldn't imagine anyone she knew leaving their door unlocked after midnight. Not unless they had a serious desire to lose all their worldly goods. She stepped cautiously inside, pushing the door to behind her. A faint light gleamed from the hallway, revealing that she was in a tiny kitchen. A couple of mugs sat on the draining board and a dirty plate lay in the sink, fork and knife askew.

Tenille moved into the room off the kitchen, which contained a dining table and chairs and the sort of display cabinet she'd only ever seen through the windows of antique shops. No papers there, just horrible china shepherdesses and other car boot sale tat. The door to the hall was open and, as she drew nearer, a faint smell crept towards her. It smelled like a cat litter tray that nobody had cleaned out for a while – the dark reek of shit, the sharp bite of urine, overlaid by a bitter edge of spent tobacco. She couldn't understand why people had cats indoors. They were meant to be outside, not stinking up houses like this.

The stench grew worse as she gathered her courage to move out into the light of the hallway. She crept towards the other open door, almost gagging now at the smell. She peered round the door jamb and nearly added her own contribution to the smell.

Half-facing the door, mouth hanging open and eyes staring at nothing, an old man lay sprawled in an armchair. The bright overhead light revealed dark stains on his grey flannel trousers. It wasn't the explanation for the foul air that Tenille had been expecting. For a long moment, she was frozen in place, staring at the dead body opposite, her heart thudding so loud it sounded like a drum in her head.

'Oh shit,' she said. What the hell was she supposed to do now?

But the same serpent that ensnared the first Adam also reared its head to strike at us. From the start, our numbers were unmatched. We were fifteen men to twelve women. It was agreed that the white men should have a woman each for their exclusive companionship & that, according to their own custom, the six native men should share the remaining three women. But soon after we made our home on Pitcairn, Williams' wife died & he demanded the right to a wife for his exclusive use. Although I was opposed to this, I was overruled by the majority and the decision was taken that the natives must lose one of their women. It came as no surprise to me that the natives took this to be a humiliation. But I did not expect they would take it as occasion to plot against their masters. Two natives proved to be ringleaders in this wicked connivance & we were forced to take action to protect ourselves and our families. By dint of persuasion, I arranged to have them killed by their fellow natives. Thus peace & harmony were restored to our little world. Or such was my belief, at any rate, & it was some little time before I was proved to be wrong.

33

Jane turned over and checked the clock. Ten past two. Nine minutes since she'd last looked. Sleep seemed as elusive as the Wordsworth manuscript. She kept almost nodding off, but then the events of the day would combine in an uncomfortable kaleidoscope that made her start awake. She had that uneasy feeling that she had missed something crucial, something to do with Donna Blair's visit. But it remained elusive.

At some point, the shallow dozing gave way to proper sleep. When she finally woke, she couldn't believe she'd slept till quarter to twelve. They had work to do. Why hadn't Dan called? Even in her sleep-fuddled state, Jane knew the answer to that one. She threw back the covers, grabbed her dressing gown and hurtled downstairs. 'Why didn't you wake me up?' she demanded as she burst into the kitchen. It was empty. A note propped against a vase of late roses read, *Dad and I have gone to Dalegarth to look at a litter of puppies. Toad in the hole in the fridge, just needs heating through, put it in the bottom oven while you're having your shower. We'll be back by teatime. See you later. Love, Mum.*

Tutting in exasperation and muttering curses at Dan, Jane did as she was told. Twenty minutes later, she returned to the kitchen, clean and dressed, her damp curls a corkscrew cascade over her shoulders. She took the hot dish out of the oven and divided it between two bowls. She covered them with a cloth then headed out for the slaughterhouse, apprehensive about what might await her.

This time when she opened the door, she could see Tenille sprawled on the stone bench, fully dressed inside her sleeping bag, one arm thrown back over her head. She looked absurdly young to be fending for herself. 'Rise and shine,' Jane called, closing the door with her hip and taking the food over to Tenille.

The girl woke up, rubbing her eyes and yawning. She said something that sounded like, 'Wagwan?' which Jane translated as, 'What's going on?'

'Wamcha?' Jane replied, a response she'd learned from Tenille which corresponded to, 'What happened to you?'

'Last night,' Jane continued. 'Where were you?'

'Man, is that hot food?' Tenille's eyes widened and her nostrils flared. 'Smells good.'

'I thought we could have brunch together. Since we were both apparently awake till late last night,' Jane said, a dark warning in her voice.

'You stopped by?' Tenille sounded surprised. 'I figured you couldn't get out. Thought you'd gone to bed.' She stretched luxuriantly. 'You going to share or just torture me?'

'I'm not sure you deserve it. What the hell were you doing, going out like that? Anyone could have seen you.'

Tenille shook her head, reaching for a bowl, which Jane smartly snatched out of her reach. 'There's nobody out round here that time of night,' Tenille said dismissively. 'They all tucked up in bed. I think they turn off the electricity at midnight. And even if anybody does see me, all they're going to see is somebody on a bike. It's not like they're going to clock that I'm black.'

'A bike?' Jane said faintly.

'I borrow your bike. I didn't think you'd mind. Now, are you going to give me that food or what?'

Jane handed over the dish. Tenille looked at it suspiciously. 'What the fuck?' she said.

'Toad in the hole.'

'Looks more like turd in the hole,' Tenille said. 'I never saw a sausage curled up like dogshit before.'

'It's Cumberland sausage. A local delicacy,' Jane said. 'Eat it, or I will. I can't believe you took my bike out in the middle of the night. What if a cop had stopped you?'

'Why would they? It's not against the law to ride a bike round, even in the middle of the night.'

'It is if you haven't got any lights. And I know for a fact that the lights for my bike are on the shelf in the hall.' Jane glared at her.

Tenille shrugged, her mouth full of sausage and feather-light batter. 'I'll take my chances,' she mumbled when she'd finally swallowed. 'Hey, this is good.'

'Luckily my mother thinks I have the appetite of a small army,' Jane said. 'But why have you been cycling round the district in the dead of night?'

Tenille looked guilty. 'I had to get out. Man, I was

going stir crazy. You try being locked up in here twenty-four seven. See how long you can stand it.'

'It's more than that,' Jane said. 'I can tell. There's something you're not telling me.'

Now the girl was definitely looking shifty. 'Don't ask and you won't get told no lies.'

'I want the truth, Tenille. Stop being so bloody evasive. I'm putting myself on the line keeping you here, the least you can do is be straight with me.' There was no pretence now; Jane was genuinely angry.

Tenille refused to meet her eyes. 'I was trying to be helpful,' she said.

'Helpful how? What's helpful about wandering around in the middle of the night?'

Tenille shuffled her feet inside her sleeping bag. 'I been visiting the old people,' she said.

'What? What old people?'

'The ones you've been talking to about this manuscript. I figured you're too soft, Jane. Anybody could lie to you and you wouldn't know they were doing it if you trusted them. So I figured they might be lying when they said they didn't have no papers.'

Jane looked aghast. 'You've been breaking into their houses?'

'I never broke nothing,' Tenille protested. 'I just found a way in. Then I took a look round.'

A horrible suspicion bubbled up in Jane's head in spite of her knowledge of the girl. 'You didn't scare them, did you?'

Tenille looked contemptuous. 'Course I didn't. When I went to that Edith woman's house, she was already dead and gone, the house was empty. And so was the house in Grasmere. If anybody's been doing the scaring, it's been them. Man, I nearly crapped myself last night. I went to that guy Edward Fairfield's house in Keswick. Soon as I walked in the door, I thought there was something hinky going on. It smelled funny. Like shit. Anyways, I walked into the living room and there he was, sitting in his chair, dead as a fucking dodo.' She shook her head. 'I tell you, I've seen enough dead people lately to last me a lifetime.'

Jane finally recovered the power of speech. 'He was dead?' she yelped. 'Eddie Fairfield was dead?'

Tenille nodded. 'I touched his hand, just to make sure. He was freezing cold, Jane. It wasn't nice. His mouth was hanging open and I could see his false teeth and everything. And he'd shat himself. That's what the smell was.'

'What did you do?'

Tenille shovelled more food into her mouth. 'Wasn't anything I *could* do, was there? He was long gone. So I just did what I went for and searched the place.' She glanced up at Jane. 'Don't look at me like that. Fuck's sake, what was I supposed to do? He was already dead, Jane. Old people die all the time, it's what they do. I went there with something in mind and I did it. It didn't hurt nobody and I never found anything, so it's like I was never there.'

Jane put her head in her hands. 'I can't believe it.'

'I was trying to help,' Tenille whined.

'I mean, I can't believe another one of these old people has died. That's three, all in Dorcas's family line. Three in the space of four days. That's not natural.' Her words were muffled by her hands, but Tenille heard them clearly enough.

'It's how it goes, Jane. They get to where they feel

like they've nothing to live for, somebody else close to them passes and it's like they lose the will to live. It happened to my gran's cousin. When my gran passed, her cousin died two days later. And it's not like they were big buddies, just family, you know?'

Jane shook her head, like a swimmer emerging from water. 'It's just too weird, that's all.' She pushed her bowl away, suddenly lost for appetite.

'You done with that? Can I have it?'

'Help yourself.' Jane waited till Tenille had finished eating, then took her bowl from her. 'Promise me you're going to stay put. Otherwise I'm going to take the key off you.'

Tenille grinned. 'You'd have to find it first.' She held her hands up, palms outward. 'OK, I submit. I'll stay home. But you got to figure something out because I am going to die if I stay here much longer.'

'That I doubt,' Jane said drily. 'I'll see you later.'

She walked back to the kitchen, shocked and bemused. She couldn't take it in. Eddie Fairfield had been frail, but he'd been full of beans. Jane couldn't believe he'd just slipped out of life so easily. She picked up her mobile, considering whether to alert someone to Eddie's death, when she noticed there was a voice-mail message. She dialled the service and heard Dan's voice. Her relief turned swiftly to dismay as his words sank in.

'Hi, Jane. It's Dan. Jimmy just called me.' He cleared his throat. 'I've got some bad news for you. Eddie Fairfield – the guy you went to see yesterday – Jimmy just heard that he passed away last night. Jimmy had been planning to go round there and ask him about the manuscript. He reckoned if the papers had ended up on that side of the family, Eddie's the one who would have known. So we're fucked on that score. Anyway, I just thought I'd let you know. Phone me when you can.'

Jane ended the call and dropped her head into her hands. She might be off the hook as far as letting anyone know about Eddie's tragic end. But she was starting to feel like the Angel of Death and it was scary. Her expression troubled, she dialled Dan. He picked up right away.

'You get my message?' he said abruptly.

'Yes. I can't believe it. That's the third person on our list who's died. It's too much of a coincidence, Dan.'

'Why? Old people are frail, they die – it happens all the time. The death certificate's usually signed by their own doctor, isn't it? Well, if there'd been anything suspicious, the doctor would pick up on it right away and order a post mortem. If those three hadn't died of natural causes, you'd have heard. For a start, they wouldn't be allowing the funerals to go ahead.'

'You think?'

'I think.'

'It makes me feel funny, that's all. They were on my list, and they died in the same order.' She let out a sigh, pushing her hair back from her troubled face. 'So did you have a nice time with Jimmy?'

'You don't want to know how nice,' Dan said smugly. 'Let's just say it was very late when he headed back to Alice's.'

'Well, I'm glad one of us is having a good time,' she said tartly.

'What's the plan for today?' Dan asked.

'I don't know. I'm feeling pretty shaken. I'll call you later when my head's straight. You could always ring Jimmy, see if he wants to help you pass the time.'

'I might just do that. Catch you later.'

Jane tried to tell herself Tenille and Dan were probably right. Edith, Tillie and Eddie were all in their eighties. Old people did die, and sometimes they just threw in the towel when the aches and pains and frailty got too much for them. But she wanted to mark their passing in some way. Her experience with Alice Clewlow had made it clear to her that she'd better steer clear of wakes and funerals lest she be tarred with the graverobber tag again. But she could still pay her respects. Families tended to stick to the same undertaker. She wouldn't mind betting that Tillie Swain and Eddie Fairfield would be at Gibson's in Keswick.

A little later, Jane walked into the large Victorian pile that had been a funeral home for as long as anyone locally could remember. A depressingly unctuous young man in a black suit met her in the hall. She couldn't escape thoughts of Uriah Heep as she explained the purpose of her visit. 'Mrs Swain is in Derwent, just down the hall,' he told her. 'But I'm afraid we're still preparing Mr Fairfield for viewing. You'll have to come back tomorrow to see him. If you'd like to follow me?'

Jane let him lead her down the panelled hall and usher her in through a door marked 'Derwent' in Gothic script. The room held a dozen chairs upholstered in red velvet and, set on polished oak trestles, a simple pine coffin. Uriah closed the door behind her and Jane walked slowly across to the coffin. She'd had little experience of the dead and was surprised by how mundane Tillie Swain's corpse appeared. She was expertly made up, but her pallor was hard to hide. She wore a dress with a mandarin collar in peacock blue silk with matching necklace and earrings. She looked like a rather unappetising mannequin.

Jane tried to empty her mind and find something meaningful to focus on. But her brain refused to offer her anything but cliché and, after a few minutes, somehow disappointed in herself, she decided to leave. As she walked back towards the front door, a tiny young woman came bounding in the door in a most unfunereal manner. Long dark hair cascaded round her face and she grinned at the young attendant as she passed. 'Hi, Chris,' she said cheerily.

'Good afternoon, Dr Wilde,' he said, his grave tone a reproach to her energy.

Startled, Jane stopped short. As the woman drew level with her, she said, 'Excuse me? Are you Dr Wilde, the forensic anthropologist?'

River paused. 'That's right, yes.'

'You're dealing with the bog body?'

River gestured towards a flight of stairs leading downwards. 'He's right here on the premises.'

'Can I ask you a question?'

River smiled. She was always happy to share her expertise. 'Of course.'

'The tattoos. Are they typical of the South Sea islands? Tahiti in particular?'

'They are, as a matter of fact. Why do you ask?'

'I've a theory that your bog body is Fletcher

407

Christian.' Seeing River's frown of curiosity, she added, 'You know? Mutiny on the *Bounty*. Mr Christian –'

'Here we go again,' River said impatiently. 'Yes, I know who Fletcher Christian is. You're not the first person to mention that very possibility to me. I'm beginning to wonder if there's something in the water that has everybody wondering if my Pirate Peat was Fletcher Christian.'

'Pirate Peat?'

'My nickname for the bog body. We're making a TV programme, they like something catchy. So what's your interest?'

'I'm a Wordsworth scholar. I'm exploring the possibility that Fletcher came back to his native land and told his story to William.'

'Sounds pretty vague to me.' River glanced at her watch. 'Look –'

'I've got a lot of circumstantial evidence. And a couple of letters that back it up. I don't think there's anyone around here who knows more about Fletcher Christian than me. If you want accurate historical detail for your TV programme, I could help.'

River grinned. 'But actually, what you want is to know if this is your man?'

Jane nodded. 'Yes, but the offer still stands. Any chance of it being him?'

River made a decision. 'Come on down and I'll show you what I've got so far,' she said, heading for the stairs. 'What's your name, by the way?'

'Jane Gresham.'

River turned and they exchanged a clumsy handshake on the stairs. 'Did you come here to see me?'

'No, I came to pay my respects to someone I interviewed a couple of days ago. Not anyone close, but I just wanted to . . . oh, I don't know. Everybody seems to be dying.'

'Everybody?'

'Well, only the ones I interview for my research project.'

'What? The Wordsworth thing?' River swung round at the foot of the stairs to face Jane, a vaguely incredulous look on her face.

Jane paused on the bottom step and sighed. 'Yeah, the Wordsworth thing. I drew up a list of people to interview – descendants of the last person to have had the manuscript. And all these old dears on the list seem to be slipping away. It's a bit spooky, that's all.'

'Unexplained clusters of elderly deaths do occur from time to time. There's always a reason – heart, whatever – but often no particular thing that points to why today as opposed to any other day.' She put a hand on Jane's arm. 'Don't let it get to you. Come on, I'll introduce you to Pirate Peat. We've finished filming for today and the students won't be back for a bit, so we can have him to ourselves.'

Jane followed River into a room that could have provided a film set for a Victorian operating theatre. On a table in the centre of the room lay a surprisingly small bundle. Without muscles and flesh, Pirate Peat looked like a human-shaped leather bag filled with bones. The tattoos were evident, their decorated bands circling his waist. Jane looked for the other tattoo she knew Fletcher Christian had possessed, the star of the Order of the Garter on the left side of his chest. But that area was missing, rough tear marks round the edge of a hole roughly eight inches in diameter. 'What happened there?' she asked, pointing to it.

'Probably eaten by animals at some point,' River said.

'Could it have been deliberately cut away? By the killer?'

River frowned and examined the tear more clearly. 'I don't think so, it looks more like it's been torn by teeth. What makes you think it might have been deliberate?'

'Because Fletcher Christian had a distinctive tattoo just there.'

River raised her eyebrows. 'You're as good as your word, Jane. Full of interesting gobbets of information. Tell you what, I'll take another look under the microscope, see if I can come up with a definitive answer . . .' She paused, as if struck by a thought. 'This manuscript of yours – is it something a dealer would be interested in?'

'You bet,' Jane said. 'If there really is a poem in a holograph manuscript, it would likely fetch over a million at auction. Which would mean a tidy commission for the dealer. Why do you ask?'

'A guy came up to me the other night, over in the hotel bar. He said he was a document dealer, that he was following up reports of a possible manuscript connected to Fletcher Christian. And he was interested to know whether I thought this could be the man.' She gestured at the body on the table.

Jane felt her heart sink. 'His name wasn't Jake Hartnell, was it?'

'You know him?'

'Only too well,' she said heavily. If she'd needed confirmation that Jake was more interested in the manuscript than in her, here it was. 'Let's just say we don't see eye to eye on most things.'

River raised one eyebrow. 'Can't say I took to him myself.'

Jane gave a wry smile. 'Then you're at least as good a judge of the living as the dead.' She glanced at her watch. 'I'd better be going. Thanks for showing me this.'

'My pleasure. And I'll keep you posted. If this turns out to be Fletcher Christian, you'll be the first to know.'

Ewan Rigston was briefing his team on an armed robbery at a petrol station when the message came through from the front desk that Alice Clewlow was waiting to see him. He wound up the briefing and had her sent up to his office. He remembered Alice. She was a few years younger than him, but he'd once asked her out to a rugby club hop. She'd laughed, not unkindly, and told him he was wasting his time. He'd been offended at the time, but over the years, it had gradually dawned on him that her rejection had been generic rather than specific. Not that she broadcast the fact. Discretion, that was always the name of the game in a small town.

He hadn't seen her except at a distance for a few years, and he was pleasantly surprised to see how little she'd changed. A few more lines, a few silver hairs. But still the same old Alice. She'd retained the air of confidence and competence that he remembered as surprising in a teenager. As she sat down, he noticed a tension round her eyes that he hadn't spotted at first glance. 'Hello, Alice,' he said, waiting till she was settled before he sat down.

'Thanks for seeing me, Ewan. Or should I call you Detective Inspector Rigston these days?' There was a genuine enquiry beneath the light tone.

'Ewan will do fine,' he said. 'I was sorry to hear about your grandmother,' he added, remembering the mention of Edith Clewlow's death in the weekend report.

'That's what I'm here about,' Alice said.

Rigston frowned. 'You think there was something suspicious about Mrs Clewlow's death?' His heart sank. There was nothing more troublesome than relatives who got a bee in their bonnet about perfectly natural deaths.

'I didn't at the time,' Alice said. 'But since then, two other relatives have died. Both elderly, it's true. But one was my gran's sister-in-law, Tillie Swain. Over at Grasmere. The other was Tillie's second cousin, Eddie Fairfield. He lives here in Keswick. They all died in the night, and they've all been certified as natural causes.' She paused, her expression one of caution. 'You think I'm daft, don't you?'

'No, Alice, I'd never think that of you. But I'm struggling to understand why you think this is police business. I know it's hard to accept, but old people often pass away without there being any sinister implications.'

'I understand that, Ewan. But would you feel the same if I told you there was something else linking them?'

'What sort of something else?' he asked, leaning forward, his interest piqued.

'There's a woman called Jane Gresham –'

'From Fellhead?' Rigston interrupted. 'Gresham's Farm?'

'That's right. You know her?'

'Let's just say our paths have crossed in a professional capacity. What's Jane Gresham's connection to your gran?'

'She's looking for a manuscript that she thinks one of our ancestors might have got from Wordsworth. She came to my house with some bloke she's working with when my gran was barely cold, pretending to offer her condolences. But what she was really after was finding out whether Gran had these papers. Her brother – he's the headmaster at the primary school in Fellhead – he'd rung Gran about it the day she died. Helping his sister, I suppose.'

'I'm still not quite sure where this is taking us,' Rigston said, his interest seeping away.

'You remember my little brother Jimmy? Plays drums?' Rigston nodded and Alice continued. 'He was pally with Jane when they were kids. They hooked up again at the wake. They went out for dinner last night. Jimmy didn't get home till the small hours, and when I told him about Eddie this morning, he looked really shocked. He said Jane Gresham had a list of people she thought might have this manuscript. Gran's name was top of the list. The next name was Tillie Swain and after her came Eddie Fairfield.' Alice stopped and gave Rigston a level stare. 'Now do you think it might be suspicious?'

'It's odd, I'll grant you that. But are you really suggesting Jane Gresham is running round the district killing old people just to get her hands on some old manuscript?'

413

Alice shrugged. 'I don't know what to think, Ewan. All I know is that members of my family keep dying. And I think you need to look into it.'

While we remained on the ship, I had been able to exercise the authority of a captain. But once on land, my shipmates cleaved to the conviction that no man should be their master again. They perceived themselves as the landed gentry of Pitcairn, & some discovered in themselves a need to oppress others in order to savour their power fully. Quintal & McCoy were prime among this tendency, & they were wont to flog their natives at the least excuse. Bligh's fate had taught them nothing; they could not comprehend that such cruel & arbitrary treatment might justifiably recoil against them. However I pleaded with them that such behaviour was both unnecessary & provocative, they would not change their ways. I began to fear for all of us & decided to take precautions accordingly.

34

Jane's phone started ringing on the doorstep of Gibson's, making her start guiltily. Just as well it hadn't rung while she'd been paying her respects to Tillie Swain. She pulled her mobile out of her backpack and glanced at the display. An unfamiliar mobile number. Only one way to find out who was calling. She hit a key and put it to her ear. 'Hello?'

The voice on the other end was deep and formal. 'Dr Gresham? I believe you wanted to speak to me? Bearing in mind that cellphone to cellphone is not what you could call secure . . .'

The Hammer, she realised, looking around instinctively to make sure nobody was watching her. *Thank you, mad Mrs Gallagher.* 'Thanks for calling. I need to speak to you about the matter we discussed last week.'

'Again?' There was a chuckle in his voice, which frightened her more than any threat could have.

'The solution you came up with last time appears to have created some fresh problems,' Jane said, choosing her words carefully.

'So I heard.'

'Our friend now refuses to solve her problems in

the obvious way because she feels too much loyalty. And she's adamant that you too must avoid taking that particular course of action.'

'I think I understand you. Neither of us wants to talk to William, right?'

The name threw Jane off balance. Why was the Hammer talking to her about Wordsworth? It took her a moment to make the connection; William, Bill, Old Bill. 'That's about the size of it,' she said cautiously.

'You're very close to our friend, right?'

How did spies manage this sort of cloaked conversation, Jane wondered. She felt completely out of her depth in shark-infested waters. 'Yes, but I don't know how long that's going to last,' she said, hoping he would understand.

'If you can manage to make it last till the weekend, I'll get it sorted.' Hampton sounded calm and confident.

'You'll both be OK?'

'Oh, you can count on that, Dr Gresham,' he said, and ended the call.

Jane stood staring stupidly at her phone. She needed a drink, she decided. It wasn't normally her first recourse, but then it wasn't every day she had a killer on the other end of her mobile. She left the car where it was and walked down the hill towards the town centre, turning into the first pub she came to.

She bought a Southern Comfort and Coke and found a quiet corner where she could turn her back to the room and recover herself. So it was that she had no advance warning of Jake's presence. One minute she was alone, contemplating John Hampton's inscrutably dark world and fervently hoping she never had to come closer to its epicentre than she had just done. The next, Jake was beside her, one hand on the back of her chair, the other touching the edge of the table. 'Jane, what a surprise,' he said.

She whirled round so fast a curl whipped into her eye, making it smart and water. Rubbing her eye fiercely she said, 'Stalking me again? How much clearer can I make it? We. Are. Through.'

Jake looked discomfited, casting a quick glance over his shoulder to see if anyone in the half-empty pub had picked up on their personal drama. Happily they were all deep in conversation or Sudoku. 'I didn't follow you,' he said. 'I was out for a walk when it started raining. I dived in here to get out of the rain.' He held out the arm of his jacket, stained with dark circles. 'Look, rain.' He gave her the grin that had once made her stomach flutter. Now it made her stomach turn.

'Whatever. Doesn't change the message.' Jane pointedly looked away, staring at her drink on the table, trying to avoid looking at his hand. He took his hand away and she thought for a moment he was going to take her at her word. But no. Instead he sat down next to her. She pushed her chair back, preparing to leave. He grabbed her wrist, his fingers a handcuff round her bones.

'Let me go,' she hissed, still bound by the English convention of never making scenes in public places.

'I accept what you said.' Jake spoke quickly. 'About us. It's not what I want, but I accept it. I want to talk to you about something else.'

'You want to talk me into helping you get rich quick,' Jane said contemptuously. 'Now let me go.'

Jake released her wrist and she rubbed it with her other hand. 'It's not like that,' he said.

'No? Then what were you doing asking Dr Wilde if the bog body is Fletcher Christian? And why are you still here? You're trying to cash in on my hard work.'

'I'm not trying to do you out of anything,' Jake protested. 'Yes, there's money to be made. But please don't pretend you're indifferent to money. I know how much you hate doing two jobs to make ends meet, and how much you'd love to be able to do nothing but your own work. Well, if we work together on this, all that would be within your grasp. I'd get the commission on the sale, you'd get first crack at the poem.'

'Stop it, Jake,' Jane said. 'I'm not interested in your little schemes. You sit there and talk about commission, but what you're really about is trying to con people. I know you. If you find this manuscript, you'll make whoever has it an offer they can't refuse. They're not smart London operators, they're straightforward Lakeland people – they'll be blinded by the zeros. They won't know you're only offering them a fraction of what it's worth.'

'That's bullshit,' he protested. 'I'm not here to rip anybody off. I want to play fair.'

'You might, but I bet your precious Caroline doesn't. Jake, watch my lips. I really don't care about the money.'

At this, Jake snapped. He got to his feet and thrust his face close to hers. 'Maybe not, Jane. But other people do. And they will go to extraordinary lengths to cut you out of the process.'

He turned on his heel and marched out into the rain. Jane stared after him, stunned. For the first time since she'd heard about the body in the bog, it dawned on her that there might be personal danger in what she was doing. There were, it seemed, bad people out there who were a lot less obvious than John Hampton.

Rigston stared through the rain streaking his window to the grey rooftops beyond. Bloody miserable afternoon, he thought. Better things to do than sit on the end of a phone waiting to be connected to some bloody doctor who clearly still subscribed to the view that the only people whose time had any value were those in the medical profession. It wasn't as if he expected anything earth-shattering from the conversation. Not if the two previous calls were anything to go by.

'Yes? Is that Inspector Rigston?' the voice in his ear said, sounding peevish and about twelve years old.

'Speaking.'

'Jerry Hamilton here. Dr Jerry Hamilton. My receptionist said you needed to speak to me about a patient. Now, you must be aware I can't discuss medical records –'

'You can when they're dead,' Rigston snapped, running out of patience. 'Especially when it's you that signed the death certificate.'

'Ah yes, well, that does rather alter the situation,' Hamilton said, his tone more emollient. 'And the death in question would be . . .?'

'Edward Fairfield. I believe you attended him this morning.'

'Ah yes, Mr Fairfield. Perfectly straightforward, Inspector. Heart failure.'

'Did Mr Fairfield have a history of heart trouble?' Rigston doodled heart shapes in a line across his pad.

'He had a minor heart attack just under two years ago. He'd been keeping reasonably well since. But this happens with the elderly all the time. The heart just runs out of beats.'

'So you'd say it wasn't an unexpected death?' Rigston asked, adding arrows to the little hearts.

'On the contrary, Inspector. I would say it was un-expected – but not surprising, given his age and general health. Does that make it any clearer for you?' The peevish tone was back.

'And there were no suspicious circumstances?'

'I don't know what you mean by suspicious.'

'Signs of a struggle? Petechial haemorrhages consis-tent with smothering? Any indications of a fatal in-jection?' Rigston said, trying to keep the irritation out of his vôice. Bloody doctors.

'None of the above. Nothing that was in any way inconsistent with natural causes. Why are you asking these questions, Inspector?'

'I'm pursuing a line of enquiry, sir. You've been very helpful. Thank you for your time,' he said mechanically, ending the call. Rigston leaned back in his chair. Three dead old people. Three different doctors. Three unequivocal verdicts of natural death. He should be satisfied.

But he wasn't.

Dan leaned back on the sofa and shook his head. 'I don't know what to say. On the one hand, you'd think somebody would notice a maniac bumping off old people all over the place. On the other hand, Harold Shipman was murdering elderly patients for years before anyone noticed.'

'Living where they did, Edith, Tillie and Eddie would have had different doctors,' Jane said. 'So it's not some crazy doctor doing his own form of euthanasia.'

'So we're back to natural causes.'

'Maybe they were scared to death,' Jane said, pushing her foot against the floor to build up momentum in the rocking chair that sat in the corner of the cottage living room.

Dan pulled a face. 'I don't think you can scare someone to death very easily. And you couldn't rely on doing it time after time. I think Dr Wilde is right – they just turn up their toes when they've had enough. Maybe when somebody in the family dies, it sort of turns their mind to it. What do I know? I'm just a simple student of language.'

'Do you think we should get Jimmy to warn Letty? I mean, if there is something dodgy going on, she's the next on the list.'

Dan snorted. 'Oh yes, let's make sure we scare her to death. "By the way, Letty, somebody's out to get you." That'll be helpful. Jane, if there's no murders, there's no murderer. And so no risk to Letty.'

Jane scowled. 'It wouldn't do any harm for her to be on her guard. And Jimmy's family.'

Dan gave a little cat-like smile. 'He's family, all right.'

'I don't want to know,' Jane said firmly. 'Harry's my friend too, remember?' She got up and stretched.

422

'I'm going to get some fresh air. Ever since Jake accosted me, I've felt like I should be looking over my shoulder. Like there's someone watching me.' She looked out of the window to the valley below and shivered. 'It's not a nice feeling. I wish I could shake it off.' She turned back to face him. 'It's cleared up nicely now. I think I'll drive up the fell and take a walk. Clear my head.'

'OK. Have we got plans for later?'

Jane shook her head. 'Let's leave it till tomorrow.'

As she drove down the hill in the dying light of the afternoon, Jane spotted Matthew wheeling the buggy across the road from the Post Office. She slowed to a halt and wound down the window. 'Don't stake your hopes on Letty Brownrigg,' she called to him. 'I've seen the papers and she's got nothing from Dorcas.'

Matthew's eyes narrowed and his brows lowered. 'You are pathetic,' he snarled at her, turning into his driveway and disappearing behind the hedge.

The satisfaction was petty, she knew, but it was satisfaction nonetheless. Jane stepped on the gas and headed up past Langmere Stile. She felt a pang as she passed Edith Clewlow's cottage. *Nothing to do with me.* The thought lacked conviction.

A mile further on, she swung left into the National Trust car park for Langmere Force. Hers was the only car there at that time of the afternoon and Jane felt calm creep over her as soon as she cleared the stile and walked up the woodland path to the forty-foot waterfall that cascaded from the high fell into Dark Tarn below.

After a short, strenuous climb, the path emerged

from the woods on to a small limestone pavement, its irregular cracks and fissures giving the appearance of giant crazy paving. As was her habit, Jane walked right up to the edge and carefully sat down with her legs dangling over the lip of the rock shelf, just as she'd done since the first time Matthew had dared her to as a child. The rock formed a shallow U-shape round the waterfall that roared amber and white to her left, and her vantage point provided a breath-taking view of the cascade and the tarn below. Jane couldn't remember a time when Langmere Force hadn't mesmerised her, taking her out of whatever ailed her and making her feel healed. That afternoon was no different. Things slowly slid into perspective and she began to feel the pressure lifting.

The great advantage of an area with few roads was that it made tailing someone very easy. You could hang well back, knowing there were no turn-offs, then narrow the gap when the rare junctions approached. But he hadn't needed to be even that sophisticated as he tailed Jane that afternoon. She'd driven up the hill towards Langmere Stile, an easy follow. And as he'd climbed in her wake, he'd spotted her car in the Langmere Force car park. It would have been hard to miss, really, sitting in splendid isolation near the start of the path.

She was already out of sight by the time he pulled in. Nevertheless, he was careful to park his car in the furthest corner, more or less hidden from sight of the road. He took a deep breath, wiping his hands on his trousers. Killing anonymous old people was one thing. What he was planning now was a different thing altogether – if you could call this flying by the seat of the pants planning. Still, he'd done all right so far. No living witnesses to date. He had to make sure it stayed that way. Eliminate Jane, clear the path to the manuscript.

He got out of the car, shivering as the chill air hit him. He glanced at the information board at the start of the path, understanding that the waterfall might give him the perfect opportunity. If he caught up with her there, the roar of the water would cover the sound of his approach. And it would be the perfect place to dump the body afterwards. He needed a weapon, though. As he climbed through the trees, he scanned the ground on either side of the steep path, looking for something suitable. At last, he saw what he needed. A fallen limb had been cut into sections, presumably by one of the park rangers, and stacked alongside the track. He chose a section that was about three feet long and six or seven inches in diameter. He put one end on the ground and leaned into it, testing its strength. It wouldn't do to attempt murder with a rotten piece of wood.

He carried on upwards, his chest tightening with anxiety as well as the climb. He didn't want to do it, but it had to be done. As the trees thinned out, he slowed, not wanting to come upon Jane unawares. He'd been right about the water; its rushing filled the air, covering the stealthy sound of his feet on leaves and twigs. When he caught sight of Jane, his heart jumped. The gods were playing right into his hands. She was perched on the edge of the limestone pavement, all her attention focused on the water below her.

He crept forward, holding the wood like an unwieldy baseball bat. His soft footfalls were swallowed by the water's rush. A fine mist fell on his hair and face, making him blink. He gripped the wood tightly, battening down any qualms about what he was about to do. It had to be done. He inhaled deeply, raising the wood above his shoulder as he turned sideways on to Jane.

When the branch crashed down on her head, it came entirely without warning. So sudden she had no possibility of grabbing anything to hinder her fall, the blow stunned her. Before she had even registered it, she was in mid-air, falling through water, drenched, deafened and dizzy. She tumbled through water, treacherous rock on all sides, too stunned to offer any defence.

The plummet into the tarn took the breath from her lungs. Bubbles trailed from her nose and mouth as she sank under the power of the waterfall. The blood pounded in her ears, a red film obscured her sight. A flicker of consciousness told her to strike out for the surface but the message didn't make it through to her limbs.

The distance between life and death was shrinking by the second.

Tenille was almost beginning to enjoy herself, though she would have died before she'd have admitted it to anyone. OK, it was frustrating not to be able to go out in daylight, but she had books to read, music to listen to, food to eat and it was warm enough tucked up in the sleeping bag. She'd never had a problem with her own company, and Jane came by often enough to save her from feeling completely cast adrift.

Jane had brought good news earlier that day. She'd seemed kind of remote, like she was trapped in her own head and it was too much like hard work to get out. But she'd been clear enough about her conversation with the Hammer. Now he knew Tenille wasn't going to grass him up. And Jane had told him Tenille didn't want him making pointless gestures, taking the blame on himself to get her off the hook. Tenille didn't have a clue what her father had planned, but she trusted him. Though he'd kept out of her life for thirteen years, he'd proved his devotion when it mattered. She had no doubt that he would stick by her now. He would come up with some plan that would put them both in the clear. In a few days' time, she'd be able to come out of hiding and get back to her old life.

She wondered where Sharon was staying now the flat was burned out. Would the council have rehoused her in one of the empty flats on the Marshpool? Or would she be camping out with one of her mates, drowning her losses in booze and weed? Tenille didn't mind the idea of going back to live with Sharon. Her aunt had mostly left her to her own devices. They'd evolved a way of life that more or less suited them both. But maybe her dad would step into the frame now. She didn't think he'd want her living with him – she knew enough about the kind of life he led to realise he wouldn't want his daughter in the thick of it. But maybe he'd keep an eye on her, make sure Sharon didn't bring home any more deadbeat pervs like Geno.

And maybe, with her dad in the picture, she could let herself have the dreams she'd always pushed away because they were beyond impossible. Dreams of study, of university, of maybe even writing her own poetry one day. If she knew there was a real point, then she could make herself go to school, play the game and follow the path Jane had shown her. She could make her dad see that tossing a few quid in the pot wouldn't be money wasted. She could make him proud.

But that was for the future. Right now, she was focused on paying Jane back for the way she'd stuck her neck out for her. It didn't matter that she'd made a promise; in her world, promises were flexible. You kept them when they made sense, you broke them when they didn't. Jane was too soft to see that you couldn't take people at their word. That was why she was getting nowhere with those old people. Nobody volunteered anything to anyone, whether information or possessions, unless there was something in it for them.

Tenille waited for midnight, then set off. She'd meant to go to Letitia Brownrigg's house the night before, but finding Eddie Fairfield dead in his chair had left her more shaken than she'd admitted. She couldn't face doing Mrs Brownrigg's place after that.

She found the address on Chestnut Hill easily enough, though it took her a few moments to figure out that 12A was the low extension that thrust out from the left-hand side of the big stone house numbered 12. She hid her bike behind some shrubs by the entrance to the drive and walked softly up the grass verge. A couple of windows in the main house showed the gleam of a light, but otherwise it was in darkness. Tenille guessed at a landing light left on for children who might wake up needing to go to the toilet. She wondered what it must be like to live somewhere big enough for there to be any chance of missing your way from bedroom to bathroom. She kind of liked the idea and wondered if maybe one day she would live somewhere like that.

The door was round the side, a rustic construction of sturdy wooden planks with square iron nail heads. But the handle and the mortise lock just below it were modern. Tenille gently depressed the handle and pushed, to check if there were internal bolts as well as the lock. To her astonishment, the door opened and she almost tumbled inside. So it really was true that, out in the country, people still left their doors unlocked. How mad was that? Her heart pounding, she slipped inside, leaving the door ajar behind her.

She moved stealthily down the hall towards the first closed door. Again, she took infinite pains not to make a noise as she opened the door. What she saw made her gasp out loud. A man was standing by a bureau, rifling through papers by the narrow beam of a torch held in his mouth. Hearing Tenille's strangled, 'Fuck,' he started and swung round, the light bouncing over her. Tenille backed out of the room and hurtled down the hall, yanking the door open and slamming it behind her to buy a few precious seconds.

She sprinted down the drive, dragging the bike from the bushes and into the road. She threw her leg across the bike and set off down the hill as fast as she could pedal. Through the rush of wind in her ears, she listened in panic for the sound of a car in pursuit. If he had wheels, she'd have to abandon the bike and leg it through the gardens that flanked the road. But luck was on her side. No car loomed behind her, though she still didn't stop till she made it back to Fellhead, sweating and exhausted. She replaced the bike and ran back to the slaughterhouse, making sure she locked the door behind her.

Panting, she leaned against the door and tried to calm herself. He couldn't have seen her properly, not with the baseball cap pulled down over her brow and her jacket zipped right up to cover the lower part of her face. Even if he had seen her, he couldn't have known who she was or where she was staying. He obviously had no more right to be there than she had. So it wasn't like he could go to the cops and tell them about seeing a young black burglar. Just as well. If the local cops were smart enough, they'd soon be putting two and two together and coming up with Tenille Cole and Gresham's Farm. She was safe. She really was safe.

She wasn't so sure about Letitia Brownrigg, though. If somebody else was after Jane's manuscript, then maybe there really was something funny going on with all these old people dying.

Tenille felt her chest constrict. What if she'd come face to face with a murderer? If he knew about the manuscript, chances were he knew Jane. And if he knew Jane, he might know about Tenille. And if he knew about Tenille, he might be able to work out where she was hiding. Was he really going to leave her alive to tell the tale?

Maybe she wasn't quite as safe as she'd thought.

When we sank Bounty, we made sure to keep safe the cutter & the jolly-boat. At 20ft & 16ft in length, they made ideal vessels for our fishing parties. We kept them on the shingle, drawn up beyond the tideline available to any who wanted to fish from them. As my apprehension of some sort of violent rebellion grew, I began to take secret steps to secure my own survival & that of my family. I made a hiding place near the boats & there I began to build up supplies. Dried fish & meat, cocoa-nuts, dried fruit & skinfuls of fresh water, enough canvas to rig a sail, the sextant I had kept by me; all of these I secreted away, along with a substantial portion of the gold we had carried off from the Bounty. It was a fine irony that the one metal that had no value at all on Pitcairn might yet earn me my liberty. I said nothing of my preparations to anyone, not even my dear wife Isabella, for though I doubted not her love for me, the women loved nothing more than to gossip about us men as they went about their daily business. I could not risk my preparations being discovered & so I left her out of my confidence.

35

That Thursday displayed the sort of weather that Jane yearned for when she was in London: high blue skies raked with fragments of thin cloud; leaves green, gold, russet, chestnut and oxblood; skylines etched clear and rugged; birdsong and the smell of autumn on the air. She could hardly believe she was still alive to see it. She was bruised and stiff, there was a long gash down one arm and a lump on the back of her head. But, that apart, she seemed to have survived her ordeal with remarkably little physical damage.

The real injuries were internal, she suspected. Jane had never been the victim of violence, never known the visceral fear that comes with knowing that someone is out to harm you – and having no sense of who her attacker was made it even harder to deal with the fear.

She owed her life to a shepherd and his dog, a man like her father who knew the lines of the fell as well as his jaw under the razor. He'd been walking back to his Land Rover with the dog when he'd seen Jane fall into the tarn. Man and dog had raced across the hillside and he had sent the animal into the water.

She had no recollection of the dog seizing her collar in his teeth. She remembered breaking the surface in a panic, convinced the dog was her attacker, struggling to free herself from his grip. Only when the shepherd waded in did she stop struggling and allow herself to be towed to shore. She was groggy but conscious enough to make it back to the Land Rover, her arm slung round a man she vaguely remembered from sheep sales and summer barbecues.

Her mother had risen to the crisis with customary calm. Judy's fretting was always in the abstract; faced with concrete calamity, she simply got on with what had to be done. Jane was stripped, inserted into a hot bath, supplied with sweet milky tea. Her wounds were cleaned and she was wrapped in a warm towel before being put to bed in a pair of flannel pyjamas she had never seen in her life. Only then did her mother pause to ask what had happened.

'I don't know,' Jane had prevaricated. 'I must have slipped.' Now the practicalities were over, she didn't want to tell her mother the truth. It would terrify Judy, but it would terrify her even more to relive the moments after the blow struck, moments when she'd plummeted downwards half-stunned, her mouth and nose full of water, no sense of which way was up as she tumbled through the column of water. But when Dan had shown up in response to her phone call, she had told him the moment they were alone.

'Do you have any sense of who it was?' he demanded, his hands clenched into fists.

'I've no idea. I told you I felt like I was being followed, but I can't think who'd do a thing like this. Not Jake, not Matthew.'

'Whoever did this was serious,' Dan said. 'You should tell the police.'

'But why would anyone want me dead? I haven't got the manuscript.'

Dan reached for her hand. 'Maybe they want to eliminate the competition.'

'In that case, they could be coming after you too.'

His face froze in shock. 'Christ, I never thought of that.' He exhaled loudly. 'Well, from now on, no more solo interviews. No more wandering around on your own. We stick together, right?'

Jane nodded, weary of thinking and puzzling. 'Maybe you're right. Maybe I should talk to Rigston.'

'Sleep on it,' he advised. 'We'll talk again in the morning.'

Now morning was here and her concerns still plagued her. It seemed as if every area of her life was in turmoil. Judy had tried to cheer her up over break-fast, but Jane's secrets weighed too heavy. Dan's arrival felt like the cavalry.

Judy tried to dissuade Jane from going out, but she was adamant. She and Dan were heading for Coniston and Jenny Wright, younger sister of Letty Brownrigg, née Fairfield. It was a relief to be out of the house, out from under her mother's smothering concern.

'How are you feeling?' Dan asked as he drove out of the yard. 'Really feeling, I mean.'

'Like shit,' Jane said. 'I'm aching all over. But I've no intention of giving up.'

'What about talking to Rigston? Have you thought any more about it?'

'I don't know, what if he doesn't believe me?' *Or worse, what if he does believe me, and suggests staking out the farm or offering me protection? There'd be no hiding place for Tenille then.*

'Why wouldn't he?'

Jane sighed. 'If there is something odd about these deaths, he must be thinking of me as a possible suspect. He might think I made up the attack to divert suspicion away from myself.'

Dan threw her a quick glance. 'You have a very devious mind,' he said.

'So do coppers,' Jane said drily.

They drove for a while in silence, skirting Ambleside and heading out through Clappergate and Skelwith Bridge, the looming bulk of the Old Man of Coniston rising before them. Jane had always liked Coniston village. There was something plain and unselfconscious about it. It felt like what it was – a post-industrial village with few pretensions. It had sprung up because of the seams of copper ore in the mountain behind, and most of the grey stone houses were small and unassuming. Somehow Coniston had resisted the prettification of tourism rather better than most villages in the area; it still seemed a place where local people lived and worked.

Jane directed Dan off the main road on to the narrow track that led to Coppermines Valley. She almost wished they'd brought her father's Land Rover as Dan's Volkswagen Golf bounced and groaned its way up the valley and over Miner's Bridge. Ahead was a terrace of tiny cottages which had originally been built to house the miners and their families. Irish Row had been abandoned and left derelict once the mining had ended, but then modern roads and disposable incomes made the Lake District achievably desirable for weekends and holidays. Property in the area became valuable again and the stone terrace had been gutted and turned into sought-after weekend and holiday cottages that no local labourer could imagine being able to afford. Jane remembered coming up here in her childhood for days out, exploring the remains of the old mine workings under the watchful eye of her father. She couldn't remember Irish Row at all, but she did remember the cottage a hundred yards further on where Jenny Wright lived.

The memory had not persisted for aesthetic reasons. Copperhead Cottage was a tall, narrow building, its natural stone covered with battleship grey rendering. It sat sinister as a toad in the landscape, the square panes of its blind windows shrouded in net curtains. The first time they'd come up there, she and Matthew had run on ahead of their parents. As they'd rounded the bend, Matthew had grabbed her arm and stopped her in her tracks. 'That's where the witch lives,' he whispered. 'She likes to eat little girls. If you wander off on your own, she'll come up to you disguised as a sheep and she'll gobble you up.'

As far as she could remember, Jane had only been about five, and Matthew's words had been all too convincing. So the edge of her pleasure had always been blunted whenever their family outings had brought them to Coniston. So in spite of the glorious weather and her adult sensibility, Jane still felt a faint sense of trepidation as she walked ahead of Dan up the path of Copperhead Cottage.

When the door eventually opened to her knock, Jane felt an ancient tremor of fear. The woman who stood on the threshold bore an eerie resemblance to that childhood image of witchery. Her grey hair was an untidy nest, her eyes dark and sunken on either side of a hooked nose which curved towards a strong chin. One shoulder was higher than the other and she leaned on a knobbly stick. As if to complete the picture, a grey cat rubbed against her ankles. 'This is a private house,' she announced. 'No bed and breakfast, no cream teas. And I don't allow people to use my lavatory.'

'Mrs Wright?' Jane asked, spirits sinking.

The woman peered at her through her little round glasses. 'Who are you?'

'My name is Jane Gresham. I'm a friend of Jimmy Clewlow – David and Edith's grandson,' Jane said, instinctively going for the family connection. Anyone this unwelcoming of strangers wasn't going to be moved by her credentials. 'And this is my friend Dan Seabourne.'

'Also a friend of Jimmy's, ma'am,' Dan said, ingratiating smile at the ready.

'You're a day early if you've come to take me to the funeral,' she said ungraciously.

'That's not why we're here. Jimmy thought you might be able to help us with a research project. Jane and I work together at a university in London,' Dan cut in, his charm to the fore.

Jenny Wright frowned. 'What sort of research project brings you up here?'

'I come from up here. I grew up in Fellhead,' Jane said, trotting out the rest of her credentials.

'More fool you for leaving. So what's this project that Jimmy Clewlow thinks I might be able to help you with?'

'Maybe we could come in and tell you, rather than keep you standing on the doorstep in the cold?' Dan suggested.

The old woman shook her head. 'Dropping a name or two won't get you across my door. How do I know you're who you say you are? How do I know you're not here to rob an old woman?'

Dan hid his exasperation well. 'You could always phone Jimmy and ask him.'

Jenny snorted derision. 'I don't have his number.'

'I do.'

'And how would I know it was him? Nay, you can state your business well enough out here.'

'Whatever you prefer,' Jane said politely. 'I specialise in the works of William Wordsworth. I understand one of your ancestors, Dorcas Mason, once worked for the Wordsworth family at Dove Cottage. And I believe she may have acquired some of his papers.'

'Are you saying she stole them?' The woman sounded even more hostile.

'Not at all. We think she was given them for safe-keeping.'

'Well, if she was, she would have kept them safe. We understand about duty in our family.' She pursed her lips and nodded with self-satisfaction.

'That's what we're hoping. We're trying to find out if the papers survived and, if possible, to have a look at them.'

'What's your interest?'

Jane smiled. 'If I'm right, this is an undiscovered poem by Wordsworth. A long poem. I would like to be the first person to read it. And I would like to have the opportunity to study it. To write about it.' She tried to make her tone even more placatory. 'It would be a very valuable manuscript. Whoever owns it could become rich as a result.'

'See? I said you were out to rob me. Well, I've nothing worth stealing, young woman. No manuscripts. No jewellery. No money, neither. You and your young man are wasting your time here. I've nothing for you.' The door began to close, then it opened again. 'And tell Jimmy Clewlow to make sure somebody comes for me tomorrow. I don't want to miss Edith's funeral because somebody forgot I exist.' This time, the door closed completely, leaving them staring at an expanse of black paint.

'And a very good day to you too,' Jane muttered, turning on her heel. She felt as if the windows of the house were staring at her as she walked away. Another wasted journey. At this rate, she'd be back in London with nothing to show for her two weeks of study leave. Nothing apart from a throbbing lump on the back of her head, assorted cuts and bruises and nerves shredded to tatters.

After Dan dropped her at the farm, Jane seized the chance to go and check on Tenille. She found her curled in a corner, wide-eyed and twitchy. 'What's the matter?' she asked, settling down beside the girl and putting an arm round her shoulders.

'Bad shit,' Tenille muttered.

'Are you freaking out, stuck in here?'

Tenille leaned into her. 'You know you made me promise I'd stay in?'

Jane could hardly bear the thought of more trouble.

The attack had left too many nerve endings exposed. 'What happened?'

Tenille hunched into herself under Jane's protective arm. 'I went to that Letitia Brownrigg's house last night. I got there round one in the morning. The door was unlocked so I just walked in. Only, there was a man in the living room.'

'Oh, shit, Tenille. What if he called the cops?'

'No, you're getting the wrong end of the stick. He was a burglar. He had a torch in his mouth, he was, like, going through this desk thing in the room. Looking through papers. Like I would have been doing if I'd have got there first.'

Jake's words came back to her in a rush. Someone a damn sight more unscrupulous than her was intent on finding the manuscript. And Tenille had walked into the middle of it. Her heart was in her mouth; could it be the same man who had tried to drown her? 'Did he see you?'

'Well, he saw, like, a person. I don't think he actually got a good look at me, not enough to know I was me, if you get my meaning.'

'Did you recognise him?'

Tenille pulled a face. 'I didn't see his face. I just got an impression of him, you know? Like, he was quite tall, not fat, not thin. I think he was wearing a beanie. Like, just a geezer. Could have been anybody.'

'Could it have been Jake?' She had to ask but didn't want to hear the answer.

'I don't think so, but I couldn't say for sure. Like I said, it could have been anybody.'

'What did you do?'

'I legged it. Didn't stop pedalling till I got back here.

Man, I was scared. I thought, you know, what if he saw enough to see I was black? Cuz there's not many black kids round here, right? And, like, if he's chasing the same thing you're after, chances are he knows you. And that means he, like, knows who I am. Cuz maybe you talk about me, right?' Her voice rose, the fear obvious.

'I do talk about you, you're right. But even if this person did figure out it was you, they wouldn't know where to find you.'

Tenille snorted. 'Sure they do. They know to look where you are.'

It was hard to argue with her logic. 'All the more reason to stay inside, then,' Jane said, trying not to show her own fear. 'There's nothing we can do about this. We just have to keep our heads down. I'll try and get hold of Jimmy, see if he's heard anything about a break-in at Letty's.' She gave Tenille a final squeeze then stood up. 'Let this be a lesson to you. Stay inside – this time I mean it.'

'Yeah, yeah. You got it.' She yawned. 'I'm too tired for any more adventures anyway. Man, I feel like I ran a marathon last night.'

Jane walked back across the yard, her brain in a whirl. Who was the mystery man? It had to be connected to her search. Anything else was too much of a coincidence. But however much they might want to beat her to the manuscript, she couldn't imagine Matthew or Jake having the nerve or the appetite for burglary, never mind murder. Or was it someone else she knew nothing about, someone whose existence Jake had hinted at? Before she could get completely tangled in her thoughts, she was jerked back to the present by the ringing of her mobile. 'Hello?' she said.

'Is that Jane Gresham?' The voice was vaguely familiar.

'Yes. Who is this?'

'Detective Chief Inspector Ewan Rigston. We met at your parents' farm on Saturday night.'

'DCI Rigston. How can I help you? Has Tenille been found?'

'No, it's nothing to do with Tenille. I need to talk to you about a sudden death.'

And yet, despite my best preparations, when the end came, I was as little expectant as anyone. One black day in September 1793 a native servant borrowed a gun, saying it was his desire to shoot a pig to provide dinner for the white men. This was nothing out of the ordinary of itself. We had often previously allowed them firearms for such purposes with no ill result. The women left the village as was customary to collect the eggs of seabirds. The white men went to work on their plantations, while I remained close to home. My wife was large with our third child & I wanted to be at hand. As I worked on my yams, I heard a gunshot & foolishly rejoiced because I believed this to herald roast pork for dinner. My joy was short-lived, however. Some little time later, the rebellious natives crept up behind me & shot me in the back, the shot passing clean through my shoulder. I fell to the ground with a cry. Then I felt a blow to the head & blackness descended upon me.

36

Jane fought the feeling of dread in her chest and said a small silent prayer. 'A sudden death?' she said, trying to sound as if it were the least likely thing a police officer might ask her about. 'Who's dead?'

'An elderly woman name of Letty Brownrigg. She lived up on Chestnut Hill on the outskirts of Keswick. The thing is, she had your name and phone number written on the pad by the phone in her living room.' He let the words hang.

Jane felt as if she'd been punched in the chest. She fought to stay calm. 'Yes. She wrote it down on Tuesday when I went to see her. But I don't understand why you're calling me. Is there something wrong? Something suspicious?' Jane was desperately struggling for the words of an innocent person. She knew already she wasn't going to reveal Tenille's presence at the scene. Better to withhold evidence than to expose her to suspicion of involvement in a second death.

'Now, why would you think that?'

Jane sighed in exasperation. 'Because if she just died in her sleep, there wouldn't be a DCI involved, never mind one phoning me up to ask me what seem like pointless questions.'

'Fair enough. What it is, Mrs Brownrigg hadn't been to the doctor for a little while, so we need to make some enquiries to make sure everything is as it should be. You say it was Tuesday that you saw her?'

'Yes. She seemed fine. Quite chirpy, in fact.'

'Aye, well. She did have heart problems, but she'd been fine lately. But anyhow, you're not the last person to have seen her alive. Her daughter-in-law took her out to lunch yesterday, so we've got a more recent account than yours. It just seemed strange, that's all.'

'How do you mean?' Jane's skin turned to goose-flesh. Something in the very casualness of his tone unnerved her.

'It's just that this is the fourth death this week that connects to you,' he said bluntly.

Jane said nothing. There was nothing she could think of to say that wouldn't sound disingenuous.

'Edith Clewlow, Tillie Swain, Eddie Fairfield and now Letty Brownrigg. I believe those four names feature on a list in your possession.'

'That's because they all appear on the same family tree. The only one of those four I had ever met before was Edith Clewlow. And she was dead before I had the chance to talk to her. If there's something funny going on, don't you think you should be looking a bit closer to home?' Jane could hear the defensiveness in her voice, but she knew it was a strong argument.

'That might be a valid point if this hadn't all kicked off when you turned up asking about a lost manuscript.'

'All the more reason to look at the family. If the manuscript exists, it's worth a lot of money. Seven figures, we're talking here, Inspector. If I was the killing sort, I might think that worth the candle.'

'Maybe so.'

'And it's my understanding that the first three deaths were deemed to be from natural causes. So I'm not quite sure why you're asking me these questions.'

Rigston cleared his throat. 'They say three's the charm, don't they? Well, I'm looking at four now, and my instincts tell me there's something here that goes beyond coincidence. And whatever it is, you're at the heart of it, Dr Gresham. We'll be talking again.'

'And my answers will be the same.'

'Heard anything from Tenille?' he added, throwing her off balance again.

'No,' she replied firmly. 'Goodbye, DCI Rigston.' Jane's heart was thudding in rhythm with her head. Edith, Tillie, Eddie and now Letty. All dead. The first four names on the list, all dead. Jake's words echoed in her head: *And they will go to extraordinary lengths.* Who were these people? And surely they wouldn't commit four murders in pursuit of what might yet turn out to be little more than a figment of Jane's imagination? Hell, one murder would be too much for a poem. Four was beyond belief.

But there was the additional evidence of the attack on her. An attack she couldn't tell Rigston about now, that was for sure. He was already treating her like a suspect. She could see no prospect of him believing in her unseen assailant.

She lurched into the kitchen and collapsed into

446

a chair. She needed to talk to Dan. She dialled his number and he answered on the third ring. 'I can't talk now,' he said straight away. 'Can you meet me in Keswick in an hour?'

'Yes,' Jane said wearily. 'Where?'

There was the sound of muffled conversation. She thought she recognised Jimmy's voice. 'Down by the lake. The car park on the road to Friar Cragg. OK?'

'I'll see you there in an hour.' Jane stared at her phone as if expecting it to give her some irrefutable guidance. Her suspicions weighed heavy on her and she didn't know who to talk to. Certainly not Rigston. She recognised in him a man who was far too smart to be fobbed off with the half-truths that were all she could offer him. But she couldn't just keep her mouth shut either. If someone was killing off old people, she had to make sure the deaths didn't all drift past without anyone acknowledging what was going on.

Then it came to her: the one person who would be more interested in the deaths than in whatever Jane might be hiding.

Half an hour later, Jane was sitting in the basement of Gibson's funeral parlour, keeping company with a two-hundred-year-old corpse and a forensic anthropologist. *If they could see me now,* she found herself thinking absurdly. She'd just caught River, who was on her way out to grab a sandwich.

'This is going to sound pretty weird,' Jane said.

'Oh good, I do like weird,' River said, settling herself on a lab stool.

'Bear with me. I know I told you some of this before, but I need to get it straight in my head. It's to do with the manuscript I'm looking for. The last person I know to have had it in her hands was a servant called Dorcas Mason. I figured she might have decided to keep it safe rather than to destroy it. So, if it still exists, the chances are it's been passed down to one of her descendants.'

'Makes sense,' River said.

'I drew up a family tree and then I listed the surviving descendants in order of likelihood, based on primogeniture.'

River nodded. 'Soundest principle, especially back then.'

'The first person on my list died the night before I was going to see her. The second person on my list died the night after I visited her. The third person on my list died the night after I visited him. And I've just had a call from DI Rigston to tell me that the fourth person on my list died last night. Two nights after I visited her.' She produced her rough family tree and illustrated her point.

River studied it with interest. 'It's bizarre, I'll grant you that. But, like I said before, old people die.'

'I know. And none of these deaths has been treated as suspicious. But they're all related to each other. OK, a bit distantly, but still in the same extended family. The same extended family who might just be in possession of a very valuable and very portable piece of property. And since old people don't go out very often, if you want to search for something like that, killing them's the most certain way of making sure you won't be disturbed.'

'It does feel suspicious,' River said slowly. 'It's not unheard of to have a cluster of deaths in a family, but this cluster is rather too close together.' She tugged at her ponytail. 'This woman Ewan Rigston called you about – why was he ringing you?'

'He said he wanted to know if I was the last person to see her alive. Something about a sudden death, she hadn't been to see the doctor recently. But he ended up acting like I was a murder suspect or something.'

River's eyebrows shot up. 'Really? Well, if she hadn't seen the doctor recently, there'll have to be a post mortem. I tell you what I'll do, I'll have a word with my colleague in Carlisle. Normally he'd be called in to do it. But I'm here on the spot, I'm a qualified pathologist, and it'll get me some Brownie points with my boss if I step into the breach. And I can take a good look around your little old lady and see if there's anything at all suspicious. How does that sound?'

Jane grinned. 'You have no idea what a weight you've just taken off my back.'

'Don't hold your breath,' River said. 'Chances are I'm not going to find anything.'

'I'd be very happy if you didn't. This all started because I was determined to find a manuscript that might not even exist. The last thing I want is four deaths on my conscience as a result.'

The two men were already there, sitting on a bench, staring out across the silver glitter of the water. Dan looked round as she approached, his smile as cheerful as the sunshine. 'Sorry about cutting you off earlier,' he said, pushing off from the car and pulling her into a hug. He kissed her lightly on the mouth. 'You know how it is. So, how are you?'

'Still aching. And there's something I need to talk to you about. I don't know how to say this except to come straight out with it,' she admitted. 'Letty Brownrigg died last night.'

Jimmy's face registered shock. 'Granddad's cousin Letty? Lives up Chestnut Hill? She was at Alice's on Monday. She looked fit as a fiddle. What happened?'

'They think it was natural causes, but there'll have to be a post mortem.' Talking about it seemed to increase the burden of Letty's death, not reduce it. Jane had let herself be charmed by Letty, and now she was dead. Perhaps because of Jane.

Jimmy covered his face with his hands for a moment. He ran his fingertips over his eyebrows, dropped his hands to his lap and sighed. Dan put an arm round his shoulders. 'Poor Letty. Jesus, it's like all the oldies just decided to lie down and die together.' He gazed bleakly at the water for a few minutes in silence. He turned to Jane, a question on his face. 'But how come you know all this?'

'The police phoned to ask why my name and number were on her phone pad. I was there on Tuesday, remember? They wanted to check that I wasn't the last person to see her alive.' Then the dam burst and Jane's emotions spilled over. 'It's like everybody I need to talk to about the manuscript is dying. First your gran, then Tillie, then Eddie. And now Letty. It's scaring me.'

Dan put his other arm round her, instinctively pulling her close. 'I can see why.'

'And now Ewan Rigston is treating me like I'm a suspect. Just because it's my list they're on.'

'Well, it is too much to be coincidence,' Jimmy said. 'And I suppose you are the obvious connection. Have you got any better ideas?' There was nothing hostile in his question; it was more a plea.

'Somebody who believes the Wordsworth manuscript is out there and wants it very badly. But see, here's the thing about old people. They don't go out much. People come to them. The family takes care of them. They're always home and they sleep notoriously lightly. Consequently, they're hard to burgle. If you want to search their houses properly, you need to shut them up. And this guy shuts them up for good.'

Dan shivered. 'Fuck, Jane, that's cold.'

'I know. But it's the only explanation I can think of.'

'Surely somebody would have noticed if they were all murdered,' Jimmy said, fighting the logic of her argument because to accept it was too monstrous.

'Not if there weren't obvious signs of a struggle or injuries. They were all old. All pretty frail. Not hard to terrorise. Maybe that's what killed them.'

Jimmy shook his head, as if trying to dislodge something. 'So what are the police going to do about it? Apart from acting like you're the suspect.'

'I don't know. But Ewan Rigston seems to be taking it seriously.'

'So he should.' Jimmy turned sideways to face her, anger in his eyes. 'These are people I've known all my life, people I care about. My kin. Is there nothing we can do?

'I'm trying. I spoke to Dr Wilde, the pathologist who's working on the bog body. She's going to do the post mortem on Letty. If there's anything, anything at all to suggest foul play, she'll be all over it.'

Jimmy's face cleared. 'That's a start, at least.'

'There's one other thing. Dan and I went to see Jenny Wright down at Coniston this morning. She was next on my list. I don't think she should be left on her own down there until we know what's going on.'

Jimmy pulled a face. 'God, that old witch.'

'She was very insistent that someone should fetch her to the funeral tomorrow. Maybe you could go down this afternoon and bring her back with you?'

'That's not a bad idea.' Jimmy groaned. 'But she's such a disagreeable old bag.'

'Even so, you don't want her murdered, do you?'

'I suppose not. Couldn't we get the cops on it?'

'They're not going to care for her like her family will,' Dan said.

'OK, I'll go now.' Jimmy looked stricken at the thought.

'I could come with you,' Dan said. 'Lighten the load.'

Jimmy shook his head. 'Thanks, but I can live without the Spanish Inquisition that would provoke.' He got to his feet, patting Dan on the shoulder. 'I'll call you later.' He leaned down and kissed the top of Dan's bald head.

In silence, they watched him drive off. 'He's a nice guy,' Dan said.

'I know.'

Dan screwed up his eyes against the sparkle of the

water. 'I admit, I started it because I thought he might be a useful source for us.' He gave a deep sigh. 'But I'm getting to like him far too much.'

For once, Jane couldn't be bothered with the self-indulgence. She got up and started back to the car. Halfway there, she turned and said, 'You know what, Dan? Four old people are dead. Somebody tried to kill me last night. When it comes to your love life, you're confusing me with someone who gives a shit.'

When I recovered my senses, I quickly understood that they had left me for dead. I knew that, if I remained, they would surely return & finish what they had started in so cowardly a fashion. A terrible pain beat in my head & my shoulder was bleeding profusely. But I knew if I did not remove to some other place, I would surely die. I struggled to my knees & almost fainted with the agony. It was then I saw what I took at first to be an apparition. It took the form of my wife Isabella & I thought myself closer to death than I had at first believed. But when the apparition spoke, I understood it was truly Isabella in the flesh. 'Husband, I am come to help you,' she said. 'They told me you were dead but I did not believe them. They are killing all the white men.' With her help, I was able to find my feet & together we stumbled into the banyan trees nearby. I was safe, but I feared it would not be for long.

37

River had developed a knack for getting her own way. It had something to do with determination, but even more than that it had to do with a profound understanding of what made people tick. Judicious flattery, professional courtesy and the willingness to grant favours, often before they were even asked – all these helped her to bend the world to her will. By the time she'd finished her phone call, the pathologist on the other end was convinced she was doing him a favour by performing the post mortem on Letty Brownrigg.

Since Letty's body had already been transferred to the hospital mortuary, it didn't take long to have everything set up. By the time Jimmy set off for Coniston, River was preparing to examine the dead woman. Her assistant and the uniformed police constable Ewan Rigston had asked to be present were discussing football with casual disregard for what was about to take place. River looked across at the nonchalant policeman and said, 'Have you witnessed a post mortem before?'

'Aye, I have,' the stolid young man replied. 'More

than most. They always send me. My dad was a butcher. Bodies don't bother me.'

'I'm glad about that,' River said. 'I hate having to hang about while people run off to lose their lunch.'

'No chance of that with me. It's just meat, isn't it? I mean, whatever it is that makes you human, that's long gone by the time they hit the slab,' he said casually. 'We're all just bags of blood and guts once we're dead. I've never understood the way people get all squeamish about their loved ones having to have post mortems.'

'Some people do have religious objections,' River pointed out as she began to probe the woman's skull with her fingers for any signs of contusions or abrasions.

'And that makes even less sense, when you think about it,' the policeman said. 'OK, I accept some people believe in the resurrection of the physical body. But if you've got this all-powerful god, surely he's capable of putting the pieces back together the way they were? It should matter even less to the religious because they're the ones that're supposed to have faith that their god can do anything. That's the trouble with religion. You bring God in the door and logic flies straight out the window.'

River grinned. 'How come you're still just a constable? I'm not used to philosophical discussions from men in uniform.'

'I like being a grunt,' he said. 'This way, I spend more of my time with people, not paper. I don't have to worry about the politics of policing or keeping the brass happy. When I go home at night, I don't have to fret about the burden of command. It's not a bad life.'

'Some might call that a lack of ambition,' River said. Suddenly something caught her attention and she stopped listening. She bent over to look more closely, reaching for a magnifying glass. 'That's interesting,' she murmured.

'What is?' the policeman asked.

'A very faint bruise right above the carotid sinus,' she said, pointing it out to him.

'Funny place to have a bruise,' he said. 'I mean, it's not like you're going to knock yourself there. What do you think caused that? Has somebody tried to strangle her?'

River shook her head. 'I don't think so. There are no other corresponding marks. Well, we'll have a better idea once we open her up.'

But River's confident prediction was not entirely borne out by events. As she left her assistant to close the Y-incision, she shared her conclusions with the PC. 'Heart failure, pure and simple. Her heart showed signs of cardiomyopathy, arteries pretty furred up. Heart stopped beating.'

'Isn't that what happens to all of us, ultimately?' the philosophical policeman said.

'Yes, but for a variety of reasons. Absent any other obvious cause of death, like massive gunshot wound or signs of poisoning or asphyxiation, all we're left with here is heart failure.'

'OK. So the death certificate will be forthcoming, will it?'

'I'll see to that.' River peeled off her latex gloves. On the face of it, there was nothing suspicious about

Letty Brownrigg's death, but a niggle of unease troubled her. Jane Gresham's concerns hadn't dissipated into thin air as she had hoped. What she planned to do next was entirely outside her remit and against professional protocol, but she wanted to satisfy herself.

Once the policeman had left and she had changed back into her street clothes, River walked back to Gibson's. She nodded to the young man who greeted the grieving and headed for the viewing rooms. When she looked in on Tillie Swain, a middle-aged woman was sitting in a chair, head bowed. River slipped back out into the corridor and made for Eddie Fairfield.

The coffin sat in splendid isolation, a wedge of afternoon sunshine splashing the body with colour. Swiftly, River crossed to the coffin and looked inside. A white ruff shrouded Eddie's neck but it took only a moment for her to move it out of the way and study his neck. She pulled out her magnifying glass and looked more closely. It was very faint, but it was there. A small bruise on the carotid sinus, about the size and shape of a pair of fingertips. 'Oh, shit,' she muttered. She took out her digital camera and shot a range of pictures, from close-ups of the bruise to longer shots that established it as being indisputably a feature of Eddie Fairfield's body. 'Oh shit,' she repeated, rearranging the ruff.

Back in the hallway, she collared the young man. 'Where's Edith Clewlow?' she asked.

'All screwed down ready for the funeral tomorrow morning,' he said laconically.

River smiled winningly. 'Any chance you could open her up for me?'

He recoiled slightly, as if she'd suggested some

improper sexual act. 'What for? I thought you were just supposed to be doing the bog body?'

'Call it professional curiosity,' she said. 'I've got this theory, and I want to check something. Just five minutes, that's all I need.'

He looked doubtful. 'I shouldn't, really . . .'

She laid a hand on his arm. 'I realise that. But I need you to trust me. If I'm wrong, nobody need ever know. But if I'm right, we'll be sparing the family a lot of heartache. Nobody likes having to order an exhumation . . .'

He looked startled. 'Exhumation?'

'Shh,' River cautioned. 'Not a word people like to hear in a funeral parlour.'

He stole furtive glances up and down the hall. 'Promise you won't tell?'

'I won't tell.' She followed him into a smaller room at the end of the corridor where Edith's pine box rested on trestles. From a cupboard, he took a ratchet screwdriver. Unscrewing Edith took only a couple of minutes and it took even less to lift the lid off the coffin. River studied the old woman's neck through her magnifier and nodded to herself in confirmation. 'Bollocks,' she muttered. Out came the camera and again she framed a sequence of shots.

The young man was dancing from foot to foot by then. 'Are you done?' he kept saying after every photograph.

River stepped away from the coffin and pocketed her camera. 'I am now. Let's get her boxed up again.'

They were back in the hall within ten minutes, just in time to see the single mourner leave Tillie Swain's room. 'I'll be right back,' River said to the young man as he headed off to usher the other woman out and she returned to Tillie.

Tillie was a disappointment, however. Because of the position in which she'd been lying after death, the blood had pooled under the skin, causing post mortem lividity in the very area that interested River. It was impossible to tell whether there was a bruise. 'Three out of four, though,' she said under her breath. Jane Gresham had been right. There was something going on here.

Two hours later, River walked into Ewan Rigston's office. His face lit up when he saw her, then almost immediately became guarded as propriety kicked desire into submission. 'I wasn't expecting to see you,' he said, his delighted tone removing any negativity from the words.

'I wasn't exactly expecting to be here.' She sat down heavily. 'You know I did Mrs Brownrigg's post?'

'Aye. I was a bit surprised, I thought the professor would have done it. He usually does.'

'Yeah, well, I'm qualified and he thought it would be straightforward.'

Ewan raked around the papers on his desk. He pulled a handwritten note out with a flourish. 'Which it supposedly was. Heart failure, you said.' He gave her a shrewd look. 'But that's not right, is it? You wouldn't be here if it was straightforward.'

'There was a reason I wanted to do the post myself. I had a visit this morning from Jane Gresham.'

'Now that's interesting.'

'She said you'd been on her case. She was more than a little freaked out when she came to see me.

She's scared someone is bumping off these old people to try and get their hands on this manuscript.'

There was a long pause. 'She's not the only one. And did you find anything to support that idea?'

River nodded bleakly. 'There was a strange little bruise on Mrs Brownrigg's neck. Not something that would set off alarm bells, but enough to give me pause for thought. So I went back to Gibson's and took a look at the other three cadavers. And I found a similar bruise on two of them. I couldn't be sure of the fourth one just by looking because of post mortem lividity.' She pulled some papers from her satchel. 'I took a few pix.' She fanned them out for Rigston. 'Letty. Eddie Fairfield. Edith Clewlow.'

'What does it mean? This bruise? Is it an injection site or what?'

River shook her head. 'No sign of a needle mark in any of them. But it seems to be over the carotid sinus.'

'Which is what, exactly?'

'Your common carotid artery runs up the side of your neck, here –' River pulled aside the collar of her shirt to demonstrate. 'And just down here, more or less in line with your ear, it splits in two. The external carotid stays on the surface, the internal goes under your skull. Now, if you apply pressure to the carotid artery at the sinus . . .' she paused to indicate what she meant – 'it can cause bradycardia. That's slowing of the heartbeat, in lay terms. But there is a school of thought which maintains that, in cases of the elderly or those with underlying heart disease, pressure on the carotid sinus can provoke fatal cardiac arrhythmia.'

'A school of thought?' Rigston said weakly.

'It's what's called a postulated mechanism, because obviously you can't do experiments to see if it really does kill people or not. So nobody is entirely sure if it works. There have been documented cases of people using it for heightened sexual pleasure, though not with fatal results. But then, you tend not to want your sexual partner to end up dead, so you'd stop applying pressure at the first sign of them losing consciousness. If it does work in the way that's been postulated, it's a very good way to kill someone who's elderly or has heart disease. No traces, you see. No petechial haemorrhages like you get with asphyxiation, no broken hyoid bone like you get with strangulation. It just looks like a heart attack.'

'Would you need to be strong to kill someone like that?'

'Not really. I don't think it would take a lot of pressure. And it wouldn't be hard to subdue the victims. It would probably be enough just to hold them down.'

'So a woman could do it?'

'If she was reasonably fit and strong.'

Rigston rubbed his jaw. 'And you think these old dears have been murdered in this way?'

'I'd say it's certainly possible. It's too much of a coincidence that I'm seeing the same odd bruise in three out of the four.'

Rigston's expression hardened. 'I had a feeling in my water about this. That's not coincidence. That's suspicious.'

'I agree. On their own, the bruises would be relatively insignificant, but taken in tandem with what Jane told me. . . well, you have to take it seriously.'

Rigston smiled grimly. 'I am. Thank you for coming

straight to me with this. I'm bound to say, it doesn't look good for Dr Gresham.'

'You can't seriously think she's behind this?'

'She's connected to all our presumed victims. We both know that.'

River shook her head, bewildered. 'That doesn't make her a suspect. Ewan, nobody would have had any evidence that there was something dodgy going on if Jane Gresham hadn't come to me. She's the one who initiated this. Why on earth would she draw attention to the fact that she's been getting away with murder?'

Rigston shifted in his seat. 'With this fourth death, it was bound to come out anyway. This way, she makes herself look good by being the one that draws attention to it. From what you tell me, she's changed her tune since I spoke to her earlier.'

'That's because you're a scary cop and I'm not.' River sighed in exasperation. 'Ewan, I know it's your job to consider every possibility, but I'm damn sure the only attention Jane is interested in is what she'll get if she discovers her precious manuscript. She showed me the family tree with her interviewees marked in order of priority. I know the name of the next person on her list. Why would she let me see that if she was the killer?'

'You've got the name?'

River passed him a slip of paper. 'There you go. Ewan, you need to ask her who else might be after this bloody poem that wants it badly enough to be killing people for it.'

Rigston frowned. 'And that's another thing. How does killing people get this murderer any nearer to the manuscript?'

'Jane had a theory about that. She pointed out that old people don't go out very much. If you want to search their homes for hidden treasure, you have to incapacitate them first.'

'See? She's got it all worked out. I'm telling you, River, Jane Gresham knows more than she's letting on.'

'She's stubborn as a mule,' Jimmy said, pacing up and down the track outside Copperhead Cottage. 'She won't budge. She doesn't want to leave her cats, she never gets a wink of sleep outside her own bed, she doesn't like being among strangers – you name it. I don't want to frighten her out of her own house, but I don't know what else I can try.'

Jane stared out of her bedroom window, her mobile to her ear. 'Why don't you offer to stay over at the cottage? That way she'd be safe without having to leave home.'

Jimmy whimpered. 'I thought you liked me. Jane, she's a bloody nightmare.'

'I know. I met her, remember?' Jane suddenly had a chill thought. Someone cold-blooded enough to kill four people might not be deterred by Jimmy's presence. The last thing she wanted was to put him at risk too. She had to find a way to backtrack without making him feel his masculinity was under challenge. 'Mind you,' she said slowly, 'I suppose you staying over is no guarantee of her safety. It's not as if you'll be sleeping across the threshold of her bedroom like Gelert.'

'Not bloody likely.'

'In that case, there's nothing else for it. You're going to have to tell her it's not safe for her to be there. Not till all of this is sorted out.'

Jimmy sighed. 'I thought you would say that. I really didn't want to frighten her, you know? Behind all that bluster, she's just a lonely old lady who loves her home. I don't want to make that a place where she doesn't feel safe any more.'

'I know. But better scared and safe than dead.'

'Wish me luck,' he said heavily. 'If you don't hear from me later on, you'll know she's eaten me alive.'

Once in the trees, I instructed Isabella to remove my shirt & tear it into strips. Under my guidance, she fashioned a bandage for my wound that would staunch the bleeding. This being done, I insisted we make our way deeper into the banyan grove. As we rested, I told Isabella the time had come for us to leave Pitcairn. We could never be safe, not now the natives had tasted power of their own. But she put my hand on her swollen belly & reminded me of her condition. *You must go if you will, husband. But I cannot.* The force of her argument was undeniable & I knew that she would be safe where I could not be. My children too would suffer no reprisal; the Otaheitians have a high regard for children, & the paler their skins, the higher they are prized. *Then help me to the base of the cliff,* I said. This she did, & when we were still some distance from my hiding place, we made our tearful farewells. (I did not want her to know where I was to be found. It was a truth hard-won among us that the natives were not to be trusted, not even those we counted among our own families & I did not wish to put temptation in her way.)

38

Ewan Rigston had never been a Boy Scout; nevertheless, he always liked to be prepared. In spite of
everything River had said, he still felt unsure of
Jane Gresham. But he intended to be forearmed
before he confronted her about her list. And there
were precautions to be taken too.

He was going to have to go back to the houses of
the dead and treat them like crime scenes, even though
any evidence would have been compromised by the
emergency services and family members trampling
over the scene. Still, the fingerprint team might just
come up with someone whose dab had no business
being there. He was also going to have to talk to the
families. Or family, rather, since the dead all seemed
to belong to one clan. He knew the Clewlows and the
Fairfields, the Swains and the Brownriggs. Decent folk,
local roots, community-minded mostly. He'd never
had cause to arrest any of them, not even a teenage
lad falling foul of too much drink.

He'd seen River out to the car park, and promised to call her later. They'd had plans for the
evening – a curry and a folk night in Carlisle – but

that was history now. They'd agreed that there needed to be post mortems on the other three victims, and River had been adamant that she would do them right away. A quick call to the coroner had established his agreement. That was one of the advantages of working in a small town, Rigston knew. The machinery could be made to work faster than in the big cities. Still, neither of them anticipated being finished before midnight.

Then he'd gone back to the office, organising the deployment of the handful of SOCOs he had at his disposal that late in the day. He wanted to move fast, but equally he'd have to be careful about authorising overtime ahead of a formal murder inquiry. Bloody bureaucracy. People wondered why the police didn't seem able to keep the lid on crime. They should spend a week in his shoes, shuffling paper and balancing budgets, then they'd have a better idea.

A couple of phone calls to his local contacts and he'd established that the entire clan seemed to be gathered at Alice Clewlow's house. He arrived unannounced and alone. Alice answered the door, her face shifting from welcome to satisfaction as she realised who was calling. 'An inspector calls,' she said drily. 'Hello, Ewan. So you decided to take me seriously after all. I'm just sorry it took another death in the family for you to get your act into gear.'

'Come on now, Alice, that's hardly fair. I've been making enquiries.'

'An arrest would be even better.'

'I could use a few words.'

She glanced over her shoulder. 'It's mob-handed

in there. Come round the side, there's a bench in the garden.'

He followed her through a wooden gate in the fence into a spacious, well-kept garden. A few late roses hung their bedraggled heads from a trellis, next to which was a wrought-iron bench. They sat down and there was silence for a moment. 'Spit it out then, Ewan.'

'I just wanted to keep you posted. Although we still haven't established a suspicious cause of death in any of these four instances, we are investigating the circumstances,' he said carefully.

Alice shook her head sorrowfully. 'They were just ordinary, harmless old people.'

'I know. And if this turns out to be murder, I won't see evil like that go unpunished. The thing is, we think somebody believes a member of your family has something very valuable in their possession, and –'

'I told you. Jane bloody Gresham,' Alice interrupted angrily. 'Is that what this is about?'

'It might be. But Dr Gresham's probably not the only person who knows about it. So I need to make some enquiries about your relatives. Who saw them last; anything they may have said about Jane Gresham or anybody else asking about this manuscript. Now, I know you're all grieving and I know Edith's funeral is tomorrow, but I could really do with talking to people tonight.'

'But the funeral – surely you have to do a post mortem or something? If she was . . .' Alice tripped over the word. Rigston understood; he'd seen that same denial before.

'That's all in hand,' he said. 'The funeral service

won't have to be postponed. But I'm afraid you won't be able to bury your grandmother.'

'What do you mean, we won't be able to bury her?'

Rigston spread his hands helplessly. 'I'm sorry, Alice. The rules say the body has to be available to the defence in case they want to do their own autopsy.'

'But what if you don't arrest anyone? How long do you expect us to wait to bury my grandmother?' Alice's voice was growing more shrill.

'If we haven't arrested anyone after a month, we arrange for a second, independent post mortem. Then we release the body to the family.'

Alice's head dropped into her hands. 'This is terrible, Ewan.'

'I know, Alice. And I'm very sorry. But I would really appreciate your help right now. The best way you can serve Edith and the others now is to work with us. It's our job to speak for the dead. But we need your help.'

She looked up, her eyes heavy with tears. 'Whatever you need. Just give me five minutes to break the news. I'll come and fetch you.'

Rigston watched her walk into the house, head bowed and shoulders slumped. He felt for her. Taking that walk back into the heart of the Clewlow clan wasn't something he was looking forward to either.

Jimmy Clewlow was not a happy man. It had taken some time to convince Jenny Wright that her life might be in danger if she remained alone in Copperhead Cottage. Once convinced, it had then taken hours to effect the departure. Cats had to be supplied with adequate food and water. Deciding what to pack apparently involved combing Jenny's entire wardrobe, including a trunk that looked as if it hadn't been opened since the Napoleonic wars. All the electrical appliances had to be turned off, including an antique fridge whose contents had to be transferred to plastic bags so they could be removed to Keswick. Jimmy was a patient man, but even he had his limits and Jenny had exceeded them long before she was ready to leave.

It didn't help that she was the worst passenger he'd ever driven. Whenever he exceeded thirty miles an hour, she drew her breath in sharply and demanded to know whether he was trying to kill them. If he came within three feet of the verge on her side of the car, she would yelp that they were about to crash. By the time he turned into Alice's street, Jimmy was beginning to wonder why he hadn't left her to her own devices.

To his astonishment, when they walked into Alice's living room, Ewan Rigston was settled in an armchair, a mug of tea in his hand. He hadn't seen Rigston for years, but he recognised him instantly. Alice jumped up from the floor and steered him and Jenny into the kitchen. 'What's he doing here?' Jimmy demanded.

'I know this is going to come as a shock, Jimmy, but the police think Edith and the others might have been murdered,' Alice said, throwing a concerned look at Jenny.

'That's why Jenny's here,' Jimmy said. 'Jane Gresham thinks she might be next.'

Alice looked ready to burst into tears. 'Christ, Jimmy, what's going on?'

'It's a long story,' he said. 'And Jenny's tired. She needs to stay here for a few days.'

'You don't have to talk about me as if I'm not here, young Jimmy,' Jenny snapped. 'I can speak for myself. Alice, I need somewhere to stop. Can you put me up?'

'Of course,' Alice said distractedly. 'I'll show you to the spare room.'

'All in good time,' Jenny said. 'Jimmy, be a good lad and get me a brandy.'

Jimmy cast his eyes heavenwards and went back into the living room where Alice had set out the drink. This time, Ewan Rigston caught his eye over the heads of what Jimmy thought of as the council of elders. 'Jimmy,' he said in greeting.

Jimmy nodded. 'Shouldn't you be out there trying to catch the person who's killing my family?' he asked mildly, reaching for the brandy.

'I'm trying to do just that.'

'You won't find them in here.' Jimmy poured a generous measure into a glass.

'Your family are filling in some background for me. I'm trying to get a picture of what happened before the deaths. Funny thing is, your pal Jane Gresham keeps turning up like a bad penny.'

If Rigston had intended to needle Jimmy, he hit the mark. 'Yeah. And her and Dan are victims here too,' he said defiantly.

'Who's Dan?'

'Her colleague, Dan Seabourne.' Jimmy could feel the colour rising in his cheeks and hoped Rigston would put it down to anger.

'How do you reckon them as victims, then?' Rigston asked.

'Somebody's hijacking their work. And they're making Jane look like the villain of the piece in the process. You should be getting her to help you, not insinuating that she's part of the problem.'

'Jimmy,' his mother said, her tone a warning. 'Ewan's just doing his job.'

'Is he? Then why was it up to me to take care of Jenny? If he had the sense he was born with, he'd be getting Jane's list off her and making sure nobody else dies.'

'Don't tell me how to do my job, Jimmy.'

'Somebody needs to,' Jimmy said contemptuously. 'If it wasn't for Jane, Jenny would be sitting in her cottage waiting for a killer to show up. Now, if you'll excuse me, I need to take her a drink.' He turned to find Jenny in the doorway, smiling at him for the first time all day.

'Well said, lad. I expected better from you, Ewan Rigston. If it hadn't been for Jimmy here, I could be dead in my bed. It's time you put a stop to this nonsense. Now, Jimmy, suppose you show me to Alice's spare room?'

Tenille was at war with herself. She'd had two major shocks on her most recent excursions and she didn't want a third. But she still felt like she owed Jane for taking care of business. Besides, she couldn't take constant confinement. So if she was going to go out anyway, didn't it make sense to do something useful at the same time? And what were the chances of running into another burglar two nights running?

The decision made itself in the end. She'd become accustomed to sleeping at times other than the dead of night and now sleep just wouldn't come when it was supposed to. She gave up tossing and turning just before midnight and headed out towards Coniston. Copperhead Cottage took a bit of finding, but she was relieved to discover it had no near neighbours, especially once she realised it wasn't going to be easy to get into. After lengthy attempts to pick the locks front and back, she finally gave up. All of the windows were locked. She circled the house again, desperately looking for a way in, on the point of giving up altogether.

It was a cat that showed her the way. A long-haired white cat came shooting out of the shrubbery, leapt on to a garden bench and from there, on to the roof of a lean-to shed that abutted the gable end. The cat scrabbled up the slates and on to a window sill. As it disappeared inside, Tenille realised the window was open a few inches. She clambered up on to the back of the bench and reached for the guttering. It wobbled, but it took her weight. She managed to haul herself on to the roof at the third attempt, then crawled gingerly up the slippery slates, swearing under her breath.

When she reached the window, she clung to the sill as if it were a lifebelt in a stormy sea. She peered in, not wanting to raise the window if it was some old biddy's bedroom. She couldn't see much, but it was enough to know the room was empty, a bare mattress on an iron bedstead the only indication that this had once been a place where people slept.

Bracing herself against the roof, she pushed the window sash upwards. It creaked and groaned, but not enough to freak her out. Tenille slid across the sill and landed softly on the carpeted floor. Cautiously she crossed the room, almost tripping over the white cat, who was weaving round her ankles purring.

On the landing there were more cats, their yellow eyes gleaming. There was a faint aroma of cat piss and stale meat in the air. To her surprise, all the doors off the landing were open, and she could see that none of the curtains had been drawn. A quick circuit upstairs and down revealed that the house was empty. She breathed a huge sigh of relief. For once, it was going to be easy.

She started in the only bedroom that showed signs of occupancy. A thorough search revealed nothing of interest. The second bedroom told the same story. In the third room, however, Tenille found an old brass-bound chest. It seemed to contain nothing but old photographs. But when she lifted them out, she noticed the chest seemed shallower on the inside than it ought to have been. She risked carrying it through to the landing, closing all the doors and turning on the light. When she looked more closely, she saw a thin leather loop in one corner of the bottom. She yanked on it and the whole base lifted up, revealing an inch-deep hiding place.

Tenille lifted out a thin bundle of papers. The paper was thick and brittle, yellowing round the edges. It smelled of dust and dry cleaners. It was covered in old-fashioned handwriting, all loops and curls. She could hardly make it out at first. Then the opening words jumped out at her. *I am minded tonight of the time we spent at Alfoxden, & the suspicion that fell upon Coleridge and myself, viz. that we were agents of the enemy, gathering information as spies for Bonaparte. I recall*

Coleridge's assertion that it was beyond the bounds of good sense to give credence to the notion that poets were suited for such an endeavour since we see all before us as matter for our verse & would have no inclination to hold any secrets to our breasts that might serve our calling.

There should be trumpets or drums or something, she thought stupidly. Trumpets or drums or the Hallelujah chorus. This was the real deal. What she was holding in her hand had been written by one of the greatest poets the world had ever seen. Hardly anybody had ever set eyes on it. And she was touching it, smelling it, reading it. She'd have died before she admitted it, but Tenille felt exhilaration and exultation. She sat back on her heels and drank it in greedily.

She had no idea how long she crouched there, overwhelmed with it all. She felt drunk with excitement. But at last she came to herself and realised she had to get back to Jane with this news. She was tempted to walk out with the whole manuscript, but she knew instinctively that was the wrong way to play it. She thumbed through the papers, checking to see if there was a poem tucked in between the prose jottings. But no. All she could find were notes. What if she took one of the pages from near the middle? Then Jane would know she was telling the truth. And it would be worth all the hassle to see the look on her face when she realised what she was looking at.

Tenille chose a page at random and carefully placed it between her T-shirt and her sweatshirt. Then she put everything back as she had found it, carefully replacing the chest exactly where it had been so as not to disturb the dust around it. She felt giddy with delight as she made her way back to the cat window.

The chill night air and the prospect of getting down from the roof sobered her up. She eased the window back down and spreadeagled herself on the tiles. Inch by careful inch she made her way down the roof. When she reached the edge, she realised she was going to have to drop to the ground; the bench was too far from the wall to lower herself back on to it.

Tenille didn't care. She felt invincible. She hung from the guttering then let go. It was only a few feet, and she landed safely in soft earth. As she staggered upright, heavy hands descended on her from both sides. Snarling, she struggled to free herself, but it was pointless. Her assailants were bigger, stronger and heavier. Within seconds, she was face down in the dirt, her arms pulled roughly behind her.

She felt cold plastic against her skin as a voice said, 'I am arresting you on suspicion of burglary.'

Tenille's face screwed up in frustration. 'Ah, shit.'

My hiding place afforded me some sense of safety, which was needful to me as I was in no condition to load a boat & set sail on the treacherous waters that beset Pitcairn. For some days I had little choice but to remain in hiding, feverish & weak. My head throbbed constantly & my shoulder burned. Under cover of night, I forced myself down to the water's edge to bathe my wound, but that was the only sortie I dared. I knew my best chance of survival was to disappear completely from sight. The natives were too simple to understand that I might have survived to escape after they had taken me for dead. As to the disappearance of my body, I trusted Isabella to concoct some tale & this she must have done for I never saw nor heard any signs of a search party.

39

Rigston glowered across the table at the mutinous child opposite. He'd had to wait for an appropriate adult to arrive before he could interview her, and the duty social worker had taken his time to get to the station. The kid had had three hours in a cell to contemplate her options. He hoped it had softened her up a little.

He'd gone through the formalities with the tape, but Tenille had refused to confirm her identity. 'I ain't saying one damn thing to you, Mister Man,' was all she had offered.

'You're doing yourself no good,' Rigston said. 'I know you are Tenille Cole. I know you're wanted by the police in London in connection with a murder and an arson down there. We've taken your finger-prints and they match the ones the Met sent us. It's only a matter of time before they arrive to take you back down there. Unless of course you'd care to explain your connection to four suspicious deaths up here, in which case I'll be hanging on to you.'

She glared at him from under lowered brows. He couldn't fathom her. Most thirteen-year-olds he dealt with were sufficiently intimidated by their surroundings and his presence to fold like a house of cards. But she was a tough customer, no question of that. Not much older than his own daughter, but she could have been from another planet.

'We've been processing crime scenes all night, Tenille,' he said, more gently this time. 'We found your prints all over their homes – Edith Clewlow, Tillie Swain, Eddie Fairfield and Letty Brownrigg. You were in their houses. But there's no sign of anything having been stolen, so you weren't there for any ordinary burglary. And now we find you climbing out of Jenny Wright's cottage with a sheet of paper that looks pretty old to me. Would you like to talk about that?'

Tenille shook her head.

'For the benefit of the tape, Tenille Cole has shaken her head to indicate a negative.'

Rigston rolled up his shirtsleeves and leaned his meaty forearms on the table. He dropped his voice confidentially. 'See, here's how I think it went down. Jane Gresham's been hiding you. I mean, why else would a London sparrow like you come up here? And Jane Gresham is on a quest. A quest she's roped you into. She thinks somebody up here has something she wants very badly. And when she couldn't dig it out the conventional way, she sent you in to look for it. Is that how it went down?'

Tenille made a small noise of contempt and shifted in her seat so she didn't have to meet his eyes.

'Only, things got out of hand. In all of those houses where Jane got you searching, somebody died. You're in big trouble, Tenille. But we can maybe find a way to make it go easier for you. I think Jane Gresham put you up to this. She told you what to do, how to do it so nobody would know it was murder. And that lets you off the hook a bit. You're just a kid. You were doing what Jane Gresham asked because you were frightened that, if you didn't, she'd hand you over to the police for Geno Marley's murder. That's called coercion, and it would make things easier on you.'

Tenille turned her face back to him, defiance written on her features. 'That's called bullshit,' she said. 'And that's all I have to say.' She turned to the social worker. 'You better get me a lawyer. You're no use to me, man.' She folded her arms and leaned back in the chair, studying the ceiling.

'You going to take the rap for Jane Gresham?' Rigston said. 'Very loyal. I wonder if she'll be as loyal to you? I bet you're going to end up carrying the can for all of this, Tenille. You're an easy target. Truanting black kid, bastard love child of a big-time gangsta. You're going to take the fall for your nice middle-class university lecturer. While you're spending the foreseeable future banged up, she's going to be making a name for herself with the manuscript you found.'

She flashed him a quick look of contempt.

Rigston laughed. 'You reckon that's not how it's going to play? I thought you'd have more street smarts than that. Jane Gresham will walk, and you will not. That's the bottom line.'

'I think you're badgering her now,' the social worker said. 'If you've got some evidence, let's be having it.'

'I've got evidence of burglary,' Rigston said. 'My men were staking out Jenny Wright's cottage. They were waiting for a killer. Looks like they got one too. But until we can firm up that part of the case, we've still got Tenille for burglary. And we'll be keeping her locked up for now.' He pushed back his chair and stood up. 'Interview terminated at three fifty-three a.m., Inspector Rigston and Constable Whitrow leaving the room.' He suited his actions to his words and walked out into the corridor.

'You didn't pull any punches there, guv,' Whitrow said.

Rigston ran a hand over his face, rubbing his tired eyes. 'For all the good it did me. Can you believe that kid is thirteen? Hard as nails and tough as old boots. Doesn't even need to get lawyered up to know to keep her mouth shut.' He set off down the corridor. 'Let's shake the tree a bit and see what falls out. Send a couple of uniforms out to Fellhead and bring Jane Gresham in.'

'You want them to arrest her, or just ask her to come in for questioning?'

'Arrest her. Let's get her on the back foot. Conspiracy to burgle, that should do it. She's not got the equipment to stonewall us like Tenille Cole. Let's scare the shit out of her. I've got four dead bodies on my patch and I want some movement.' Rigston swung into his office and closed the door firmly behind him.

Shocked awake by the ringing of the bell and the hammering on the door, Jane winced as she sat up in bed, stiff and disorientated. The bedside clock showed four twenty-three. What the hell was going on? She struggled out of bed, groaning as her bruised muscles complained. Grabbing her dressing gown, she opened the bedroom door. Her mother stood at the top of the stairs, her face blurred by sleep, her expression bewildered. She could hear her father's tread on the stairs. 'I'm coming,' he bellowed.

She heard the door open and Allan's startled, 'What's going on?' over the clatter of boots on the stone flags of the hallway.

'We're looking for Jane Gresham,' a male voice said.

'Is she on the premises?' a female voice added.

Judy turned a startled face on her daughter. 'It's the police.'

Jane pushed past her and took a few steps down the stairs. Her father had his back to the wall. He kept repeating his original question. Two uniformed police officers occupied the rest of the space, the confined area rendering them even more unnerving than their uniforms and bulky utility belts.

'I'm Jane Gresham,' she said quietly. 'What's all the commotion?'

The woman officer stepped forward. 'Jane Gresham, I am arresting you on suspicion of conspiracy to commit burglary. You do not have to say anything but it may harm your defence if you fail to mention when questioned something which you later rely on in court. Anything you do say will be given in evidence.'

Jane stared open-mouthed, too astonished to feel anything other than shock.

'What?' Allan said. 'Are you out of your minds?'

Judy followed Jane and clutched her hand. 'There must be some mistake.'

The woman pushed past Allan and began to climb

the stairs. 'Please step away, Mrs Gresham.' When she reached Jane and Judy, she said, 'If you'd like to get dressed, Dr Gresham, I'll have to accompany you.'

'This is an outrage,' Judy wailed. 'How dare you march into my home and arrest my daughter?'

'Please, Mrs Gresham. We have a job to do. I'd advise you not to make it any more difficult.' The woman kept coming, forcing Judy back and to one side without actually touching her. She took Jane's arm in hers, not ungently, and led her upstairs. 'Which is your room?'

Jane recovered the power of speech enough to say, 'That one.' She shook her arm free and walked in, leaving the door ajar for the police officer to follow her. Under cover of her dressing gown, she stripped off her pyjamas and dressed in jeans and a shirt. 'You're making a terrible mistake,' she said as she followed the policewoman downstairs. Her mother was huddled into her father's protective arm, tears spilling down her cheeks. 'It'll be all right,' Jane said, feeling useless. 'This is a cock-up,' she added.

'What can we do?' her father asked anxiously.

'Try not to worry. I'll be home soon.' As she passed her mother, Judy reached out to clasp her hand briefly.

'I hope you're bloody pleased with yourselves,' Jane said bitterly as she was escorted out of her own front door to the waiting police car. 'Are you trying to make a point here? Or is it one of the perks of the job, terrorising innocent people in their own homes?'

'Shut it,' the male officer said as he pushed her head down to avoid her hitting the door frame of the car. 'You'll get your chance to sound off when we get you to Keswick.'

484

The journey was long enough for anger to be subsumed by fear. What did conspiracy to burgle mean? It had to be something to do with Tenille, but what exactly? Jane cursed her failure to tell Tenille about the attack on her. She'd thought she was protecting her, but telling her might have had the salutary effect of keeping her from wandering around on her own after dark. What had she done now? And how was it tied into Jane? Somehow, she couldn't imagine Tenille telling a cop that Jane had known what she was up to. It had to be a trumped-up charge.

By the time she was ushered into an interview room, Jane was battling fear with self-righteousness. As soon as Rigston walked in, before he even had the chance to greet her, she was on the attack. 'How dare you send your storm troopers to my parents' home in the middle of the night,' she said. 'I can't believe whatever you have to say to me wouldn't wait till a more reasonable hour.'

'You're under arrest, Dr Gresham,' Rigston said sarcastically. 'We don't arrest people at their convenience, we do it at ours. Now, whatever you've got to say, save it for the tape.' He set the tapes running and sat down opposite her.

'I want a phone call. I'm entitled to a phone call,' she said.

'Why don't we have a little chat first?'

'I've nothing to say to you.'

'No? We've got your friend Tenille just down the hallway. Caught her red-handed in the middle of a burglary. She was coming out of Jenny Wright's cottage. The next person on your list, unless I'm mistaken.'

Jane's eyes widened. Where had he got that information from? Then she remembered showing the family tree with its list to River. She opened her mouth, then closed it again.

'Nothing to say? OK. Let's keep going. We've conducted post mortems on all four of the recent deaths in Edith Clewlow's extended family and we have reason to believe there may be suspicious circumstances.'

Jane gave him a fierce look but said nothing.

'We've also examined the premises where those people were found dead. Care to guess whose fingerprints turned up at all of them?' He paused. 'No? Your pal Tenille again. The same little pal who is already wanted for questioning about another murder. Starting to see a pattern here? The thing is, the only connection between a black London teenager and four elderly corpses in Cumbria is you, Dr Gresham. I can't help thinking that you're the one who put Tenille up to her nocturnal wanderings. Wanderings that have left four people dead.'

Jane's eyes were squeezed shut. This was a nightmare and she wanted to wake up from it. She dug her nails into her palms, but all that happened was pain. 'I want to make a phone call,' she said again.

'All in good time. You know what the irony is? The one night Tenille gets herself caught just happens to be the night she found what you were looking for.'

Jane's eyes snapped open. 'What?'

Rigston opened the folder he'd brought into the room with him. He took out a transparent plastic sleeve that held a small sheet of writing paper and pushed it towards her. Jane was transfixed as she read the familiar hand. *That night, I lay awake considering the import of Bligh's words. It was clear to me that if I did not endure his iniquitous and unwarranted treatment, I would be forced to suffer a different sort of torture . . .*

Ever since she'd found the first clue, she had refused to allow herself to believe in it completely. She had tried to treat it like a research project, not some romantic quest. Now at last she could let down the barriers and feel. The depth of her emotions surprised her. She was moved almost to tears by this simple piece of paper. She ran a finger over the letters, tracing the movements of Wordsworth's pen. The heretical thought came to her that she could understand someone killing to possess this.

And with that thought came guilt and remorse. Her search had opened floodgates whose existence she hadn't even suspected. And now four people were dead.

Rigston waited patiently, his eyes never leaving her. When she finally looked up, she could feel the tears in her eyes. 'I want to make a phone call,' she said, her voice unsteady.

'If it's not you and Tenille, Jane, who is it that cares enough about that piece of paper to want to kill for it? Who else knows the starting point for your search?' Rigston's voice was softer now, his body language less threatening.

Even in her daze, she recognised the slide into her first name. He was trying to soften her up. And this was something she could give him at no cost to either herself or Tenille. 'Most of Edith's extended family,' she said. 'There was a roomful of people there when I spoke to Alice.'

Rigston shook his head. 'Nice try, but that was after Edith's death. We need names of people who knew *before* she was murdered.'

'My brother phoned Edith on the Saturday morning to ask her if she had any family papers. I'm sure she would have told other members of her family then. They were close. And I bet they're not going to be admitting it now if she did tell them.'

Rigston pounced on the solid fact. 'Matthew knew?'

Jane sighed. 'Yes. As did my colleague Dan Seabourne, Anthony Catto at the Wordsworth Centre, and a document dealer called Jake Hartnell. I'm not sure how much he knows or when he knew it, but he does know something. And that's about the least likely list of murderers I can think of. There must be someone else, someone a hell of a lot more unscrupulous.'

'Someone like Tenille?' Rigston said.

Jane stared down at the sheet of manuscript. She'd dreamed of holding this in her hands. She just hadn't expected it to be in a police interview room. How had it come to this? She looked up at Rigston. 'Somebody tried to kill me yesterday and that certainly wasn't Tenille,' she said.

Rigston looked sceptical. 'How convenient. Another drunk driver trying to run you down, was it?'

Jane clapped a hand over her mouth. 'Oh my God, it never occurred to me. That must have been his first attempt.'

'You're really clutching at straws now,' he said sarcastically.

'I'm serious,' she insisted. 'I went for a walk up to Langmere Force. I was sitting on the edge of the rock outcropping, like I've done for years. And someone crept up behind me and hit me over the head. I fell into the waterfall. I was lucky that Derek Thwaite saw me fall. He and his dog got me out. I would have drowned otherwise.'

'You could have waited till you had a rescuer to hand and thrown yourself off,' Rigston said, just as she'd predicted.

Jane leaned forward, parting her curls to show the tender lump. 'I couldn't have done that to myself, could I?'

'It's not impossible,' Rigston said. 'You could have smacked your head into a tree or something.'

Jane banged her fist on the table. 'Why won't you believe me?'

'Because you're not very credible, you and Tenille.'

'Right. That's it. I'm not saying another word until I get my phone call.'

'You're sure about that?' Rigston said. 'Because now's your chance to get Tenille off the hook of a quadruple murder charge. You stick to your guns and she's going down. With her background, she's a good fit. Unless you admit she was doing what she was doing at your instigation, she's not going to have a leg to stand on. She'll be carrying the can all by herself.'

For an instant, Jane almost fell for it. Guilt and responsibility almost swamped her good sense. But at the last moment, she stopped herself. 'I want my phone call,' she said.

Rigston stood up. 'Have it your own way. Someone will escort you to the custody desk. You can call from there.'

At length, I felt myself enough recovered to effect my escape proper. I waited for the first night when there was little wind & the sea was calm & then I loaded the jolly-boat with my provisions. I still had little use of my left arm, & dragging the boat to the water's edge was hard going. Once aboard, I had some difficulty in handling the oars. By good fortune, the natives had fashioned paddles for the boats since they found our methods alien to them. I was better able to manage the paddle, & though my progress was painfully slow, by the time dawn's first light streaked the horizon, I was well clear of Bounty Bay & able at last to raise my jury-rigged sail. I took a last look at my failed Eden, then resolutely set my back to it & faced the Pacific Ocean, my heart filled with a mixture of relief & terror.

40

It was, Dan thought, like being in a house where someone had died recently. The inhabitants shocked out of the ability to communicate, desperate for something to do but unable to figure out what that might be, the core of the room an absence. Judy and Allan Gresham sat at the kitchen table, hands clasped, mugs of tea untouched and cooling in front of them. Matthew paced restlessly, unable to settle.

'I don't understand why she called you,' Matthew had said when Dan explained he'd come to the farm in response to a phone call from Jane.

'Because she thought your parents would be too upset to take it in. She didn't know you were here.'

'Of course I'm here. Who else would Mum and Dad call?' Matthew actually grabbed a handful of his hair and tugged at it. 'So what did she tell you?'

Dan pulled up a chair and sat opposite Judy and Allan, who looked at him with mute fear. 'It turns out she's been sheltering Tenille – her friend from London.'

Judy looked puzzled. 'Why would she do that? And where?'

'Because she believed in Tenille's innocence. I'm not sure where she was hiding her. One of the outbuildings, I think.'

'Bloody madness,' Matthew muttered, throwing himself into a chair. 'But I still don't understand what happened tonight.'

'The police caught Tenille red-handed in a burglary. And apparently Tenille finally found what we've been looking for.'

'What? Where did she find it?' Matthew interrupted.

'Does it matter?' Dan said, unable to keep a momentary flash of anger from his eyes. 'Jane didn't have time to give me any details. What matters is that the police put two and two together and made five. Jane was looking for the manuscript, Tenille burgled the cottage and came out with a page of manuscript, Jane knows Tenille, therefore Jane must have put her up to it.'

Judy shook her head. 'That can't be right. Jane wouldn't do something like that. She wouldn't.'

'We all know that,' Matthew said impatiently. 'We need to get her a lawyer. We need to get her out of there.'

'That's what she asked me to do,' Dan said.

'Why you? You don't know any lawyers up here,' Matthew said.

'She asked me to talk to you and your parents,' Dan said mildly. 'Matthew, she only called me because she didn't want to give you guys any more hassle than you're already having. So, who do we call?'

Matthew threw his hands upwards. 'I don't know. I don't know any criminal lawyers. I'm a teacher, for fuck's sake.'

'I can't bear to think of her locked up,' Judy whispered. 'I can't bear it.'

Allan released Judy's hand, patted it and pushed his chair back. 'I'm going to call Peter Muckle.'

'He does land and contracts, Dad. He doesn't know anything about crime,' Matthew said.

'He'll know someone who does,' Allan said stolidly.

'It's barely six,' Judy said weakly. 'He won't thank you for it.'

'I was at school with Peter, he won't mind.'

Dan watched him shuffle out of the room, diminished by fear and uncertainty. He leaned across the table and put his hand over Judy's. 'It'll be all right, Mrs Gresham,' he said.

Judy gave him an uncomprehending look. 'You've got no idea, have you, lad? No idea at all.'

Although it was after eight when Rigston called Anthony Catto, he sounded half-asleep. When Rigston introduced himself, there was a momentary silence, then Anthony cleared his throat. 'Sorry, I had a very late night. I'm not quite with it. You're with the police in Keswick?'

'That's right. I was wondering if you could help me with something.'

'That sounds rather ominous, Inspector – helping the police with their enquiries.' Anthony sounded cautious.

'It's nothing like that, sir. A piece of manuscript has come into our possession and I wondered if you might cast an eye over it and tell me whether you think it might be authentic.' Rigston rolled his eyes, annoyed with himself. He always became formal to the point of pomposity when he was dealing with people he felt were his educational superiors. It was a miracle it hadn't scuppered his relationship with River.

'I'm not a manuscript expert by any means,' Anthony said hurriedly. 'My field is a somewhat narrow one.'

'I appreciate that, but if this is what we think it might be, it's your field.'

'I'm intrigued now, Inspector.' The voice was warmer, the tone more interested. 'When would you like me to come and take a look at it?'

'No time like the present, sir. I could send a car for you.'

A short pause. 'No, that won't be necessary. It'll be quicker if I drive myself. I should be with you in, say, forty minutes?'

'Perfect.' Rigston replaced the phone. Another brick in the wall. Before he could make another call, the phone rang.

'Custody suite here,' the voice said. 'Neil Terras is here. Says he's representing Jane Gresham.'

The family weren't hanging about, Rigston thought, trying not to feel pissed off at this exercise of Jane Gresham's rights. He was probably screwed now as far as getting anything out of her. Terras was the shrewdest operator of the criminal law for miles around. He was surprised the Greshams knew that. 'You'd better let him see her, then,' he said.

'He's asking for disclosure,' the custody sergeant said.

'I'll be right down.'

*　　*　　*

Half an hour later, Rigston felt like he'd been gutted and filleted and stitched up like a kipper. Terras's forensic questioning had left him without a leg to stand on. 'It's all suspicion,' Terras had said. 'I wouldn't even grace it with the term "circumstantial". You've got nothing against my client whatsoever. I'm going to talk to her now, and when I come out of there, I expect you to be ready to let her go.'

Rigston knew his case against Jane Gresham was weak, but he had been hoping her unfamiliarity with the legal process might have provoked her into revelation. There was no chance of that now. If he bothered to interview her again, he knew she'd be going 'no comment' while the ticking clock imposed by PACE ran down. Best to put off the interview until he had more leverage. It was the end of the game.

He watched Terras go off to commune with his client then turned to the custody sergeant. 'When he's done, bail her pending further enquiries.'

He walked back to his office, feeling every minute of the long night in his bones. He was getting too old for this kind of thing. Working through the night was a young man's game.

Anthony Catto was waiting for him in the CID room. Looked more like a superannuated hippie with a hangover than a world expert on Wordsworth, Rigston thought sourly as he showed him into his office. 'Thanks for coming in,' he said, waving him to a seat.

'How could I resist?' Anthony said, crossing one long leg over the other.

'Feeling a bit more chipper now, eh? You sounded rough when I spoke to you on the phone.'

495

'As I said, late night. I was over in Newcastle giving a lecture, then a group of us went out for supper. It was after two when I got back,' he explained. 'But the thought of what you might have to show me has perked me up.' He gave Rigston an expectant look.

Rigston handed over the plastic folder that contained the manuscript page. Anthony held it carefully by the edges and studied it. After a couple of minutes, he looked up. 'Might I ask where this came from?'

'I'd rather not say at this point. It's part of an ongoing inquiry. Does it matter?'

'Ultimately, yes, it does. It's a question of provenance. You see, Inspector, this appears to be part of something whose existence until now has been nothing more than rumour and theory. But it has been the subject of . . . shall we say, some interest lately.'

'Who's been interested?' They were going all round the houses here, but Rigston didn't mind. Information was always potentially useful.

'There's a young woman called Jane Gresham who comes originally from Fellhead. She's an academic based in London, and a good friend of mine. But she recently uncovered some material which suggested there might be an undiscovered Wordsworth manuscript in existence. And she's been looking for it.' He tapped the paper with his finger. 'This appears to be precisely what she was searching for. If it's authentic.'

'You still haven't said what you think it is,' Rigston said.

'The handwriting is either that of William Wordsworth or of an expert forger. One would need to test the paper and ink to be certain whether it's the real thing. One would also need to know the provenance to assess how likely it is to be authentic. The subject matter appears to be a first-person account of matters relating to the mutiny on the *Bounty*.'

'And you were aware that this was what Jane Gresham was looking for?'

'Oh yes, I knew all about it. The new material she found was in our archive. I was able to give her a little assistance right at the start.'

'What sort of assistance?'

Anthony met Rigston's gaze. 'Why are you so interested in this, Inspector?'

'Humour me. I like puzzles.'

Anthony shrugged. 'It wasn't much, really. She came across a reference to some papers being entrusted to a servant. All Jane had was a first name. I was able to provide her with a surname, which gave her a direction in which to focus her search.'

'So you knew she was looking at the Clewlow family?' Rigston asked.

'Was that the name of the man Dorcas married? I didn't know that,' Anthony said absently, studying the paper again.

'You weren't interested in making your own enquiries? It being your field?'

Anthony looked startled. 'Good heavens, no. It was Jane's discovery. She's a very competent researcher and she has a huge passion for this particular project. Even if I was so inclined, I have far too much on my plate with the new Jerwood Centre to spare the time for chasing something so fundamentally unlikely. I was happy to offer any help I could, but this is her baby.'

Either he was a very good liar or he was telling the truth, Rigston thought. Somehow, he couldn't see Anthony Catto burgling and murdering his way to anything. The man was too wrapped up in his own world.

'This is really very exciting,' Anthony said, as if to reinforce Rigston's judgement. 'I can't tell you how rarely one makes a really important find in this field. And if this is what I think it is, and there is more of it, it's probably the most significant discovery in English literary studies for a few generations. I'd love to see the rest of it.' His smile was wry. 'Are you sure you can't tell me where it came from?'

'Maybe you should ask Jane Gresham,' Rigston said, unable to keep an edge of bitterness out of his voice. 'We should be letting her out of the cells any time now.'

Jane followed her lawyer out to the car park in a daze. 'I can't thank you enough,' she said. 'Rigston had me really scared.'

'He was trying it on. He doesn't have anything on you. And he's not going to get anywhere unless Tenille Cole starts trying to lay the blame on you. Even then, it'll be your word against hers, and yours will carry more weight,' Terras said, glancing at his watch.

'She won't say a thing, she's loyal to a fault,' Jane said. 'Is there anything I can do to help her?'

'She's got her own lawyer.' He grinned. 'Not as good as me, but not bad for a duty solicitor. She might want to talk to you. If she does, I should be with you.' He looked at his watch again. 'I'd drive you home, but I'm due in court. Will you be OK?'

'She'll be fine,' a familiar voice interjected.

Jane swung round. 'Anthony? What are you doing here?'

'Waiting to give you a lift home. I've been helping the police with their enquiries,' he said.

'I'll be off, then,' Terras said. 'Stay in touch.'

Jane nodded, distracted by Anthony's presence. 'Surely they don't think you had anything to do with the murders?'

'Murders?' Anthony's face registered surprise. 'Murder wasn't mentioned at all. In fact, now I come to think of it, I don't recall a single crime coming up in the conversation.' He moved towards his car and Jane followed. 'But what concerns me is what they were doing arresting you.'

'In a minute,' Jane said, impatient to hear his story. 'You first. Tell me what went on with you and the cops.'

As they drove out of Keswick, Anthony filled her in on his interview with Rigston. 'I can't tell you how extraordinary it felt to hold that piece of paper in my hand,' he said. 'I'm damn sure it's the real thing.'

'I think so too.'

'So it was you who found it?' He looked away from the road, his excitement palpable. 'But why is it in the hands of the police? And what's this about murder?'

Jane groaned. 'Four murders and a burglary. And from what you've been telling me, it sounds as if Rigston has been checking you out as a potential suspect.'

Anthony's mouth fell open and the car swerved alarmingly. '*Four* murders?'

'Don't forget the burglary. Which is where the manuscript page comes in.'

'I don't understand any of this. Can you begin at the beginning?'

Jane sighed. 'It all started with a teenager called Tenille,' she said. By the time she got to the end of her tale, Anthony had run out of exclamations and had settled for astonished silence. 'And that's where we're up to,' Jane concluded.

'But you simply have to find the rest of the manuscript,' Anthony said. 'Do you know where it is?'

'All I know is that it came from Jenny Wright's house. That's where the cops picked up Tenille.'

'You have to talk to this woman, have her show you the rest of it,' Anthony said as they pulled into the farmyard.

'I'm too tired to think about it now,' Jane said, getting out of the car. Anthony followed her into the house, still trying to talk her into it. She had barely stepped into the kitchen when her mother was upon her, enveloping her in a warm embrace, tears running down her face. Her father, Matthew and Dan joined in a kind of group hug and it took Jane some moments to free herself.

Her ears were assaulted by a chorus of demands to know what had happened. Jane put her hands over her ears and shouted, 'One at a time! I know you're pleased to see me, but give me some space here.'

It took a few minutes for everyone to calm down, but before too long they were all seated round the table drinking tea and Jane was forced to tell her story all over again, the narrative disjointed by incredulity, disapproval and outrage from her several listeners.

'So did Tenille kill these old dears?' Matthew asked.

'Of course she didn't,' Jane said. 'What do you take me for? You think I'd shelter someone who was capable of that?'

For once, Matthew was placatory. 'I'm not questioning your judgement. Just trying to make sense of what's going on.'

'Apart from the fact that she's not a killer, Tenille didn't know about any of this until after Edith Clewlow's death,' Jane said. 'So that lets her off the hook.'

'Frankly, I see no point in us trying to play an Agatha Christie parlour game,' Anthony said, cutting across the discussion. 'It's the job of the police to sort this mess out. Your real responsibility, Jane, is to the manuscript. You have to persuade this Jenny Wright to let you see it.'

Jane stifled a yawn. 'Somehow, I don't think that's going to happen. Don't forget, I'm the prime suspect in the murder of four of her relatives. I don't think she's going to be handing the manuscript over to me any time soon.'

'Maybe not,' Dan said. 'But Jimmy's her favourite nephew right now. I could talk to him, see if he can get her to let me take a look.'

Jane tried to hide her disappointment. 'If you think that will work,' she said despondently, feeling her dream slipping out of her grasp.

'I know it's your thing,' he said. 'And I'm not trying

501

to steal your glory. I could get her to let me make a copy of it, maybe? Then you could make a start on it.'

'It's not a bad idea, Jane,' Anthony said.

'And it means you can stop here, where I can keep an eye on you and make sure you don't get into any more trouble,' her mother added ominously.

Jane sighed. 'OK. You go and see Jimmy.' She stood up. 'I'm going to bed. I am knackered.' Before she could leave the room, the phone rang. She paused while her father answered it.

'Just a minute,' he said. 'It's for you,' he added, passing the phone to Jane.

'Hello,' she said impatiently.

'Dr Gresham? This is DI Blair from the Met.'

Jane groaned inwardly. Not more hassle about Tenille. 'How can I help you?' she said wearily.

'I wanted to let you know that we're no longer looking for Tenille Cole in connection with the murder of Geno Marley,' Donna said baldly.

Jane could hardly believe her ears. 'What?' she said. 'Why? What's happened? Have you made an arrest?'

'A young man died in the early hours of this morning during police pursuit of a stolen car,' Donna said, her clipped voice the perfect vehicle for the officialese. 'Among his effects was Geno Marley's wallet. The passenger in the car admitted that the driver had in fact boasted to him about blowing Geno away. So the case would appear to be closed.'

'That's great news. I mean, not that somebody is dead, obviously, but that Tenille is in the clear.'

'She's not quite in the clear. There is the matter of the arson.'

Jane's spirits plummeted as quickly as they'd risen. 'But . . .'

Before she could go on, Donna cut across her. 'Dr Gresham, can I speak frankly to you?'

'Of course,' Jane said.

'I think Tenille's one of those rare kids who can be saved. Everything I've heard about her suggests that she could make something of herself. Prosecuting her would destroy any chance she has of that. I don't believe there's much prospect of her reoffending. Unless of course we push her through the system and offer her no alternative. But she's going to need somebody in her corner if she's to make good on that promise. To put it bluntly, are you going to be there for her?'

Jane didn't even have to pause for thought. 'She's like a kid sister to me. I'm not going to walk away. I promise you, DI Blair, if you give her this chance, I won't let her waste it. And I don't think her father will either.'

'Yeah, well, the less said about him the better. Let her know it's safe to come home, will you?'

'Um . . . it's not quite that simple,' Jane said. 'You're going to have to talk to DCI Rigston.'

'In Keswick? Is there a problem?'

'I'd rather you heard it from him. I'd appreciate you giving him the same message about Tenille that you just gave me.'

'That doesn't sound very promising,' Donna said, her doubts about her own judgement obvious even over the phone.

'She's a good kid, DI Blair. She's redeemable.'

'I'll talk to DCI Rigston. I hope our paths don't have to cross again, Dr Gresham.'

'I hope so too, in the nicest possible way. Thank you, Inspector. I'll do my best to make sure your leniency isn't wasted.'

'Good luck.' Donna hung up.

Jane looked around the room, her face cheerful for the first time in days. 'That was the police in London. Tenille's off the hook for the murder and arson down there.'

'That's great news,' Dan said.

'Maybe now Rigston will leave you and Tenille alone and start looking for the real killer,' Matthew added.

'Let's hope so. Now, I really am going to bed,' Jane said. 'Perhaps when I wake up, this will all make sense.'

Dan grinned. 'I wouldn't bet on it.'

I was naturally alive to the irony of my situation. I had been responsible for setting my captain adrift in an open boat. Yet here I was a scant four years later in precisely the same predicament. Poetic justice, indeed. Now I would find out if I had truly absorbed Bligh's lessons in navigation. I set my course to bring me upon the western coast of South America & prayed to God for fair weather. My prayers were answered for I was fortunate in that the weather looked kindly upon me. What rain I endured was a blessing in that it allowed me to replenish my fresh-water supplies. I sailed for twelve days & nights & saw neither sail nor land on the horizon. On the thirteenth day, a whaler from Newfoundland hove into sight & I made for her. My gold was sufficient to buy me passage without questions being asked & my seamanship made me a welcome addition to the ship's complement. I felt like a free man again and resolved to make my way home to England to clear my name.

41

Jimmy slid into the passenger seat of Dan's car, parked up at the end of Alice's street. 'Mysterious phone call,' he said, leaning across to kiss him. 'I feel like a spy.'

'I didn't want to come to the house without talking to you first, what with the funeral preparations and everything. Have the police been in touch with Jenny?' Dan asked.

Jimmy's monkey face screwed into a frown. 'No, should they have?'

'The cottage was burgled last night.'

'No way,' Jimmy breathed. 'Man, I'm so glad we got her out of there. That could have been the killer, Dan. She could have been lying dead this morning.' He shook his head.

'We don't think the burglar was the killer, Jimmy.' Briefly, Dan outlined the events of the previous night. 'I don't think it was Tenille. That means the killer is still out there. Frankly, the best thing Jenny can do right now is to hand over the manuscript to us. Once it's out there in the public domain, there's no point in any more deaths. If Jenny wants to make sure she stays alive, she needs to take herself out of the target circle.'

Jimmy nodded, seeing the force of his argument. 'Let's go and talk to her now,' he said. 'Alice is round at Gibson's so the coast's clear.'

They found Jenny sitting in the conservatory drinking tea, watching the birds feasting on Alice's bird table. She peered suspiciously at Dan. 'You're that lad was with Jane Gresham the other day,' she said, no welcome in her voice.

'Dan's a friend of mine,' Jimmy said.

Jenny raised her eyebrows. 'Oh, aye? You want to let your head rule your heart a bit more, young Jimmy. Handsome is as handsome does and he's out for what he can get, this one.'

'Auntie Jenny,' Jimmy protested. 'That's not fair. If it wasn't for Dan and Jane, you could be dead in your bed. There was a burglary at your cottage last night.'

Jenny's hand clutched her chest. 'Oh my God. What did they take? Did they vandalise the place?'

'The burglar only took one thing,' Dan said. 'A piece of paper. Just one. A sample, you might say.'

'What are you on about?' Jenny looked every inch the timorous, confused old lady, but Dan wasn't buying it.

'You've got the manuscript, Jenny. We know that now.' He crouched down so he was level with her. 'I really don't want to frighten you, but four people have already died so someone could get their hands on this manuscript. As long as you keep it hidden, you're next on that person's hit list. But if you get it out in the open, entrust it to Jane, or Anthony Catto at the Wordsworth Trust, you protect yourself. I don't want you to die for a bundle of papers. Nobody does. Give it up, Jenny.'

The old woman's lower lip thrust out in an expression of defiance. 'I don't know what you're talking about,' she said.

'The sheet of paper came from your house. The police were watching the house, they caught the burglar as she was leaving. She had it on her.'

Jenny's head came up in defiance. 'And what's to say she didn't have it on her when she went in? What's to say it's not all some clever bluff? You and your university friends, you're all so bloody clever-clever, that's just the sort of thing you'd come up with. I'm telling you, I don't know what you're talking about and I'll thank you to leave me to drink my cup of tea in peace.' She turned away, pointedly studying the birds again.

'Auntie Jenny,' Jimmy said, his voice a plea. 'It's for your own good.'

'It would be if I had the papers he's talking about. But I don't, and that's that. Now be a good lad and get him out of here before Alice comes back and has a come-apart at the sight of him.'

Jimmy followed Dan out to the street. 'What can I say? She's a stubborn old biddy.'

Dan shrugged. 'We tried. Work on her, Jimmy. For her own sake.'

Matthew glowered at Ewan Rigston. 'I don't believe my sister tried to make out I'm some sort of fiend who goes around preying on little old ladies. We might not always see eye to eye, but she knows me too well to entertain a thought like that.'

'When people are in a tight corner, they have a way of speaking the truth,' Rigston said.

'So why are you quoting lies at me and pretending Jane said she suspected me?'

'I never said she suspected you. I said that she told us you were one of a handful of people who knew she was interested in the Clewlow family. And that you knew what she was looking for. It's my job to talk to people in possession of that information, Mr Gresham. Four people are dead.'

'Well, it's got nothing to do with me. I was just trying to help Jane.' He pouted like a child. 'Fat lot of good it did me.'

'The person we caught burgling a cottage last night was just trying to help Jane too, we reckon. There seem to be a lot of people willing to give your sister a helping hand.'

'Stop treating me like an idiot, Rigston. You're not going to trick me into some stupid admission because there is no admission to make. Like I said, I was only trying to help. And this is the thanks I get. Up half the night trying to get my sister out of jail. Police turning up at the school, making me look like some sort of criminal.' Matthew shifted irritably in his chair. 'Are you done now? Only, this is supposed to be my lunch hour and so far I haven't had any.'

'I'm done for now, yes. But I'll be checking what you've told me and I may have some further questions for you.'

'Fine, ruin my reputation. Look, I don't murder people. I'm just a country schoolmaster, dull and boring. People like me don't go on killing sprees.'

'I'm sure people said the same thing about Harold Shipman,' Rigston said drily as he walked out. He didn't like Matthew Gresham. He thought the man was a vain, pompous prick. But that didn't make him a murderer. Nor did the fact that he'd spoken to a couple of the victims. He wasn't a likely killer. But, in Rigston's book, he wasn't off the hook yet either.

It was mid-afternoon by the time Jane surfaced. Dan and Judy were in the kitchen, drinking yet another pot of tea. 'Any joy?' Jane asked Dan as she poured herself a cup.

'Stubborn old witch wouldn't give an inch,' Dan said. 'She won't even admit she knows what we're talking about. Jimmy's going to work on her, but don't hold your breath.'

'I wish I knew how Tenille is doing,' Jane said. 'I asked if I could see her, but they wouldn't let me near her.' She looked thoughtful for a moment, then gave her mother a speculative look. 'You could go,' she said. 'Take her some food, something to read. So she doesn't think she's been abandoned.'

'Me? You want me to go and visit her? After the trouble she's caused you?'

Jane sighed. 'She's a good kid. Please, Mum. You'd be taking a load off my mind.'

Judy looked uncertain. 'What would I talk to her about?'

Jane rolled her eyes. 'It doesn't matter. Just being there will be enough. Please? For me?'

Judy pursed her lips. 'I don't know why I let you talk me into these things, I really don't. All right, I'll go and phone the police and see if they'll let me talk to her.'

As she left the room, Jane's mobile rang. 'Hello? Jane Gresham speaking.'

The querulous voice on the other end was vaguely familiar but she couldn't place it at first. 'I want to talk to you about something important but I need you to promise me you won't tell another living soul,' the voice said.

'I'm sorry, I don't know . . .'

'It's Jenny Wright,' the woman said impatiently. 'Promise me you won't tell anyone what I'm about to tell you.'

Jane's eyes flicked towards Dan. He had picked up the paper and was apparently reading. She turned her head slightly. 'I can do that,' she said.

'I'd go myself, but it's Edith's funeral and I've no way of slipping away. And I think it's urgent. Your pal, Jimmy's young man – he said my life was at risk while the papers stay hidden. He said I'm on a hit list. I don't want to die, lass. It might not seem like much of a life to you, but it suits me fine.'

'I can understand. I feel the same,' Jane said gently. She was desperate for Jenny to get to the point but knew there was no point in hustling her.

'I know he's your pal and all, but I've never trusted nancy boys,' she said, apparently off on a tangent. 'I don't understand how our Jimmy turned out that way, but he's family and he's a lad that knows family comes first. But I don't trust any of the rest of them. So even if he is right, I'm not letting him near it.'

'Fair enough,' Jane said. 'It's up to you.' Her heart was thudding in her chest now, anticipation making her feel light-headed.

'I want you to fetch it. There's an old privy at the bottom of the garden with some old paint tins on a shelf. The spare key to the back door is under a tin

511

of white gloss paint. Go upstairs to the spare bedroom and you'll see an old brass-bound chest. It's full of junk, but underneath all that, there's a false bottom. Lift it, and you'll find the papers. You go and get them and take them to the Wordsworth Trust. They can make a proper song and dance about it. That way the killer will know to leave me alone. Have you got all that?'

'Clear as crystal. Thank you. Thank you so much.' She tried not to sound too enthusiastic, not wanting to alert Dan to the momentous nature of the call. She hated keeping him out of the loop, but a promise was a promise.

'And not a word to anybody. That way, you stay safe too.'

'Don't worry. I'll let you know how things go.' She heard Jenny hang up the phone but she kept her mobile to her ear, pretending the conversation was ongoing. 'OK, Neil. My mum's going to try to see her this afternoon, but I'll make sure she doesn't talk about the case. Thanks for calling.' She put the phone down.

Dan looked up enquiringly.

'My lawyer,' she said. 'He's been talking to Tenille's solicitor. He thinks I should give a statement saying Tenille didn't know about the manuscript until after Edith was dead. It can't hurt me and it can do her a lot of good.'

'I would have thought so,' he said, stretching and yawning. 'I think I might go back up to the cottage and take a nap. Will you be all right here on your own?'

'Yeah. I think I might go back to bed. I feel wasted.'

As Dan got up, Judy returned. 'That's all sorted, then. I can see her in an hour. Jane, you need to help me with a care package.'

'I'll leave you ladies to it,' Dan said, heading for the door.

It took twenty minutes for Jane to get her mother out of the door. She was in a fever of impatience. Then it dawned on her. With her mother gone, she had no car. And her bike was presumably still at Copperhead Cottage from Tenille's excursion. 'Fuck,' Jane muttered. She found her wallet and checked her cash level. She had enough for a taxi to get her to Coniston, but not enough to get back. 'Sod it,' she said, reaching for the phone book. She could call Anthony on her mobile once she had the manuscript. She didn't think he'd mind in the least coming to collect her and her precious cargo.

Jake was sitting in the bar of his hotel, nursing a pint and wondering why he was still kicking his heels in this godforsaken hole. He'd grown tired of knocking on doors where there was no reply and he'd finally given up altogether when his arrival for the third time at Eddie Fairfield's had coincided with a police Scene of Crimes team. He hadn't even stopped the car, just cruised on past and headed straight back for the hotel. He'd tried telling Caroline he was wasting his time, but she had insisted on him staying put. 'You never know what will turn up,' she'd said mysteriously, then refused to be drawn further.

If this was working in the private sector, he couldn't help feeling he'd made a mistake. He'd expected much more action, much more hands-on contact with the old manuscripts that had always fascinated him. Not all this hanging around in hotel rooms waiting for directions like some errand boy.

As if to confirm him in his thoughts, his phone rang. 'Hi,' he said, trying not to sound as bored as he felt.

'Let's have a little hustle, Jake,' Caroline said. 'It's showtime.'

'What?' He sat up straight in his chair.

'I know where you can find a Wordsworth autograph manuscript,' Caroline said.

'How the hell . . .'

'Jake, you're not my only set of eyes and ears,' she said. 'But you are my only pair of hands. I know where it is, and I need you to fetch it. I'm flying back tomorrow. We'll enjoy the spoils together.'

It was all moving too fast for him. 'OK, OK, I'm on my way.'

'Don't let me down, Jake. This is what I need you to do . . .'

I sailed with the whalers for some months until they called at the port of Valparaiso. I rejoiced at being back on dry land, but my journey was still only barely begun. I signed on with a trading ship that was headed for Savannah, Georgia. There I hoped to make passage back to England on a cotton trading vessel. But although my actions on Bounty may speak otherwise, I am not a man given to rashness & having made Savannah, I took lodgings in the town & sent word to my brother of my whereabouts & asked whether he considered it possible for me to return safely to these islands & to broach the reasons for my actions in respect of Bligh. You will imagine the impatience with which I awaited his response & my horror at his account of Bligh's voyage, his hero's welcome in England & of the courts martial of the notorious mutineers. I could have conjured up no worse outcome for myself. Instead of returning home, I could envisage nothing other than cruel & perpetual exile from both of my families, the one in England & the other on Pitcairn. It seemed almost too much to be borne.

42

The last of the light was fading behind Langmere Fell when the taxi turned up. By the time they reached Coniston, the only light came from windows where curtains had not yet been drawn. There were a few people making their way to and from the pub, and Jane asked the driver to drop her there. She didn't want to draw attention to herself by having him take her right up to Copperhead Cottage.

It was a brisk fifteen-minute walk up to the cottage and Jane enjoyed the feel of the fresh air on her skin. Even a few hours behind bars had been enough to reinforce her need to be out of doors. There was an autumnal tang to the air, made up of leaf mould and the smoke from coal fires. It was a smell that made Jane nostalgic for the autumns of her youth – Hallowe'en guising, Guy Fawkes bonfires and fireworks, cosy evenings in the kitchen doing her homework to the background sounds of her mother baking and making preserves.

She was so lost in her memories that she was on Copperhead Cottage almost before she realised it. Glad that she'd remembered a torch, she picked her way through the garden, its bare stalks and tender plants wrapped in sacking a sad remnant of what must have been glory in the summer. The outhouse wasn't hard to find, and the key was exactly where Jenny had told her it would be.

Jane let herself in and felt for a light switch. She clicked it on, but nothing happened. Cursing, she remembered Jimmy's tale of Jenny's elaborate preparations for leaving the house. She must have turned off the electricity at the mains. Jane was too impatient to go searching through the dim house for the fuse box, so she climbed the stairs by torchlight.

The room with the chest was the third door on the landing. As she swept the room with her torch, Jane noticed an old-fashioned oil lamp sitting on a chest of drawers, a box of matches next to it. That would make things easier, she thought, lifting the glass and turning the knob that raised the wick high enough to light it. The flame guttered and smoked, but Jane lowered the wick a little and replaced the glass. It wasn't as good as electric light, but it was a damn sight easier than trying to juggle the torch and the contents of the chest.

Jane crouched down and raised the lid. Her eager hands hurriedly lifted out the jumbled contents and dumped them on the floor next to her. By the light of the lamp, she could see the thin leather loop. Holding her breath, she lifted it and set it to one side.

'Oh, my God,' she murmured, reaching out and letting her fingers caress the brittle, yellowing pages. It was real. She lifted the bundle out and stared at it. *William Wordsworth wrote this. Dorcas Mason kept it safe.*

'Thank you, Dorcas,' she said, getting to her feet, her eyes still fixed on the familiar handwriting.

'I'll take that now.' The voice was as shocking as the chill waters of Langmere Force.

Jane whirled round, clutching the papers to her chest. 'It's fine,' she gabbled. 'I've got them safe, it's fine.'

Dan shook his head, his mouth curling in a pitying smile. 'Just hand them over, Jane.'

'Why? What are you doing here?'

'Did you really think I was going to fall for that line about a call from your lawyer? You've never had an emotion that wasn't written all over your face. There's not a lawyer on the planet could make you look like that. Now, just give me the fucking papers.'

'But why?'

'Because I want them. Because I'm tired of my crappy life. Because I'm tired of being a nobody going nowhere. Because I deserve something better and this manuscript is my ticket to it.' He made an impatient movement with the hand that wasn't holding the heavy rubber torch. 'Because I can. Now give me the fucking papers.' He took a step closer and Jane backed up, almost tripping over the chest.

'This is crazy, Dan. We can work on this together, that's enough to make a great career for us both.'

He snorted. 'You think I want to be a fucking academic for the rest of my life? You really think that's how I want my life to be? What a tiny, pathetic ambition. I want things you can't even imagine.'

Cold creeping fear had its hand on her now. She had never suspected this viciousness existed within a man she had counted a friend. 'Things worth killing for?'

'It was an accident, the first time. I just meant to scare her. But –' he snapped his fingers – 'she went out like a light, and it made things easier. It's no big deal, Jane. They were old. I've seen how death creeps up on people and it's not pretty. You might even say I did them a favour. Saving them from a slow and lonely decline.'

'You don't have the right to make that decision. They valued their lives, how dare you presume to play God?' She had no idea how she was going to escape him, but she knew she had to try to keep him talking. 'And what about me? I'm not old, but you tried to kill me.'

'I'm not getting into it, Jane. Stop playing for time. Give me the papers.' He lunged towards the manuscript, but she fended him off with her free hand.

Sudden rage erupted in his face, turning his lips to a snarl and his eyes to narrow slits. 'Stop fucking with me,' he screamed, slamming the torch into the side of her head.

A brilliant light exploded behind her eyes. Then everything went dark.

It was the acrid smell of burning that acted on Jane like smelling salts, helping her make the last steps on the upward spiral into consciousness. Bleary and groggy, she pushed herself up on one elbow, unsure of where she was and how she had come to be there.

The flames were what drove her disorientation from her, sharpening her consciousness. Jane pushed herself to a crouch. A line of fire extended from the spilled oil lamp across the floor for about eight feet. The carpet was burning, and the paint around the door frame was beginning to bubble. The air was already thickening with smoke, sparks shooting upwards like baby fireworks. Through the shimmering haze above the flames, she could see Dan, his face attentive, watching the fire take hold, making sure the blaze across the threshold kept her at bay.

'You should have given it to me,' he shouted above the roar and crackling of the fire. 'I'd have made it easy on you. Burning's a bad way to go, Jane. A bad way to go.'

Still crouching, Jane turned her head towards the window to see if there was an escape route there. But heavy wooden shutters were bolted shut top and bottom. There was no way of reaching the top bolts. The only furniture in the room was too heavy for one person to shift. She looked back at Dan. 'You bastard,' she screamed. 'You bastard.'

He grinned at her, the familiar open, careless expression she knew so well. It was like a physical blow. 'I've always admired your spirit, Jane. Just despised your ambition.' The fire was rising now, and she could hardly see him. 'I'm off now, it's getting a little too hot around here for my taste.'

And he was gone.

'Fuck this,' Jane said, coughing as the smoke caught the back of her throat. She wasn't going to let this happen. It was now or never. She moved crabwise as close as she dared to the blaze. She blinked the tears from her eyes, pulled her coat over her head and launched herself through the flames in a diving forward roll.

Jane scrambled to her feet, pulling off her smouldering coat. Dan had barely made it to the top of the stairs and she went for him with a scream of pure rage. Dan stopped and turned back, taking the full force of her charge in the ribs. He grunted in anger and drove into her, landing a punch to the side of her head that made her dizzy. She lashed out again and caught him in the ribs. This time he yelled and she felt a moment's grim satisfaction.

But still he was coming at her. He smashed a fist into her stomach, forcing the air from her lungs in a sudden whoop. Jane staggered backwards and his hand was on her wrist, forcing it back, threatening to break it. He pushed her and she felt herself falling. But just in time, she grabbed hold of his jacket, catching him off balance. They crashed to the floor together, their momentum carrying them back towards the stairs. Jane scrambled away from him, trying to get to her feet, but he was faster than her, lurching forward and grabbing her leg. She kicked him in the face with her free foot and he yelped as he let her go.

This time, she made it to her feet. Three steps and she was at the top of the stairs. She chanced a look over her shoulder just as he launched himself at her. Instinctively she threw herself to one side.

He crashed into the newel post at the top of the stairs then spun away from it. For a long moment, he seemed to hang immobile, one foot on the top stair, the other in space. Then his balance went and he tumbled sideways, completely out of control. One foot caught a stair tread, pitching his whole body into a cartwheel. He landed head first at the bottom of the stairs with a sickening crunch.

Jane was frozen with shock. She couldn't move a muscle. Then she began to shake, her whole body shivering from head to foot. She clutched the banister for support, staring down at the unmoving heap below. This time, it was the crackle and hiss of the fire that got her moving. Step by step, she made her way downstairs. Even in the gloom of the hallway, she could tell he was dead. Nobody's head could be at that angle to their body and still be alive.

A sob caught in her throat. It didn't matter that it had been Dan who had made it a matter of life or death. What her head knew hadn't yet filtered down to what her heart comprehended. At that moment, she was looking at her friend with his life snuffed out.

A loud crack from upstairs galvanised her into action. She stooped over his body and tried to figure out where the papers were. It was no good; she was going to have to turn him over. Grunting with the effort, she managed to push him on to his side. His jacket fell open, revealing a plastic folder rolled up in the inside pocket. Hastily, she grabbed it, checking it was truly what she sought. She glanced upwards, in time to see the balustrade crumpling under the weight of flame and falling into the hall scant feet from her. She had to get out of there.

Jane raced for the back door, still unlocked as she had left it. She burst into the cold air, chest heaving, pulse hammering in her head. She knew she had to get away from the house, knew it wasn't safe to stay close. Staggering after her effort, she rounded the corner of the house and made for the track. *Fire brigade, police.* Stupidly, she patted her pockets. *Jacket.* That's where the mobile was, in the jacket she'd discarded on the landing.

Her head swimming and her legs rubbery, Jane staggered off down the track towards Irish Row.

Jake had been sitting in the car at the end of Irish Row for a good twenty minutes when he realised he couldn't wait any longer to pee. He got out of the car and turned to walk behind it when he saw a faint orange glow against the skyline. At first he thought it was a bonfire but as it intensified and grew bigger, it dawned on him that this was something much more serious.

He zipped himself up and headed for the track, almost tripping over a mountain bike stashed behind a bush. Catching himself before he fell, he stumbled on to the track and headed in the direction of the fire.

As he rounded the bend, he saw tongues of flame shooting out of a couple of upstairs windows of a lone cottage. 'Jesus Christ,' he exclaimed, reaching for his mobile. When he was connected to the emergency services, he explained he needed the fire brigade. 'There's a cottage on fire. In Coniston. You go up past Irish Row, it's maybe a quarter of a mile further on. It's a huge blaze,' he said, raising his voice as another window exploded like a bomb, showering the air with shards of glass that glittered in the red glow of the fire.

In normal circumstances, the instinct for self-preservation would have driven Jake from the scene for fear that this fire was something to do with his acquisition of the manuscript. But the ancient fascination of fire held him fast. Enthralled, he watched the flames thrusting like blades into the sky, the cinder trails snuffing out as they fell to earth, the billows of smoke shifting like clouds on fast forward. The figure that came staggering down the path from the house was almost upon him before his trance was broken.

At first, he registered only that the escapee from the fire was dishevelled and filthy, bleeding and stumbling, coughing and gasping. He saw the glint of eyes in a smoke-blackened face, then a voice he knew as well as his own rasped, 'You too? You were in it too?'

'Jane?' was all he had time for before she was upon him, raining blows against his chest, sobbing and shouting incomprehensibly. He tried to fight her off without hurting her, but she was like a woman possessed. She just kept hitting him.

The next thing he knew, strong hands were gripping his arms and shoulders. Jake struggled, but he was held firm. He realised there was a man on either side of him, clearly determined not to let him go. A third man had his arms round Jane from behind, holding her tight and saying meaningless words of reassurance.

'What the fuck's going on here?' one of the men said.

'I've got no idea,' Jake said desperately. 'I saw the fire and called the fire brigade. Then Jane came staggering out of the fire with some crazy notion that I was involved and started beating up on me.' As he spoke, he realised how unlikely his version appeared.

'That sounds like a right load of bollocks to me,' his other captor said. 'Reckon we'll wait for the cops to come and sort it all out.'

'Are you all right, love?' the man holding Jane asked, loosening his grip and turning her to face him.

Jane burst into a fresh bout of sobbing and leaned against him. 'Nay, lass, it's all right,' he said, looking over her head at his mates with an expression of bewilderment. Before anyone could say anything more, the night was split open by blue flashing lights and sirens.

He was, Jake realised, well and truly fucked.

I lived in Savannah for five years, signing on with trading ships for short voyages when I needed money. But my heart cried out for home & at length I decided I must take my chances. The country being in the grip of war against Bonaparte, I believed my return might go unnoticed. I informed my dear brother Edward of my decision & placed myself in his hands. When I landed at Bristol, he sent word that I was to meet him at an inn near Bath. When we embraced for the first time in more than ten years my heart felt swollen in my chest & I could scarce breathe. We were agreed that I should journey to the Isle of Man, where our friends & relations would be happily complicit in keeping my identity a secret from outsiders. My brother had papers for me in the name of John Wilson & I made my way safely back to a place that felt akin to home. But I confess this life of quiet chafed with me. I am not a man built for idleness. Furthermore, the sea called me like a siren song. I dared not sign on with any regular ship under a British flag for fear of being recognised even after all these years. In conclusion, I was faced with only one possibility, & for the past two years, I have earned a fine living as a smuggler. I have become a familiar of the shoals of the Solway Firth, bringing brandy & claret to the gentry & the commons without the intercession of the exciseman. I do not pretend that this is a noble calling. But it suits my temper & it presents me with the opportunity to exercise my one skill of seamanship. However, mine is a life not without risk & rivalry & I fear that I will not make old bones. For that reason, I have come to you that you might set down the true tale of Fletcher Christian, mutineer of the Bounty, that men may know my true fate.

43

Jane decided she liked the hospital room. It was
white and it was quiet and she didn't feel ill enough
to be scared by what being there might mean.
According to the doctor, she'd suffered minor smoke
inhalation, a painful but medically minor blow to
the head, plus assorted cuts and bruises. They were
only keeping her in for observation because they'd
thought her incoherence on arrival had to do with
concussion. But then, doctors were not trained to
diagnose grief.

There was, she knew, a police officer outside her
door. The one on duty first thing had been really
helpful, calling Rigston and telling him she was
ready to make a statement. She knew she wasn't
going to be able to hold her emotions at bay for
long and she wanted to get the events of the night
off her chest before they became blurred by her
reactions to them. The inspector had been there
within twenty minutes and in spite of the attempts
of the nursing staff to thwart Jane's desire to talk,
he'd taken a statement from her. He hadn't given
her an easy ride, threatening at one point that he

would charge her with police obstruction if only to make sure she stayed in one place for long enough for him to complete his enquiries without any further catastrophe. But by the end of their conversation, she felt from him a grudging acceptance of her version of events.

'You need to stay here while I examine the evidence and decide whether you're telling the truth,' he said firmly when they were done. 'I'm leaving an officer on the door. He'll have orders to arrest you if you try to escape.'

'I promise I'll stay put if you answer two questions for me,' Jane said.

'I'm the one who asks the questions.'

Jane pulled a face. 'Spare me the hard-boiled cop routine. First thing I want to know is what happened to the papers that I had tucked into my waistband last night?'

'Your precious manuscript is back in the hands of its owner,' Rigston said. 'It's up to Mrs Wright now what she does with it. And I don't want her pressurised in any way. She's an old lady and she's just lost her home in traumatic circumstances. Are we clear on that?'

Jane closed her eyes and sighed. 'I'm not in any fit state to go round monstering old ladies. Trust me on that.'

'What was your other question?' Rigston asked.

'Will you please pay attention to what DI Blair has to say about Tenille? She needs a break. I know she broke the law, but look at it this way: what she did triggered what happened last night. Without her intervention, you might never have solved those murders.'

Rigston shook his head in exasperation. 'I'm not making any promises. It's not my job to let criminals walk away from their crimes.'

She'd pushed him on the point, but he would say nothing more concrete. And she was too tired to carry on. Seeing that, he made his escape, leaving her to silence and white and the insistent nag of grief.

Her isolation didn't last nearly long enough. The nurse granted her parents twenty minutes. Judy wept for eighteen of them while her father sat gripping her hand as if he would never let it go. Matthew, Diane and Gabriel were given ten minutes. Little was said that didn't revolve around Gabriel but it felt like the start of something different between them.

None of this eased the terrible ache in her heart. Dan's treachery was terrible, but her conviction that Jake was complicit only compounded the bitter taste of betrayal. And somewhere in the middle of all this, Tenille had got lost. She had made promises that she had failed to keep, and that hurt almost as much as what Dan and Jake had taken from her. And who, she wondered, had broken the news to Harry that his lover had been killed by one of his closest friends? The occasions for grief just kept piling up around her.

Rigston came back late in the afternoon, bringing an air of satisfaction into the room with him. 'I think we're there,' he said. 'We found Dan Seabourne's prints in Edith Clewlow's house where they had no business being because you were never there with him. No joy so far at any of the others, but, if you're telling the truth, those later deaths were premeditated and he probably had the sense to wear gloves. We checked with Jimmy Clewlow and although he gives Seabourne a partial alibi for a couple of the deaths, he had enough of a window of opportunity to commit the murders.

'We also checked out his computer. As well as the email address you were using for him, he had another anonymous account. And we found an exchange of emails with Caroline Kerr, your pal Jake Hartnell's boss. They were negotiating for her to handle the sale of the manuscript. That's what Jake was doing parked up by Irish Row. He was supposed to have a rendezvous with the vendor, though neither he nor Ms Kerr will admit to knowing the vendor's identity. Nor that what they were negotiating for was going to be stolen property.'

'Stupid greedy bastard,' Jane said. But at least stupidity and cupidity were better than conspiracy to commit murder. It was small comfort, but it was better than nothing.

'They usually are. Unfortunately I can't find anything to charge him with.' He sighed, staring out of the window with a glum expression on his face. 'Can't bloody find anything to charge you with either. This job's a pain in the arse sometimes.'

'What about Tenille?' Jane hardly dared ask.

'Her auntie's coming to fetch her tomorrow.' He shook his head. 'I'm a fool to myself sometimes. I'm counting on you to keep her honest.'

'Thank you,' Jane said. 'I won't let you down.'

'Mind you don't.' He got to his feet. 'Oh, and

Dr Wilde says she'll be in touch when she's got something concrete to report.' He paused on his way to the door and turned back. 'Get yourself some counselling,' he said gruffly. 'Five deaths is a lot to carry on your conscience. Especially when they're not your fault.'

Rigston had been followed in short order by the doctor, who pronounced her well enough to go home and free up his acute bed. To her surprise, when she had emerged from the room dressed in the clean clothes her mother had brought, her father was sitting on a chair further down the hall, twisting his cap in his hands. He jumped to his feet as she walked unsteadily towards him. 'I sent your mother home with Diane and Matthew,' he said. 'She was doing everybody's head in.'

Jane felt the prickle of fresh tears. 'I love you, Dad,' she said, linking her arm through his. By the time they arrived back at the farm, Jane was so tired she could barely climb out of the Land Rover and walk indoors. The stairs looked like a mountain, but she dragged herself up. At the top, she looked down at the anxious face of her father. 'I need to sleep for about a week,' she said. 'Tell Mum to please let me sleep.'

Jane took the stairs one at a time, steeling herself for a major smother attack from her mother. When she opened the kitchen door, she was astonished to see Alice Clewlow sitting at the table with the inevitable mug of tea. Her mother was nowhere to be seen. 'Judy's just popped out to the shops,' Alice said, as if her presence was as routine as the view from the window.

'I didn't expect to see you here,' Jane said weakly, slumping into the nearest chair.

'Somebody needed to talk to you and Jimmy's too wrapped up in his own bloody psychodrama to be any use to man nor beast so I thought I'd better pick up the baton.' Alice gave her an appraising stare. 'You look like shit.'

'Feel like it too. Look, I'm sorry about Jenny's house. I . . .'

'I didn't come here to get an apology. I came here to make one. I'm sorry I was so bloody rude to you at Edith's wake. I should have known a Fellhead Gresham wouldn't be out to cheat my family. If I'd listened to you then, we might have saved a few lives.'

Jane shook her head. 'I've been over this in my head so many times. Dan was set on his course. I don't think anything would have stopped him till he got his hands on that manuscript. There's no point in either of us beating ourselves up.'

'Not that that will stop us,' Alice said drily. 'Anyway, I'm sorry for what I said.'

'It's OK, Alice.' Jane managed a weak smile. 'And I should apologise for introducing Dan to Jimmy.'

Alice snorted. 'He's always had appalling taste in men.' She took a drink of tea.

'Can I ask you something, Alice?'

Alice looked slightly wary. 'Sure.'

'How did Jenny end up with the manuscript?'

Alice looked relieved. 'That's easy. It passed down from Dorcas to her eldest, Arthur, and he entrusted it to his eldest, Beattie. And Jenny was Beattie's favourite. So she got the family heirloom with strict injunctions to keep the Wordsworth family skeleton firmly locked away in the closet. It was only when she understood people were dying for it that she realised she had to give it up.'

'That makes sense,' Jane said.

Alice fiddled with the handle of her mug. 'Jane, I didn't just come here to apologise to you. I came because I've got good news and I've got bad news for you.'

'Oh Christ,' Jane said. 'I don't know if I can take any more bad news. This has been the worst week of my life.' She pushed her hair back from her face. 'Better let me have the bad news first. Then at least I have something to look forward to.'

'Jenny wasn't totally frank with you,' Alice said, her manner halting and awkward. 'She's cautious by nature, is Jenny. So she let you have the notes, to see how you behaved. Like, could you keep a confidence? Would you try to talk her into selling them? Would you treat them with respect, or would you just try to make a name for yourself off the back of them. It was a kind of test . . .'

Jane suddenly felt cold. 'Oh God, Alice. Oh please, no . . .'

Alice blinked hard. 'I'm afraid so. She had the poem too, Jane. About sixty pages long, loosely bound between leather covers. Handwritten. She kept them separate in case she was ever burgled. So that, if she lost one, she'd have the other as a sort of insurance policy. She kept the poem stuffed inside a pillow in her bedroom.' She took a deep breath. 'So, yes. There was a poem. But now there isn't.'

Tears spilled from Jane's eyes. 'Oh God, no,' she wailed. 'This is a disaster.'

'The thing is,' Alice continued, 'it's a disaster nobody's going to know about. Nobody blames you. The family's talked about this and we're all agreed, nobody's going to say a word about what's been lost. Your reputation's not going to suffer.'

'To hell with my reputation,' Jane stuttered. 'The poem's lost forever. And it's all my fault. If I hadn't got so het up about it, it would still be safe. Your relatives would still be alive and so would bloody Dan.' She sniffed. 'How am I going to live with myself after this?'

Alice got up and put an arm round Jane's shaking shoulders. 'Stop it, now,' she said, her low voice genuinely comforting. 'That kind of talk is pointless. What's done is done. You couldn't have known any of this would happen. I meant it when I said nobody blames you, and we're the ones with the right to dish out the blame. And here's the good news. Jenny wants you to have first crack at the notes. You can still make something marvellous out of all this mess. Please, don't get eaten up with guilt.'

'I can't help it,' Jane snivelled. 'I feel so bad about all of this.'

Alice pulled up a chair so she could hold Jane against her shoulder. 'There's something else I have to tell you that might help you look on the bright side. I took Jenny out to her place yesterday afternoon. And half a dozen cats came out of the undergrowth as if by magic, rubbing themselves against her legs. And you know what she said? She said, "I always hated that house, Alice. Bloody miserable place. But it had been in the family for generations, it wasn't my right to walk away from it. Now I can have a nice little bungalow with big windows so I can see the view. I can see out my days in comfort." So you see, it's truly not all bad.'

The burden of my friend's story contains all the elements necessary to compose a thrilling yet moral narrative of man's vanity & fallibility. I cannot but feel it is the ideal subject for a poet with my gifts, & I feel it singing in my veins even now. The tragedy is that I will not enjoy its praise in my lifetime, for to publish it would bring calumny upon me & my family. Yet after my death, it may please the world to learn the truth of the matter that so exercised the public prints at the time of Bligh's return. I vouchsafe that any man who reads my words will not fail to be moved by the tragic case of Mr Fletcher Christian, a man more sinned against than sinning.

Post Scriptum: After that last day in the garden at Dove Cottage, I never saw my friend more. His brother reports that he has sunk beneath the horizon of his family's awareness. Whether he be alive or dead, none can say. Thus does Fletcher Christian leave us with yet one more mystery that has no easy resolution.

44

January 2006

The Viking was in its customary state of somnolence ahead of the lunchtime rush. Instead of serving behind the bar, for once Jane was sitting at a corner table. She'd quit the Viking to spend more time working on the Wordsworth manuscript. Now that Jane was the custodian of the *Bounty* narrative, Professor Elliott had miraculously found enough money in her budget to retain her in a full-time position.

Jane glanced at her watch. She was ten minutes early, no need to fret yet. Harry brought her glass of white wine and sat down opposite her. 'It's not the same without you here,' he said. 'I'm thinking of looking for somewhere else.'

To Jane's surprise, since Dan's death and the exposure of the full extent of his crimes, Harry seemed to crave her company. She'd expected him to blame her, to hold her responsible for seducing his partner from the straight and narrow, and ultimately for his death. But the opposite had happened. Harry cleaved to her because she was the only other person, he claimed, who really understood Dan in all his complexity. She had loved him enough to be his friend, but nobody knew better than her now how perfidious he could also be. 'You should think carefully about that,' Jane said. 'Anywhere else, you might actually have to work the hours they pay you for. No more leaning on the bar reading while you wait for customers.'

'Yeah, right. So, any news?' he asked.

'Jenny's new bungalow's nearly done. She can't wait to get moved in. She's having the place decked out like a palace with all mod cons. She's even building a cat house for the felines. "Bugger the grandkids," she says. She's planning on spending the lot. And I spoke to Anthony yesterday. He thinks they're going to be able to raise the money to match the auction price and keep the manuscript in this country.'

'That's good, I hate to think of it ending up in some millionaire's collection in the States.'

'Oh, and Anthony passed on a juicy bit of gossip he picked up on the grapevine. Apparently Caroline has ditched Jake. Both professionally and personally.'

'Couldn't happen to a nicer bloke,' he said, looking cheerful for the first time that day. 'And how's Tenille?'

Jane grinned. 'All very unofficial, but we're doing OK. It's a bit cramped, but I don't really mind giving up my study now that I've got a proper office at work. And she spends a couple of nights a week with her dad, so I do get time off for good behaviour. The best news is that she's actually going to school. Her dad's talking about trying to get her into a private school, and I think that might be the best answer. At least then she won't get the piss ripped out of her every time she hands in her homework.'

'And she's proved she's tough enough to handle anything those posh totties can hand out.'

As he spoke, River Wilde dropped her satchel on the floor, put her glass of wine on the table and sat down. 'Nice to see you again, Jane.'

'You too. And this is my friend Harry,' Jane said, wondering anxiously whether River knew where Harry fitted in the jigsaw of the past months.

'Pleased to meet you, Dr Wilde,' Harry said courteously, extending his hand. 'Now, if you'll excuse me, I need to get back to work.'

'Is that . . .?' River asked as he walked away.

'Yes,' Jane said.

'Right. Just so's I know.' She leaned down and took a folder from her satchel. 'Pirate Peat. The mystery man.' She opened the folder and took out a bundle of papers.

'The question: is the body in the bog Fletcher Christian, *Bounty* mutineer.' She glanced up at Jane. 'This has been bloody fascinating,' she said. 'Thank you for putting it my way. Now, the first thing I had to do was to gather as much information as I could about your man Fletcher and then compare it to what I had on the table. Did you get the tape I sent you?' she asked Jane, referring to a videotape of the session where River had outlined the first points of comparison for the camera.

'Yes, it was really exciting to watch. I'm very much looking forward to seeing the final version.'

River pulled a face. 'I look like such a moron,' she said. 'I had no idea how much time I spend with my mouth hanging open when I'm working. Anyway, you'll remember that from those early examinations there was nothing to contradict the possibility of this being Fletcher and quite a bit of supporting evidence. What I've got now are the results of the tests from the big boys' toys.' She pulled out a single sheet. 'The teeth. According to the cement annulation, our guy is the right sort of age. And the stable isotope analysis of the teeth tells us that he lived in Cumbria at the time his teeth were formed. So, like Fletcher, he was living here when he was around six, seven years old.'

'You can tell all that from teeth?'

'Yes. It's called science,' River said, her grin taking the sting out of her words. 'And then,' she continued, fishing out another sheet of paper, 'more stable isotope analysis, this time on the femur. And I can tell you that in the last fifteen years of his life, he had lived in the South Pacific.' She grinned. 'Pretty cool, huh?'

'This is amazing. What about the DNA?'

'Patience, patience. I'm coming to that. Now, he had long hair, which is pretty useful for telling us about diet. And his hair indicates periods where he was eating a good, well-balanced diet rich in vitamins and minerals interspersed with a much less healthy diet. So, maybe a sailor who had some long spells on land where he was eating well, followed by long voyages with nothing much in the way of fruit or vegetables. Again, very suggestive.

'Then there's that wound on the chest where the star tattoo would have been if it was your Fletcher. Remember I said when I did that first superficial examination that I thought the flesh and skin had been ripped out by an animal? Well, when I took a closer look, I realised I'd been mistaken. The skin had been hacked away by a serrated knife. So yes, we could be looking at a primitive version of permanent tattoo removal.'

She put the papers to one side and steepled her fingers. 'There's not one piece of evidence that contradicts the theory that the man who was murdered in Carts Moss was Fletcher Christian. Balance of probabilities? Well, there were a lot of sailors around then. We'd just fought a war and also trade routes had opened up hugely in the eighteenth century. But if I was a betting woman, I would have put a few bob on Pirate Peat and Fletcher being one and the same. Apart from that inconvenient little thing about him being murdered on Pitcairn.'

'Which, according to the *Bounty* manuscript, was absolutely not what happened,' Jane said.

'Quite. Which leaves the DNA.' River stopped to take a sip of her wine. 'I really did have high hopes of this. So much so that I arranged right from the off to have some comparison samples from Fletcher's direct descendants sent from Pitcairn and New Zealand. Now, there's a big problem with bog bodies. The DNA in any bog body will be badly denatured because of its environment. The bog is acidic – that's why the bones tend to "melt" and the skin is essentially tanned. The acid in the peat denatures the double helix of the DNA strand and effectively strips the base pairs away. So DNA detector kits can see that DNA is there because they see the phosphate backbone, but it is no longer replicable because the base pairs have gone. And it is replication of the DNA through PCR – that's polymerase chain reaction to you and me – that allows sufficient quantity to be duplicated to allow fingerprinting and therefore comparison. So although, if you're very lucky, you can get bits of DNA, you generally can't get enough to sequence it. And that makes comparison impossible. But I was hopeful with this body, I really was. We used every available technique. I even pulled some strings with a lab in Switzerland who are doing some stuff with DNA that is way out there.' River shook her head.

'I'm really sorry, Jane. I just couldn't do it. I couldn't harvest enough DNA to make a comparison.'

'So we'll never know for sure?' Jane looked stricken.

River nodded. 'We'll never know for sure.'

Bibliography

I consulted many works of reference in the preparation of this book. Notable among them were:

The Bounty, Caroline Alexander (HarperCollins, 2003)

Wordsworth, A Life in Letters, Juliet Barker (Viking Penguin, 2002)

Wordsworth, A Life, Juliet Barker (Penguin, 2001)

The Mutiny of the Bounty, John Barrow (Blackie, 1961)

The Bounty Mutiny, William Bligh, Edward Christian (Penguin Classics, 2001)

Fragile Paradise, Glynn Christian (Hamish Hamilton, 1982)

William Wordsworth, Hunter Davies (Sutton Publishing, 1997)

William Wordsworth, Stephen Gill (Oxford University Press, 1989)

Mutiny on the Bounty, ed. Rolf Harris (Rolf Harris Productions, 1998)

The Spirit of the Age, William Hazlitt, ed. Robert Woof (The Wordsworth Trust, 2004)

Captain Bligh & Mr Christian, Richard Hough (Chatham Publishing, 2000)

Captain Bligh: The Man and his Mutinies, Gavin Kennedy (Duckworth, 1989)

Life and Death in Eden, Trevor Lummis (Phoenix, 2000)

The Way of a Ship, Derek Lundy (Jonathan Cape, 2002)

The Bounty Trilogy, Charles Nordoff & James Norman Hall (Back Bay Books, 1985)

The Wake of the Bounty, C.S. Wilkinson (Cassell, 1953)

The Grasmere and Alfoxden Journals, Dorothy Wordsworth, ed. Pamela Woof (Oxford University Press, 2002)

William Wordsworth: The Major Works, William Wordsworth (Oxford Paperbacks, 2000)